i

Devil's

Prince

Louise Furley

Devil's Prince

ISBN- 978-1-7363452-0-7 (Paperback)
ISBN- 978-1-7357712-9-8 (eBook)

Cover design by Pixel Mischief Design

ALSO BY LOUISE FURLEY

Solitar

Halo Valley

Isle of Orainn

Anastasia

The Kissing Number

Distilled Duplicity

The Poser

Wrath of Wolf

Devil's Seed

Adara

Jungle Treasure

Jancarlo

His Winnings

Jezábel and the Assassin

DEVIL'S
PRINCE

Chapter One

Although the room teemed with a grand variety of different species, some innocuous, others lethal, surreptitious glances from males flagged Devilos Dravidian as he moved through the crowd. Never direct stares, just fleeting uneasy glimpses.

A felon-hunting warlord, the aura of bestial violence clings to Dev like a savage cloak and no one at the party wanted to draw that menacing notice. Men fear him, and only the truly wanton females that preferred the darker, more brutal side of males endeavored to get near him.

Right now, one of those women batted thick lashes at the warlord while dragging her nails down his sleeve of black leather. "Ah, Dravidian," her sigh a gush of sultry invitation, "you are so damned tall, what, over six and a half feet of pure muscle? The legends tell that when you are enraged, your body morphs into... they say you become like a goliath man-eating monster."

People drank and danced and wandered around the couple, none dared to come too close to the demon warrior.

Tall herself, even in six-inch heels, Rianna still had to bend her head back to look in his eyes. Her attention shifted to his head. "Oh, yeah, and those crazy ears, slightly pointed, makes you seem so..." her suggestive tongue swirled over wide lips, "mysteriously erotic," she giggled, "I mean exotic." Her fingers twittered toward one of his ears, but at the narrowing of his eyes she drew her hand back.

Something at the party already had his attention thus he ignored the woman. That didn't slow her down a bit. Leaning close to him, Rianna raised her hand to dally her nails down the side of his darkly bronzed, hard face. Her breath drifted over the skin of his neck, right over the enigmatic tattoo that curled up the side.

She murmured in hushed excitement, "They say your fangs elongate and can tear flesh and muscle, gut even the vilest of creatures."

When he didn't respond, exhaling a purring breath, Rianna nuzzled her breasts against his huge bicep. "And your claws," she uttered, looking down at his big hands, the claws were retracted, his blunt fingers curled into his palms, "can gouge through meat and crush bones, your supreme strength decimating them." Shivers rippled over her heated skin in fantasy imagining the carnage he could wreak.

Hooded lids hid the gleam of rich darkness beneath, concealing the object of his interest. Devilos stood as a statue, the full harsh mouth remained closed, the only movement was the flexing of his jaw, he still did not respond to the woman pawing him. His gaze stayed fixed beyond the scores of people.

"I'd love to feel those fangs and claws on me, and those horns, star spheres above," Rianna drawled, running her palms down over her breasts, "they're big, like rams' horns."

Wriggling in sharp desire, her coo a breathy shiver, "I bet you're big and hard like that…all over." She gazed up at the horns, the points curved towards his back. Currently retracted like his claws and fangs, they were only about five inches long.

She looked like she was considering if she dared touch one. The tip of one pointed ear twitched, making Rianna resist the urge to stroke a horn. "I hear tell they grow to at least nine inches and are thick as a man's wrist when you battle, and during…" she mewed, "*sex.*"

Rianna Malone hit on Devilos whenever he was on the space station, Protostar. He'd blown her off each time. Rianna's voice an annoying buzz in his ear, he squinted across the room.

His black hair bound in more than a dozen warrior braids springing from all over his head fell past his shoulders.

She stroked one, murmured, "I can picture these braids flying when you're charging after outlaws, while slashing your rapiers, slicing off heads and stabbing through hearts, those braids swinging and arcing, they would be their own terrifying sight." Her palm stroked over a broad shoulder with another lusty inhale and heated wriggle.

Without moving his head, Devilos looked down at the woman pawing him. A human female. Long wavy dark hair, blue eyes flashed under the faux lashes at him but they appeared to be an unnatural color.

His gaze traveled further down. Her huge tits ballooned out of the low décolleté, and she was rubbing them all over his arm.

The scarlet dress she wore clung like skin over the breasts, the wide waist and bumper-sized ass. Obvious that she would like a dangerous rough ride with elements of pain, something he could definitely give her, she would make a hardy quick tumble. But. His gaze slid from her back to the far side of the room.

"Darlin'," Rianna whined slightly at his lack of attention to her, it was not something she was used to with her beauty and voluptuous figure. The busty woman's hands were now roaming his leather pants moving to below his belt. "What say you, we slag this party and find a dark," she writhed against him, "private place we can, indulge in our...kinky fires?"

Her hand skimmed lower to cup his bulge outlined in the leather. "Zues," she moaned, "*big*, ah, come with me, Dravidian, *now*." Her breaths oozing fast and shallow, she raised her arms to slide her hands up his chest and nestle her body into his.

Pushing her hands off him, he turned from her with a growl, "Not interested."

Her huff of displeasure made no impression on him as he stared across the crowded room. Beyond the Albino Taws, the drunken Alpas, past the clique of humans that were obviously denigrating the rest of the species that flocked the room judging from their sniggers and mimes, something pulled at him.

Rianna slid her hand over Dev's ass with another invitation on her tongue; he snatched her wrist and bent it. The pain was piercing, Rianna gasped.

Dev released her, snarled, "Do not touch me again, get lost."

Holding her injured wrist, the thick lashes flopped up in down in disbelief and pique. With a snort of irritation, she stalked off to find other robust meat.

Ignoring the anxious glances shooting at him by people that were frightened by his looks alone, he was used to it, he continued his perusal under lowered lids. He didn't care what people, of whatever species, thought about him. At the moment, his jetting eyes were tunneled to a female at the far side of the crowd.

"Ah," his best friend and 1st Lieutenant, Bowie Busoni, moved to stand beside him, nodding with a slight grin, "you've noticed the fair Prinţesă?" Almost as tall as Devilos and also with shoulders and arms like a bull, Bowie combed long fingers through his thick blond hair. Devilos was a warlord hence the long braids, Bowie as a warrior kept his hair much shorter.

The crescendo of noise increased as more liquor and drugs were consumed, laughter and conversations bounced off the neon pink alloy walls. An alloy floor and the many windows surrounding the party hall on the space station did nothing to conduct the din.

Outside the windows billions of stars and planets blinked pinpricks of light in the infinite black galaxy. Cosmic vehicles buzzed in a constant stream around the station taking off or landing.

Devilos grunted, "Who is she?"

"I'm not surprised you have never seen her before. Ever since he took her from her parents, Krystian Ritrova keeps her under tight wraps on Qoph. She is Prinţesă Svetiessa Emita Ritrova."

Bowie looked from the female to Devilos and back. He smiled. "Extraordinary, eh? I mean for a human. Quite *ádainn*, uniquely beautiful."

When Devilos made no comment, Bowie chuckled. "I've only seen a brief glimpse of her once before myself. But there's no forgetting that hair, like a brilliant swirling flame, a *lasair* of a flickering candlelight. You can't see it because of the crowd, but it waves and curls like a glowing ribbon to her waist. Skin like silken pearls, and that mouth, tiny but plush as shit, hell Dev, I have dreamt about it."

Bowi'es brows drew down. "Can't see her figure in that gown. But-"

"Who is that man with his hands all over her? What is he to her?" Not that Devilos cared who the man was. Or her for that matter. He couldn't explain his interest, he shrugged, must be bored curiosity.

They both watched the man, a foot taller than the female, with red hair but darker, auburn, not a flickering flame like hers, cradle her face, lean in to kiss her but she lowered her head and his lips landed on her forehead.

The man chuckled. His laugh was mirthful, but the dark glower indicated he was not happy about her avoidance.

"That is her brother."

Devilos' brows arched, his attention twitched to take in Bowie's blue eyes twinkling with mischievousness. "Her *bráthair* touches her like he's her lover?"

"Aye. Krystian Ritrova is more accurately her *leasbratháir*, her half-brother. It is well known that he is infatuated with his young sister. She appears to be barely out of her teens."

As they watched the siblings, Krystian put both hands to net her face and hold her immobile while he lowered his lips to hers. Her fear was tangible as was her subtle struggle, as if she didn't dare draw attention to them but wanted to be released.

His expression incredulous, Devilos spat, "He kisses his own *deisfiúr*? He is a *séantóir*."

Bowie nodded. "Aye, the pervert as you say, is kissing his sister. And she clearly objects to being manhandled by him. But, he has ownership over her as her guardian. As a female on her planet, especially a prinţesă, she has no rights."

He could feel Dev turning rigid with heat roiling off him. Bowie warned him, "Nay, *má bráthair*, don't get involved. He is a powerful Sautarine. He's not pure human like her."

His chest pumping, Devilos took a step in their direction- but the siblings turned to vapor, and in a poof, were gone. "What the fuck?" his rumble resonated coarsely with his stunned glare.

"I told you, Dev, he's a Sautarine. He has limited transporting power. His ship must be right outside the station. I've heard rumors he's trying to sell Sveti's *maidenlacht,* her virginity, to obtain a greater power, one that will open wormholes to him. He is," Bowie glanced at his friend, "conflicted between his lust for power and his lust for his little sister."

They stood staring at the empty space where the siblings had been.

"Come on, Dev, there are females abounding here that have been giving both of us the eye all night. You turned down the ribald Rianna. I guess she's too…much? Tawdry is her middle name, eh? No worries, there's plenty of other kitten chow out there.

"Let's get us a couple of those Nymphin Plintins, or better yet," he grinned seeing half a dozen Nymphins floating towards them, "let's take a handful of 'em and hit the upstairs?" He clapped Dev's back as the Nymphins circled them.

Curvy, ebony-haired females like mermaids giggled and flashed the men their breasts as they floated around them. Unlike true mermaids, they could separate their legs when having sex.

"They chatter like incessant magpies, Bow," Dev groused, his gaze still arrowed to where the Ritrova siblings had vanished.

Bowie reached out for one of the floating girls. "Aye. I had five sisters you know, I learned how to tune the chatter out. Come on now, the Nymphins are as damned insatiable as their names imply, grab a bunch of them and let's go."

Chapter Two

*W*eeks later, Dev stood in front of the main command center on his flashjet, the Grisail, with Connar Basque, one of his lieutenants at his side. The men faced the window that spread across the tip of the bow. The bridge was cluttered with people manning instruments, communications, computers and a myriad of other technicatics.

Through a stretch, Connar yawned. "It's good to be heading back to Protostar." Specks of bright lights flashed as they tunneled through the galaxy.

Another yawn and he went on, "Seems like we've been gone for ages, it took forever to capture that bastard, Ja'an Ukrenna. I don't know how he got away so long with those serial murders. I mean, the missing prostitutes weren't noticed until the political councilmenes started disappearing."

Dev pushed his long braids off to his back. Instead of his normal leather he wore a long sleeved black shirt, pants, and heavy boots. "Aye. If it weren't for his girlfriend fearing she would be next and squealing," he shrugged one shoulder, "it would have been a helluva lot longer."

"What are your plans for tonight, Dev?"

Devilos glanced at one of his closest friends and lieutenants. Connar's thick shiny chestnut hair was a draw for the ladies. Every time Dev saw one near him, she was forking her fingers through the heavy locks groaning like she was coming.

The same as Bowie and Dev, Connar was as big and strong as a tank. All of Dev's lieutenants, true bred warriors, were immense, powerfully built males without an ounce of fat. Heavy chests and lean hips, they were continuously barraged by brazen women.

"Ah, I have work to do. The Naledi-Sarkastodons, Nal-Sarks, have been raiding the smaller planets again to capture slaves for their mines. I have a request from L-Rign to look into it. I need to spend the night researching."

A low thrum of hubbub filled the bridge from conversations between staff as they prattled to each other and as they spoke into communication devices.

"Craw Dev, you work too fucking hard. I know you're the rough tough kill 'em and chill 'em guy, but even the devil needs to take a break." He grinned at Dev. "Besides, *má bráthair*, you don't take orders from anyone."

Devilos nodded in agreement. "True that. But you know it's easier to work with the L-Rign than against them and incur planetary sanctions. Basically we're after the same things. I want to take out every one of those fucking Nal-Sarks."

"So-"

"Sire." Connar was cut off by Elvana, a spectra officer. Sitting at Communications, she swiveled on her chair and said, "There is a request from a Svetiessa Ritrova of Qoph." She turned back to her monitor not catching the flicker in Dev's dark eyes.

He walked over to her and clipped sharply, "What is it?"

Exceptionally tall, Elvana, part human Asian and part Ulexia, crossed her willowy legs and tapped the monitor. "Um, she says she would desire to- to trade one of our captured lieutenants, Miles Dontour."

A raven brow rose. "For whom?"

She tapped his words on the monitor. Her head cocked as she read the response. Tucking black hair like stiff oil that fell past her shoulders behind her ears, she nodded and said, "Ms. Ritrova indicates she wants to transport here with Miles and trade him for Kaeto Kincaid."

His face remaining impassive, Dev looked over at Connar. His lieutenant expressed his surprise.

Connar trod quickly to his Sire and friend. "That Spireling assassin? Why would she want him?"

Crossing his burly arms, Dev answered, "He has minimal powers that under rare, certain circumstances can be taken from him by those that have the same level powers thereby increasing the strength of the stealer's powers."

Bowie had entered the bridge with another lieutenant, Lukas Martial.

Overhearing the request, Bowie said as he approached, "We hadn't been able to locate Miles for months. We didn't know if he was dead or alive. Dev, he's worth a million Kincaids."

His skewed glance at his friend filled with a cagey tease, he added, "Ah, and the Prinţesă Ritrova in person as the bonus cherry on top? How can you refuse?"

Dev was silent. The thrum of noise desisted. All attention was on the four strapping warriors. Several silent seconds passed.

"Sire?" Elvana prodded. "She has resent the request and is waiting for your response."

Dev was looking at the spectra but wasn't seeing her, his dark eyes were blank discs as he thought. Recalling the extraordinary woman from the party, while hunting the latest villain, he had kept eyes and ears out for word of the location of the Prinţesă. As well as Miles was a good and loyal lieutenant. Two in one.

"Tell her yes. When?" He waited while Elvana transmitted his response.

Minutes passed before she said, "Ms. Ritrova says she knows Kincaid is on board here in our brig. She says they can be transported here in fifteen minutes." She turned to Dev. "What say you, Sire?"

"Confirm."

"Aye Sire." Elvana transmitted the information and gave the navigational coordinates for the transporting.

Dev ordered, "Connar, get Tomi and retrieve Kincaid. Make sure the chains are secure."

"Copy." The light splashed on Connar's chestnut hair as he nodded and immediately left the bridge. The doors whooshed open before he reached them and closed directly after he passed through.

His blue eyes twinkling, Bowie grinned at Dev. "So, we're gonna get a second visual of the Prinţesă. This time we should get a better view of her up close and personal. There won't be a crowd of people hiding her, we can see her figure, get a gander at those tits and ass. If we're lucky, her skirt will be really short and the legs will be on display."

One hand on his lean hip the other rifled through his thick blond mane, Bowie pondered, "I wonder what color her eyes are?"

Brows curving up over hazel eyes in curiosity, Lukas looked from Bowie to Dev. Bowie smirked at the man with short buzzed tawny hair. Lukas was brawny like the others but his muscles were angular, edged, he looked like an ancient human Marine.

Only Devilos was from the obsidian planet Nasitar. His friends and lieutenants were all from Resh but they'd all known each other since their early military training. When their planets had enlisted them at six-years-old, Dev had already been there for years.

Through ages of severe training and dangerous, deadly missions the men had become *compánach cogaidh*, brothers-at-arms.

His hands clasped behind his back, Devilos said without inflection, "This is work, Bow, a trade to get a member of our team back. Not a porn show."

"Ha!" Bowie barked out a laugh. Through his grin he said, "Don't you think it's funny your thoughts went to porn? Come on, you've got to be as curious as I am. She sticks around long enough I'm going to try and finagle a date out of the wench. I think I have a shot if her perverted brother isn't around." His grin grew bigger at Dev's jaw gritting.

Connar entered the bridge with the prisoner Kincaid and another lieutenant, Tomi Thomason. Mammoth with dark skin the color of Earth's core, his smooth pate shaved clean, Tomi flanked the prisoner's other side.

Kincaid was enveloped in chains. They had chained his wrists behind his back and around his waist, neck and down to wrap around his ankles forcing him to walk with stunted shuffling steps.

The chains chinked around him as he moved. The lieutenants maneuvered him to an open space away from the cluster of staff and technicatics.

An uneasy quiet permeated the bridge as everyone was on alert awaiting the people to transport over. Bowie, Connar, Lukas and Tomi stood with weapons drawn in a guarded circle around the prisoner. Dev waited several feet from them, near to where the female and their missing comrade would evolve.

Tense moments passed, then, a wavering vaporous image within feet of Dev solidified into two people. His missing lieutenant and the prinţesă appeared.

Dev forced himself to keep his gaze on his man, Miles Dontour. "Lieutenant," Dev's deep gravelly voice sent shivers over the newest rookies on board, he asked, "you are well?"

He was much leaner than when Dev had last seen him, straight black hair swished over his grey eyes, but except for bruises and cuts, the man looked relatively uninjured.

Miles nodded, the hair flopped. He pushed it aside, his eyes slid sideways at the Prinţesă before returning to his liege. "Yes, Sire, I have been treated..." he glanced at her again, but her eyes had flit to Dev then around the room, then she fettered them by lowering her lids. "Uh, fairly well," he said with a shaky smile to Dev.

Then she spoke, all eyes were already on her, including now Dev's. "Sir, Captain Dravidian," her soft voice was so hushed she was barely audible. The prinţesă nervously pushed her long curls over her shoulders. "My...I mean, I am here to trade Mr. Dontour for," her eyes flicked anxiously to the prisoner.

His mouth hooked in a smirk, bright green psychopathic orbs gleamed lewd barbs at her. Kincaid deliberately strolled his gaze down her like a lewd lick, from the top of her flaming hair, over the heart-shaped face with plush lips and searing crystal blue eyes, over the gown that draped her full breasts, and sifted in at her tiny waist then curved over her small rounded bottom to pool on the floor.

Kincaid's tongue slicked the outside of his lips. He said with a lustful rasp, "Ah, Mistress, as soon as we're alone I'm going to fuck the heavenly shit out of-"

Bowie slapped the prisoner cutting off his words while Connar yanked out a handkerchief and tied it over Kincaid's mouth. The green eyes flashed furor, then shifted back to the woman where they tangibly raped her.

Due to Bowie and Connar's distracting movements, everyone shifted positions. The woman and Miles were inches closer to the prisoner.

Dev's brows drew together in a frown. His hand out to her he said, "Prințesă, you need to move away from-"

The woman, Miles, and the prisoner started wavering.

Dev barked, "*Fuck no-*" He grabbed at her, clutched her face with both hands, and bizarrely covered her lips with his in an inexplicable kiss. The thought, *velveteen roses*, flickered through Dev's brain as she faded in his hands; the shocked, confused, dazzling blue eyes were the last things he saw.

"What the hell?" Bowie burst out taking a step towards the disappearing threesome.

To the empty space Connar yelled, "Miles!"

The room reverberated in stunned silence.

Dev stalked over to Elvana who sat in stupefied shock with her mouth hanging open. He ordered, "Get her, *now.*" Sparks of orange flames shot up around the enraged warlord's boots.

Blinking dumbfounded teardrop dark eyes at him, Elvana didn't move.

"Now!"

His bark jolted her. She turned to her monitor and typed rapidly. Waited. Nothing.

"Again," he snapped.

She typed again and again, but there was no response from the prinţesă.

Dragging a hand down his face, Dev scrubbed his skin hard with his fingers. "Keep trying. And I want a locate trace put on her. Find out where she transported from. Advise me as soon as you know."

He turned from her, strode across the bridge and out the door, flashing flames popping and lashing behind him.

Bowie tracked after him. "Shit, Dev, what the hell was that all about?"

He shook his head, the braids swept his back and shoulders. "I don't know. A trick to get Kincaid, I assume."

"Why take Miles back then?"

One shoulder bumped. "So she can use him again."

The corner of his mouth cut up in a half-grin, Bowie said, "You kissed her, Dev, what the hell-"

"I was trying to hold her from evaporating. I should have grabbed her fucking tits and ripped them off her. When I see her again, I will do just that." Enraged steam poured from him, fire blazed in ferocious flames around him.

He was as surprised and confounded as the others that he had kissed her. When he gets his hands on her, and he will, he'll beat her within an inch of her young life, then throw her over his knee, lift that gown and spank the fucking humiliation out of her bare bottom before terminating her life.

His growl fierce and quiet he swore, "That bitch is on my hunting list."

Chapter Three

As she was materialized in front of her half-brother, Sveti was fuming. She and the two males had been transported to Krystian's ship. The ship fled to their planet, and then the trio was transported to the castle.

Krystian stood there with a smug smirk. Dressed in black, his belt and cuffs were gold, his boots polished to their pointy gold toes, the dark red hair swished over his ruffled collar.

"Ah! It fucking worked! I can't believe it," Krystian crowed as strode to where the three bodies were solidifying.

At the same time, half a dozen guards in black and red uniforms rushed over to make a wall around Kincaid. The gag over his mouth, the prisoner glanced around at everyone with a wary, puzzled look.

Krystian said to two of the guards, "Return the prisoner Dontour to the brig."

The two guards instantly grasped Miles' arms and dragged him away.

"Krystian, no!" Sveti cried with quick steps to her half-brother. "When you forced me to do this you said you were freeing Miles, you can't keep him prisoner!"

The doors opened, Miles twisted his neck to look back at Sveti. "Don't worry, Prinţesă, I'll be all right. Now that he knows where I am, Devilos will come for me. I don't blame you, you were kind to me and he tricked-" He was jerked out of the room and the doors swished shut.

Sveti swung from staring aghast at the doors, to her half-brother. His nasty smug grin chased away her normal fear of him. "Krystian, I don't understand," she said as she moved closer to him but stayed out of reach since he loved to touch her.

Released from a prison colony after years of incarceration for committing dastardly deeds, Krystian had gone to his and Sveti's father's home, and was instantly besotted with his beautiful half-sister. Whenever he could get near her, he stroked, fondled, groped anything he could get his hands on.

He made his obsessive interest in her clear. As far as he was concerned, he wasn't around while she grew up so they were basically strangers, and they were only half-blooded, therefore, they could marry if he chose.

"Darling," Krystian drawled, stepping closer to her. His gaze always lecherous when it settled on her was just as intense as ever. "I knew Dravidian would be willing to release a low level convict like Kincaid for his lieutenant."

His hands clasped behind his back lest he give into temptation and jerk the top of her gown down and fondle her with all the guards present, he swiveled to Kaeto Kincaid.

The malevolent smile creasing Krystian's handsome face drove visible willies right through the prisoner. The bright green eyes tapered in unease over the gag at the gleeful Sautarine.

Seeing Kincaid's expression tightening drew Krystian's grin wider. "You get it yet, Kincaid, why I wanted you?" He waited but the prisoner blinked in bafflement at him. "I want your power. I have equal level as you and with the right circumstances, and I have them here, I can take it from you."

Kincaid's eyes popped, beads of sweat burst around his hairline and ran down the sides of his face. He shot his gaze at Sveti as if asking her for help. She stood bewildered. As a human, she had little understanding of the aliens and their various kinds of powers.

Sveti said, "Krystian, you aren't going to hurt him, are you? I mean, why would you take his power when you have your own?"

Rolling his eyes, her half-brother frowned at her denseness. "Really, Sveti, get a clue already. You know my powers are quite..." he tugged slightly embarrassed at his shirt sleeves. "Let's say, inadequate. I can take equal level powers from another person and that will double the little bit that I have."

"But how-"

"It would take too long to explain. Chemicals, spells, and the help of a stronger-powered person. Jessen of Jupiter-solarium will be here to manifest the procedure."

Her lips pulled in, Sveti was still confused. She looked at Kincaid who was now sweating bullets. "Please, Krystian, don't do this to him. Be satisfied with what you were born with, it's wrong to covet another's...uh, possessions."

Krystian held a hand up. "It's already done, darling, don't worry your pretty little head, he'll hardly feel a thing, right Kincaid?" He swung his wicked face from Sveti back to the prisoner. His smile deepened as he saw Kincaid coming to the comprehension that he had just been given a death sentence. The shell of the body would have to expire for the principé to suck the power out of it.

"But, Krystian, you're not going to hurt him-"

"Hush, sweetness, it's none of your concern." Krystian snaked out his hand and snatched her arm pulling her in close to him. He stared down at her cherry lips. His brain turned to fuzz as lust for her charged from his loins, streaking up his body leaving a trail of heat behind, like it had since the first time he had returned home and laid his eyes on her.

There have been too many people around and too much activity going on for him to take her as he desired. And he still hadn't decided if he was going to sell her. He was working on a scheme to sell her *and* keep her.

But that didn't mean he couldn't play with her until then. Holding his sister immobile in his strong grasp, he lowered his head to kiss her.

The prisoner Kincaid went nuts. He thrashed his body trying to get loose of the chains; under the gag, his roars of fury and fear were muffled. The guards jumped to control him.

Krystian released Sveti and shouted, "Get ahold of him, shut him the fuck up!"

In the sudden chaos, Sveti used the distraction to slip away.

Grabbing up her long skirt Sveti hustled out of the room and to the elevator. She didn't go to her room, it's the first place Krystian will look for her. Instead, she hurried to a back staircase and jogged from the eighth floor down to the fifth.

As she rounded the corner, she saw the guards that had ushered Miles from the bridge leaving, already passing out of the corridor. They had put Miles in a room temporarily.

When the guards returned with other prisoners, they would transport them with Miles to the cell cages buried deep beneath the castle.

Scurrying silently to the room, Sveti whispered, "Miles?"

A second, then, a hopeful, "Prinţesă?"

She could hear him move nearer to the door. "Yes. Hold tight, I have a key." Earlier she had snatched several key cards out of security, managing to grab the one to the temporary holding cell.

She unlocked and opened the door, and with trepidation Miles poked his head out. His face lit with a grateful smile when he saw her.

Sveti gestured, said quickly, "Come, hurry."

He stepped out and she pointed to another staircase seldom used as everyone was lazy and utilized the lifts. "Go to the stairs, take them to the first floor. There is a door to the outside that everyone forgets about. Outside the door is a faint trail, follow it and it will lead to the woodlands. Here." She handed him a remote.

"I stole this from Krystian's room when he was away. There is a flashjet stashed on the far west side of the castle. Use it to escape. It will take you as far as the Fantar Station and you can call for help from your people there. The GPS will delete immediately so your captain will be unable to trace you back to here."

"But what about you, Prinţesă? Your brother will undoubtedly figure out it was you who helped me to escape. His wrath will know no bounds, even with you. My captain will shield you. You must come with me!"

Recalling his captain, the livid beast with braids all over his head that had kissed her to hold her, the fierce onyx eyes that glittered promised death to her, Sveti shook her head with a smile. "Don't worry about me, Miles, just go, hurry, don't look back."

When he still hesitated she urged, "Please, run!"

He took her hand, kissed it, then with a slight bow and grin, he was gone.

Sveti ran back down the corridor to the elevators, her soft slippers silent on the carpet.

"Sveti," a young man's voice stopped her at the elevator.

She spun around and smiled. "Ryen, hey, what are you doing here?" She hugged the fair blond man then stepped into the lift and he followed her.

He said, "I brought Krystian's May-Aunt, Mrs. Ells to the castle. Hey," he said, gently setting a hand on her arm. "You look upset." Yellow brows rippled in a frown over pale blue eyes. Worried, he asked, "Krystian didn't-"

"No." She shook her head, the shiny curls fluttered across her back. She didn't know how long the power sucking thing of Kincaid would take; she needed to find a place to hide for a while, let her brother's rage cool at her fleeing him, and helping Miles escape.

They stepped off the elevator together.

She sighed. "No, but every day, every minute, Krystian comes closer to claiming me." A shiver shook her entire body at the thought of wedding and bedding her blood brother. "I think he's trying to figure out a way of selling my virginity for powers, yet keeping me at the same time."

"I'm sorry. Sveti, the principé is notorious for his sick and torturous sexual predilections. People have tried to tell him it would be incest with you."

"I know, but he blows them off. You know, the strongest protesters he literally blew off, as in blown off out to space to die. The only thing that has saved me so far is that as much as he wants me, he wants powers almost more." Pink flushed her fair complexion.

Ryen's boyishly handsome face lost its cheerful smile. "We all know he has said that he could sell you, uh, your virginity to be exact, to a powerful prince. And it has to be a prince for the spell to work. Krystian could actually trade you for more superpowers from the prince, and as the prince would be a stronger being, he would not lose his life in the process. I've read that Krystian has put the banners out there to see if he can elicit interested buyers."

Her nod carried the despondence that was becoming too familiar. "Yes, and dozens of princes of differing species from around the nearest galaxies have responded with affirmations.

He just has to decide which one to accept, or keep me for himself. I think he will institute bids next. He exiled the rest of our family from the castle and forbade them to contact me, under penalty of death, so they can't help me."

The pair stepped outside into the warm day.

A gentle, kind young man, Ryen cupped her face and settled a chaste kiss on her lips, then sighed forlornly. "If only, Sveti, we could marry, you could have a normal life, children, with me."

The mild several suns' light glistened on a tear in her eye. She laid her palm on his smooth face and forced a weak smile. "We've been childhood sweethearts, Ryen, the little bit our families have allowed us to be together. But," she stroked his face sadly, "Krystian would never allow it, and I would never let him hurt you."

On tiptoes she gave him a swift kiss. "I need to…go. He will be looking for me and you can't be seen with me. He has vowed to kill any man that ever touches me, unless he has sold me to him. Funny, huh? Selective jealousy. Anyway, I will see you as soon as we can manage it. Okay?"

Sveti gave him another quick kiss then made her way to the chapel down the lane.

Leaving the voluminous, ivory granitium castle behind her, she hurried along, choosing to run over the flowing blades of grass instead of on the moving travelelator.

As soon as she entered the tiny, dim, quiet building, the tenseness shed from her shoulders. The chamber was empty.

She walked quietly to a pew and knelt on the prayer bench. Her hands clasped and head bowed, she struggled to pray for the prisoner Kincaid, for Miles, and for Krystian to do the right thing with her.

Shaking her head in chagrin, that was not going to happen. Krystian was more powerful than their father who was only a human. Krystian gained his powers from his mother, Khrisstya.

Khrisstya and their father met while she had come to his planet on an intergalatical vacation, but she had died bearing Krystian. Sveti's half-brother was a narcissistic sociopath.

The rumors that filled the castle of Krystian's decadence and depravity, and the enjoyment he got out of torturing his sex partners chilled Sveti to the core.

As she tried to concentrate on her prayers, the picture of that...man? Beast? Devilos Dravidian came to her mind. Assuming the warlord Dravidian would be suspicious of Krystian but less so of a female, Krystian had sent transmissions for the trade of Miles in her name. A full body shudder shriveled her skin as she recalled the...creature. The warlord.

The men standing in a circle around him had looked fairly human. He was different. Sort of human but...beast-like. He was big, massive, all mammoth lean muscles, and he had...horns, like a ram's that faced the back of his head, and, he had pointed ears. Numerous, long black braids covered his head and swung around like tentacles as he had reached for her.

At first he had regular hands, human fingers, big and thick and strong, like iron pegs that clutched her face. Then as he reached for her while she was fading she saw claws unsheathe from his fingertips in his rage.

Her heart pounded as she recalled those claws, the behemoth chest, the horns, and the unleashed wrath on his roughly carved face, fierce and frightening, yet oddly...handsome.

With a quiver, Sveti thought she'd also seen...fangs, along with the fury and vow of death in his dark eyes as they turned to...blazing white...as she faded from him.

She touched her lips with her fingertips. As hard as his full lips were, his rough kiss...was...unnerving, almost...painful, she had felt the brush of his fangs as she was dissipating. Yet, something deep inside her, she couldn't put her finger on it, stirred.

Exhaling a deep sigh, she pushed him from her mind and tried to focus on her prayers, but those deadly eyes bored right back into her brain. Sveti knew, if he found her, he would kill her.

And, she had a feeling, he was going to hunt her, like wild game. He wasn't the kind of creature that would let the trickery committed against him go without retribution.

"Prinţesă," a quiet voice called to her.

It took a strong effort to pull her thoughts from the...ferocious beast, Dravidian, to attend to Gillian, one of the castle tenders. Lifting her skirt, she wiped her eyes with the hem of the dress, then resettled the skirt around her ankles and turned to the woman. "Yes, Gillian? What is it?" It had to be important to interrupt her in the chapel.

Gillian, in her thirties, would have been prettier if her chin wasn't so long and square, and her poor wispy hair that grossed out Krystian. He told her if she didn't get it under control he would remove it, with a knife. Starting at her eyebrows. She hurried over to where Sveti knelt. "Prinţesă, it's Samson."

Sveti's hand flew to her chest. "My little brother, what, Gillian, what has happened? Is he all right?" Grabbing handfuls of her skirt to pull it out of the way she scrambled to her feet.

"No, I mean yes, I mean no," the woman panted, she'd run all the way from the castle.

Sveti grasped her arms. "Take a breath, Gillian, tell me." She waited, growing more scared by the second as Gillian struggled to get a grip.

"He- he's been taken, Prinţesă -"

"Who? Who has taken him? Answer me, Gillian!" Sveti shook her hard.

"Uh," she stammered, "Illyios Gha'auvin, Priest of the Amphicyonids, the bear-dogs. A messenger sent notice," she gasped for breath, "he is going to sell him to the Ochlos."

The words shook from Sveti's frozen lips, "From the planet Ochlo for- for Ochlocracy- meaning mob rule. They are the ones stealing people, other beings, aliens, to work the Naledi-Sarkastodons' mines. Oh my Goddess Satrine!" Sveti pushed past Gillian and rushed out the door.

She didn't stop running until she was in the castle and to the communications center.

Sveti forced herself to stop outside the door and draw a deep breath; if she flew in all frantic and disheveled they would call Krystian before complying with her instructions.

Her half-brother would never attempt to rescue their little brother Samson.

She took a panicked moment to smooth her fiery fat curls down, then her dress, wiping her damp palms on her gown she willed her pulse to slow.

As she moved in front of the automatic door, it swished open. She stepped inside the center.

There were eight people within the room consisting of several species working at various controls. They glanced up at her.

When they went to rise, she held out a hand and said, "Please, stay seated." She walked on wooden legs to the orator transmitter.

"Dennison." She smiled at the orator.

"Yes, Prințesă." The Acksand from third galaxy of aurora nodded his long horse-like head to her.

"I need you to send a transmission for me. Right now."

"Yes, Prințesă. To whom?" His four tiny, hooved fingers hovered over the inlaid tablet.

Sveti cleared her throat, calmly said, "To Illyios Gha'auvin."

His hooves halted in mid-air. Dennison's big nostrils flared, snorted, super long lashes swept down then up, his chocolate eyes rolled sideways up at her. "Ma'am? Not the-the Priest of-"

"Yes," she said firmly. "It's all right. Krystian asked me to forward a message to him. There is a planned ransom to be made between them. Go ahead." Sveti gestured with her head for him to type.

The round brown eyes stared at her for so long Sveti thought he would deny her. If he called for Krystian, her brother would flat out refuse, and quickly lock her up. But, then Dennison nodded his long head and typed.

Releasing her held breath, Sveti said softly, "Let me know when you access him, Denn."

"Yes ma'am."

Several taut moments passed before Dennison nodded at the tablet. "I have the speaker for his head captain."

"Fine. Scoot out of the way." Sveti pumped her hip at him to move him off his chair.

"But-" It was highly irregular for anyone but the assigned communicator to utilize the tablet. However, he would lose his head if he angered any of the royals in the castle, so Dennison shoved off the chair and stood to her side.

Sveti leaned over so he couldn't see what she typed:

'Illyios Gha'auvin. I wish to trade, immediately, myself for my young brother, Samson. I am older and thus will last longer, therefore be more valuable. I await your response, Prinţesă Svetiessa Ritrova.' She sent the coordinates for her exact location.

Sucking in an anxious deep breath, Sveti sat on her hands to still their trembling. She'd signed her own death warrant.

Illyios would either kill her after they entertained themselves with her torture, or sell her to another species to be sexually assaulted for as long as she survived, or be sold to the animal Nal-Sarks to work in their mines until she collapsed and died.

The Nal-Sarks were always seeking slaves as no one lasted too long in the mines. Some beings were stronger than others and lasted a while. Sveti knew she wouldn't last long, humans were the first to expire.

Getting a bad feeling, Dennison said nervously, "Mistress, perhaps we should wait for Principé Krystian to deci-" But he was too late. Sveti was fading before his eyes. Illyios Gha'auvin was taking her.

While he blinked like crazy, another form materialized.

A boy, more a bloody broken pulp than a human, lay crumpled on the floor.

Dennison ran for the com to call the principé.

Chapter Four

Earsplitting noise embroiled with shrieking pandemonium bombarded throughout the iron and rock fortress. Warlord Devilos Dravidian led his men battling their way through the rudimentary stronghold.

Screams and cries resonating in the very air around him, Dev slashed and thrust his Black-Noachian sword hacking off heads and arms, stabbing into bellies. The blood groove on the shaft of the blade caused increased bleeding, blood gushed like red rain hailing around them.

His team splintered out to the tunnels and stone corridors. No one used firearms as they could shoot each other accidentally with ricochets.

Creatures called amongst other names bear-dogs along with more alien fiends circled Dev, howling and screeching in a whirlwind, they hacked at him with ax-type weapons.

Chains whipped and swords slashed at the warlord trying to cut off his head, he ducked and dodged knives and spears flying at him.

Then, in an almost invisible cyclone of movement, Dev whisked around the room chopping and stabbing, punching and lancing until all but one of the creatures was lying dead or dying.

Ceiling-tall, the grizzly-canine came at him, mouth wide in a thunderous roar, every razor-sharp tine dripping with saliva, monstrous arms raised to bring his slashing trowel-sized claws down to slice Dev into pieces.

In less than a nano-second Dev morphed, growing hulking huge. His muscles burst into boulder-size, chest massive slabs of steel, he towered over the grizzly. Face a snarling mask of beast, Dev's own claws raked across the grizzly's gut as he smashed his fist into its face.

All around the charging Devilos, his body ignited fire that sparked and flamed then raged into a wildfire blazing through the chamber burning everything including the bodies to ash.

The creature fought back. Like two gigantic leviathans thundering over the earth they clawed and punched, kicked and snarled, slashing and hitting until Dev finally overcame the animal, pounding it into the ground until it was nothing but a bloody mess of entrails and crushed bones.

"Hey, Dev," Bowie huffed as he ran up to him sheathing his own Damascus sword. Like Devilos, he was smattered in blood and guts, but his grin was ever cheerful.

Dragging a sleeve over his eyes to clear the muck from them, he said panting, "I think we've got most of them. Our men are checking every room. Gha'auvin wasn't here that we can tell. We liberated the captured victims up here. Hey where you going?" he called out as Dev strode from him heading down one of a dozen spindled stone corridors.

Connar came tromping out of another corridor looking the same as Bowie, filthy, bloody, proud, and exultant. "Where is Dev going?"

A big smile covered Bowie's handsome face. Swiping the back of his wrist over his sweaty blond locks to push them out of his eyes, he replied, "The prințesă. Word was she is here, a prisoner. It's why we came. Gha'auvin captured her younger brother, Samson, and was about to sell him for the mines when the info reached the Prințesă."

"Aye, the rumor is true then."

Nodding, Bowie affirmed, "They say that she," the smile straightened into a solemn line, "traded herself for Samson. I heard the boy was returned," he grimaced, "in less than the perfection he was when he was taken."

Connar dropped his hands on his hips and matched Bowie's somber mien. "The prințesă is screwed."

Bowie shuddered with desolate sorrow. "Undoubtedly, she has been screwed to death."

"Well, the Amphicyonids are bear-dogs. I don't think they can, you know, fuck with humans. If she's still alive, she was probably to be sold. She wouldn't last but a minute in the mines, so Gha'auvin likely put her on the block. But, he and the other hounds would have had their torturous fun with her first."

"If she's still here, and lives, which is highly doubtful," Bowie said grimly, "Dev will find her. That's why he brought us here, he has unfinished business with the girl."

Nodding, Connar dragged his sleeve over his face clearing a path through the sweat and blood. "Uh huh, and then he will kill her for her trickery."

Dev moved quickly, stealthily down the stone steps into the bowels of the bastion, his heavy boots silent on the stones. Lanterns on the walls lit the way. The creatures that resided there were not into technology. They hadn't the brains or hands needed to utilize it. When transporting and communicating they used captured victims or other alien mercenaries to do the work.

He slowed when he reached the last step and adjusted his eyes to the dimness. All stone; walls, ceiling, dirt floor, the dampness clung to his skin, the stinking air cold. Desperate cries and tormented wails echoed over the barely lit, dank, harsh chamber.

Hesitating, Dev stood and looked around.

In the murky, pungent soil smelling, chilled gloom, all kinds of beings were chained to walls, poles, the ground. Most looked on their deathbeds, beaten to little but crushed bones and flesh.

Methodically scanning each prisoner, his eyes flicked over to a body hanging by a chain from the ceiling, the feet dangling a few inches from the floor.

The wrists were above her head clamped in chains; her emaciated body hung limp, head hanging down. The vibrant hair, a dirty tousled mess draped over her face.

Near her, a mercenary guard, he appeared human, had his hands on the hem of her ruined gown and was pushing it up to the tops of her thighs. When Dev approached, the guard turned.

"Halt," the guard ordered, "do not come any closer or I will kill you. You can do her after I'm done." His hands moved up under the dress.

The long braids dangled down his broad back, Dev's body was shifting almost back to normal, yet still double the guard's size, he kept advancing.

One hand on the hanging female, the guard pulled out a gun. Before he could aim it, Dev was on him. He threw his hands out, grasped the guard's head, dug his claws into his neck and tore the head completely off. The carcass fell, and he tossed the head.

Dev stepped over the body to Sveti. Fire burned in his gut at the way she'd tricked him, cheated him. But, Zues, she was hanging by her thin wrists.

His stomach churned, she was likely dead. He stuck his bloodied claw in the back of her thick, knotted hair and pulled her head back.

Sveti's colorless lips parted, her lashes fluttered so slightly Dev thought he'd imagined it. He saw her bosom rise slightly. She was alive, barely. He slid a burly arm under her and lifted her while hacking at the thick chain she hung from with his sword.

"Godsdamn, Dev, is she gone?" Bowie strode into the room, the sound of metal grinding as he thrust his sword into the sheath at his side, his heavy boots clunked across the stone floor.

"Not yet. See to the others," Dev commanded. The chain cut, Sveti slid into his arms.

Bowie looked down at her. "God's breath, Dev, they did a number on her."

Sveti's face was battered, so bruised and swollen she was barely recognizable. Her neck, arms, every visible bit of skin was bruised and slashed, bites pocked between the other injuries.

"Aye. Free the others, destroy the fortress and meet me at the Grisail." Carrying Sveti in his arms, Dev strode rapidly across the stone floor and up the steps two at a time.

He didn't stop moving until he'd reached the flashjet. When he got inside he saw everyone but Bowie was already there.

"Whoa, Dev, you got the prinţesă," Tomi crowed from his seat. He was belting in his huge body preparing for flight. Blocks of muscles covered his chest and arms. His shaved head gleamed with sweat under the bright lights.

Everything on Tomi was thick and black, his head, his neck, his body, his clothes.

Dev didn't respond. He moved to a captain's chair and sat down with Sveti draped in his arms on his lap. He looked down at the frail, delicate female.

She hadn't opened her eyes, her breathing was thin and shallow. The flaming hair darkened with filth whirled, arraying messy ringlets over his arms. Brushing the dirty locks off her battered face, he barely felt her slight weight on his legs. She'd been torturously beaten, starved, brutalized by the bear-canines.

Her gown was in shreds, he struggled to keep his eyes off her breasts more exposed than not in the torn fragments. It was doubtful she was going to make it.

He hoped she survived. Dev had punishment planned for her for making a fool of him. Lies, and cheating, faults that he abhorred the most. She'd done both. To him. No one got away with that.

Connar sank into the 2nd command chair and flipped levers and pushed buttons, stroked the digital pads, firing up the flashjet. He twisted his head to look at Dev with Sveti dying in his arms. "We're only waiting on Bowie."

His eyes on the critically injured woman on his lap, Dev mumbled, "He is liberating the civilian captives, and triggering the demolition devices you guys placed in the hold. As soon as he's here we leave. Be ready."

It wasn't long when Bowie trampled on board with a group of ragtag beings tramping behind him. "I'll get them settled in the board room," he said, as he motioned for the people to follow him. They were in pitiful filthy shape, so ill and injured they had to help each other to the lifts.

The outside door closed up and the engines fired.

The flashjet swooped straight up, then shot like a rocket into the stars.

Chapter Five

The ship landed smoothly on the space station. After they docked, Dev unbuckled his safety belt and left the ship carrying the prințesă. She hadn't once opened her eyes. Dev decided he must have only imagined how radiant and crystal blue they were.

As he made his way along foam-carpeted corridors and vast open spaces where people, humans and other species, hung around or traveled about, some who knew Dev waved, most quickly lowered their eyes and scurried out of his sight.

There were plenty of other immense and scary looking species on board, but Dev speared intense fear into even the most formidable hearts.

He strode for fifteen minutes before he finally reached the sickbay. The auto-doors flashed open before he reached them and closed as soon as he passed through.

Entering the first room Dev called out, "Geffry!"

A female Tron, a nurse with a body like an anvil, she was quite tall and strong with dark webbing hair, amphibian-like skin, several eyes, hurried over to him. She held her arms out to take Sveti. "Sire, give her to me I will put her on a gurney."

Dev strode past her, barked, "Get Geffry," and kept going until he reached an infirmary room. Most everything was white; walls, ceiling, beds, linens, chair covers. The floor was white and beige diamond shaped tiles.

By the time Dev reached a bed, a husky man came striding in. Also in white; coat, shirt, pants, his brown hair was tufted with grey, Dr. Geffry Jamez bustled into the room.

"Ah, Dev, what have we here?" He looked down at the battered woman in Dev's arms barely clinging to life. He told him, "Set her on the bed. Lynya," he called out to the nurse who had followed them into the room.

"Take her vitals and," he called out again to a male assistant that had followed him in, "Jaspin, bring me the relconsitation."

Dev gently laid Sveti on the bed. The mattress didn't even dent she was so slight. He stood staring down at her.

"Uh, Sire, uh," Lynya said nervously, "you uh, could you please stand back so I can take her vitals?" She had seen the Dravidian plenty of times when he brought in injured warriors but she was still just as terrified of him as the first time he'd drilled those incising fathomless eyes at her.

Dev didn't move as if he hadn't heard the nurse's request.

"Devilos," Dr. Jamez gruffed at him, "you aren't helping the injured young lady." He nudged his body against Dev easing him aside so the nurse could get to Sveti.

When Dev wandered over to the other side of the bed to observe, Lynya drew her hand-held auto-vital tac over Sveti's body.

A young human male hurried into the room wheeling a machine on a cart.

The doctor immediately unwound wires and suctioned them onto Sveti's head, chest, abdomen and hands then flipped switches on the machine. It whirred and blinked as information was fed from Sveti's body into it.

"So," Geffry Jamez murmured as he worked, "who is our guest and how did she get in such dire condition? Besides obviously beaten, kicked, bitten, and caned no doubt, she appears to have been…stomped on and starved." He peered into a screen that was clicking out a diagnosis.

His eyes on her, Dev explained, "She is Prinţesă Svetiessa Emita Ritrova. Apparently Illyios Gha'auvin captured her younger *bráthair* and was selling him to the Ochlos for the mines. When the prinţesă got wind of it she traded her life for his."

Geffry's brows hit his hairline. "Is she insane? Twas cerain death."

Dev nodded. "Truth. However, apparently her young brother's life was worth more to her than her own."

The doctor looked upon the uncouncious woman with grim eyes and tightened lips. "Brave lass," he commented softy. But you got her out in one piece?"

"My team invaded his lair, killed his soldiers, Gha'auvin wasn't present. I found her like this. The Amphicyonids as you know are grizzly-canines, they like to make their captives run so they can chase them and take them down, then they enjoy repeatedly pouncing on and batting them around, and throwing them at each other in games, cutting them and biting them."

Geffry shook his head, his lips pursed. "Hard to fathom creatures so evil and deranged they get a thrill out of submitting henious injuries upon a sentient being."

"And aye, you are correct, they get off on caning captives too, amongst other delights. I found the prinţesă in the dungeon hanging from the ceiling by her wrists. If she had survived the vicious brutality she would have been sent directly to the mines."

Jamez shot a glance at Dev. Shaking his head again he muttered, "Shit."

"Aye," Dev nodded agreeing, his eyes on the young woman. "Do you think she'll make it?"

The doctor ran his palms over Sveti's body incurring an inexplicable growl and frown from Dev.

Geffry ignored him. As the doctor ran his hands under her skirt up her legs, Dev's body pumped, the growl deepened, he moved imperceptibly.

Geffry glanced at him again with a slight smile. "What is she to you that you're reacting that way?"

Dev crossed his arms and glared at the doctor then lowered his gaze back to Sveti. "Nothing. Only a prisoner. My prisoner."

Stifling a chuckle, Jamez continued his examination. "I see." Then he turned serious. He leaned back and instructed Lynya, "Get plasma into her stat, AB pos, and electrolytes."

As the nurse hurried to do as he bid, the doctor sifted his palms over Sveti's ribs, she whimpered, her body pulsed.

Dev took a step closer to the bed. "What did you do? Did you hurt her?"

Shaking his head, pushing aside the shreds of her gown to expose her top half, Geffry said quietly, "Her ribs are broken. Every one of them."

The nurse blanched, whispered, "Oh my Zues' sons."

Sveti's entire torso, limbs face, neck were solid black and blue. Even the breasts that plumped over the torn peach bra were a mess of lacerations and bruises.

Dev's expression remained impassive, but his lids lowered over his eyes. "Geffry," his heavy voice low he asked, "what are her chances of recovery?"

Studying the relconsitation indicator, Jamez shook his head again. "I don't know. Right now it's iffy that she will survive the night. Now," he turned to Dev, said sternly, "I can't work with you in here glowering at me. You need to leave. I will contact you with information as it happens." He glared at Dev when the big man stood stolidly.

He had business to attend to or he would observe, for a while anyway. Rough and low, Dev commanded, "Someone is to stay with her every second, night and day. That will be only you or Lynya."

His fluffy grey brows rose then pushed down, Jamez said, "Devilos, Jaspin and Roy are quite satisfactory to watch over her." His flaccid face burrowed into a frown. "Besides, no one would attack that child in the condition she's in. She will be safe-"

Dev's words hard and cutting, brooked no further discussion, "Only you or Lynya."

The doctor raised his palms. "All right, fine. Now, get out so I can work on her."

Casting a lingering look from the top of Sveti's dirty curls down the length of her broken body, Dev spun and strode out the door.

Chapter Six

A few weeks passed when Bowie slid onto a barstool next to Dev. He raised a hand at the bartender then clasped his hands together and set them on the bar. "So, how's she doing?"

The strong, pale-leasant green liquid went down Dev's throat smooth as silk.

The bartender set a beer in a frothy draft in front of Bowie. The lieutenant picked it right up and chugged half of it before setting it down. Dragging the back of his hand over his mouth he made a satisfied, "*Ahhh*," sound.

Without looking at him, Dev said, "Jamez says she's on the mend. He kept her in an induced coma because the pain she would be suffering healing would be…unbearable, excruciating. He brought her out of it yesterday but," he chuckled mirthlessly, "he wouldn't let me see her. Said he didn't want his fragile patient frightened back to death."

Sucking his beer, Bowie laughed. "I can see that. Besides your fearsome looks, she's gotta know you have a personal vendetta hit out on her."

His brows drew down with a scowl. "I do not have a *hit* on her, Bow."

Bowie cocked his blond head at his friend. "Yeah? You need to tell her that, because moons to stars she's going to think that. Besides, you pretty much said those words. Everyone knows how she tricked you, us, with that ploy. But," his grin straightened, "Miles is back now. He told you she got him out, snuck him out, and assuredly, *bráthair* or not, Krystian Ritrova will punish her for that the second he gets her back in his clutches."

"Huh," Dev snorted, took a deep drink.

"You need to cut her some slack, bro, Miles said her *bráthair* sent that transmission to us in her name, and he forced her go with Miles. You saw at the party how he used his strength to manhandle her and how much she resisted. Hell, Dev, the fear and dread of him was plain as rain on her face."

Nodding grimly, Dev grumbled, "Aye, we, *I* should have been suspicious that it was not a visual transmission." Granted, Dev had thought about it at the time, but he wanted to get Miles back as soon as they could knowing he might be in bad shape, so he allowed the rushed transport.

It certainly wasn't because he had wanted to see the prințesă again. See what color her eyes were, see those lips-he shook his head of the nonsense filling it. "Geffry has cleared me to see the female in the morning."

"And then what? What will you do with her once she's recovered?"

Dev arched his neck letting his head fall back for a second, the braids dangling, before pulling it back upright.

"Doesn't matter the ins and outs of it, she was involved in the subterfuge, she was personally on board, on the bridge. She was complicit in the dupe."

"Uh, huh." Bowie shrugged. "But think about it, she looked scared as shit and didn't say a word, in fact she looked as shocked as us when Miles transported back with her. She's human, she can't transport, Ritrova would have had to do it. He undoubtedly didn't fill her in on the fraud he'd planned.

"And again, I repeat, she helped Miles to escape at the risk of her own neck. It's well known Principé Krystian Ritrova is a ruthless vicious psychopath.

"By Zues, Dev, she traded her life for her younger brother's, fully aware she would be tortured and then die at the hands of the bear-dogs, or work the mines until suffering an equally agonizing death. The females in the mines are granted no protection from the males, guard, prisoner or otherwise."

Devilos was silent as he finished his drink. Two females from Bowie's planet, Resh, approached the men, one slid onto the stool beside Dev, and the other turned her wide engaging smile to Bowie as she joined him on his right.

The woman next to Dev gave him a sparkling smile, her blue-red eyes shining in explicit invitation. She stroked her hand over his forearm then tucked it around his upper arm. Her elongated body was slender with enhanced breasts and matching derrière. She cuddled a breast against Dev's big arm.

"Sire," her words slurred slightly. "They say you don't bang chicks that are on the station, but when women from other planets gossip," she took a heavy lurid breath, "I hear you are like a fucking warhead in the sack. That you are a different kind of male, sex with you is...different. Rough and...punishing, with that steely body and other...aspects."

Wearing a tiny, tiny dress that almost didn't cover her bosom or butt, she plucked at the top pulling it down further aiming her rack at Dev. Any lower and she'd get arrested for public nudity. "I," she licked her enhanced lips, "l-o-v-e it rough, honey. How 'bout you take me right now and show me how tough you can be?" She tugged at one of his braids.

Dev didn't look at her, he glanced at his friend.

Bowie had his tongue down the throat of the female next to him and his hands up her top.

Shoving from the woman that clung all over him, Dev stood up, imprinted his wristband on the ticket in front of him paying his tab, and without a word, left the bar. Bursting constellations of aggravated flames ripped behind him.

The next morning, after showering and shaving, Dev pulled on black cargo pants and a black thermal shirt and headed to the infirmary. He ignored Lynya's scared cringe as he strode past her and went straight to the room Sveti was in.

He stopped dead in the doorway. The scowl prowling inside him didn't show on his stoic face as he observed Connar, Bowie and Lukas standing around Sveti's bed. They were laughing and grinning at her.

Even the serious science whiz Lukas with his Marine buzz cut was laughing.

And Sveti, still terribly thin but with roses in her round cheeks, in a clean gown, her hair washed, the curls shiny, was sitting up against a stack of pillows. Much of the bruising had faded and the cuts healed.

Judging by the stiff way she sat, he assumed she still had the wrapping around her ribs to hold them while they knit back together. She wasn't laughing or talking, she appeared to still be in pain and was just smiling in weak politeness at the men.

Bowie saw Dev in the doorway. "Hey, Dev, come on in. We thought we should see how our patient is doing. I mean, after all, we did rescue her."

Dev took a few steps into the room mutter, "No, *I* captured her."

He noted as soon as she saw him the color seeped out of her cheeks turning her pale face into soft alabaster. She shrank back against the pillows. The huge eyes were as crystalline as he had remembered, even more so. They were wide with terror at him.

"Geez, Dev, cut it out, you're scaring her." Bowie stepped in front of him with a warning frown.

"I didn't do-"

"Nay," Bowie hissed in a whisper, "it's your natural implacable scowl, and it's worse than normal. Lighten up."

Dev glared at him then lowered his head, generating a centering calm over himself. He growled to Bowie as he elbowed past him, "Get the fuck out of my way. We don't coddle goddamned *coiriúil,* criminals."

He moved in front of Bowie, catching his and all of his friends' displeased frowns, and the female looked about to expire from fright. She had obviously heard him.

The three men came together to stand like a wall between Dev and the girl. It was symbolic only, each man was aware it would be a helluva a fight but Dev could take them all out at the same time if he chose to.

Bowie said under his breath, "She's still sick, Dev. You can see how frail, skinny and tired, and in pain she is. You don't need to be scaring the fuck out of her." Indeed her plush lips tightened as a flash of pain crossed her face.

"You should have taken Esmeralda up on her offer last night and you wouldn't be so cranky now," Bowie joked. "I had to be a gentleman and step in for you and take them both to bed." He grinned broadly at his friend with a wink.

"Seriously, Dev," Connar said, "give her some time before you go all ballistic on her."

"Aye," Lukas chimed in. The three men stood immovable, their arms over their chests. Lukas added, "And you need to rethink the brig. It's freezing and uncomfortable, and filled with lethal men, she would be in danger, and she won't get well in that dank pit."

Dev knew he could take his men out if he chose to, but, his eyes narrowed in menace at Sveti. He stated coldly, "I'll be back tomorrow to talk with you, alone." Satisfied at the terror that flickered over her beautiful face, he turned on his heel and left the room.

Stalking down the hall, Dev was furious. The fucking bitch was a felon, a *coiriúil*. She had conned them and further endangered Miles' life with her false trade. His lieutenants had no business protecting her from him like she was a fragile child- shaking his head, whatever.

He went to the garage where the Grisail, his flashjet was parked and spent the next few hours burning off his anger doing routine maintenance on it, then afterwards he hit the gym because he was still fuming with ire.

Dev got up early the next morning, showered, shaved, and went straight to the infirmary. As he moved through the office, he nodded at Geffry but held a hand up as the doctor started to warn him off. He kept going until he stepped inside the small recovery room.

Sveti was as yesterday leaning against pillows. A tray was on a stand next to the bed. The plate of food looked scarcely touched. Her pallid face was strained with pain that she worked to clear the second she saw him in the doorway.

When he moved closer to her, she braced herself, her body stiffened, her eyes went to his horns, blinked hard like she was hoping she imagined them, and the pointy ears.

Although her half-brother was part alien, he looked fully human, she had come in very little contact with other aliens as isolated as they were on their planet.

"Prințesă Svetiessa," Devos muttered. He stopped a few feet from the bed. She looked so panicked he could hear her heart beating frantically from where he was. Literally could hear it. He had powerful hearing. "Can you please get a grip, I'm not going to eat you for fuck's sake."

Although the blue eyes were wide with fright, she whispered with faint sarcasm, "Are you sure about that?"

Dev's lip twitched, he stuffed his hands in his pockets. "I am here to discuss your status."

She clutched her hands together to still their trembling, and appeared to physically will herself to calm down. Her mouth opened as if to say something, but she closed it without a word.

Pulling his hands from his pockets, Dev set them on his hips. His upper body was so stacked with blocks of lean muscles it made his body more an extreme V with his tapered hips. The belt on his pants hung just slightly from his sinewy hips. A firearm in a holster pulled the side of the belt down a hair more.

His gaze rolled over the bright curls then back to the brilliant blues trained anxiously at him.

When she said nothing, he cleared his throat, his voice low and rough he said, "You are a *coiriúil,* a criminal. You are my prisoner. When you are well enough you will be confined in a suite."

Flame-colored brows arched in apprehension. "You mean, the uh, the brig."

He moved his hands to cross his arms over his bulky chest. "The brig currently is filled with dangerous…male outlaws. I have no space for a female." As she was a princess, she wouldn't have been housed there anyway but he chose not to tell her that.

"So, uh," she visibly swallowed hard before stammering, "what, uh, then? Will I be sent to prison?"

Dev covered the twitch in the corner of his mouth with his hand, shook his head. "Nay. You would have to stand trial first."

He studied her as the fear of the unknown and the possibility of lengthy incarceration rippled across her thin and still bruised, but lovely face, her thin shoulders trembled.

"However, your *bráthair*, uh, that is your brother, Principé Krystian Ritrova, has forwarded a warrant for your return." His brows drew down low at the strike of deeper thudding fear that rushed her expression.

She blinked rapidly as if to hold back tears, the tiny bit of color that she had, left her skin again. Dev wondered what she feared more, him, prison, or her brother.

Her weak voice shook, "W-" she took a breath and swallowed, "when will I go?"

He rubbed his brows with fingers and thumb. "When you are completely healed we will procure a ship to take you to your planet. My flashjet is too small to go the entire way. I think tomorrow you should be well enough to be moved to your suite. There will be a guard posted outside of your room. You will not be allowed to leave, unless you are with me."

Watching her as she struggled to control her anxiety, he said, "Do you have any questions?"

Long curly lashes swept down her cheeks where they paused before rising. Her gaze direct at him did not waver. "No, sir."

He waited, staring silently at her until she lowered her eyes as if it hurt to look at him. "Fine then. I will be back tomorrow to move you."

Her lids flew up and she blanched again. Oh aye, she feared desperately being alone with him. As she should. She said nothing.

Without another word he left the room.

Dev waited until the noon hour had passed the next day before he went to retrieve her. His friends had twittered at him all last night to not be so hard on her. She was frail, fragile, really a sweet little thing.

Bah. She was a felon who had them all fooled with her beauty and soft ways. Well, she wouldn't be pulling the wool over his eyes again, goddammit.

His prideful rage rose as he neared the infirmary, infuriated that he'd let a tiny slip of a girl, a human, get over on him.

When he reached the lobby, she was sitting in a chair in a medical green smock top and pants with her hands folded in her lap. Geffry was speaking quietly, almost fatherly to her. Great. She's taken another male hostage with those big, sorrowful blues. "Are you ready?" he snapped.

Geffry turned to him with a frown.

The woman blinked hard and started to get to her feet. Her knees buckled, Geffry threw an arm around her.

"There, there, Sveti, honey, remember I told you to take it slow. You move fast like that and you will get dizzy, lightheaded, having had more than one concussion incurred, you might pass out."

Dev watched them through narrowed lids.

When she was standing more steadily, Geffry patted her on her shoulder. He said, "There you go, honey, easy now. Take your medicine as I instructed you," he nodded to the small bag she clutched in one hand, "and-"

"Let's go," Dev snapped again, leveling a look at Geffry that shut the salt and pepper-haired doctor's mouth.

With a weak but friendly smile, Sveti said politely to Jamez, "Thank you, so much, Dr. Geffry. I will do everything you said. I am sorry you've had to go to such trouble to save my life when he is only going to take it." Her gaze flashed to Dev. His brows rose. The doctor sputtered.

She spoke softly, "Thank you for being so kind to me, doctor." Before the doctor could respond she started for the door. She didn't wait for Dev, just started down the hall.

"Dev," Geffry said, "she is not really recovered, you shouldn't-"

Without a word, Devilos trod out of the room. In only a few steps he reached her. The strain of walking turned her face red, her jaw clenched, crinkles tightened in the corners of her eyes.

He strode silently beside her, keeping to her slow pace until she put her palm against the wall and used it to brace herself as she struggled to keep putting one foot in front of the other, but she was slowing with each step, her breathing labored, tears of pain blurred her eyes.

With a beleaguered sigh, Dev shoved both hands under her and lifted her up in his arms.

"What- what are you doing?" she cried in surprise.

"I don't have all day," he muttered striding quickly down the corridor.

"But- but I think your other men offered to take me-"

She held herself so rigid in his arms he thought she would shatter. He murmured quietly, "Lay your head on my shoulder, Prinţesă, rest."

When she didn't move, her body shaking from the effort to keep herself away from his chest, he growled roughly, "I said lay your head on my shoulder, *do it.*"

Sveti gingerly set her head against his shoulder. It took a few minutes before he could feel her relax. Long flaming locks strew over his arm and fluttered behind them as he headed down a wide staircase.

When they passed people, Dev glared so blackly at them they averted their eyes and hurried away down corridors. As bone-thin as she was, she was still soft in his arms, her hair tickled his chin and the arm it tumbled over.

Her natural fresh feminine scent rolled over him, he made an effort to keep from inhaling it.

Without lifting her head, she said quietly, "I'm sorry to be such a burden, I can walk, please put me down, you must be weary."

In fact, he held her high and tight to his chest and wasn't even breathing hard or slowing his pace. He carried her as if she was made of paper.

He didn't reply or set her down, just kept going until twenty minutes passed and he reached a suite amongst an endless row of suites. A guard stood at stolid attention to the side of the door.

Dev nodded at him. The guard opened the door with a sly sneak peek at Sveti's chest.

Dev carried her in and the guard closed the door behind him. Dev went straight through the living room, down a carpeted hall and into the bedroom. Everything was unadorned white. Floor, walls, furniture. He set her down on the bed.

Setting her medication on the blanket, she wriggled to sit on the edge of the mattress. Her head turned slightly away from him, her eyes closed as if prepared for him to strike her.

He stepped a few feet from her, his attention on her face still pale from her ordeal and losing even more color as she held her breath waiting for the beating she clearly thought he was about to initiate.

A corner of his mouth quirked, he towered over her in height, weighed 100 plus pounds more than her and was stronger than ten bulls. If he struck her once with his fist she would be dead.

He crossed his arms over his powerful chest and remembered he had planned to smack her butt until she couldn't sit for a month, humiliate her like she'd humiliated him. But, right now, she looked so frail that a slight breeze would knock her over.

His voice coldly dispassionate, he said, "You know how to work the controls to decorate the chamber any way you desire. There is a kitchen supplied with a week's worth of food. The maid will see to the cleaning of the suite and your," he took a breath, she had no clothes.

"I will have the maid bring you whatever incidentals you need and some clothes."

He swiveled heading for the door then paused. "Doctor Jamez will be by tomorrow to check on you. Otherwise, as I said before, you will not leave this suite unless you are with me. And, only the maid will be allowed in. Do you have any questions?"

She faintly shook her head, warily watching the angry beastlike man. His threatening dark eyes under a low ridged brow raked over her, huge biceps bulged under the tight shirt when he moved his hands to his hips. With a flick of his head he tossed back the long braids that were all over his head.

"All right. You need anything, you intercom Keldon the guard, or call me. My number along with Dr. Jamez's is in the wall cell-com." He waited. Her lips stayed closed, she just stared at him.

He turned and walked out of the room, down the short hall, through the stark living room and out the door, where he let out his held breath.

Chapter Seven

$\mathcal{D}$ev attended a variety of meetings, reviewed research on some outlaws he was going to hunt, and hung with his lieutenants in the evenings. When any of them tried to bring up Sveti, he shut them down.

He waited a week before going to see her. The guard, the maid and the doctor reported back to him daily. She was healing, eating a bit more, she caused no trouble and was sweet and kind to them. Sure, he thought, and Adam thought Eve and her pet snake were sweet too.

When he reached her chambers, the guard was planted against the wall. Dev nodded to him, the guard did not blink or respond. Dev knocked on the door and waited. Nothing.

He knocked again, then again.

She didn't open the door.

What the hell- He had the guard open the door and close it behind him.

Inside, soft music played. He glanced around. She had decorated the suite. It was filled with verdant leafy plants, vibrant with flowers of pinks and purples.

The entryway was soft neon shades of greens, blues, tiny tiles made up the lower half of the walls. In the living room, soft blue lighting illuminated the pastel lavender walls. Hearing sounds coming from the kitchen, he made his way there.

The kitchen was done in pastel yellow and corals, and ochre. Herbs in small pots clustered on a shelf over the sink.

Sveti was standing on a crate that was on a chair and she appeared to be trying to get a knee up onto the counter. The cupboard above her was open, and she was reaching for something way above her head on the top shelf- she started teetering, then her arms flailed as the crate shifted, then the chair-

Dev rushed over and slapped his big hand on her bottom to hold her steady. At her yelp, he barked, "What the hell are you doing? What the fuck is the matter with you? Why didn't you ask Keldon the guard-"

He broke off recalling the leer the guard had slipped her when he thought no one was looking. Picturing the guard with his hand on her ass like Dev's was, for some crazy reason made his blood smolder.

"I couldn't reach-" The crate shifted, she jerked her feet trying to keep her balance, her arms flailed and she toppled from his hand, yelped again and dropped in his arms with an, "*oof!*"

Blue eyes pinned wide collided with his rich black orbs. He quickly lowered his lids shuttering his eyes. When she landed she threw her arms around his neck, her breasts pressed against his strapping chest. His already smoldering blood ignited, flooding his groin with heat.

He quickly set her on her feet and took a step back. She'd put her hair up on top of her head in a messy bun but much of the tresses had tumbled out and curled around and down her shoulders.

"What were you thinking climbing up there like that?" He reprimanded her like she was a child. "Standing on a fucking crate on top of a chair? How stupid-"

"I- I didn't want to bother Keldon, the uh, guard. I just needed to put the-"

His voice grated through his clenched jaw, "You need something you call me. No one else. And no more goddamned boxes on top of chairs. You got that?"

Sveti took in his skin darkening with his eyes, his hair was not in braids, it hung straight down his back past his shoulder blades. Her gaze rose to the top of his head and she blanched. The horns on his head were growing bigger, thicker.

Seeing her looking to the top of his head, Dev ran his hands over the horns as if trying to flatten them like he would an erection. Her eyes glued to his horns, she inched away from him.

"Knock it off," he groused annoyed, "if I was going to harm you right now, I would have let you fall."

"Um, that was probably reflexive," said Sveti inching a bit further from the dark glower like a black laser cutting at her.

His gaze flickered down the front of her body. If possible, his glower hardened more, the dark orbs heated with flames of white. He barked, "What the fuck are you wearing?"

"What?" She crossed her arms in an X over her front with her hands on her shoulders.

His gaze shot down her clothes to her bare feet and back up, brows knifed between his eyes.

The top she wore was just a bit of a cropped t-shirt that fit very snuggly to her breasts. He could see her nipples poking through the thin material before she crossed her arms over them. She was so skinny from being starved her breasts looked swollen compared to her tiny waist and slight frame.

She had on a miniscule pair of shorts that showed brief flashes of the bottom rounds of her butt.

He looked at the slender legs that were shapely but thin and childlike showing she was only recently out of her youth. His groin burned and swelled more, he resisted tugging at his pants to loosen them.

Raking her with angry scrutiny, brows down hard over his surly eyes aimed at her chest, he ground out, "You look like a slut. Your tits show right through that shirt and your ass is hanging out."

Dumbfounded, her mouth fell open, arms dropped. Then her brows lowered, lids narrowed, she responded with her own anger, "First of all, Sire, you are aware I have nothing to wear. The maid is washing the one gown she brought me."

Setting one arm around her waist and resting her elbow on the forearm, she tapped a finger on her lip, "And two, I am here alone. I see no one but Mara the maid, it's not like I'm parading around in front of an audience."

Her hands moved down, curled on her hips and one lid lowered further over an eye in a squint of reproof. "I sure didn't expect you to come barging in unannounced. That was rude, so you deserve to see the ignominious me. Suffer it. I'm sorry I disgust you, so don't look at me." She moved her arms to cross under her bosom with a huff.

His gaze still on her breasts, pupils dilating, he growled, "You aren't even wearing a bra?"

Uncomfortable, she moved her arms back up over the front of her. Licking her lips, she said, "You are very vulgar and too familiar to talk to me like this, and it is none of your business what I do or don't wear. Besides, I have only one and it's in the laundry. Again, I was not expecting to see anyone." His huge intimidating body looming over her, she backed away.

Following the trail of her tongue, his teeth grit. "I knocked. You didn't answer. I thought you might be ill or injured," the corner of his mouth curled. "As it happens, if I hadn't come in you would have fallen. You were up high enough you could have broken your foolish neck.

"Which brings me back to, don't let me see you do that shit again. When you're pulling a chair over to climb on it, think twice and call me. You need something fetched that you can't reach or lift, or a lid you can't twist off, you call me. Only me. I don't want the guard in here. Do you understand?"

She backed from him wrapping her arms tighter around her body. Even though she spoke to him with rebuke, clearly her fear of him hadn't lessened a whit. Which wasn't surprising considering beings like him were rarely seen.

Plus, he realized his skin had darkened, shoulders inflated, he was so much taller than her and she knew he was infuriated over her illegal stunt. His pointed ears twitched with irritation.

"No," she replied, shaking her head, "I don't understand. You should have let me fall, that would have solved your problem of punishing me or having to take the time to take me to my," a catch in her throat, "anyway, if I broke my neck all our problems would be solved, and it would save you a lengthy trip. Right?"

His attention was on her lips. The remembrance of their kiss came unbidden to his mind. Unfortunately, it wasn't the first time. Or the second or third, the kiss had plagued him since it happened. He didn't know the fuck why.

He blinked away the thought. "What was it you were trying to reach? I will get it for you."

A slim smile softened some of her angst. "Actually, I was putting a bowl back up. I had used it to make pasta fungiello. You know, mushrooms, eggplant, cherry tomatoes, other stuff in a light, slightly spicy saffron sauce."

His raven brows rose, gaze still on her lips. "That sounds…good. You can cook?" He sounded disbelieving. "A princess cooking?" He shook his head as if the idea was ludicrous.

The plush lips pushed out. "I happen to be a very good co-"

Someone was knocking on the door. His eyes in a stupor on her mouth, Dev didn't move but Sveti hurried out of the kitchen and into the living room.

Her hand was on the button when he came from behind her and threw his arm across the front of her jerking her back against his chest. His palm slid over the top swell of her breasts before it got across to her arm. Her nipples instantly popped from the contact.

He fought looking at them. "You never open the damned door without seeing who it is first. What's the matter with you?" he scolded harshly.

His arm over the front of her held her petite soft body taut against his hard chest, her little round bottom pushed into his already hardened groin, her hair sprawled over his arm. Thinking, *soft as Earthly pussy willows*, he quickly released her.

Moving her behind him, he peered through the peephole then opened the door.

Sveti stepped from behind Dev to stand beside him. The maid was there with some clothes for her. Next to her, Keldon was blatantly leering at Sveti's breasts, his gaze delved to between her legs and back to her tits.

Dev gave him such a threatening look the man withered and quickly turned his head. With a deep scowl at Sveti, Dev moved her back to stand behind him, and waved the maid in.

Once she came into the room, Dev closed the door and said to Sveti, "Mara will bring you more clothes and a case to put them in. We're leaving day after tomorrow to go to, ah" his ebony eyes flicked to hers then dropped, "to take you home."

Again, she looked even more horrified than she did when gaping at his fierce face. Her skin paled, she bit her lips to stop them from trembling.

Observing her obvious anxiety about returning home, he said, "I will come for you in the next morning. It's a very long way to your planet. There will be others on the large airship we're taking to visit their relatives and friends at stops along the way."

He watched her but she stared blankly at the floor. Her lids seemed heavy and she swayed slightly. "What is the matter, Svetiessa? Are you ill?" He wound long fingers like iron rivets around her upper arm to hold her steady.

She wiped at an eye that had a purple shadow under it. "I'm fine."

"No she isn't, Sire," Mara stated firmly. "She insisted on cleaning this entire place and has worn herself out being still in recovery from the hell she went through."

Dev turned Sveti to face him. She looked so weary, about to drop. He asked the maid, "Why was she cleaning?"

The forty-something Mara tucked brown hair up in a chignon and straightened her black bodysuit with lacey collar over her plump figure. "She said she did not want someone having to clean up after her. I argued, but," she lifted her palms, shrugged, "she did it anyway."

She added with a whisper, "Plus, her nights are punctuated with nightmares of the Amphicyonids, the torment, what she endured. Between that and her fear of going home, well, she hasn't gotten a lot of sleep."

Sveti's lids were rolling down over her tired eyes, she looked thoroughly done in.

He could understand the nightmares. He had taken her out of hell that day. Dev started to ask her why she was afraid to go home to her brother, but shook himself, it was none of his concern. He didn't care what she was afraid of. Right now, she needed to go to bed. "Come," he said and drew her from the door.

"Where-"

"You're going to bed for the rest of the day." He walked her across the carpet to the hallway.

She tried to pull her arm from his grasp but his hand was like a thick steel clamp. "I am fine, please, I haven't finished tidying, I need to-"

He ignored her, dragging her to the bedroom. Inside, he let her go and pulled the lavender blanket and white sheet down then stood aside.

She tried to glare at him but was too tired to make it look stern. Instead, she turned from him and started for the door, saying, "Don't be ridiculous, it is early, there is so much more work to do, the floor still needs mopping. I am not going to bed now."

His gaze fell to the butt cheeks showing under the shorts and remembered how he'd thought to toss her over his knees, lift her gown and smack her behind until she screamed, for the con she'd pulled. He could jerk those little shorts off that curvy ass with no effort- He shook his head.

"Svetiessa," his voice a chilled warning, "you get back here, right now. You do not want me to come and get you. Get in the bed and lie down."

She halted. Sighed. "I need to undo my hair, and," hearing his deep rumbling growl, she turned and moved gingerly back to where he stood by the bed. Keeping her eyes off the hulking warrior, she sat down on the mattress with a vexed sigh.

He hovered over her staring down at the top of her head. Speaking in cold even spurts, he snarled, "I said, get in the bed and lie down. *Now*. All the doctor's hard work, and I am not returning an ill woman to her *bráthair*."

Again, her features paled, her head lowered and there was a faint trembling in her hands. Her fear made no sense, before he left her with Krystian Ritrova, he would get out of her why she feared him so much.

But for now, he waited while she slid thin bare legs in the bed and lay on her back with her head on the pillow.

Looking up at him under lowered lashes, she mumbled through a yawn, "Your hair is unbraided."

His long black hair hung down his chest and shoulders making him look more like a medieval warrior instead of his normal demon warrior. His smile crooked, he said softly, "Aye, it is."

"Hmm." She rolled over partially on her side and closed her eyes, murmured, "You're kind of bossy you know."

He smiled, said quietly, "Because I am the boss." Dev watched her for a minute. When she didn't move, he bent and pulled the pins from her hair and set them on the nightstand. Then he combed his long fingers through the curly locks, spreading them over the pillow.

Exhaling a soft sigh, Sveti rolled and lay on her back, the blanket fell to the side. Her hands moved up beside her head like she was surrendering. She was asleep.

Dev's gaze fell to the tiny tight shirt that cradled her breasts like they were round pillows. Her beaded nipples had relaxed into soft nubs.

His eyes drifted down to the tiny shorts that outlined her young womanhood. His pants grew so tight he had to tug at them for relief. He pulled the sheet and blanket up to cover her. Then quickly left the room.

"Mara," he said to the maid, "I do not want her out of that bed until morning. She argues with you, you tell her you will be punished if she does. I have a feeling that would have more impact on her than if I threatened her harm."

Seeing Mara's smile that he was correct, he nodded. "All right. No one comes in, and she does not leave the suite. In the morning you may leave to take care of your own needs. Right?"

She bent her head respectfully. "Aye, Sire."

Closing the door, Dev said to the guard, "No one, except Mara, not even you, goes into her room. Clear?"

Keldon nodded sharply. The guard with short wheat colored hair combed to the side, kept his hawk nose level, he knew the Dravidian had seen him ogling the sexy little miss and was very displeased about it. His light blue eyes unblinking, he stared straight ahead

Dev strode down the corridor to another, and another, up some stairs, more corridors before he reached his own suite. Dragging a hand through his long locks as he entered the room, his majordomo presented himself.

"Sire," he bowed his head. Then smiled. "You were with the human woman?" He had been with Dev for hundreds of years, long enough he was almost like a father to him.

"Aye." His expression impassive, Dev went to a counter containing bottles of liquor. He grasped a bottle, pulled the stopper off, and poured the blue-tinted liquid into a glass.

"Is it true, they say she is extraordinarily beautiful, even beaten and emaciated?" Brahms followed behind Dev with his hands behind his back. He always wore black tails and a starched white shirt, his silver hair combed straight back.

One shoulder rose in casual disinterest. "Aye." Dev tipped the glass to his mouth.

"And, they say she's as sweet as the morning dove. True?"

Dev frowned at his glass, said nothing. He left to go to his office, knowing Brahms was smiling amused at his back.

****

Very early the following morning, Brahms had just finished braiding the dozens of Dev's war braids when there was a rap at the door. Brahms went to open it.

Dev stood up starting to button his shirt, then stopped when he saw Keldon at the door.

Dev moved quickly to him, his brows down. "What are you doing here?"

Keldon looked confused. "Ah, you sent for me, Sire."

His forehead furrowed, the ridge of brow hardened. "I did not. Explain yourself."

Color crept up Keldon's thick neck. Over the hawk nose his pale blue eyes darted to Brahms who always remained cool and composed with a slightly satirical smile. "Uh,"

Keldon said to Dev, "Rianna Malone told me you said to come to you immediately. I uh, said I wasn't to leave the prinţesă's door, not leave her alone, as the maid Mara had gone to-"

Grabbing the keycard from the guard's hand, Dev shoved Keldon out of the way and sprinted down the hall.

Outside of Sveti's door he heard a woman's strident voice; it was not the young prinţesă's soft lilting tones. He threw the door open.

Sveti was on the floor holding her palm to her face where a bright red splotch marred her fair skin. Rianna stood in front of her in body clinging tights and a thin sweater that cut down the front almost to her navel.

A sharp move and he would know the color of her nipples. Not that he cared to. She clutched a knife in her hand.

"What the hell is going on?" Dev strode to Sveti, bent and grasped her arm pulling her to her feet. He moved her hand to see her face. Tilting her chin, he could see the mark was clearly a handprint.

He turned to Rianna who was nonchalantly studying her nails. "Rianna, what the fuck are you doing here?"

The voluptuous woman took a menacing step towards Sveti, she had a good ten inches on the petite prinţesă. "That bitch, Devilos, she is a criminal, she belongs in the brig with the other crooked convicts."

She took another step towards Sveti, her arm raised with the knife in her hand ready to slash at her.

Dev moved in front of Sveti, his big body blocking her, tough hands planted on sinewy hips. His voice gruff disbelief, "You fucking hit her?"

Seeing his harsh face harden into sharp planes, the dark eyes flickering white, wisps of flames flashed around him,

66

Rianna backed up, but said with a sneer, "Yes, she needs to know she can't get away with her illicit behavior on our journey to her home. She puts the rest of us, you especially, my handsome prince, in danger."

Holding the knife in one hand, she lifted the other to stroke his bare chest through the unbuttoned shirt.

His eyes blazed blinding white and narrowed, he grasped her wrist and twisted it, the knife fell to the carpet. He threw her hand in disgust.

Stunned, now nervous at his painful aggression, the tall brunette backed several feet away from him.

The furious warlord hissed, "Leave. Now. You touch her again and I will forget you are a female," his lip curved in a snarl, the fangs descended and glistened in threat.

Rianna's olive skin paled. She pulled in her wide lips and left the suite with a huff, slamming the door behind her.

Dev turned to Sveti, flames leaped at his feet.

The pastel ceiling lights gleamed off the wetness in her big blues. "I- I'm so sorry, uh, Sire. I didn't mean to cause any more trouble, I swear." She stepped away from him, her hand still over the red stain on her cheek trying to hide it in her embarrassment.

In frightened awe, she gawked at his fangs, the horns had also grown bigger, claws curled from his fingertips, his face seethed dark and fearsome.

Her gaze dropped, he had only buttoned one button on the bottom of his shirt. His massive chest covered with dark hair was partially visible. His torso so powerful she looked with vivid fear at it, yet, enthralled.

The flames disappeared. Murmuring, "Svetiessa," he clasped his hands behind his back to move his claws from her sight, and willed his fangs and horns to retreat. "You did nothing wrong. She should never have come here much less strike you, or brandish a knife at you. She is lucky her cousin is a friend of *má bráthair* or she would cease to exist for that offense. I will, however, see to her discipline."

Sveti's mouth dropped, she paled. "No, please, you wouldn't," seeing his stoic expression, it was clear he would. "I- it is not worth a person's wellbeing, I am not worth it."

She moved to him and without thinking set her palm on his chest like Rianna had and appealed, "Please, Sire, don't hurt her, please. I'm sure she didn't mean anything, she probably...uh, already regrets it."

Dev didn't move, not even to look down at the small warm hand on his bare chest. His skin tingled under her innocent touch, and the tingle rifled down his chest, through his abdomen, straight to his shaft. Feeling it harden, he knew he needed to get away from her.

Rianna's hands on him repulsed him, disgusted him. A trivial, light touch of Sveti's and his body burned raging out of control.

Wide pure blue eyes studied him, she bit her bottom lip as if discerning was he going to hurt her and should she try to run now. But she didn't move and the heat kept radiating across his chest from her small palm.

As his manhood continued to swell, his heavily hooded dark eyes flared at her. Devilos Dravidian wasn't a nice being; he could, and possibly would, take her against her will. He has never raped a female before, he'd never had to, they throw themselves at him.

But, he knew this little human would deny him, and for some reason he couldn't fathom, she turned him on like no other ever had. His demon's lust razed his brain, whipping him into an uncontrollable fury that normally fed him in warring.

He could feel his eyes burning white, fangs descending again, and his horns along with his dick, enlarging. He had to get the hell out of there. The overwhelming desire to take her was consuming him, shredding his control, he felt the beast rising.

She was small, delicate, still fragile in her injuries; he could do irreparable damage to her in the frenzied sexual onslaught he would besiege on her, especially if she fought him.

He broke from her; his heavy boots clomped over the carpet to the door. Flinging it open, he said over his shoulder, "I will send one of my lieutenants, Bowie, to collect you for travel," he sure as hell didn't trust himself at the moment to be alone with her.

"He is blond with blue eyes, and has an annoying sense of humor. Allow no one else in but him. Keldon will be back at your door. I will see you on board the ship." Before she could say a word he left.

Chapter Eight

At the knock on her door, Sveti went straight to it but Mara was already there looking through the peephole. The Sire had instructed her to keep the prinţesă away from the door. He didn't want a repeat of yesterday.

Mara's stomach roiled at what happened to the young woman. That whore Rianna had waited until Mara was gone and tricked Keldon into leaving then actually struck the girl! And she had a knife! What more would she have done if the Master hadn't come? She let out her held breath and opened the door. The charming Bowie was there with the usual twinkle in his eye and grin on his handsome mouth.

"Hey, Mara, what's doing?" the blond man greeted her cheerfully as he entered the room.

"All is well, at least at the moment, Lieutenant Busoni." Mara smiled her welcome. Both looked over as Sveti came in. She trod warily to the lieutenant.

Shyly she asked in a hushed voice, "Lieutenant, are you Mr. Bowie? I remember you from the infirmary."

He grinned at her and bowed. "At your service milady. I've come to escort you to the Sennseen." At Sveti's perplexed look he said, "The airship we're to travel on. Dev will of course be captaining it." More perplexity. He clarified, "Devilos Dravidian. His friends and brothers call him Dev."

"We commoners call him, Sire," Mara said with a short grin.

"Uh huh." Sveti smiled absently, she called him Beast, and went to pick up her small case of clothes and toiletries. But Bowie was quicker and snatched it out from under her hand.

"I've got it, honey. You ready?" His lips pursed at the stricken look on her pretty face. Dev had told him there was something up with her and her half-brother. He'd seen for himself the asshole was inappropriately all over her.

Dev had intimated the prințesă was terrified of going home.

"Prințesă," he started to ask her but she turned her back and made for the door. He followed her out and they walked side-by-side down the hall.

"Um," he said, "that's Bowie, Prințesă, not Mr. Bowie," and grinned broadly at her.

Her own smile was bleak and forced. "Oh, okay. Please call me Sveti." She chanced a quick glance at him.

He was quite handsome with thick blond hair and dark blue eyes, and a mischievous smile. He seemed friendly.

Mara appeared comfortable with him, so maybe he was safe, no, she shook her head. He was one of the beast's lieutenants and therefore likely just as lethal and dangerous. Just not as scary looking. All of the lieutenants looked human, but Mara had told her they were from Resh so they were tons more powerful than humans, and they were immortal.

The beast was from Nasitar. Mara said they are a very private species. Not that much is known about them other than most of the men born there, and some females, train almost from birth as *gaiscíoch*, warriors.

They are a league of vicious hunters. Sort of waratorio bounty hunters. They were sought out by differing planets to retrieve the worst of the worst nefarious miscreants.

The ones that were too monstrous, too powerful, too deadly, for the regular policing agencies to capture, or kill.

Sveti thought to herself, that creature, Devilos Dravidian, looked to be the kind that would be savage enough, contain the raw strength and ruthless violence necessary to bring in the most dangerous, depraved felons in the universe.

His eyes, she shivered, enigmatic obsidian under hooded lids, like a predatory croc's. All she saw in them was merciless aggression.

He looked almost human, except he had an exceptionally powerful build; his lieutenants were near his muscular size. But he had horns, and claws, and fangs.

Recalling the flames that flounced around him when he was disturbed, a shiver of alarm rippled through her. And, again, those formidable black eyes that had blazed blinding white.

She'd seen it twice now. Once that time she was transporting out of his hands on the ship, and the second time was when they were aimed in fury at Rianna. He must be concerned about bringing Sveti in one piece to Krystian.

Keeping pace with Bowie, Sveti wondered, hoped, she would not be anywhere near the beast on the ship. Besides scaring the life out of her, he confused her. She touched her lips. He had kissed her that day she was on board his ship with Miles, for the life of her she could not figure out why.

He had caught her when she fell off the chair, he insisted she go to bed when she was so weary yesterday, and he'd been furious with Rianna for attacking her. And, she took a deep breath; he had rescued her from torture and certain death at the hands of Illyios Gha'auvin and the Amphicyonids.

Though not actually a rescue, he had taken her prisoner for the believed deception he thought she'd played on him.

Why he would storm a fortress and wipe out the entire evil occupants just to take her prisoner made no sense to Sveti. If he'd left her there, Dr. Jamez said she would have been dead by day's end, and he would have been avenged by her death without all the trouble.

But, she pressed her hands against her eyes, now he was taking her back to Krystian. An involuntary shudder raced around her body shaking her bones. She needed to keep herself at the ready for the first opportunity to escape.

"You okay?" Bowie asked glancing down at her.

"Uh, yes. Just a chill. I'm fine." She flashed him a gaunt smile.

"Hmm." Bowie stared at her for a couple of seconds. Dev had said if Bowie thought the prinţesă appeared at all fatigued, or ill, he was to carry her to the ship. A grin tugged at the corner of his mouth. No doubt Sveti would not care for that.

He glanced down at her again, almost as if she was reading his mind, she straightened her spine to appear less weary.

The Sennseen was a huge ship. Dozens of people were boarding with them. Most of them appeared human, but these days it was really hard to tell with inter-species mating and physical modifiers and the like.

Bowie greeted people with a nod and a wave but kept them moving when anyone tried to stop and talk. All eyes were on Sveti. She knew her cheeks were blushed with mortification. They all thought she was a criminal that had tricked the warlord beast and kept Miles in danger.

Bowie saw things differently. The men were blatantly ogling her and many tried to stop him to get an introduction. He warned them all off with a harsh frown.

He felt bad for the girl. There was no way this fluff of sweet female had any involvement in the fraud. Miles told them she had snuck food and items of comfort to him, and had managed to help him escape at the risk of incurring her brother's devastating wrath.

Feeling her suddenly go rigid beside him, he followed the direction of her gaze. Crap. That bitch Rianna was in a huddle with her girlfriends and glaring daggers at Sveti.

Her actions against Sveti could have meant a brutal whipping or even death, but Dev had let Sveti's compassionate pleas seep in, and he only confined Rianna to her stateroom and put a freeze on her money band. She could not shop, only purchase food.

Her payment and reservation had already been made for the trip before she'd assaulted Sveti, or Dev would have refused her passage.

Bowie wished his sisters could be on board to give Sveti some female support. She's going to basically be an island alone. The females weren't going to be friendly to her, and Bowie had seen the way Dev looked at her, there was no way he was going to let any other men near her. He only had Bowie bring her this morning because he couldn't.

"Ignore her, honey, just smile that pretty smile up at me and pretend she isn't there." He dropped his free arm around her shoulders. Sveti did as he said. She looked up at him with a tremulous smile she strove to make steady.

Peripherally as they passed Rianna, Bowie saw the blowsy woman look even more thunderous. That witch had made it clear ages ago she wanted Dev.

What scorched her big ass worse than being rebuffed by Dev, was his interest in Sveti that was obvious to a blind man. Everyone could see it except the big man himself. And the prinţesă who obviously feared and disliked Dev.

"This way, Sveti." He led her through the huge busy atrium of the ship.

It was buzzing and bustling with people making their way on board while visiting and getting instructions to their rooms. Bowie brought Sveti through the crowd and to the lift. Inside, he pressed the second floor button and they were there in an instant.

They walked down the hall until they saw Keldon standing outside a room.

Her brows boomerangs, Sveti said in dismay, "I'm to have a guard here too? I certainly can't get off the moving airship!"

Nodding at Keldon as he opened the door, Bowie caught the bruise under Keldon's pale blue eye. It looked like Dev had that talk with him about gawking at Sveti, or coming near her unless she was in trouble and needed help. Inside, the cool air rushed them. It was dim in the chamber.

Bowie pushed a button and the steel shade went up to reveal the loading dock teeming with people outside the one-way window. The room brightened pleasantly.

He took her case into the bedroom and set it on a stand and came back out to join her.

"Yeah, sorry. Dev feels besides the fact you might recklessly try some perilous escape, that you need protection. You must see that yourself after Rianna's attack on you." Then there were the men who would take a chance and come after her if they thought she was alone and unprotected.

"Keldon will be outside that door whenever you are inside. Dev has set up a relief guard for him as well."

Her pained expression pricked his heart. "I uh, have to go. Everything you need is here. Dev says you need anything you are to call him." He motioned with his head to the wall-com on the wall by the door.

"Um, he said do not let anyone in, and obviously, you can't leave without being with Dev or one of his team lieutenants, that's me, Lukas, Tomi, and Connar. Our names and numbers are on the wall-com as well."

Her voice strained and reedy she sighed. "I understand, Bowie. Thank you so much for your assistance. I appreciate you being so kind and friendly."

She walked Bowie to the door. He patted her shoulder. "Buck up, hon." He grew serious. "You know, Sveti, I realize you are afraid of him, but if you tell Dev why you are so terrified of your *bráthair* he can help you. I promise."

Her smile saddened. "Thanks, Bowie, but no one can help me."

"Ah." He opened the door. "Well, at least think about it, okay?"

She nodded mildly. "Sure."

Bowie's wristband buzzed. He lifted his wrist, answered, "Busoni," and listened. Looking at Sveti he nodded, then said, "Aye." He picked up the wall-com and handed it to Sveti. "There is an incoming from a Ryen

Rembrandt." His blond brow arched at the thrilled smile that lit her face.

"Oh, thank you, Bowie. He is my," her cheeks shone with pink, "childhood sweetheart. I guess he would be my boyfriend if Krystian allowed it, but-" She broke off, the thrill dimmed. Accepting the phone she said quietly, "Thank you."

Bowie smiled and stepped out of the suite to give her privacy. "Remember, do not open the door to anyone except for us. See ya later, sweetie." Keldon would ensure she stayed in and no one would enter. He'd taken a beating after letting Rianna trick him. Dev expected his guards to be smarter than that.

He grinned and closed the door. Wait until Dev hears about the boyfriend.

The takeoff was smooth and uneventful. After they were airborne for several hours, Sveti was sitting on the couch reading a book she'd taken from the many on the bookshelf in the cozy room.

Occasionally she looked out the window but there wasn't much to see. It was of course pitch black. The only illumination was the stars and sometimes other ships that passed near them.

Her stomach started rattling and she was just thinking about seeing what was in the kitchenette when there was a light rapping at her door.

"Great. There's no reason for someone to be here, so it must be trouble. God, I hope it's not that woman again." Sveti left the couch and tiptoed to the door and carefully looked out the peephole. Her stomach did summersaults. It was him. The beast. "Oh no, what could he want?"

Her heart started pounding, maybe he was here to mete out the punishment he'd mentioned. Maybe if she ignored him he would go away. Sure he would. She jumped when he knocked again.

"Prinţesă, open the door. It's me, Dravidian," his deep voice rumbled through the door shearing chills up her spine.

The guard was right there, she thought, why doesn't he just have him open it?

"Svetiessa." He didn't sound angry, just tough. Her name on his lips sounded foreign with his unusual accent.

Wiping her damp hands on her jeans, Sveti unlocked the door, pushed the button and let it slide open a crack.

Staying behind the door, she whispered, "What do you want?"

Chapter Nine

$\mathcal{D}$ev's mouth twitched and his brows lowered. "I want to come in. Step out of the way." He waited. She didn't move. "Svetiessa," he said, "I'm coming in regardless. I don't want to hurt you, move away from the door."

Her fear of him exuded from the big eyes. She had eyes like a doll's. Round and like cut crystal. He'd never seen anything like them. His domineering growl wasn't making her any less afraid.

More quietly, he told her, "I said I won't hurt you. You know I could smash the door in if I wanted to." He waited again.

She stepped back from the door panel but didn't open it. He put his palm on the steel and pushed it aside into the wall. Her eyes widened, no human being could do that.

The door closed automatically after he entered. In a long sleeved, dark blue shirt and black cargo pants, so big and brawny he took up most of the doorway, his hair was loose again, it hung fairly straight down past his shoulders.

Her skin pale as a daisy, Sveti moved away from him and pawed at a few locks of her long curls.

"Thank you," he said, checking out what she was wearing. Thank Zues, the shorts and that fucking wet dream of a top were replaced by a frilly, pale yellow blouse and jeans. His eyes narrowed at the blouse, ah, good, she was wearing a bra.

He didn't need her lighting any fires in him or any other males on board flitting around with those plump, unfettered breasts bouncing everywhere.

The jeans outlined her small but curvaceous rump and sexy yet too thin legs. The dark eyes nudged back up to the blouse.

Seeing where his gaze paused, Sveti's face filled with color. She nervously drew her hair down to cover her front. "Mr. um, Captain Dravidian," she cleared her throat inserting more strength in her voice, "why are you here?"

His lids levered up to her flushed face then his gaze flit to the wall-com and darkened. Bowie had told him a boyfriend or some-shit had called her. "I've come to bring you to dinner."

At her quizzical look he said, "There is a main dining room on the middle floor. Most of the people on board dine there."

"Oh, uh, I believe I have sufficient food here, I mean, I haven't looked but Bowie said…"

The black eyes glanced at the kitchenette and back to her. "It wasn't a request." The tone of his rough voice told her she had no choice. He rolled his shirt sleeves up to his elbows exposing burly forearms laced with dark hair, and set hands that could crush a skull on his lean hips.

"That is," he glanced pointedly at her kitchen again, "unless you would prefer to provide a meal for me here. You said you were a good cook. A home cooked dinner would be a damned nice treat. My majordomo provides most meals for me, however," he sighed, "he tends to cook strictly scientifically, there is no depth of," he thought for the words, "savory flavor." Hunger flared in his pupils aimed back at her bosom.

A hint of a smile almost broke his austere face when he saw her alarm at the suggestion that he stay there alone with her. "Aye," his gaze swept down her body, lips now curled in a cold smile, "there's nothing like a beautiful woman wearing nothing but an apron at the stove-"

"I uh, just need to wash my hands, I'll be right back." She turned in a flurry and fled to the bathroom.

A picture of Sveti in only an apron that was nothing but a swathe of material down her front barely covering her nipples and stopping just below her privates fueled his mind as he ushered her down the corridor.

Dev felt the urge to put his hand on the small of her back to guide her. But judging by the rigidity of her spine and rapid blinking, she'd pop if he touched her. He had thought he wanted her to fear him, she should. But now it annoyed him.

When they neared the dining room he did put his hand on her back to guide her and felt her stiffen under it.

He brought her to a buffet type set up. Handing her a tray and a plate he said, "Choose what you'd like."

Looking over the array of food, she hesitantly picked up a shrimp quesadilla, and caught his raised brow. "What? I love them. Cheesy and gooey and-" She broke off, surprised when he chose the same thing, but quadruple the serving, and he added french fries and a huge hunk of chocolate cake.

He got a beer and waited while she filled a soda.

All eyes followed them as they made their way to a table where Bowie, Tomi and Lukas were sitting.

Setting his tray down, Dev pulled a chair out indicating for her to sit. She set her tray on the table and gracefully slid onto the cushioned chair.

Ignoring Bowie's mocking grin, Dev plopped down next to her.

Everyone in the room was gawking at Sveti. "Ignore them," Dev said gruffly to her as he picked up a quesadilla and took a big bite, "they'll grow tired of staring." The four men however, unconsciously nudged their chairs closer together making a wall of muscle blocking Sveti from most of the occupants' view.

Feeling a million eyes on her, Sveti lost her appetite. She pulled and pinched at her sandwich but didn't eat much.

Bowie and Lukas were talking together about Sveti's planet, Qoph. Bowie had been there a few times but Lukas had never seen it.

"What's it like?" Lukas asked, forking a stack of ketchup drenched fries.

"S'alright, mostly humans, a few others mixed in, but nothing else like," Bowie shoveled in barbeque shredded modified meat and baked beans, tipped a nod at Sveti, "her." He felt Dev's frown and smirked at him.

Bowie went on, "The structures are mostly white with a lot of pale green, it used to have a," he scooped up some beans, "cozy, garden kinda feel, but since Ritrova took it over-"

At the color leaving Sveti's face, her eyes dropped to the table, he flushed, his voice skittered off. "Uh, it feels somewhat, an anxious cold, now." Quickly changing the subject, he said, "Anyway, Luke, you been back to Dominia?"

Dev looked from Bowie to Sveti picking apart her sandwich. He'd already put away three of his quesadillas and half of the fourth. "You lost a lot of weight, Prinţesă," Dev murmured, nodding at her plate, "you need to get your strength back."

Staring at her plate she mumbled miserably, "Doesn't really matter."

"Svetiessa, what-"

"Hey," a man interrupted. Nice looking, tall with sandy hair and green eyes, he smiled at Sveti. "My name is Charlie, everyone is going upstairs to the lounge for drinks and dancing. I'd like to get my shot in first to dance with you-"

"Nay," Dev snapped tersely without looking at him. The other men at the table looked as surprised as Charlie at Dev's harsh response.

Charlie's eyes darted around the table, the other guys were all eyeing him relatively amiably.

Sveti raised her head, her expression towards Dev disturbed at his rudeness, and for speaking for her.

Charlie looked at Dev who had finished his sandwiches and was stabbing at his chocolate cake. "But, Sire, I'm sure she'd like to dance."

Stuffing a hunk of cake in his mouth, elbows on the table, his shoulders hunched, Dev stared off to the crowd, chewing. "I said no." His gaze rose briefly to Charlie when the man didn't move off, then he looked away, his voice a growl, "She does not dance. Get lost."

Still, Charlie hesitated, his eyes flit from Dev to Sveti whose face was staining pink, back to Dev. Dev's eyes rolled up to him, under his heavy brow, his lids were so low barely a speck of black eked out.

Charlie gulped loudly, mumbled, "Perhaps later," and quickly slipped away.

Mortified at Dev's dictatorial treatment of her, Sveti pushed her plate away and glared at him, he studiously ignored her.

"Ah," clearing his throat, Bowie awkwardly struck up a conversation about a new ship being produced that used a unique type of fuel. "The uh, Empire Wing they're calling it, there's one on display at Station Comp II. Maybe on the way back from," his eyes flicked to Sveti, her lips tightened, "uh, we can make a stop. What do you think, Dev?"

One shoulder shrugged with Dev's noncommittal grunt.

Lukas jumped into the awkward silence. "Yep, I read about it. What do you think of the roadstal pinions? They the max, huh?"

Bowie, Tomi and Lukas discussed the new ship with enthusiasm. Dev concentrated on his cake and beer, Sveti sat silently and fumed, embarrassed and angry.

After dinner, the group made their way together to the lounge. The bar area was just as crowded as the dining room had been, and louder.

The cocktails were flowing and the people were zealously imbibing. Music streamed from a speaker, people gyrated on a small dance floor.

Tomi dropped his arm around a woman who had sidled up next to him, bumping him with a hip as bounteous as her hello.

Lukas grinned at the dancers, a variety of species dancing in a variety of interesting ways. The walls neon pink, blue lighting illuminated under the bar counter and along the walls giving bright yet mellow light.

Bowie said to Sveti, "What would you like to drink? Wine or something stronger?"

She opened her mouth but Dev brusquely cut her off, "She will have a soda, get me an anfira," a blend of scotch, cognac, and a strong, dusty green spirit from the planet Zeper.

Golden brows down, handsome lips pursed, annoyance marring his normally devil-may-care tone, Bowie said tersely, "A little liquor isn't going to hurt her, Dev. We're with her. Give the girl a break." He glared right back at Dev's scowl at him.

"Um, I don't care for anything," Sveti said, glancing around. "I need to go to the ladies room."

This was one of the times Dev wished he had female warriors but none had been available for this trip. He said coolly to Tomi, "Take her."

Mouth dropping, Sveti's brow furrowed with her protest, "Oh, really, I'm sure I can find it with no prob-"

Tomi was already getting to his feet. Smiling with a wink at the woman he had his arm around, he patted her abundant bootie and said, "Later, hon," and held his football sized hand out to Sveti. "Come along Prințesă," he grinned big, showing all his pearlies.

Sveti looked up, way up. Tomi was a bulldozer of a man. Huge and hulking. With dark skin, tattoos swarming around his neck and down his arms, there was even one on the back of his shaved head, if she saw him on the street she'd run for her life.

She glanced at Bowie who nodded to her with a smile, she didn't see Dev frown at him, annoyed that Sveti looked to Bowie for assurance. She got up and went with the giant.

After he ordered their drinks, Bowie snapped, "Shit, Dev, what the hell? You know damn well she was just as much a pawn as everyone else in the games of her *bráthair*. Stop treating her like she's a renegade felon and a prisoner."

"She is a prisoner, my prisoner." Unbidden, a picture of a naked Sveti cuffed to his bed flashed through Dev's mind.

Rolling his blue eyes, Bowie said, "Cripes, a few drinks and a couple of dances aren't going to hurt anything."

Dev grunted, "She doesn't need to dance." They gathered their drinks and made their way to the table Lukas had claimed.

"Come on, give the girl a break. You afraid to see *your prisoner* in another man's arms?" Bowie teased sitting on a micron-plastic chair, then before Dev could rip his head off with his dastardly scowl and swift denial, he said quickly, "You know, I saw the bulletin Krystian Ritrova put out, you know, the one about selling her, or rather actually selling her virginity."

Dev remained impassive but his jaw worked.

"Aye, yeah, so, I hear for the spell to work for him to get the power to transport through wormholes, the guy that takes her virginity has to be a full bloodline prince." Bowie watched for Dev's reaction but his face was as unreadable as a rock. "Oh yeah, and the man who takes her virginity becomes legally married to her."

His grin big, Bowie went on, "Actually, per the laws of her planet, the guy that marries her, owns her. Like I said before, as a female, and as a prințesă, she has no rights but what her father, male guardian, or," he chugged part of his beer, smacked his lips, "husband, give to her."

Not even a grunt this time.

Snickering, Bowie turned to Lukas beside him and fell into a minor argument about the Galaxie Warrior Games. They each had bets on rival teams.

Bowie swung his head to ask Dev who he was backing in the tournament but he bit back a grin instead. Dev's hooded eyes were trained on the beauty threading her way across the room towards them.

Tomi hulked behind her snarling scowls at any men who attempted to stop her, and grinning lasciviously at hot women. He steered her wide of Rianna's foot out in the aisle ready to trip her.

His grin taunting, Bowie said, "Aye, that beauty needs a strong keeper. In this half-lawless universe, I see too many males insanely desiring her that would just grab her and run. I think I'll apply for the job."

Not jumping to the bait, Dev watched Sveti and Tomi approach.

When they reached the table, Dev stood up and pulled her chair out. Warily, she sat. After he pushed her in, she swept her balletic legs to the side, and he sat back down without a word.

The lieutenants stared in surprise at their warlord captain who normally barely grunted at a female. They'd never seen Dev exhibit such gentlemanly courtesy.

He was respectful and held doors open, but that was about the extent of his manners. Unless he was banging a female, or working with one, he generally ignored their existence.

Connar joined the group bringing a tray of second round drinks for everyone. He set a glass down in front of each person and a glass of rosé wine for Sveti. He said to her with a smile, "I didn't know what you'd like so I took a chance with this, it's sweet, like you."

Not catching the look Dev shot him, Connar stood between Sveti and Dev to give Dev his drink. At the same time, the man who had approached Sveti at dinner was at her side asking her to dance.

Before Dev noticed him, Sveti stood up defiantly and let Charlie, with his big grin, take her hand and lead her to the small dance floor. He slipped his hand around her waist as they blended into the crowd.

When Connar moved, Dev saw Sveti sliding into the group of dancers. He put his palms on the table to push his chair back and stand up, but Bowie set a hand on his arm. "She's not going anywhere, bro, and no one's going to hurt her."

Dev paused, face set hard, sat back and glowered at the dance floor.

When the first song ended, another man tapped Charlie out and swept Sveti across the floor, her flaming hair a frill of brilliant color swinging around her. The next dance another man was there with his hands out to take Sveti, laughing and slightly breathless, into his arms. But a muscled arm blocked him.

"This dance is taken," Dev pronounced with a low growl.

The man took one look at the big warrior with the dangerous face and moved quickly away.

A tense crease in her forehead, her smile gone, Sveti stepped back from Dev and said, "I uh, think I'll sit this one out. I'll just go back-"

Dev caught her arm to stop her. He put his rough palm on her small waist and pulled her to him. Sveti stood stiffly not moving. Looking down at the top of her flaming hair, he said quietly, "Svetiessa, relax, put your hand on my shoulder."

She was staring at a button on his dark blue shirt, her gaze lowered to his cargo pants. A firearm was at his hip, and he assuredly had numerous weapons stashed all around his body, a shiver rolled over her shoulders.

He curled a finger under her chin lifting it to force her to look up at him. "Svetiessa," he murmured, "it's just a dance. I am not going to harm you."

She tried to move her chin, but he held her firm, yet gently. The corner of her lip pulled in wryly. "Oh yeah? Maybe you're going to twist my head off like you did that soldier in the dungeon."

His black brows arched in surprise. Releasing her chin, he lowered his hands, his strong fingers tightened on her waist drawing her closer.

Sveti's gaze rose to his then drifted down. "I was barely conscious when you...retrieved me from that...place."

The skin around her eyes and lips whitened remembering the torture of the bear-dogs bashing her, jumping on her, beating her with sticks, and doing other things she couldn't stomach remembering...until eventually blessed unconsciousness had claimed her.

Afterwards, she gained shreds of consciousness, flickering in and out she realized she was hanging by her wrists in a cold grim place with bleak cries all around her in the harrowing dark.

Her pained eyes had cracked open at a male's voice near her, it was a guard. Abjectly helpless, she could feel his hands on her thighs, pushing her long skirt up. Then she saw Dev entering the dungeon, war braids flapping against his back as he strode towards her.

Before passing out again, she saw him kill the guard. Ruthlessly, viciously, without remorse or hesitation. His body behemoth, he had wrapped his enormous hand around the guard's head, stuck his claws into his neck and just ripped the man's head off and casually tossed it aside like it was a soccer ball.

Seeing that and remembering how enraged he'd been when she'd vaporized with Miles, she'd been mindless with fear the day he came to the infirmary to check on her recovery progress. Her thoughts were that he must want her well enough to withstand his punishment before he enjoyed killing her himself.

And here she was in his arms. Again. He'd carried her to sick bay, to her suite, caught her when she tumbled off the chair, and now, he had her pressed up against him. He must have some motive, was planning on how to carry out his revenge on her.

Unnerved, she said in a low voice, "Uh, I did see what you, did to that, to that…man, the guard."

Dev slid his hand like a gentle web under the side of her face and said softly, "That was reflexive." Using her prior words, his mouth turned in a dry half smile. "Unlike catching you when you fell in your kitchen; that was deliberate."

He pitched his head tossing a lock of long black hair off his shoulder and studied her confused face.

"I am a warrior, Svetiessa, I kill, yes," he shrugged, "sometimes brutally, and ruthless without pity. It's instinct at this point. But I kill only when necessary. It is not necessary to kill you. So, relax." He stroked her jaw with his thumb, watching her digest what he said.

"When it becomes necessary, then what?" Pink stained her cheeks at his perplexing caress. Was he seeing how tender she was before he took a bite out of her with those fangs? Or would he cook her first?

Black brows slanted down with his frown of irritation, he moved his hand from her jaw to stroke his long fingers up the back of her neck.

Deep voice quiet, gravelly, he replied, "I am not partial to killing females." That reminded him of how he had planned to...punish her, over his lap with her bare ass meeting his palm.

Strangely, it took an effort as it was for him to keep his hands where they were. They were irresistibly drawn to cup her round little bottom, play with it for a while before pulling her hard against his burgeoning erection.

The usual women he spent time with would have relished him feeling them up, in public, private, they weren't particular. But this wee woman, a sigh lumbered out, he would likely get slapped before she flounced off.

As much as he wanted to cram her pelvis against his hard-on, he placated himself with feeling her lush tits pressed on his chest, and kept his hips slightly turned so she wouldn't feel his erection and end the dance.

"But, you vowed vengeance," she reminded him, her big blues swept over his dark eyes in hushed fear.

"Enough talk," he growled, grasped her hand and set it on his shoulder. He moved his palm under her hair to her nape, and drew her to lay the side of her face against his powerful chest.

Spreading his fingers on her back, he took her hand that wasn't on his shoulder, and held it to his chest. Settling his chin against the side of her head, inhaling deeply, he drew in her fresh scent and nudged his chin deeper into her hair. Being part animal, her scent aroused him.

They didn't move very much, swayed mostly. As the minutes passed, her body lost the stiffness and she nestled in his muscled arms.

Dev rested his head lightly on hers still languidly inhaling her scent, his loose black locks blended with her light tresses. She smelled of flowers, not perfume but a natural scent, her skin was petal soft with just the faintest hint of floral.

The music played pleasantly, couples drifted around them. No one bumped them, everyone gave the couple a wide birth, Dev's lethal temperament was legend.

A new song started, Dev felt a tap on his shoulder. He held Sveti tighter and growled without moving his head, "Take off."

"But sir, you need to let some of us other guys have a chance to-"

Barely turning his head, Dev peered at the man through Sveti's curls, his eyes blazed wickedly white. The man's eyes hopped from the blazing white irises to the horns swelling on Dev's head, he blanched, and quickly walked away.

Tightening his arms, Dev drew her closer, one hand splayed on her nape, his fingers stroking her skin, the other hand clasped her small hand to his chest. A silent growl roiled inside him at the feel of her breasts rubbing his hard chest with their slight movements.

He didn't know what possessed him to dance with her, but now that he was, her sexy little body fit like a curvy satin ribbon against his steely frame. He willed his horns, and dick, to calm while he snuggled her deeper into his embrace.

The song ended, Sveti tilted her head back to face him. She had the drowsy look of a woman who was sated from a long night of decadent sex, her eyes heavy lidded, lips slightly parted, light tendrils of flames wisped over part of her face.

Dev gently pushed the wisps off her face, pulled her back to nestle against him as the next song started up. Her face still tilted up at him, his head canted and his lips lowered to hers.

Then the ship rocked. A few people stumbled, gasped. Sveti leaned back, a trace of concern on her soft face.

His arm a strong band around her, Dev ran a finger down the side of her cheek, murmured, "It's all right, Svetiessa, must be a bit of meteor-" The ship rocked harder, sharper, causing glasses and plates to slide on tables.

"Fuck-" Dev cursed. Taking Sveti's arm he moved swiftly through the shaken crowd bringing her back to their table.

When they got there the lieutenants were already on their feet.

Dev ordered, "Tomi, send out the alarm, everyone goes immediately to their cabins and stays there until the all clear. I'm going to the bridge." The ship jerked another hard slant, people shrieked. His boots planted solidly on the floor, holding tightly to Sveti's arm, Dev handed her to Bowie.

Tomi took off. Grasping Sveti's upper arm, Bowie asked, "You want me to take Sveti to her room?"

Dev was already starting for the door. "Nay," he said, "bring her, I want her on the bridge with me, us." Black hair fluttering behind his strapping back, he jogged out of the room.

"Come on, honey." Bowie took her arm leading her out of the sudden chaos foraying in the room. People panicking ran into each other shouting and crying.

Tucking Sveti under his arm, Bowie ushered her down juddering corridors and up the stairs to the bridge.

Chapter Ten

$\mathcal{A}$ tense quiet pervaded the bridge as the airship floundered. Traction and speed slowed as it shifted to one side.

Over Dev's head, Lukas scanned the control panel monitors, asked, "What is it?" Scraping hard fingers through his tawny short buzzed hair, he looked up as Bowie, Sveti and Tomi entered the bridge.

Dev skillfully pushed buttons, flicked levers, and typed into the ship's engineer computer.

His eyes on the monitors, he replied, "One of the engines is out. I need to make an emergency landing. When we get back to base, I want to know who the fuck serviced this ship."

"What are our chances of not crash landing, Dev? Not that I don't have faith in your piloting ability to get us down safely, but," to the right of him, Connar raised his palms with a small shrug.

Concentrating on what he was doing, Dev didn't answer him, he said to Tomi, "Lieutenant, see to the engine room." Tomi immediately left the bridge.

Bowie hovered behind Dev's chair next to Connar with Sveti. Seeing her lips tighten with nerves, Bowie smiled and said with confidence, "Don't worry honey, we have the best captain in all of the universes. Dev won't let us down. Whoa," he caught Sveti's hand when she stumbled as the ship dipped crazily as it sped downward.

"Belt her in, Bow, you too, what the fuck, you think this is a party? Get to your position," Dev barked at the blond man.

"Come on, honey," Bowie said, ushering her to a chair, "let's do as the big bad wolf commands." His grin reassuring, he buckled Sveti in before going to his own seat beside Dev. He turned his attention to monitors and three-dimensional, digital moving graphs, and worked in tandem with Dev.

Sveti faced the window watching the stars flash past as the ship rocked and shook, bumped and tilted as it raced to the nearest planet.

The quiet strum of the airship's engine was the only sound on the bridge.

Everyone was belted in, half the occupants calmly watched Dev preparing the hurtling airship to land, the rest of the crew stared out the window anxiously observing the rocky planet that they were seeming to head straight at in breakneck speed.

The planet rushed up at them, Dev turned the ship's nose slightly up as they were seconds from impact. The ship's vapor stream barely jounced on the rough terrain as Dev brought it in to land.

He didn't land the aircraft as quickly as usual but let it ride in softly for a longer time to smooth out the landing.

When it came to a completely non-jarring stop, collective held breaths exhaled relief in unison. Quiet murmurs of praise for Dev's amazing skills at so gently landing the handicapped ship railed around the deck.

Unbuckling and getting to his feet, Dev instructed Lukas, "Give me a report on any injuries." His hazel eyes as serious as ever, Lukas nodded.

Dev said to Connar, "Go to Tomi, I want a report on the engines." Both lieutenants strode out of the bridge.

To the communicator Dev snapped, "Contact the base station, tell them our situation and to send pickups."

A male that, judging by skin stretched too tight over oddly angled bones had struggled into his human form; nodded and started tapping on his monitor.

Reports came back with no injuries, but the ship was not flyable. The warriors and crew retrieved supplies; packs of compressed food, water, disposable toilet paper, blankets, tools, etc.

Everyone evacuated the craft and stood in a loose crowd murmuring their concern and complaints.

Tomi strode to the front of the crowd. One behind the other, the planet's several suns beat down, light glanced off his cinnamon skin and shaved scalp with his movements. He wore a beige t-shirt and brown camouflage colored cargo pants as did all of the warriors except Dev who wore black.

The huge man's biceps flexed under the short sleeves as he raised his arms for attention. "All right," Tomi said loudly, "please, give me your attention."

He waited until everyone settled down. "This is what is going to happen. The airship is not flyable so we have to make our way to the pick-up stations, which are a couple of days' walk from here. The land is too unstable at this location for a second ship to land here. The only way to get to solid ground is across water." He paused as moans and complaints shuffled from person to person.

Rianna spoke up, her strident voice scratching shivers down many a backbone, "What the hell, Lieutenant? Where are we expected to- to sleep? This is totally unacceptable, you can't expect us to-"

"We don't expect you to do anything, Ms. Malone," Dev's cold dark voice caused everyone to turn towards the open walkway of the ship as he was striding out.

At Rianna's dropped mouth and antagonistic expression, he said, "You may stay here, but the ship will be locked up and no one will be allowed to stay on it. It may be months before they come and repair the ship and return it to the base. So," Dev's smile chilled, "feel free to stay here."

He kept walking past her to where Bowie was with Sveti. He didn't see the annoyed and hateful look Rianna shot at his back, but he was well aware of it.

"So," Tomi continued with a big toothy grin, "as I was saying, the group will be split as we need to access boats and they are located at two different stations. There is not one boat that we can all fit on so a larger group will go to Station A which is closer and where there are numerous water craft but not enough to transport all of us, and a smaller group will go to Station B, which unfortunately is further away.

"When we reach Protostar, we will send recruits to retrieve your bags. For now, you can only bring what you can easily carry, like a toothbrush."

He spoke over the grumbling, "I'm going to call off your names, you all have been randomly assigned by computer to the groups. And," he grinned broadly, "as Captain Dravidian said, any of you that wish to stay here, we will give you some supplies, but no weapons. You will not have access to the ship."

Tomi's grin slightly mean he told them, "Just to let you know, this planet is rife with savage wild animals. That said, I am going to call off your name and either the letter A or B. All A's will gather there," he nodded to an area where a series of enormous boulders were clustered, "and B's," he indicated a second area, "go there. We leave in fifteen minutes. Be ready, or stay behind."

Dev told Bowie, "I will stay with the prinţesă; you go get your gear."

Bowie gave him a surreptitious frown, and glanced at Sveti who was watching Tomi call off names. "How about she stay here with Tomi, he's already got his supplies, or she can come with me-" Bowie shrugged at Dev's silent, narrowed eyes, shut his mouth and headed back to the ship.

Uncertainty in her unsettled voice, Sveti said, "Um, Mr. Dravidian, uh, Captain, Mr. Tomi hasn't called my name, should I just join a group?"

Her wellbeing ambiguous, Sveti wasn't sure if Dev planned on leaving her behind to stay by the ship, or have her in the group he wasn't heading, or…

His arms crossed over his rocky chest, Dev didn't look at her, he said, "Nay. You will not leave my side until I deposit you with your bráthair."

She squared her body to bravely face him. "Captain, I choose to stay here."

Not used to anyone balking at his orders, Dev's head swooped down to her so fast his hair swung over his shoulders. "Must you debate everything I say? I will do whatever I see fit. As my prisoner, you have no say in the matter."

Her lips clamped shut and she lowered her head.

He gripped her jaw and raised her head. "You understand me? I am telling you that you will not leave my side until we reach your *bráthair*."

His fingers were digging into her soft skin when he realized he could damage her and lightened his grip. "You try to escape and you will face the unpleasant consequences when I catch you. Am I clear?"

Avoiding looking directly into his blades of angry obsidian eyes, Sveti whispered, "Everyone is staring at us," and watched his skin darken.

Positioning his head inches from hers, his voice so low it was barely audible, he ground, "I don't give a fuck. I am talking to you. Do you understand my command? Because I don't want you later to say you didn't know."

Sveti braced herself to look him calmly in the eye and said, "He is my half-brother, not my brother. And, I am not one of your *people* to be barked at with orders." If she thought he looked ferocious before, he looked about to detonate now.

Apparently he didn't care for people arguing with him and not answering his questions. His eyes flickered black-white-black and his fingers tightened around her jaw.

He glared at her, she glared back. Eyes tapered with anger, he said, "You'd better-"

"Hey Dev," Tomi was advancing on them, "everyone is in groups and ready." He looked from Dev to Sveti with a smirk of humor at the pair locking horns, so to speak.

Dev held her defiant chin for another few seconds, his glower like an ice storm, but she stared straight back at him. He released her and said, "Stay here with Tomi," and he stalked off to meet with the rest of his team.

After Dev's team carried on a brief discussion of how to proceed, they returned to the waiting people.

"All right everyone," Tomi said loudly, "let's get going. Please stay with your group and keep your leader in sight at all times. Any serious issues, tell one of us soldiers immediately. Don't stray from your group, never wander off alone. Okay," he announced and gave the signal to the soldiers that would be leading each group.

People collected into their various assigned lines and each group started marching in separate directions.

Walking was fairly easy as the planet was mostly hard reddish dirt bisected by slices of lime green streams and yellowish square lakes.

The interior was comprised of forests chock full of trees with gnarly black as pitch trunks, and enormous leaves like elephant ears tangled with bushes that were spiked with thorns and needles.

The soil horizon, the ground beneath the first layer of hard packed dirt and of that below, was soft sand and that made it very difficult for any airship to land on it.

Dev had pulled off the impossible by keeping the landing gear raised and gliding in light as a feather instead of abruptly landing as the spaceships were designed to do.

To get to the retrieval airships, the group would need to head to where there were stations on solid rock.

Dev led his smaller group of fourteen civilian males and females, plus two ship personnel, Sveti, and five other warriors besides his lieutenants; Bowie, Tomi, Connar and Lukas.

The other group A contained the majority of the passengers and crew. The boats were disparate. One location had only one watercraft, whereas the other site had many but not enough to ferry everyone.

Dev's group would be traveling further to the site with only one craft; their site was twice as far as the other. He led up front with Bowie, Sveti was behind him with Connar beside her, the rest of the warriors were scattered throughout the group with Tomi and Lukas the last at the rear to ensure the most protection.

The passengers consisting of several different species but most more or less resembled humans after eons of replicating to look like them as the universal model; whined and groused until they grew too tired to complain.

They finally made camp for the night within a circle of mordant black trees. As the people dropped to the rust colored ground in exhaustion, Dev and Bowie make several fires to keep the animals at bay.

Three warriors handed out the compressed food to everyone along with tubes of water. The others set out silver thermal pads that automatically filled with an inch of air when unwrapped, with an attached light blanket.

Sitting in clusters, as they ate and rested, the group gained strength back and now the people were chatting away getting to know each other and sharing grievances.

Sveti sat quietly eating, listening to Bowie, Tomi and Connar chat amongst themselves. They talked about people and events she knew nothing about. She kept her head down to avoid being drawn into their conversation. They were all kind to her, but she didn't trust any of them.

Only a few feet away, Dev and Lukas with their backs leaning against some trees smoked thin cigars. Noticing Dev's gaze seldom left Sveti, in a low voice Lukas asked him, "Dev, you are delivering her to her *bráthair*, Krystian the Sautarine, getting rid of her, why are you scowling at her?"

Even heavily serious as Lukas was, his brain a constant science experiment, he still had compassion. "I've never known you to have any feelings one way or the other over one of your…missions, or, prisoners. What's biting you?" One hazel eye squinted as he took a deep drag. The smoke swirled around his Marine-square head and tawny buzzed hair, before dissipating into the night.

Sucking on his cigar, Dev's broad shoulders rose in a shrug of disinterest. He could not move his brain away from how she felt in his arms last night.

If they hadn't had ship trouble he would have tried to maneuver her into his bed, and she undoubtedly would have blown him off, and he would have resorted to force. And that pissed him off and made his gut churn.

Not keeping his voice low, he replied, "Ah, I am just annoyed at how…frail she is. She is not like the other women, human and otherwise. That creamy skin will burn easily on this planet with its multiple suns, the flaming hair will draw notice from the indigenous tribes that savage this land."

Uncaring that Sveti could hear him he continued, "She is too small, too slight," a grunt of irritation, "she will require constant protection. Unlike the other females that are stronger, bigger, more robust, they can take care of themselves. At least they have meat on their bones. If we had to stay here any longer than a week she wouldn't make it."

Bowie looked over at him with a frown to let Dev know they could hear him. Sveti's spine stiffened, her head was still lowered but her cheeks turning pink in shame were visible.

But Dev went on in his deep-pitched voice, "She is too skinny, except for those curves," he sneered as if her body was deformed. "Those tits will attract damned attention from the men here, I don't need brawls over the bitch." His gaze traveled down the front of her like a finger touching her skin, drawing down between the breasts he disparaged, "Nay, she will require more work than the other women. What a pain."

Her cheeks bubblegum pink, Sveti blinked back tears of mortification. Under her breath she whispered confused, "Just last night he had been so kind and gentle with me. Today he is the beast again."

Bowie didn't waste his breath telling her Dev didn't mean it or what he said wasn't true, she wouldn't believe him. "Aw, Sveti, come on, let's get you settled down." He stood up, bent over and offered her his hand.

She took it and he helped her up then brought her to the air-pad that was for her. It was placed between Dev's and Bowie's. The other warriors and lieutenants were sleeping in a circle around the rest of the group for protection.

After he got Sveti settled, Bowie trod over to where Dev and the others were. "Fuck, Dev, you bastard. What the hell is the matter with you talking about her like that? You think she has no feelings? She didn't ask to be here, and it's not her fault she's so...dainty, delicate, yet not a trace of complaint leaves her lips. On the contrary, she works twice as hard to keep up."

Dev's eyes were on Sveti who had curled into a ball of misery on her pad. His face like implacable iron, he said nothing.

Tucking his hands in his pockets, Bowie cocked his head and peered up at his friend with a knowing frown. "Deliberately being an asshole to her, bro, ain't gonna snuff the attraction you hate yourself for feeling for her."

Both men stared at Sveti lying a few yards away. His mouth turned down in a scowl at his friend, Devilos snarled, "I feel nothing for her, Bow, except hate and disgust for what she's done. If I didn't have to return her due to that warrant initiated from her brother, I would leave the troublesome package here."

The squirm of her small body indicating she heard him, Bowie grumbled, "Fuck you, Dev. There are better ways to fight your desire for her." Then he grinned slyly and suggested, "Go bang Rianna, or one of the others, get your lust under control." The grin flattened and his blue eyes hardened.

He whispered crossly, "She doesn't deserve this shitty treatment because you have a hard-on for her and despise yourself for it, for feeling weak because of it. That soft little bundle makes you feel out of control, and you aren't familiar with that concept and it makes you uncomfortable, and you're lashing out."

Putting out his cigar, Dev shrugged out of his shirt leaving his t-shirt under it on. He shot an irritated glower at his friend and sniped, "I must have missed those years you went to college for your shrink degree. How 'bout you mind your own fucking armchair psychology business and stay out of my head."

Gripping his shirt in his hand, Dev turned his back to his friend who now snickered at him, and started towards his pad. Rianna moved in front of him.

"Hey, Captain." Her finger traced his warlord's tattoo on his arm, then she raised her hand towards a slightly pointed ear, hesitated, thought better of it and said, "How about you grab your blanket thingy there and come and sleep with, uh," her smile oily coy, "by me? We can keep each other warm."

"I'm good," Dev said brusquely and strode from her. Stomping off, he thought, *that damned Tomi should have known better than to put that skag in his group, random assignment or not. She was a goddamned danger to Svetiessa.*

He threaded his way through the scattered bodies and sat down on his pad. Keeping his boots on, he lay on his side and looked at Sveti.

She stared back miserably then rolled over with her back to him and pulled her blanket up almost covering her head.

Chapter Eleven

$\mathcal{T}$he night passed without incident, the fires kept the carnivorous creatures away.

In the morning, the warriors passed out compressed food and water. Dev gave the people little time to eat and attend to their private relieving, everyone was given a toothbrush.

After the supplies were handed out, Dev brought Sveti over to one of the crewmembers, Elvana. The spectra officer was the only female on the journey that he knew wouldn't try to hurt the princess.

He nodded with a short smile to the officer. "Elvana, I would like you and the prinţesă to be, uh, bathroom partners. I don't want anyone to go into the scrub alone. Everyone should be at least in pairs. You both already know enough not to stray too far from the group." He bent his head to Sveti. "You understand what I'm saying?"

She rolled her eyes. "I am not entirely obtuse, Sire."

He said coolly, "The last person who rolled their eyes at me no longer had a head to keep them in."

Elvana's expression sharpened, her smile fled, a bolt of fear flashed in her dark teardrop eyes. She didn't doubt what he said one bit. But Sveti just glared back at him.

Dev turned back to his officer. "All right, then. Neither of you goes to the bathroom alone. Always together."

Elvana smiled weakly at him with a nod, the glossy black, webby hair swished forward over her shoulders then back.

Crossing her arms with a huff, her lips pursed, Sveti didn't acknowledge his command.

Dev said, "Elvana, you may take your place in line, Svetiessa will be right there." He waited for her to leave then with his hands on his hips he said to Sveti, "You can stuff the attitude, little girl. You are trying my patience."

"Oh?" One flaming brow rose. "You have patience?" Before he could open his mouth in retort, she turned away from him and moved to where Elvana was waiting with the others to get in line. The spectra officer was almost a foot taller than the prinţesă.

Dev saw the two women converse, then they disappeared briefly into the pocket of scrub around the clutch of wiry black trees the group was gathered in. He'd tied his long hair back with a band. Rubbing the back of his neck like it hurt, he went to join Bowie at the head of the line.

When everyone was back and in line, they resumed hiking.

They took breaks regularly, but as the day wore on, tiring, Sveti started slowly drifting back down the line until most had passed her.

Tomi and Lukas had their heads together talking and didn't notice as the group had grown loose and the trail they took became winding. They were now having to travel across big rocks and boulders, and often had to jump over holes as the terrain changed.

Sveti observed everyone easily leaping over a wide hole. It was three feet across, five or so feet deep, the length of it went on and on. If she tried to go around it she'd lose sight of the group.

She knew it wasn't likely she would be able to clear the pit, but as she saw the tail end of the group disappear around a bend, she had to jump or she would lose them. Which, she considered, wouldn't be bad.

Her plan was to run at some point and not be on that boat. But right now, she was deep in the woodlands and needed to be nearer to where she could find a way off the planet, without being in the Dravidian's custody.

Taking a deep nervous breath, she backed away from the hole to get a running approach then she sprinted and leaped, and landed with a yelp just on the edge of the pit.

One leg fell into the hole, but her other foot managed to catch the solid ground. She grabbed at rocks on the ground and pulled herself clear of the hole.

"Oh, Goddess Satrine," she cried in pain, she had landed hard and twisted her ankle, "why is this happening to me?" Sitting on the ground, she pulled her knee up and rubbed her ankle.

"Svetiessa, what the fuck did I tell you," Dev ground out as he came up from the trail.

Then he saw her ashen face and rubbing her ankle. "What happened?" The hole had meant nothing to him, but he had pictured Sveti trying to leap across it and he had turned around to help her over it, and he didn't see her. So he jogged back to find her.

"It's nothing, I didn't quite clear the hole." Keeping her head down she didn't want to look at his annoyance, hear his complaints that she wasn't as hardy as the other women was showing to be true.

Dev crouched beside her, then knelt sitting back on his heels. "Let me see." She didn't move but he grasped her ankle. Her pained gasp cut out of her.

"Sorry," he mumbled curtly and pushed the leg of her jeans up to examine her ankle. He untied her hiking boot and slipped it off. His long fingers felt under her sock all along her ankle, lower leg and foot.

As his fingers stroked her bare skin, the horns on his head increased slightly in size, the tips of his ears reddened. "It doesn't seem to be swollen. How does it feel?" he released her foot laying it down gently.

Sveti set her heel on the ground and put a little pressure on it. "It's fine, just hurts a little. I'm good." She pulled her boot back on and tied it.

"Yeah?" he snorted, standing up. "Try to keep up then, huh?" He grasped her arm, hauled her to her feet, and held her while she tested her weight on her foot. Her face flushed again at his insulting tone and crass treatment of her.

When he saw her ankle was all right, he strapped his fingers around her arm and marched her back to the group waiting in a loose line.

He said to Bowie, "Tell them we're taking a break so *some* people can get their energy back and keep up with the group." Letting go of her arm he trod away to join Lukas in a smoke.

Feeling self-conscious, Sveti made her way to a boulder and sat by herself while everyone caught their breath. Feeling cantankerous eyes on her, and hearing people, especially Rianna and her friends making comment after nasty comment about her, she stared at the ground and tried to form an escape plan.

Once they'd rested and were back on the trail, the easy level dirt path started to incline. The group had to scale up the side of a rocky mountain.

Rianna made her way to climb beside Dev. "So, Dravidian," she purred, "how much longer do we have to go? Are we to suffer another interminable night sleeping under the stars?"

Dev grunted, "We will be there soon."

"Uh," Rianna groaned, then let her gaze roll down his body. "I bet you're a better lover than a talker, huh?"

As he moved upwards, Dev periodically glanced back at the people making their way up the mountain. He watched Sveti as she struggled to climb. She was small and untrained in taming the outdoors, and she had none of the intrinsic strength of the other species, humans included.

Seeing her tumble for the third time, Bowie started towards her.

"Nay," Dev said to him. Much to Rianna's chagrin, Dev left her and positioning his feet sideways to keep steady going down the steep mountain, he made his way to Sveti.

She had one bleeding hand clutching a rock, her tiptoes perched on jagged rocks, she was trying to reach the jutting rock above her to pull herself up.

Dev crouched beside her, ordered, "Get on my back."

"What? Certainly not." She jumped to reach the rock above her and missed. If Dev hadn't thrown his hand out clapping it on her back she would have tumbled back down the mountain. Her breath chopped out in fear at her close call.

Not waiting for her to steady herself, Dev grabbed her arms, lifted her and swung her around and put her on his back. "Put your hands around my neck," he ordered as he grasped her legs wrapping them around his waist. He tucked his hands under her knees to hold her up.

"I- I can't, put me down, I can do this," she whined.

His words terse and short he said, "Lie against my back, put your arms around my neck and rest your head on my shoulder. If you don't do it, you will cause us both to hurtle down the mountain." Leaning over slightly, he started ambling with no difficulty up the mountain.

She reluctantly laid her torso on his back, wrapped her arms around his neck and set the side of her head on his broad shoulder.

Fighting a fledging hard-on from the image of Sveti's breasts pressing on his back, Dev easily trudged up the mountain.

The further he hiked, the more the overwhelming urge to swing her around so she was facing him, then lay her against the sloping mountainside, tear open her pants, and his, and plunge into her, made him almost blind with need.

It was another thirty minutes before everyone made it to the top of the mountain.

When the ground leveled out, without a word, Dev set Sveti on her feet, moved away from her. He needed to stop touching her, looking at her or he'd have her in the bushes.

The group continued hiking more easily on the level terrain.

Rianna strode over to trot next to Sveti. Her sneering appraisal of Sveti expressed her disgust of the smaller female. "Can't you do anything you feeble piece of shit?"

At Sveti's reddening face, her sneer spread in further contempt, "You are causing us all to slow down and you're making the captainos have to work twice as hard. You should be ashamed of yourself."

Pulling her lips in, Sveti kept moving.

Rianna walked beside her mimicking Sveti's shorter footsteps.

Behind them, the other women hiking together in a clique twittered at Sveti, mocking her.

"What's the problem, *Prinţesă,*" Rianna sneered her title, "you too pampered, too royal, too spoiled to ever have had to do anything physical?"

"Yeah," another woman sniped trotting on the other side of Sveti. She reached out and yanked at a long flaming ringlet, "It's the golden red hair," she winked at Rianna. "I've heard people with that color hair are weak, frail, they are practically handicapped, half-retarded and no brawn, ya know? Not like us, *real* women." The two women broke into rousing laughter.

They stayed beside Sveti taunting and disparaging her, snagging her hair and yanking it, pinching her.

Whenever Dev looked behind him, they cleared their expressions to a veneer of innocence and stepped away from Sveti so it didn't appear they were walking with her.

She couldn't move quickly enough to get away from them and she wasn't about to complain, so Sveti firmed her lips and her step and kept moving forward.

When they were settling for the night, everyone was occupied doing something. Sveti had to go to the bathroom and didn't want to bother Elvana, the spectra officer was busy being cozy with another officer.

It was growing dusk, so she wasn't even thinking of escaping into the forest. Making sure no one was looking in her direction, Sveti slipped away into the bush to do her business.

When she was done and starting back to the camp, a creature emerged from the brush in front of her.

It resembled a dog, a really big dog, but had an exceptionally long neck, big head, what looked like a million razor-sharp teeth and they were all exposed as it snarled at her, otherworldly eyes gleamed ugly yellow threat.

"Uh," Sveti gasped and froze.

It kept stalking towards her, snarling, hissing and snapping its jaws.

She bent and grabbed up a rock and threw it at the animal. The rock hit him in the back, which only made it angrier. It started moving faster towards her.

In her fright, shouting her fright, Sveti grabbed up handfuls of rocks and threw them wildly at it, but it leaped at her.

Screaming as the animal knocked her down, she cried out as it bit her arm. Scrambling over her, its jaw was at her throat about to rip it out when it was wrenched off her.

Dev grabbed the creature by its neck and threw it as hard as he could. The animal yelped as it landed yards away. It climbed unsteadily to its feet, barked at the pair and ran off.

Shoving his banded ponytail off his shoulders, Dev glared down at Sveti.

She was half lying back with her palms on the ground behind her, face white as a sheet, panting her terror. He bent and clinched her arm and jerked her to her feet then saw the blood on her arm.

"Shit, Svetiessa, it fucking bit you. Let me see."

Embarrassed that once again he had to come to her rescue, gasping for calm, she cradled her injured arm with her other arm, murmured, "It's nothing." She turned to hurry to join the group.

With an irritated growl he snatched her arm holding her back. He lifted her arm to view the bite. At her cry of pain, he handled her more gently as he inspected the bite.

He declared angrily, "It's not nothing, dammit, I need to put shit on it or you can get infected." He brushed at some of the blood to see the wound better.

Cursing while he looked, he grumbled, "Why haven't you asked for help for fuck's sake? You knew you couldn't get over that hole, you knew you couldn't get up the mountain on your own, and now you're out here just like I told you not to be, alone." He twisted her arm to get a better look.

Trying to pull her arm away, she sniffed, "I don't want to be a burden."

His eyes shifted up to hers and narrowed. "That's stupid. You're more of a burden when I have to come look for you. If you had screamed when the animal first appeared, I would have found you sooner and you wouldn't have gotten bit."

Dev's deep angry voice sifted with the fear he'd tried to stifle when he realized she was missing. His first thought was she'd run, then he heard her scream. He'd had to shut his brain down as he raced to find her not knowing what danger she was in.

"As it was, if I'd been seconds later you would be...dead."

Heart rushing with the truth of his words, she snapped, "I don't need your help, or your protection," she yanked her hand from him and ran off.

"Goddammit," cursing a blue streak in another language, Dev jogged after her.

Letting her go find a seat, he asked Tomi for the first aid kit. Tomi gave him a quizzical look but swung his backpack down and removed the kit and handed it to Dev.

Holding the medic pack he caught up with Sveti. She was sitting with her back against a tree with her face in her hands trying to hide that she was crying. Exhausted, still recuperating from her injuries, and so frustrated with her tenuous situation she was breaking down.

Wordlessly, Dev sank down and sat cross-legged next to her. When she got control of her pride and tears, he picked up her arm and laid it on his leg.

She didn't resist as he cleaned the wound, put antibiotic on it and then bandaged it. They didn't speak as he worked on her.

When he was done, they joined the others to eat and rolled out their air pads to sleep for the night.

The next day, Dev slowed the pace so Sveti didn't have to strain to keep up, and he stayed beside her to prevent any further incidents. He would have done that all along, but he was having such a hard time keeping his hands off her he'd hoped out of sight, out of mind.

It hadn't worked and now she'd been reinjured and it was his fault because he couldn't control his lust. Dev was not used to not just taking what he wanted. He had to constantly fight himself from reaching out and grabbing the woman and disappearing into a secluded spot where he could take what he wanted.

He didn't even care that the group would have to wait and wonder while he fucked Sveti behind some rock. Every ounce of his control went into keeping his hands to himself, and his randy thoughts out of his mind.

The group finally reached the location where the boat was anchored.

Connar advised the people, "This will not be a long ride, we just need to go a ways. The river is too long to hike around. The water is a little rough, so be careful and please stay seated."

The boat was rectangle and flat with a small cabin below. The bow took up most of the space with a shorter stern at the back.

When everyone was on board and seated in the bow area, Bowie started the craft heading down river.

Dev and his other lieutenants gathered with Bowie at the bow. It would be tricky to get the vessel out of the narrow rocky channel and they'd need all eyes scanning for rocks and other hidden obstacles. The rest of the people scattered around the boat.

One of the civilian men wandered over to Sveti and sat beside her. "Hey, honey, it looks like you've been having a hard time of it, huh?" As he spoke, Rianna traipsed by them on her way to her seat and deliberately stomped on Sveti's foot.

Sveti bit her lip to keep from crying out, she caught Rianna's mean smirk as she sashayed by and sat down with the other snarky women.

Except for Elvana, none of the other women would have anything to do with her after a bunch of vicious lies Rianna had told them.

But Elvana had a crush on one of the other officers and hung with him every chance she got. Right now she was cuddled on his lap and they were locking lips. Dev's men were all watching the river so Sveti was on her own.

Making no comment on Rianna's mean action, the man beside Sveti said, "My name is Lance. They say you're a princess. That's a sweet job, eh?" Crossing his legs he scooped his light brown hair behind his ears. He appeared to be in his mid-twenties with fairly ordinary looks, nose, chin, lips, height, all average.

When Sveti looked at him he was blatantly staring at her chest. She politely mumbled, "Nice to meet you."

"So," he muttered, nudging closer to her until their thighs touched, then he set a hand on her knee.

"Please," Sveti objected, brushed his hand off and wriggled down the durable plastic bench they were sitting on.

"Geeze, come on, honey, Rianna says you've already put out for the captain and his lieutenants, give me a little feel, okay?" He promptly set his hand on her stomach and started sliding it up.

"Stop!" Sveti whispered loudly not wanting to draw attention, shoving at his hand. Turning sideways from him, she crossed one arm over her chest and tucked the other between her legs. Another man sat down on the other side of her.

"Hey, Lance, you keeping the princess all to yourself?" The man chuckled while sidling close to her, his leering eyes raking her body. "Rianna says she does two guys at the same time, likes a dick in both ends while doin' it, you wanna share her? There's some space below we can duck down to. Whaddya say, sweetie?" He put his hand on her other leg.

Sveti pushed to stand up but both men held her down. "Wait for us, sugar," Lance cooed, rolling an arm around her shoulder, "as soon as everyone is looking up front, we'll take you below."

Sveti dreaded causing yet another scene by shouting for help, everyone hated her and the captain was furious at the trouble she'd already caused.

"No, stop, leave me alone." Sveti pushed at him but he grasped her wrist with a slight twist and said with a cruel grin, "Na, honey, let's go now, no one's gonna see us," he winked at the other man who stood up ready to take her to the cabin.

117

"Svetiessa," acid drenching his terse voice, Dev snagged her arm. With a searing look at each of the two men that left them trembling, he pulled her to her feet and brought her to the back of the boat where it was empty of people.

He pulled a length of rope from his cargo pocket. Holding her wrist he moved her near a metal bar.

"Sire, what are you doing?" trying to tug her arm away, her voice shook.

His gaze on her wrist he admonished, "You can't seem to stop encouraging the men to come on to you. I don't want a fight over you erupting on the boat, people could get hurt. The channel is treacherous, I need to be up front with my men to get us through and can't have you in the way."

He looped the rope around the railing complaining, "You're nothing but fucking trouble."

Wounded eyes sought his in fear. "Sire, please, what if the boat sinks? Why are you tying me?"

He made a short snicking sound. "It is the sturdiest water vessel made. I will be back as soon as we get out of this channel. From up front Tomi can look back to make sure no one comes back here and hassles you." He pulled her closer to the rail. "I am tying you so you don't do something stupid like jump overboard."

"You don't need to bother, I am a terrible swimmer." Her head lowered she stared at his chest.

Contemplating her sincerity, Dev held the rope in his hand. He let go of her arm, his lips pulled in. Stuffing the rope back in his pocket, he said, "All right. I won't tie you."

He gripped her chin and lifted it, commanded sharply, "You do not move from here, you hear me? If anyone, I mean anyone, takes one step back here, you scream. I will hear you up front and come immediately." His gaze flicked from her eyes to her lips, he waited.

She nodded.

Releasing her chin, he regarded her for a moment, then turned; his long legs took him quickly from the stern through the rest of the boat and back to the front of the bow.

As soon as he was gone, Sveti climbed up on a bench. Something caught her eye, she looked over.

Rianna was in the doorway grinning at her. She wriggled her fingers goodbye at Sveti.

Sveti put a foot on the rail, pushed up and then jumped into the water.

Chapter Twelve

ᗞev said to Bowie, "We look clear." To Lukas and Connar, he instructed, "Keep watch in front and the sides, there can be hidden boulders and fallen trees. I'm going to get the prințesă."

"Why didn't you bring her here?" Lukas asked.

"The water was rougher than I expected, I wanted her safer in the middle of the vessel. I ended up having to put her in the wider flatter stern, away from the wolves."

"So you left her alone back there?" The incredulous sarcasm in Bowie's voice was clear.

Dev glanced over to Tomi, but the big man's attention was on the channel.

His lips compressed, Dev started to the back of the boat. He strode through the middle of the vessel, people kept out of his way.

As Dev passed through the doorway, he noticed Rianna nearby with the most innocent look he'd ever seen plastered on her face. A tingle started in his gut, he hurried to the stern.

"Shit!" he exploded when he got to the back and Sveti wasn't there. He ran back out and said to Rianna, "Where is she?"

Her eyes rolled, she sneered, "I am not the puny princessa's keeper, Captain." The sneer turned sensuous, "But I wouldn't mind being yours."

His jaw flexing, Dev got in her face. "Don't fucking play with me," he threatened, "I will chuck you over the side."

Rianna held a hand up and gazed at her manicure. One of her wide shoulders rose indifferently, she drawled with zero concern, "She jumped overboard. Good riddance to the royal trash."

Dev's brows crashed into his hairline. He blurted, "What? She what? You saw her and didn't fucking try to stop her or come and get me?"

A sly grin curved her glossy lips. She smoothed her hands down her curvaceous form and replied with disinterest, "Why should I? It's none of my business what the ugly, skinny little slut does. You should be glad to have her out of your hair. She's been nothing but trouble and aggravation for you. Please, I did you a favor."

"You bitch," he snarled. Turning from her he booked to the railing, quickly scanned the water; there was no sign of Sveti.

He ran to the front of the vessel and shouted, "Bowie, stop the boat, Sveti is in the water!"

Not waiting for his response, Dev ran back to the stern, he didn't slow down, ran right up, hopped on the railing and dove.

His strong strokes cleaved through the rough waters, keeping his head up he scoured the river for Sveti. When he didn't see her, he feared she'd gone under. The boat hadn't been going very fast when she'd jumped, and they were too far from land for her to get to it that quickly, she couldn't be that far away.

With every stroke he scanned the water, panic rising up his throat threatening to strangle him, then- *"Fuck- there-"* panting, he saw her head bobbing.

Her arms were flailing, thrashing the water, she wasn't swimming, she was struggling to keep her head above the water but the rapids crashed over her, throwing water down her throat and pulling her under.

Dev stroked flat out with everything he had over the rushing waves. He raced to her, arms spinning like mad windmills, legs kicking so fast they were invisible but threw out a raging surf behind him like a charging motorboat.

In moments he reached her. He grabbed her hair to hold her from being torn from him by the hurtling water then drew her head up and back to keep her mouth clear of the river. She couldn't see him, she flailed in panicked terror.

"I've got you, Svetiessa," he said quietly near her ear, but loud enough to hear over the roar of the water. He slid his arm over the front of her. "Don't move, don't struggle, you'll make it harder for me to swim. Just stay limp, honey, can you do that for me?"

Sputtering, she nodded, her teeth chattered. He tightened his hold on her and started to swim for shore. He could see the boat kept moving with the momentum of the river's current.

It would be some time before Bowie could find a wider stretch to turn it around and come back to look for them. There were too many sharp ground swells to drive backwards.

When his feet touched ground, Dev lifted her into his arms and tramped onto shore.

He strode across the hard packed sand up to a slight bank and set her down to lean back against the firm slope.

She sputtered and coughed, heaved and wiped frantically at her eyes, then her head fell back as she tried to control the sheer panic from the near drowning that gripped her, stealing her breath.

Dev sat back on his haunches, his big chest rising and falling with his heavy panting. Swiping his soaking hair out of the front of his face, the band that held it was long gone. He pushed the heavy locks back, waiting for Sveti to catch her breath and her coughing to ease.

In a minute, she lay quieter. Water clinging to her lashes, she raised dazed eyes to Dev, her damp lips parted as her chest rose and fell shaky but more lightly. She had that same sultry look from when they were dancing; it spun right to his groin.

Without thinking, he leaned to her, set a hand against the sand wall beside her head, cupped the side of her face with his other hand and suddenly thrust his mouth roughly over her parted lips.

Instantly her body started, she put her palms on his chest to push him away. His barbarous kiss struck hard and hungry and fierce, torching their mouths. He pushed her lips wide and forced his tongue inside to sweep her mouth, lick her teeth, he went after her tongue.

He had been compelled to kiss her again since the day on the flashjet. The flavor of her ignited his taste buds, sending spinning shock waves to his head and his groin; it was even more damned transcendent than he had remembered. He felt her hands repelling him, he ignored her resistance.

Flames sparking around them, Dev thought he had imagined how exquisitely she tasted, like velveteen roses, how soft her lips, he could feel her innocence in the kiss and was insanely stirred by it. The essence of her natural floral scent barraged his senses. His mind went blank filling with only intense physical desire and scalding heat, there wasn't a thought in his head except he wanted more. More of her mouth, more of her body, more of her.

Sveti's hands pressing against his chest slowly curled into fists as she gripped his shirt, and now responded to his kiss. His head slanted sealing their mouths as he plundered her, tangling then sucking her tongue. At her response, his horns swelled, claws emerged, his fangs descended.

He kept his eyes closed knowing they were turning fierce white and would only frighten her. When her fingers stroked around his neck and she pulled him closer, tighter, her virginal tongue trying to match his potent fury, his body burned, cock hardened and swelled along with his horns.

Suddenly, without separating their mouths, Dev pushed his hands under her and lifted her, moving to lay her down flat. Forcing his claws to stay sheathed, he relentlessly ravished her with his torrid mouth.

He'd only needed a flicker of response from her, it was enough for him to take her.

At her soft whimper, he dragged his palms roughly down over her breasts and kept going to violently tear at the buttons on her jeans. Jerking them apart, he reached for his own belt and yanked at it, shoved his tongue down her throat briefly then growled against her lips, "Svetiessa, you don't need to consider commitment."

Shocked, she froze. Pushing at him, she cried, "*Get off of me!*"

When he leaned back in surprise, she wriggled out from under him and scrambled to her feet. Staggering at first to gather her equilibrium she then stormed off securing her jeans.

Stunned, he called out after her, "Svetiessa? Come back here, what's wrong?"

Buckling his belt, Dev climbed to his feet and dusted the sand off his pants. His body was on fire and the anger that was now descending on him fueled that fire.

He had to wait for his body to cool, return to normal or he would literally kill the first person that neared him.

His mind disoriented and confused, he tried to ascertain what happened. "Ah," he thought out loud, "she doesn't want a goddamned commitment and freaked when I said I wanted it."

Shaking his head, he shoved hunks of wet hair back, and ground out, "I would never share her with others." His hands crunched into fists, eyes burned white heat, it enraged him that she would not want to be exclusive with him. That she would desire to be with other men.

He had never cared before if the women he spent time with hopped from man to man, but Svetiessa, Dev shook his head again. He could not bear to picture her with another man's hands on her, much less between her thighs fucking- a shudder of rage rippled through his pulsating body.

Fire shot up around him. "What the fuck?" he cursed. "Damned humans, *women*, who can figure the bitches out?" He stomped along the shore following her footprints.

Shunting the guilt of being on the precipice of taking Sveti in her innocence on the shore out in the open, they had been exposed to natives and animals, it was dangerous, Dev had been out of his mind with rampaging desire for her.

If he hadn't been so shocked and stopped at her sudden departure, he would have taken her, he had been too savagely out of control, too wildly turned on to stop, even if she'd said to. And undoubtedly, in the next few seconds, when she realized how far he was going, she would have tried to resist him. It would have had no effect on him, he was too far gone. Her resistance would have been futile.

Trudging over the packed sand, less than a quarter of a mile he saw the boat anchored near shore. Tomi and Connar had set out a small float boat to the shore to collect Sveti and were already bringing her back on board.

Tomi brought the floater back out for him. Tomi's big-toothed grin disappeared when he saw the black wrath marring Dev's already hard face.

"Hey, bro, what hap-" he broke off at the murderous heat in Dev's still white eyes, flames discharging in an arc spiraled his rigid body. They didn't speak as they made it back on board the boat, and dragged the floater up on the plastic deck.

The boat traveled for a few miles before heading back to shore. Lukas lowered the anchor, and Bowie maneuvered the ship to a small dock.

After throwing down anchor, and the boat shut down and secured, everyone disembarked.

Tomi addressed the people, "We have a day of hiking before we reach the starship pickup location." At the groans and moans he glanced over at Bowie's grin, and shot him the finger.

Once everyone exited the craft, the civilians collected into loose groups and waited while the warriors and crew gathered up the supply packs.

Half dry, Sveti was standing with Tomi when Dev strode up behind her. She didn't turn around until she felt her hair lifted and the cold metal clamp around her neck.

Whipping her head around with a gasp, her hands went to the clamp secured around her neck. "What is-"

Holding the end of a chain connected to the clamp in his hand, his voice chilled, Dev said, "I warned you not to try to escape." His face hard, dark eyes inscrutable he watched scarlet shame climb up her neck and into her cheeks.

The flicker of his lashes warned Tomi against saying anything. The big black man shut his mouth, clenched his teeth, yet he still shot Dev an angry look. Dev had found the clamp and chain in the cabin storage unit.

"Sire, please, don't do this to me," her low whisper filled with humiliation was so hushed only Dev and Tomi could hear her. Everyone gawked at her.

"You lied to me, you said you wouldn't jump because you couldn't swim." The intractable gaze and tone brooked no discussion.

Her fingers clutched at the clamp, she said, "I didn't say I wouldn't jump, I just said I was a poor swimmer, which you saw was true. Please..."

Keeping his head raised, his lids tapered as he peered down at her, he declared, "You said it deliberately to trick me. It is the second time you used devious methods to trick me. That is two times too many."

"But I didn't-"

Dev put his hand around her neck over the clamp and snarled, "Enough. You are not to be trusted, you lie and deceive." His coarse voice dropped low, "And, you stupid bitch, you would have drowned with your foolish actions."

Then he snatched her arm up and slapped a clean bandage with ointment on it over the bite, replacing the bandage that had swept away in the river.

"I told you there would be consequences if you tried to escape and I caught you." His fingers curled around her throat under her jaw. Lifting her chin so she had to look at him, he brought his head low and spoke roughly, "I will always catch you. Remember that." Damp ebony strands of hair clung to the side of his infuriated face.

The threat clear in his black glare, Sveti only blinked back at him without response. Releasing her, Dev called out to Lukas, "Let's go, get them moving."

He kept to the back of the line with Sveti beside him. He didn't hold the end of the chain, it was enough that it was there. The links lined down her spine, shimmering with her steps.

Keeping his steps even with hers, Dev could hear her sniffing back mortified tears. His anger and resentment at her rejecting him suppressed his guilt about chaining her.

When they stopped for a break he told her to sit against a thicket of trees with Tomi and Connar. His two friends glowering at him for his treatment of Sveti, welcomed her with warm compassion as she knelt gracefully to sit with them.

Dev went off to the side to smoke a cigar. Bowie stalked over to him lacking his normal mischievous expression. Dev unemotionally observed his friend under low lids through a haze of smoke.

"Craw, Dev," Bowie chastised him, "you can't chain that girl like she's a dog. The others already treat her like shit because of Rianna. You are humiliating her beyond belief. Bloody Zues, *má bráthair*, she's a damned princess for cripe's sake. She deserves better than that."

Taking a long drag, Dev held it then blew the smoke out slowly. "I warned her, told her there would be repercussions if she attempted to escape, and she tried anyway. And almost died."

His lids lowered callously further at Bowie as he opened his mouth, he said curtly, "Done talking about it."

Lips firmed in a mutinous grit, Bowie knew when to stop. Shooting a pissed glare at his friend, he snapped under his breath, "She did nothing neither you nor the rest of us wouldn't have done, except we would have slaughtered everyone here, and then fled." He stalked from him to join Sveti and his friends.

Bowie plopped down on the ground and smiled cheerfully at her. "Hey Sveti, nice necklace. Expensive?"

Her sad smile wry, she said, "Quite."

"Yeah," he murmured, his smile dropped. "I'm sorry. He's my best friend but he can be a ruthless cruel brute."

The corner of her lip lifted drily. "That is an understatement." The men laughed.

She asked Bowie, "Are the females on his planet like him? Do they have horns and his powerful strength?" She shivered thinking about them. "And claws and fangs?"

Shaking his head, Bowie replied, "Nay."

He explained, "The males are holandric. Those uh, characteristics are inherited exclusively through the male descent. DNA is transmitted through genes located only on the Y chromosome. Of course his kind have a few more chromosomes than most folks."

He stuck his legs out straight and leaned back on his palms. With a chuckle he said, "Could you imagine a female Dev?" He shuddered and made a face with his tongue out. "Yikes."

Tomi and Connar laughed. "Thanks for the picture," Connar remarked, making the same eew face. Sliding a few fingers under the back of his wavy chestnut hair, lifting it out of his collar, he said, "She'd always want to be on top." The men snickered.

When not shooting arrows of hostility at Sveti and amusement at her humiliation, the females in the group stared with unabashed invitation at the warriors. When they were ignored, the women nudged each other snickering while making fun of the chain around Sveti's neck.

Rianna called out, "How the mighty fall, huh? Not so princessy now, are ya bitch? Chained like the bitch dog prisoner that you are. Should have been restrained that way from the very start. Criminals like you need to be kept away from good folks like us."

Shaking his head at their malice, Bowie looked away from the women to his friends. "Aye," he chuckled. "Picture a tall, huge, heavily muscle-bound female with the harshest bad-assed face you've ever seen, baring her fangs at you while she wraps her claws around your dick."

Turning his back to the brazen, sniping women, Tomi sniggered, "With cyclonic white eyes turning to the purest night black, war braids draping over you, ick." He shivered with a grin.

"Making love to a female version of Dev with his propensity for ruthless violence would be like mating with a killer shark. Her fierce pussy would clamp down and cut off your dick. I don't think so." They all laughed again.

Lukas snickered adding, "Aye, and Connar, she would chow down on all of those other girls you have at every station and planet to eliminate her competition."

They roared with laughter, then laughed harder at the scowl Dev sent their way.

Chapter Thirteen

After the break, before they prepared to start walking again.

Dev went over and stood in front of Sveti where she was sitting on the ground.

The lieutenants took the hint and got to their feet and rambled off to start the lineup.

Dev crouched and set his forearms on his knees; clasped his hands. "I am going to remove the chain, Svetiessa, do not do anything that will cause me to put it back on."

Her crystal blues stared unwavering at him. Keeping her back regally straight, she swallowed the humiliation and hurt. Hugging her knees she sat unmoving.

He waited for a response, thinking she would say something like, "Oh, thank you, I swear I'll never run from you again," or, "Devilos, I am so sorry I ran from you and almost killed myself, and then spurned you." But no. She had the nerve to glare angrily at him like he was the one in the wrong.

His brow furrowed in irritation. However, he also felt a pinch of admiration at her stubbornness. Like Bowie had said, if it had been any of them, they would have already tried to escape a dozen times.

But they were seasoned male warriors, not a young, petite female human. One who was still recovering her strength and health from her almost fatal ordeal.

And worse, she had tried to run on a dangerous planet with no way off. A deep sigh strummed from his heavy chest, it was also Bowie who had said the girl needed a strong keeper.

Her rejection pricked his ego. He didn't recall ever being rejected before, and he was pretty sure it wouldn't have bothered him in the least if he had. He would have just moved on to the next female, one was pretty much the same as the other.

But, Sveti, he had been so focused on her eyes; sultry fire burning in the innocent blue depths, mesmerized by the plush lips parted in confusion, every part of her was a siren's song straight to his manhood.

Dev shook his head acknowledging his guilt. So crazed with senseless lust for her, regardless of her objections, he would have pushed her on her back, yanked those jeans and panties off, spread those soft slender thighs, and slammed deep inside her. Again and again, and again.

He had been shocked at her refusing a commitment with him, if she hadn't startled him and jumped up and stormed off so quickly he would not have let her go.

Ignoring her protests, her struggles, he would have pressed...forced...himself on her, claiming her. He wasn't raised in, nor did he live in a gentlemen's world, he took what he wanted, and he wanted her.

He could admit to himself now that if she hadn't faded away that very first day on the ship he would have kept her there, heedless of her wishes, or her sick brother's commands for her return.

Her gaze remained level at him, but weariness rippled from her humiliated eyes down her still too thin body.

His eyes narrowed at her frailty, she still hadn't fully healed or gained weight from the nightmare she had suffered on her little brother's behalf.

An image suddenly flooded his mind, of Sveti in the dank dark dungeon hanging by her skinny wrists, dress torn to shreds, that bastard guard lifting her skirt to assault her, Dev's fear she may already be dead.

His stomach churned at the wretched picture of him slashing, cutting the chain, and her battered, broken body slipping into his arms.

Now he moved closer to her and slid to his knees. She blanched and tried to move away from him but her back was against the tree. Frowning, his timbre deep, he gruffed in annoyance, "I said I was going to remove the chain. Hold still."

Leaning into her, he could smell her scent. He skimmed his hard hands under her soft curls, lifted them then letting them fall down her back. Everything about her screamed soft and tender, a glaring contrast to his sheer hardness and brutality.

They were so close now her warmth and fragrance brought prickles to his skin. "Tilt your head," he ordered quietly.

Their eyes were inches apart, hers were so young and fresh, circled with long lashes, gleaming with nerves and, he was almost positive he saw desire a flourishing shadow in the depths of the vivid blue. He felt ancient and jaded looking into them.

His gaze dipped to her lips, she licked them nervously. His groin twitched. He had never kissed another woman like he had her, with such vehemence, and uncontrolled madness, but then no other woman tasted like her, had lips like hers, was as sweet as she.

Sveti closed her eyes and tilted her head so he could reach the lock on the clamp. His gaze slid to her elegant feminine neck, his fangs descended, it took effort to force them back before he sunk them into her sweet flesh.

Dev had to wipe his palms on his pants before sticking the key in and unlocking the lock. He withdrew the clamp and saw marks it had made on her fair skin. Red imprints from the heaviness on her neck, and some bruising.

His hand went to her lissome neck; he gently touched the bruises with the pads of his fingertips.

He was taken aback; he hadn't expected that the clamp would hurt her. It wasn't that heavy, it was more the symbolism than the actual chaining. He had to let her know he was serious about her trying to flee again, especially fucking leaping into the goddamned river when she can't even swim for fuck's sake.

And then, if she had actually survived and gotten away, managed to hide from him if he hadn't discovered her missing so quickly, she would have been alone and defenseless on a treacherous barbarous planet with no way to get food and no way off.

His fingers tightened on her flesh. This small woman was causing him to have feelings and emotions he was unfamiliar with, and they unnerved him greatly.

She flinched under his grip, her eyes opened and she quickly turned her face away. He figured his obsidian irises must be lightening like snow on a black lake, and his skin darkening in his renewed anger.

He knew his proximity and his hand on her neck were frightening her. A few strands of his long hair strew over his chest, her crystal eyes fell to them before rising slowly to look back up at him. The temptation to kiss her was obscenely encompassing, engulfing his entire mind and body, his smoldering gaze swept her face, her eyes, her lips.

She nervously licked them again under his intense perusal. Another second and he would drag her into the privacy of the bushes; get her on her back and her pants off. He stood up in one movement, so quickly she gasped.

Dev bent and held a hand to her. She studied it for a second, then warily took it. He pulled her to her feet. They didn't speak again throughout the final trek to the location the airship was in, or when they boarded.

He had her stay on the bridge with him while the captain that had flown the ship to the planet brought them back into space, the entire time they didn't look at or speak to one another.

When they landed on the space station, he told Bowie to take her to her chambers, and he stalked off to his.

Sveti and Bowie didn't talk on the way to her room.

Keldon was already present. Bowie opened her door and followed her in.

Once inside, Sveti let out a held breath, her tense shoulders drooped.

"Uh," Bowie muttered, standing awkwardly watching her rub her arms in anxiety and probably chill. The station was air-conditioned and they had been traipsing over a warm planet the last few days. "Can I get you anything, Sveti? We're going to be at this station for a while before we're able to get another ship to take us to your-" He broke off as her skin paled.

"No, I'm fine, Bowie," she assured him with a wan smile and small shake of her head. "You are so kind and sweet." She smiled at his embarrassed blush.

"Geez, Sveti, I'm a warrior, you can't describe me as sweet." His expression pained he glanced around to ensure no one had overheard her comment.

She laughed. Then sobered. "You aren't like...him. You have a heart, compassion, an even temper, and you actually smile. Sometimes he looks at me like he would...like to...devour me. Literally. After chopping me into bite-sized pieces." Her arms contracted in a shiver.

Bowie's lips twitched in a grin. "No one is like him." The grin straightened to a grim smile. "You don't know him like we do. I've known him most of my life. They started his training to fight almost from birth. He was not raised by your basic mother and father. His world is vastly different than ours. He was born, bred, raised to be a warrior, to be one of the most powerful warlords in the universe.

"He had no choice. So of course," Bowie tucked a hand in his pocket with a mild grin, "with all that you can't expect him to be a nice guy. He isn't. But," he smiled at her twisted lips, "you wouldn't want another man at your back. He is loyal to a fault, that's why he gets so fucked up, uh sorry, messed up over people's tricks and lies. He never lies, he's bold and honest with his words and his actions, even with the most dastardly criminals."

He didn't comment on the devouring part, all of his close friends could see how hard Dev fought to keep from throwing her down like a caveman and fucking her, willing or not. Sometimes the beast inside him was more savage animal than man, and it couldn't always be tamed. Good in battle, not so good with delicate virginal princesses.

Sveti nodded, crossed her arms and hugged her body. "I understand what you're saying, Bowie, but," color brushed her cheeks. "You don't know, he- I mean he danced with me, he…" She took a breath. "When he pulled me out of the river and we were on shore, he…kissed me."

Bowie's brows shot up. "No kidding?" He pulled his hand from his pocket and set both of them on his hips, shaking his blond head in disbelief. "Huh. He's not normally big on, uh, kissing."

His face turned slightly red. "I mean, we were in much of the same training as youths, and we've been all over universes on missions together; that made us very close, like brothers." He tugged at his collar around his neck.

"I shouldn't tell you this, but, he usually just, makes the sex quick, doesn't get emotionally involved. I mean, for him to kiss you, and, uh that's twice now, he usually keeps things more…impersonal.

"With him, sex is just an instinctual natural act, like any animal. He loathes intimacy. But," his forehead creased in question, "what happened? You came back without him and were obviously upset, and he was so pissed he could bite nails and crush rocks with his fists."

Blinking rapidly, Sveti tried to take in what Bowie was saying. Her stomach felt ill, picturing the big Dravidian having… relations with other women.

"He, well, he kissed me really…hard, and," her blushed brightened, "he suddenly laid me down and was…undoing my…clothes. Then he said," her face hardened remembering her humiliation, "he said don't worry, he doesn't expect any commitment with me."

Her gaze drifted to the floor then back up to the tall blond. "I think he planned on...trying to have sex with me, and if we did, he was saying, then I was to be just a- a- fast screw and he was moving on. I wasn't about to be ravished on the side of an alien river, but, I was," how could she explain her brain roaring with blood, buzzing so loud she couldn't think, she could only feel Dev's mouth on hers?

Like velvety cashmere and seductive quicksand sucking her in, she was absolutely mindless to stop.

Her heavy exhale pained, she said, "Anyway, when he made that comment, I came to my senses, and left him to go to the ship."

A frown pulled Bowie's golden brows down over his blue eyes. Shaking his head, he said, "I think there was a miscommunication somewhere, Sveti. Dev would not, I mean, he knows about your," this was embarrassing, "brother and selling your...ahem, virginity. We know when you lose your, uh, virginity you will be automatically wedded to that male.

"There is some kind of...chemical reaction that will tie you two together. So," he shook his head again, "Dev would not fuck- uh, have sex with you and leave you. Honey, you need to talk to him, clear this up."

Whoa, no wonder Devilos was livid when he returned to the ship. Bowie grinned inside, Dev must of have been furious, and confused, and insanely frustrated when she denied him. He's choosy and the women he chooses don't turn him down.

He must have been in a helluva stupor or at the point they were at, he would not have let her go. She must have taken him by such surprise, walking away before he could grasp what had happened.

138

Glaring at Bowie, Sveti said angrily, "The chemical reaction would only occur if he were a prince, so," she snorted dolefully, "he would have been safe from being attached to me. I'm sure he's well aware of that. No." she shook her head when Bowie opened his mouth to speak.

"He could have stopped me when I was leaving, or talked to me later to explain what he was saying, but he didn't. So either he didn't care or it was as I heard it. He had no plans to have any sort of…relationship with me.

"I mean, you said it yourself; he has sex and doesn't get involved with the women. Besides, I don't have any interest in a relationship with a big rude ox that has fangs and horns, and puts a- I mean, Bowie, he put a chain around my neck! He couldn't have done anything more humiliating to me!"

His lips pulled in, Bowie nodded, agreed, "Aye, yeah, I know. But Sveti, you have to see, he isn't used to dealing with women, at least ones like you. If you were a man he would have just put you, uh, down. By the way, didn't you say you had a boyfriend?"

Sveti felt a twinge of guilt. "Yes, no, I mean not exactly. Ryen and I probably would be together if Krystian had allowed it. But he has always threatened Ryen, or any other man for that matter, if he pursued me. So," her shoulder drew up, "we've never actually been romantically linked."

To her chagrin, she hadn't even thought of Ryen since his call. They had never really been romantic with each other, it was more of a deep liking and caring. A quiver gripped her shoulders. She doubted if Ryen had ever really kissed her would it be as…overwhelming, as the Dravidian's.

"Okay, I see. Anyway, give Dev a chan-"

A whistle blew through the intercom. "Damn," Bowie cursed. "I have to go, that's a call to all warriors to meet. I forgot we were to have a meeting today. But still," he leaned over and gave her a chaste kiss on the cheek, "talk to him." He hurried out the door.

As he was leaving, the bubbly Dr. Geffry Jamez bustled in.

Offering him a puzzled smile, Sveti asked, "Hello Doctor, why um, are you here?"

"Hello there, my dear. Devilos said you had a traumatic, ah, adventure, and it might have impacted your recovering health. He told me to come and check on you, and that bite on your arm. Come," he closed the door, motioned with his med case, "let's go have a look see, shall we?"

Chapter Fourteen

*D*ays passed. The first evening back at the station, Dev and Sveti and his lieutenants sat together in the dining room.

Under hooded lids, Dev silently regarded Sveti. She had not looked in his direction all evening, nor did she join in the males' conversations.

After that first dinner, Dev had Bowie or Tomi bring Sveti to dinner, he never joined them.

Then, after yet another meal that Dev didn't show for, Bowie sought Dev out. He found him sitting in one of the bars on the station.

Mostly just warriors went to the Lunar Lounge, only a few civilians, and fewer women were tough enough, coarse enough, to handle the company there.

The lighting was low, there were no windows, the tiled floor was dark, the walls charcoal grey, several males of diverse species sat humped over their drinks in a vaporous haze from various types of smokes.

"Hey," Bowie said as he sat next to Dev and nodded to the bartender. The bartender immediately brought a foaming beer right to him. "Thanks," he said to the bartender and took a quick swig.

Dev didn't look at him, just sipped his pale green liquor.

"So," Bowie said, "you haven't been around at dinner time."

Dev shrugged one shoulder.

"I talked to Sveti. I know what happened that day on the riverside." He gulped down a quarter of the mug, belched then exhaled with a, "*Ahh*, that's good," he wiped his mouth with the back of his hand.

Dev flicked a side-glance at him but said nothing, shoulders hunched, he took a sip and sat rocking the glass with his big fingers watching the liquid swirl back and forth.

"Yeah, so, she told me that you were all over her and then suddenly you told her don't worry, you weren't looking for any kind of commitment from her." He grinned at the angry aghast look his friend shot him.

"What the fuck, Bow, I never said that. She's just trying to cover that she is the one who said she didn't want a commitment. Probably because of that weakling boyfriend back on her planet waiting for her to return to his open fucking arms."

Dev had no respect for a man who didn't protect and rescue his woman. And if a woman needed rescuing, it was Svetiessa.

Her coward boyfriend didn't deserve her. Apparently neither did Dev. Dev had thought he could seduce all thoughts of this boyfriend of hers out of her mind. Well, for once he was wrong in his life. The one time it really mattered.

"Huh. Forget about Ryen, did Sveti say those exact words?"

Staring into his glass, Dev thought about it, muttered, "Well, no. She didn't really say anything. When I said she didn't need to worry about a commitment she pushed me away and stormed off." He turned towards Bowie.

"I told her, I mean, I meant we would be exclusive, that we were committing to each other, but she threw it in my face that she obviously wanted to be with other men, and that was it. But I," he hesitated slightly embarrassed, "would never share her with another man. She's not like other women, Bow, I couldn't handle seeing her with other males, sure as hell could never stomach her leaving my bed then go to another's."

Bowie rolled his eyes. "You misunderstood, misread her. I know you remember that the man to whom she loses her virginity is the man to whom she is eternally joined. Actually," he gulped his beer, "I think it was Sveti that misunderstood you. And," he eyed his friend, "she was peeved that you didn't come and straighten things out with her, you just let her go."

He frowned slightly at Dev, his dark blue eyes reproachful. Bowie scolded him, "Besides, you know damned well you were taking advantage of her inexperience, deliberately seducing her. I'm sure you dazed her with your kisses, and if she had a moment to gather her wits she would have stopped you before you took her. Well," his gaze rolled over his best friend's ruthless, aggressive face, his lip curled in. "She would have *tried* to stop you."

"Ah," Dev growled, slumping further over his drink. "I can't believe we're sitting here like a couple of pussies talking about broads. What are we, fucking gossiping little girls?" He snorted and motioned to the bartender for another drink.

"Hmm." Bowie roped his fingers around the bottom of his mug and looked at his dejected friend. "I can't believe a female finally got her talons in you, and you're so freaked out about it you don't know how to handle it."

Shaking his head with a wry grin, Bowie teased, "Never thought I'd see the day the baddest warlord in the stratosphere has it nutso for a chick and mucks it all up due to warbled communication. You know you have no intentions on letting her run free, so the sooner you fix the shit the better you both will be."

"Why don't you shut the fuck up," Dev grumbled. While he pondered his friend's words, a woman strolled over to him.

Setting a hand on his shoulder she said, "Hi, Captain, you look lonely sitting here." She ignored Bowie's snigger. "I thought you might like some company."

Dev didn't even glance at the shapely brunette. "Nay. I have all the company I want." He raised a head with a short nod indicating to the bartender he wanted yet another drink.

The woman stayed with her hand on his shoulder fingering a braid. "Oh." She shrugged; her loose blouse slipped off one shoulder and exposed half her breast. "I figured since that princess you were all hot and bothered over was fucking her way through the station that-"

"What?" Dev slammed his glass down and lashed his fierce expression incredulous at her. "What are you saying?" His dark eyes crunched to mere slits.

Her lip pursed and she stiffened. "Uh, well, everyone knows she's insatiable, like a nymphomaniac, you know. Right now she just left one of the warrior's room, she was with two men at the same time, and is headed to her-"

Dev shoved to his feet.

"Wait, Dev, there is no way-" Bowie got up and tried to stop him but Dev was already striding out of the bar.

Bowie glared hard at the woman who was sighing in relief and primping her hair. She wasn't as brave as her girlfriend that wanted to bed the scary Dravidian. *I mean*, she thought, *he has horns for fuck's sake.*

His eyes narrowed at her, Bowie said with suspicion, "Someone put you up to that, didn't they?"

Her bare shoulder bumped up. "So what of it? Who cares? That princess has no business poaching Rianna's territory, she-"

"Ah, fuck," Bowie swore and ran out of the bar but had no idea where Dev went. He called him on his cell, but Dev didn't pick up.

His friend was drunk and fired up or he'd realize Sveti could not have gone to a warrior's room; she has a guard at her door.

So enraged he could pound holes through the steel walls, Dev stomped through the corridors to Sveti's room.

People seeing the huge incensed warlord stalking down the hall, horns growing, long black braids flapping behind him, small cloud-bursts of flames abrading the floor around his legs, quickly got out of his way.

He didn't acknowledge Keldon, just shoved the door open and stomped in. Sveti was heading towards the kitchen; she spun around in surprise at the door slamming inside the wall.

Seeing Dev obviously infuriated, his body vibrating with rage, face a mask of brutal ferocity, she turned and started to run towards her bedroom.

He reached her quickly and snatched her arm jerking her to a halt.

Breathless with fright, she cried, "Sire, what is it? What's going on?" She tried to wrestle from his grasp but it was in vain. A rampaging elephant couldn't have gotten out of his grip.

Shoving the door that was closing aside, he marched her out of her suite, past the guard with his mouth hanging open, and down the spider-legged halls to his chambers so fast she couldn't get a word out, and he wasn't talking.

If he hadn't such a tight grip on her arm she would have stumbled half a dozen times he strode so quickly.

Throwing his door open, Dev dragged her inside. He pulled her to the big couch in the center of the room and released her.

As he stood towering over Sveti, he transformed. The flickering of a blurry wave enveloped him, his body changed, a monster was emerging. His horns continued to swell, the claws unsheathed from his fingertips.

His fangs descended, he hissed at her, "You refuse me, but you whore with others?" He pushed her until she fell, her butt landing on the couch.

Snarling with harrowing malevolence, jabbing his thumb at his hard chest he ground viciously at her, "You will damn well whore with me!"

Sveti squirmed away from him, her eyes darting around the room looking for an escape, or a weapon, not that it would do her any good. "I- I don't understand, Sire, what are you saying? I have never-"

"*Shut up!*" he roared at her and roughly pushed her down on her back.

"Wait! Sire-"

"Done waiting," he growled and flipped her over on her stomach. A huge hand pressed her shoulder down holding her from moving then he sliced a claw in her blouse and ripped it almost clear down her back.

"Stop!" she screamed, on her stomach Sveti had no way to defend herself.

Through his raging blinding white eyes, Dev saw the scrape his claw made down her back, it didn't break the skin but it left an ugly red trail. He followed it to the curve of her tiny waist.

So small, so feminine, her hair swirled in a flaming cloud around her shoulders and over the cushion. Her slender shoulders shook with terrified gasps as she struggled.

Blood rushed through his head, Dev barely heard her cries as his body enlarged further in his wrath. He lifted her again and turned her over on her back, and slit the claw through the top of her pants tearing them open.

Shoving a knee between her leg and the couch, he kept one foot on the floor and was pushing her pants down when his atavistic gaze lit on her chest.

Sveti screamed, pounded her fists at him and kicked with hysterical frenzy, but it was like a bunny fighting a starving tiger.

Through her panicked tears she saw his fierce face, his eyes wild electric white, sparking lightning; she could no longer see the man inside the savage beast, even the pointed ears grew bigger, sharper.

Grabbing both sides of her blouse he tore it apart, his predatory eyes radiated on her breasts molding full and soft over a pale peach silk bra.

"Sire, please," her voice shook with her distress, she pushed at him, hit him, but a marauding ravenous animal, he was not to be stopped.

The beast's hands closed over her breasts, he gripped them so hard she cried out. That drew his attention to her face, her lips. He lowered his head, capturing her mouth caught open in a cry, he kissed her with unleashed violence unheeding of her pleas and sobs for him to stop.

He was a raging demon, his fangs curved glinting in the light, his horns still grew, clenching her full breasts with his big hard fingers, he crushed them in his steel grasp.

She pulled from his raiding mouth and looked down, his erection strained at his pants, huge, thick, iron hard. So big, so violent, he would severely injure her, if she survived his brutal assault.

Sveti shook so hard she thought her teeth would break. She renewed her struggles but they were futile.

He sought her mouth again; she tossed her head to avoid the onslaught of his besieging lips, her curls swept over her face.

Free of his assaulting mouth, but still held trapped, she pushed her hair out of her face, her chest billowing with fear burst with fast and shallow breaths.

Roughly groping her breasts, snarls tangled in his throat, growls roiled in his heavy chest, the beast released her pained breasts to rip her pants open further, and then shoved them and her panties down to her thighs. Inhuman growls rumbled deeper, his stark white beast's eyes glowed at her exposed sex.

Sveti watched the creature in horror as he lowered his hand to her feminine folds, and drew the curve of one claw down over her woman's slit, a shudder of terror surged through her.

Keeping his monstrous eyes on her bared sex, and a hand on her shoulder holding her immobile, he jerked his belt open with prehistoric grunts, snatched open the button on his pants then unzipped them. Pushing her thighs apart he shifted his leg between hers moving his hips to hold her legs open.

He couldn't get her legs spread far enough apart for him to fit; he impatiently tore one side of her jeans and panties. She could only see the visceral beast in him as he moved his hand from her shoulder and grasped her face.

Forcing her head to turn to the side, his devouring gaze latched onto her alabaster neck. His eyes white fire, sharp glistening fangs descended to her flesh.

Sveti cried, "Please, Sire, don't take me like this!"

"Master," Brahms said calmly from several feet away.

"Go away," Dev growled a harsh snarl, digging his fangs into her neck, he opened his pants.

Brahms spoke in a language Sveti didn't understand. "Devilos, you will make her yours, forever, if you bite her while mating with her."

Growling savagely against her neck, "So what, go away," he dug his fangs deeper into her tender flesh, the long black braids covered her shoulder like sable ropes. He shoved his hand in his pants fisting his erection to tug it out.

"You can't make her yours permanently without her acquiescence or the elemental aura will taint your relationship forever."

Brahms looked down at Sveti struggling, most of her body hidden by Dev's big body, he said drily, "And she doesn't appear to be acquiescing to you raping her."

Dev snarled, "I don't fucking care," but he halted. He looked at her thrashing under him. He was so psychotic with the need to take her; he hadn't felt any of her punches.

Tears streamed out of her crystal eyes, his gaze fell to her heaving breasts, red marks bruised on them from his violent handling of her, then he looked to the pricks on her neck.

His head dropped, the claws and fangs receded, his body morphed almost back to normal. His beast's face changed as the savage animal in him shifted back to his normal hard face and body.

Still holding her head, he turned it to face him, and like the tide drawn to the moon he kissed her. Gently at first, but then his mouth moved ravenously over hers, the kiss heated him right back up.

"Sire," Brahms warned.

His sigh heavy, Dev pulled from her lips, she turned her head away from him, he saw the tear tracks on her cheeks. He drew his hands down over her breasts then pulled the torn pieces of her blouse together and slowly climbed off her.

Standing up, he reached behind his neck, grasped his shirt, pulled it over his head and laid it over her, said quietly to Brahms, "Take her back to her quarters." Without looking at her again, he left the room.

It was as if all the raging, heaving black air in the room fizzled and snapped out when he was gone. Sveti struggled to sit up.

Brahms sat down beside her on the couch and helped her into Dev's shirt.

Wiping at streaming tears, Sveti cried, "I- I don't understand him, Mr. Brahms, I don't understand." She wasn't afraid of the majordomo although she'd only met him once before. He had managed to stop Dev's attack.

"I know, honey." The older man gently smoothed her hair back. She fixed her pants the best she could.

Brahms got up and held his hand out to her. She took it and stood up on shaky legs.

His spine a rigid rod, shoulders like iron planks, the silver-haired majordomo walked Sveti back to her quarters.

Every time they passed a male that ogled her and started to move towards her, Brahms' head rose a few feet, he bared his fangs with a silent hiss of warning and they backed off.

He transformed back to normal without her ever seeing his mutation.

Chapter Fifteen

A few days later, Sveti opened her door to Bowie and smiled back at his friendly grin. "Hi Bowie, what are you doing here?" Then her brows dropped. "I'm not in trouble for something again that I don't know about am I?"

Shaking his head with a short laugh, he said, "Nay, not to worry. I'm here to take you shopping."

"Shopping? What kind of shopping?"

He laughed. "The kind girls like. Clothes, shoes, purses, whatever. Come on, let's go."

She stepped back from him with a shake of her head. "No. I'm not doing anything that is going to make that beast attack me again."

Bowie knew about Dev's assault on her. He had joined Dev in the bar later and got trashed with him. Dev told him the whole sordid story.

Bowie was surprised his hard-hearted friend expressed guilt and shame over his actions, and his worry that if Brahms hadn't stopped him he would have not only brutally raped Sveti, but would have done some serious harm to her in his beastly ferocious frenzy.

In his transformed phase he had been dangerously out of control, taken over by his animal side in primitive lusted fury.

When he had calmed down he had finally realized what Bowie had known earlier, that Sveti was always under guard, she could no way have been with anyone. But he'd been so blindly outraged that she was with other men, he'd lost his mind with jealousy and unrequited lust.

He still burned over her rejecting him on the shore, and feelings of jealousy were so foreign to him they had blindsided him.

Sexual tension gripped his brain and his balls, but he hadn't the interest in relieving himself with another female. The thought of being with anyone other than Sveti made his stomach pitch sickly.

Bowie smiled sadly at her. Dev was, as she said, part beast, part man, a warrior born and bred to kill, and to rut like an animal. He had never been with a woman like Sveti before, soft, feminine, sweet, ladylike, innocent, he didn't know how to handle her and it tied his balls and his brain into knots.

"It's okay, honey, he's the one who sent me here."

The flaming brows arched dubious. "Why?"

With a slight chuckle he said, "It's going to be a while before another ship is available for us to travel as far away as your brother, uh, that is, Dev said you would need clothes and stuff. So come on, we're going shopping on his dime."

She crossed her arms with a frown. "You are not saying that *he* is buying me clothes? Bowie, I don't want anything from him. You tell him-"

His head wagging back and forth he said, "Nay, you have to know by now there is no denying Captain Dravidian when he orders something. If you don't come with me, then he will come and take you himself. You do not want to be literally dragged through the station and the shops by a furious Devilos Dravidian. Trust me."

Sveti regarded him guardedly. Seeing his implacable expression, she let out a sigh and acquiesced, "All right. Let's get this over with."

He was right, she had only a few borrowed items to wear, and no funds of her own to purchase more. The captain was holding her prisoner, it was his fault she had no clothes, so he might as well cough up for them.

Grinning large at her, Bowie opened the door, swept his hand out. "After you, sweetness," and he closed the door after he followed her out.

He took her to shop after shop. Sveti had to argue with him the entire time. Bowie wanted her to wear scandalously sexy clothes and she told him adamantly she was not dressing as a hooker. The clothes she chose were going to be sent to her suite.

They had a leisurely lunch, then Bowie brought her to a large rec room where groups of people were playing cards and other games.

Seeing all the different kinds of people gathered there, she asked, "Why are we here?"

"I have work to do and I know you have been bored out of your mind, so I thought you might like to hang here for a while and play cards or some games."

Sveti glanced around the busy room with interest. It was filled with tables and almost every chair was full. Conversation buzzed, some people were table hopping, visiting.

"Yes, that would be great, Bowie I have been bored." She caught a flash of red near the door and saw Keldon. Her smile drooped. "I am still under guard?"

His lips pulled in, Bowie said, "Aye, sorry. With that warrant on you from your brother, anybody can, and will, take you there to collect on it. Dev is doing it because he wants you to get there, uh, safely. He's also worried you will try to make a run for it again and without realizing, because, his words not mine, you are so green, naïve, you could hook up with someone, or something, dangerous to get away."

"Huh," she snorted, "more dangerous than him? Is there such a creature?"

A crooked grin kinked across his handsome face. "Aye, well, he's not normally dangerous to innocent people. You just incite his brain and blood so much that you make him psychotic."

Her lip curled in doubt. An ashen hue took the rosiness out of her cheeks. She spoke with misery in her eyes and voice, "Bowie, you know Krystian is either going to wed me himself, or he is going to sell me to- to any kind of creature that has a prince title."

At his commiserating look, she flattened her palms on her stomach. "I've seen pictures of the...males that have responded to my brother's flyer. Bowie, half of them don't look human at all, some are like- like reptiles, and a- a thing with legs like a giant tarantula, you know what is out there."

The skin pinched around her mouth and eyes in remembered horror. "I could end up with something like those bear-dogs that tortured me." She confessed bleakly, "I still wake up screaming from nightmares of my captivity with them."

The rest of the color drained from her face. "So I am to be mated with a vicious alien creature that might even butcher me after, uh, sex, as some of the species do when uh, intermingling with a different species, or I am to commit incest with Krystian. Bowie," she put her hand on his arm.

"Krystian will insist on an heir. Our, my child, will be...damaged with our familial, our incestual blood. Ryen wanted a relationship with me but Krystian would have killed him if he had touched me."

He regarded her sadly. "Uh, yeah, I know, Sveti."

She pressed her hands together in prayer. "Bowie, can't you help me? Can't you help me escape from here? I won't tell anyone you did it, I promise, please-"

Bowie's heart clenched at the beautiful woman's dire fear. "Nay, I cannot, Sveti. You must trust Dev, he won't let you be harmed. I swear, he-"

"Yeah," she snorted, "he won't let anyone harm me. Anyone else, that is. Sure. That's why his majordomo had to stop him from violently raping me."

"I'm sorry, Sveti, his beast got the better of him. But he is more aware of it now and can control it," *maybe*. "Besides, believe me, nothing can stop Dev, not even Brahms if he didn't let him. You bring out something in Dev that he is unfamiliar with and it continues to take him by surprise. His beast comes out in battle, but not normally with sex."

"Yeah, great," Sveti choked a laugh, "I bring out the devil in him."

"Uh, aye, kind of." *More than you know.* "Anyway, Dev will help you. You need to trust him."

"I did. At least he made it clear before...you know, at the river, that he would not be wanting involvement. Believe me, Bowie; it was crazy for me too. He had me so..."

She thought about it. "I can't explain it, enraptured I guess it was. I mean, I'm supposed to wait until I am sold to a prince, or Krystian takes me himself, but, I...I don't know what came over me to- to, I almost let him have his way with me. The captain had cast...like a spell I think, over me that day."

Her voice saddened, eyes dimmed, she said in resignation, "But, I must do as Krystian deigns, he needs a prince for me or he will harm my family, my parents and brother. He is a prince of course, but the procedure for him to gain more power won't work with us because our blood is too much the same. It doesn't matter anymore anyway."

She turned her back to him. Her voice small, sad, she said, "Thanks, Bowie, for taking me shopping," she walked from him to find a table to join.

Bowie watched her impotently for a moment, then with a nod to Keldon, he left to go to work.

Hours later, after Bowie finished the last of the research graphing, he grabbed a quick dinner in his room then went to see Dev.

When Dev answered his knock, his long hair was loose and damp from his shower, although he had just shaved; his harshly angled jaw was always shadowed. A towel hung around his huge block of bare shoulders, the white of the cloth bright against the tanned skin and dark hair on his chest.

He had pulled on pants to answer the door, they were unbuttoned, his feet were bare. "Bow, what's up?" he stepped aside to let Bowie enter.

Bowie held his palms up as if to ward off Dev. "Just listen to me, let me speak before you rip my head off."

Dev crossed his arms over his massive chest and stared soberly at his friend.

Tucking the tips of his fingers into the front of his pants pockets, his hips forward, Bowie shook his head tossing his short blond hair back as he pushed his shoulders back, chest thrust out.

His blue eyes amiable on his best friend yet serious, he said, "Dev, she's going to do something, and soon. The terror of where you're taking her is eating her up, she's freaked. You know she will figure out a way to run, she's wily, and brave, she will do it."

Dev nodded, long hair swinging in front of his shoulders. "I know."

The corner of Bowie's mouth ticked up, then twisted to the side with a challenging grin. "I brought her back an hour ago from the game room. So then, what are you going to do about it? I know you have a plan."

"I do." Dev's smile as usual wasn't the most pleasant of things, he gestured for Bowie to sit down. "I have from the beginning." Over a couple of drinks Dev explained what he was planning, and what he wanted Bowie to do.

As soon as Dev concluded, he got up and opened his door. "Now, go away." He waited while Bowie set his empty glass down and got up.

At the door, Bowie stared at him for a moment, then flashed his typical impudent grin. "Okay then, bro, I leave it in your capable claws, I mean hands," with a chuckle, he saucily saluted him and left.

Dev went to his bedroom and pulled on a shirt and boots. Buckling his belt, and a holster to his hip, he dragged a quick comb through his damp hair then left his suite.

While buttoning his shirt, he strode to Sveti's room, nodded to Keldon, and knocked on the door. Dev could have Keldon unlock the door, or Dev himself could break it open like he did the other day, but right now, he wanted Sveti to feel she had some sort of control over her life, illusory though it was.

It took several knocks and many minutes before she opened the door. Reluctantly. Peering around the edge of the door she asked suspiciously, "What do you want?"

The curve of his lip twitched. "You asked me that the last time and my response is still the same. I want to come in." As he figured, she didn't move aside. So, he just started walking into the room and she was forced to get out of his way or he would have steamrolled over her.

She watched him close and lock the door, then stride right past her down the hall to her bedroom. His aura so strong and powerful, it was spine-tingling daunting to Sveti how Dev always filled the space with heat and vitality.

Warily she followed him, keeping a distance between them, as if she could really out run him if he chased her.

Her suitcase was on the stand and half packed. Just inside the lavender room, Dev turned to look at her, his lip quirked as his gaze rolled over the jacket she was wearing. Inside.

Setting his large hands on lean hips, his fingers stretched over the belt and holstered weapon, he asked amiably, "Going on a trip?"

"Uh, I um," Sveti stammered, staying outside the doorway, "am just getting ready for when we, uh, leave." Blinking rapidly at him, he was all in black; pants, shirt that covered but didn't hide the expanse of his broad chest and shoulders, black boots, long loose hair, even eyes dark as midnight. She thought, *villain*.

"I see." He looked pointedly at her jacket. "Is it chilly in here? You have control of the thermostat, Svetiessa."

For some reason he always used her full first name when addressing her. Sveti found it disconcerting, formal, yet intimately erotic all at the same time, especially in that rough deep timbre with his unique accent. He was the only one who called her Svetiessa, his tongue rolled around it like he was wrapping them together in their own private sensual cocoon.

She could tell he already figured out she was going to attempt to leave her suite. Probably knew before he even walked in her door. She said nothing and went back to the living room.

Following her, he said, "I don't know why I thought you were a good liar, because you really suck at it. Where do you think you are going?" Even from the side view of her, clear distress streaked over her soft face before it stiffened.

Letting out a big sigh, Sveti stopped, turned and faced him. "Fine. I will tell you." She plumbed light elegant strokes with her small fingers through her flaming hair, separating the curly locks.

Her voice soft, melodic even in her anguish she answered, "I do not want to mate with my brother, nor do I want to mate with...some...hideous, deadly creature." Her gaze raked him letting him know she put him in the same category.

At his passive expression, she crossed her arms under her breasts, took a deep breath.

Strengthening her tone, she continued, "The only reason for you, or anyone to take me to Krystian is because of the warrant. He wants to sell my virginity or take it himself. I have decided I will resolve the whole issue and quickly go find my own prince and give myself to him. That will negate the need for the warrant and my having to return to Krystian."

His boots braced hard on the floor, arms crossed, hair flowing over his shoulders, the only thing that moved on Dev was his arched black brows. "Oh yeah? You're going out there," he jerked his jaw towards the door, "and find the first male prince you come across, and offer yourself up like dinner on a platter?"

She nodded sharply. "Yes I am. At least it will be *my* choice, not anyone else's. Maybe the person I chose will not want me to stay with him and I can go back and be with Ryen. Now," she moved towards the door, "if you will excuse me, I am removing myself from your mission."

"Ah," murmuring, his legs longer, Dev leisurely stepped in front of the door before she could get to it. Setting his hands on strong hips, he said calmly, "Not happening."

Her lips bunched. "Get out of my way. There is no longer any reason for you to keep me prisoner. I am sorry about your loss of funds, but se la vie. Maybe my new prince will pay you my debt. Now, move. If I don't go now I will just find a way out later. Get out of my way."

She slapped her hands on her hips and looked belligerently up at him, and frowned at the placid expression on his harsh face. He should be looking angry that he would lose the money the warrant would have paid.

He moved his bulky arms to cross over slabs of steel, and smiled down at her, but it wasn't a nice smile. Sveti's skin crawled in response to it.

His age was always indeterminable to her. He looked young, but there were demonic years in the weathering of his face, and a primordial soul glimmered from the ancient, opulent dark eyes drenched in simmering danger.

Bucking up her nerve, she reached for the button to release the door, but he was in front of it. She tried to physically move him knowing it would be in vain, and it was. It was like trying to push a tank. "Sire, Captain Dravidian," she sucked in aggravated air, "step aside."

161

"You should call your lover by his first name." The smile sharpened. "That would be Devilos, or Dev if you prefer."

Her brows blew into her hairline. "What?" she sputtered, glaring at him. "We are not lovers. I am going to go find a prince, now move out of my way!"

"You are not leaving sweetheart, you are going to mate with me. Right now."

Chapter Sixteen

Sveti's eyes popped wide in disbelief. "I most certainly am not. I need a prince or the spell will not work for Krystian and he'll never let me go. Please, Sire, move."

"I am a prince, Svetiessa. Hence the title of Sire. But you will call me Devilos."

"What? Prince of what? Where?"

"Ah, there's the rub. You would actually call me the Prince of Darkness." He watched her strive to decipher his words.

She shook her head in bafflement, long bright tresses swung across the back of her frilly yellow blouse. "That makes no sense. That would be saying you are...the- the devil."

Nodding, he affirmed, "That would be correct." The features of his hard face remained impassive but with a slight rise to the edges of his harshly carved lips.

Watching him lazily unbuckle his holster and set it on top of a tall cabinet, out of her reach, she stammered, "You-you're saying that you- you *are* the devil?" Her face flushed with incredulity. Then her gaze trailed up to his horns, remembering his fangs digging into her neck, her eyes lowered to his big hands, claws had extended from them.

Recalling the flames that danced around him, the beast that rose in his anger and his lust, she bit back a gasp as she looked up at his eyes, they were flickering between black and white. She started backing away from him.

The rise to the corner of his mouth edged up further, he said with a shrug, "In a way. I am actually a great-great-great etc. grandson, the spawn of old Satan himself, Lucifer. Ergo the horns, fangs, claws, superhuman strength, hearing, sight, flames, again, etc." He moved towards her.

"But- but you are from Nasitar, the planet of born and trained killers, hunters, it can't be," she moved around furniture to get away from him. He kept coming after her, unhurried, shoving things out of his way with one hand, an easy chair, solid steel dining table.

Her hands up, she ordered him, "You stay away from me," voice shaking with her demand.

"Svetiessa, I am a prince, therefore I qualify for the requirement to bed you and thus release you from the warrant." Stalking her languidly like the jaguar slinking after the tasty soft doe that had nowhere to run, he pushed aside an oak hutch to close the distance between them.

"But- but you are a different species!" Her quarried eyes never leaving him, she felt the way behind her, maybe if she could get to the bathroom she could lock herself in. He would have to go away eventually.

He smiled with a shrug. "That's true, but we have most of the same parts, gods and angels, archangels and humans mated billions of years ago to create me, my kind, you, us, don't worry we will fit." *And in a minute you'll find out I have a few extra things to bring to the table.*

As much as it vexed her to say it, she said, "Sire, you don't understand, whoever uh, deflowers me, in my culture as the princess of my planet, owns me."

"I'll do it."

"But then you would own me!"

"Aye. I accept that." His smile leveled into a grim line, his eyes narrowed in menace at her. "But, let me warn you, my beautiful Prinţesă; I have never had nor wanted a woman of my own to keep." His shoulder bumped.

"I am afraid I will be quite possessive of you. I already am. Once we do this, you will never be with another man. I will not allow you to go home to your Ryen. You will be with me, stay, with me."

He let her see the grave threat before letting his face relax back into a mild smile. "Now, let's do this," he reached his hand to her, she slapped it away.

"No! You are not giving me a choice!"

"So what? A moment ago you were going to sashay that fine ass down the main avenue and give it to the first prince you got to. You don't need to do that, as I said, I will do it. You know me as well or as little as some other Tom, Dick, or prince out there. So why not me?"

"Because you are cruel and brutal and- and a killer, a beast, and…I am terrified of you." She stumbled a few steps backwards.

He took a step forward. "Ah, that is all true, and your terror of me will only get worse."

"You see!"

Shaking his head, he said matter-of-factly, "You'll get used to it. Come, let's seal this contract. We are doing this now. Take off your clothes. I promise, I will not be such a savage animal this time. I know you will need it gentle, careful, slow, at least until your body can take more of my...toughness, my strength. I can control the beast," *to some degree*, he reached for her again.

Again she slapped at his hand. "No! Stay away from me! You don't like me, you hate me for thinking I tricked you, and I am not even your type, why would you want to tie yourself to me? I heard the mean things you said about me being so much less than the other women."

"Ah, but my little human, a man can change his interests when he finds something he's never experienced before and finds it... extraordinary, alluring, exciting, sexy, hot, irresistible. I was struggling to fight my overpowering desire for you, I thought stupidly by disparaging you I could get you out from under my skin." He raised his palms with a shrug. "Alas, it didn't work."

"What are you saying? That makes no sense. I don't understand." As he moved closer, her back came up against the wall.

"You don't need to understand, come here, take your clothes off." Without even touching her he had herded her near the hall to the bedroom.

Bewildered, her head shook back and forth. "But why are you doing this? Why would you want to?"

"Because I want you, and you need me." He scraped his nails down his harsh face, then shoved his loose hair back with both hands.

"You got under my skin, Prinţesă, like snow under ivory. You are sweet and brave, timid and assertive, soft and shy and feminine, and have the most tempting ass I've ever wanted to bite."

Appalled, her voice squeaked strident, "Oh! How dare you-"

"Okay, sorry, aye, those plump tits are quite a draw too. I can't wait to get my hands on them, bare I mean." He smiled at her anger, his gaze dropped to her chest. "My mouth too."

As she sputtered in fury, he said drolly, "Oh, and, I kinda want to drive my cock deep and hard inside you like a fucking jackhammer until you are shrieking my name and begging for more."

When she opened her mouth to rebuke him he cut her off, his eyes narrowed, "At least I am a known danger. For fuck's sake, Svetiessa, you were just about to go out there and launch yourself at some unknown male."

A scowl pulled his black brows and full lips down. "If you're going to spread your legs for anyone, sweetheart, it will be for me. Only me."

Breathless and enraged at his audacity, she cried, "But I don't accept you. I want to live with my husband, I want to love him, raise a family, there has to be more than- than sex between us. You...are too- brutal, we would never live together. You have your planet and I have mine with galaxies in between. I assume the prince I give my virginity to will take what he wants then set me free, to go live where I please, not stay with him."

His face darkened. "Oh, but you will live with me, why would you think otherwise? You will sleep beside me in my bed every night."

"No, I- I don't want to, you are a heartless, cold, violent fiend, stay away from me!" She held a hand up to hold him off. As if she could.

"You will get used to me. Do I complain you are so soft and pretty? Now, come, stop making this difficult, go on, do as I say, take off your clothes, do a sexy strip for your male." Like a dance, he moved forward, she retreated, tripping along the wall.

"No! You are not and never will be my male. There has to more between a couple than just desire. You cannot force me to take my clothes off, to do this, I am leaving now." She turned her small nose up in the air and went to march past him.

Growing impatient with her resistance, he said, "Come, Svetiessa, this is it. We are going to mate right now. I am a true blooded prince. I will take your virginity, your *bráthair* will be satisfied," *except for the part where the sick bastard won't get to fuck his own deisfiúr,* "and we will be wedded.

"And you better get used the sex, honey, because when we are wed, I will expect my husband's due when I want it. And believe me," his heated gaze raked her body, "that will be often. I apologize ahead of time, you've already noticed, I tend to be quite…rough. But again, you will get used to it. The first few times, as I said, of course I will be gentle, careful as I initiate you into our coupling."

A lascivious smile pulled his lips up, with a lewd twinkle in his eye, he said, "Trust me, Svetiessa, you will soon become addicted to it. I am like no other male you could be with."

"Huh, a tad conceited, aren't we?" She slid her back along the wall keeping space between them. He moved a hand to her, she shoved it away.

"Stop! I said no! I am not doing this with you, you would have to- to force me, rape me, and I would never forgive you if you did. I swear, our marriage would be miserable. I would leave you first chance I got. So step aside right now." Again she tried to push past him but he stood in her way like a big brick wall.

His dark eyes glazed with sudden leaden fury, the timber deep and scary rough in his powerful chest he decreed, "You will never leave me, Svetiessa, you will be my wife and always by my side. Always." He sighed as he saw the fright slick across her face.

"Come on, sweetheart," he said more quietly, snatched up a lock of her hair, twirled it between his fingers. "I may have to help you move along, but trust me, it will not be rape, you will beg me to take you. You forget how aroused you were at the river. If I hadn't spoken that day this would have already been done. Your arms would be around me right now, not pushing me away."

"You are delusional!" Sveti suddenly made to rush past him.

Prey should never run, it always makes the predator automatically chase after it. He grabbed her, she screamed, he lifted her up holding her so she was forced to straddle him and he carried her towards the bedroom.

"Let me go!" Fighting him, she pummeled his chest with her fists, shouting, "You are too big, I need to go find a- a smaller, more gentle man that won't brutalize me- put me down!"

"Hush, sweetheart, we will fit perfectly together," *after a while*. His hands cupping her butt, he leaned her against the wall. Bracing her back on the wall, he lifted a hand and cradled her head, then lowered his and seized her mouth in a pervasive feral kiss.

Trying to turn her face from him, keeping her lips closed, Sveti hit at him. Ignoring the blows, Dev drew his thick hard fingers along the crease in her butt, she jumped and yelped, he slammed his mouth over hers and shoved his tongue inside.

Angling his head to fuse them more tightly he kissed her with relentless vehemence until her struggles lessened and she was lured in under his spell. Her tiny innocent mouth pulsed with hesitant ambivalence against his unyielding pressure and skillful strokes. Feeling her starting to respond, Dev set her on her feet and kept her pressed flat against the wall.

Fingers netting the back of her head, he again ruthlessly sealed his mouth over hers, kissing her with wild fever, growling groans rumbled in his throat. He covered her breast with a strong hand, and kneaded it over her blouse.

His kiss grew more aggressive; he sucked her tongue, then licked her lips, kissed down her jaw to her neck where he nipped her skin to just short of drawing pain. He forced his fangs and claws to stay in with sheer will, but his horns swelled along with his erection.

Dazed and sodden with passion, Sveti was carried away with his masterful fervor. Her head tilted, she moaned at his mouth sucking her neck, her hands clutched at his abdomen corrugated with muscles.

In his fanatically intoxicated arousal, he too roughly crushed her breasts, thumbed and pinched her nipples too hard. It was enough to bring her out of her fog.

Pushing him away, she said, "Sire, stop this right now, I refuse to do this." Panting, Sveti wiped her mouth, but she couldn't smother the desire flaring in her blue eyes.

Glancing down at her nipples, hard as pebbles pushing through the yellow blouse, "Svetiessa," Dev murmured through heavy breaths, grasping her head and sinking his tongue back into her mouth, he devoured her with voracious fire.

Holding her jaw so she couldn't move from his lips, he grasped her breast with his iron grip, kneaded it a shade less brutally while shoving his tongue down her throat.

Dizzy with the intensity of his harsh kisses and frenzied aggressive caresses, Sveti jerked her head back and put her palms on his chest and pushed him, cried breathlessly, "Stop, I- I need to go, let me go!"

Thick black hair flopped over one eye; Dev shoved it back with an impatient hand. Dark eyes weighted with passion and pulsating bolts of white scraped down the length of her and back up witnessing her fighting the passion mirrored in her delirious blues.

His own breathing labored, chest hitching with rapid breaths, he huffed, "All right sweetheart, have it your way, I tried to save your clothes, but," he jerked her jacket off her then before she could protest he grabbed her blouse with both hands and ripped it apart.

She gasped, shock held her frozen for a brief second before she started hitting at him, punching frantically. He turned his hips when her knees jerked up towards his balls. "You- you- how dare you-"

Her pummeling made no impression on him. He shoved her blouse over her shoulders and dragged it down her arms like she was just a ragdoll, and tore it off. Winding his long fingers around her slim arms to hold her still, he pushed her flush against the wall.

His demon's pupils swelled and glittered at her breasts mounding over the silk bra. "Shit," he groaned, "I've only had glimpses of your delectable tits, baby, they are so much more fucking plush than I even imagined, you are so perfect. So squeezable, edible, Zues, I can't wait to taste them." He released her to reach behind her to unclasp her bra.

"Sire-"

"Devilos," he growled with his big arms around her.

Sveti slapped at him, pushed him. He grabbed up an arm pulling her tight against his chest, unhooked her bra and forcefully removed it, leaving her nude from the waist up.

Dev pushed her hair back behind her and held both her arms pressing her back against the wall to look at her bare bosom. His eyes glowed pure electric white.

"Please," swallowing a sob, Sveti struggled but he held her immobile, her movements only made her breasts jiggle and kept his attention glued on them.

Absently shaking his head, Dev licked his lips. "Nay, Svetiessa, stop fighting me. You are so beautiful, so exquisite you hurt my eyes." He curled his fingers under her chin, lifting it to make her look at him. She grasped his wrist to tug his hand away, again, to no avail.

He saw fear warring with desire in the tremble of her lips, and the fog covering the brilliance of her baby blues. "Sweetheart," he said softly, "trust me. Trust me to take care of you, protect you," he lightly kissed her, "to make love to you as a man pleasures his adored wife."

Her eyes misted, mouth trembled more, but she didn't punch at him.

Slowly, cradling her head, he bent to capture her mouth, drawing her into a gentle kiss that he nourished, let her get used to, for a moment, then it rapidly effervesced into scorching arousal. When Sveti melted into him with soft purling sounds, he palmed a breast, fondled it gently then more aggressively.

At the moan that traveled up her throat, Dev left her lips to kiss along her jaw, down her neck. He moved his hands to cover both breasts, his own groan deep in his chest; his caresses grew rougher in his erecting lust.

Pressing his lips against her neck, he sucked her skin until a deep red mark pooled under his mouth, her flesh pinching in his teeth.

Clutching her breasts, he moved to kiss the full swells, rub his bristled cheek against her cleavage then pulled an entire areole into his mouth. Licking her nipple, he sucked all over her soft full mound, tasting her flesh then bit her nipple then moved to the other one.

Sveti cried out, he lathed the nipple with his tongue while kneading her breasts with his hard hands. Soft moans slid from her lips, she was turning into pudding in his hands.

Shifting his mouth back to fuse with hers, he reached down between them to her pants.

Chapter Seventeen

*H*er brain burning along with her body, Sveti could not form a word in her buzzing head. Heat gushed wet between her legs, her skin crackled and sizzled, needled and tingled everywhere Devilos kissed or touched.

The intensity of the sensations he elicited in her was thrilling, magical, her mind was spinning out of control- too fast, *he was the devil*- reeling, she pushed from him with a sharp panting gasp.

Dev's mouth dropped, dazed white eyes peered at her from under heavy lids. He moved his hands to her arms, his chest pumping with rushing breaths like a rollercoaster off its tracks. It was clear it was a struggle for him to keep his grip on her arms loose as he forced himself to stop and let her regroup.

Bending her elbows she covered her bare breasts with her small hands, they didn't cover much. Even the sight of that excited him.

"Sire, I," she panted, frantic eyes darting around his face.

"Devilos, sweetheart. Relax, Svetiessa, I promise I won't hurt you." He slowly drew her back close to him. Slipping his hand under her hair, he gently stroked her nape.

His fingers still wound lightly around her arm, his thumb brushed her bare skin. He whispered soothing, softly, "Svetiessa, just listen to my voice, feel my hands, my mouth on you, cherishing you, making love to you."

He pulled her mouth to his, kissed her gently and murmured in her ear, "Don't think, Svetiessa, just feel." Pressing his mouth on hers, he nudged her lips apart to accept his foraging tongue, when she was responding and giving back, he lowered his head and kissed her breasts. He kept murmuring against her flesh as he suckled and caressed them.

Entranced by his deep rough voice, Sveti's head arched back relishing his mouth on her soft female globes, feeling him cupping them with his steely hands, kneading them while his lips and tongue pulled at her flesh.

She looked down at his dark head at her fair bosom. His black hair waved over her skin, soft as silk teasing goose bumps to rise along her arms, her pebbled nipples tightened to hard rosebud marbles.

She didn't resist when he reached between them, unbuttoned then unzipped her pants. Her hands gripped his biceps, feeling them flex under her palms, they were so big she couldn't get her fingers even halfway around them.

Sveti didn't move when Dev pushed her pants down, then crouched to take them and her shoes and socks off, pushing them to the side, leaving her panties on.

Rising back up, his palms stroked from her calves, up her thighs, over her hips to lace around her waist. Sveti shivered under his expert touch.

"You are a *lasair ádainn,* a beautiful flame, my Prinţesă," his whisper blew the fiery tendrils around her ears, tickling her sensitive skin, more heat rushed between her legs. She felt his fingers slide over her waist and down over her hips to her panties.

"Oh!" she gasped when his big hard palm slid to cup her woman's mound over the silk. "Sire- uh, Devilos, I don't think..."

"Honey you are wet," he said with heated awe, smiling at the red that steamed her cheeks. His rumbling purr insisting, "Don't think, baby, just feel."

"Uh, no, Dev- Devilos, we shouldn't-" her breath caught when he stroked his fingers over her sex. "Uhh, that's...uh..." a soft wanton moan fluttered up her chest as he continued stroking.

He suddenly bent and scooped her up in his arms.

"Devilos! What are you doing?" Startled, Sveti threw her arms around his neck, pressed her naked breasts against his formidable chest, felt the starch of his shirt rub her sensitive skin, roughen her hardened nipples.

His hair swept down over her collarbone, she could smell his masculine scent of strength, robust virility with a hint of light cigar. Her brain blurred with the sensations he had created with his skillful hands and lips.

Sveti felt dreamlike, the back of her mind tried to tell her something, warn her, but, she couldn't comprehend it right now through the haze of arousal that lit her entire body. All she knew was, she wanted more. More of his sensuous enticing exploration.

In his arms, she said shyly, "Devilos, I am, um, almost, um naked and you," she fingered a button, "are not." Her flaming curls flowed over his arm and undulated as he moved.

He smiled down at her, his black locks sifted over his face, his gaze went from her shining passionate eyes, to her plump pink lips to her plump pink nipples. "Aye, that is true."

He strode through the rest of the hall to her bedroom. "This is how life was meant to be, sweetheart. It doesn't get any more decadent than holding a gorgeous naked woman that is hotter than Zanzi's first sun in your arms and carrying her to bed to ravish her."

A blush filled her face, then realizing he was really going to go through with it, he was taking her choice away from her, panic chased away the lethargy of her arousal. "Devilos, no, put me down," she demanded, squirming; she kicked her legs when he kept moving.

What was she thinking? He's not human, he says he's the devil's grandson, she will be tied to him forever, he's domineering, mean, deadly. "Stop, I can't, put me down."

"Trust me, sweetheart," he urged. Entering the dimly lit pale lavender and white room, he'd had this moment in the back of his mind when he first chose this suite for her, it had a king-sized bed. He wasn't going to fit in anything else. His subconscious wanted her long before his conscious brain knew and he'd prepared their nest.

He had been bought and sold the day he first saw her at the party on the space station. He didn't even know her and his hands had itched to take her brother apart for touching her, kissing her, devastating her with mortification over his shocking plans for his baby sister.

Dev set her on the bed and climbed on the high firm mattress beside her with his hand on her waist to keep her from leaving.

Sveti crossed her arms over her chest and struggled to sit up. "Devilos, we need to step back, you don't realize," her voice breathy with little catches in it, "if we have- have sex, we would be...married. For real. For heaven's sake, we don't even know each other. We can't do this."

Staying near her sitting on the bed, he untied his boots. He was done discussing it. He kicked his boots off then peeled off his socks.

As she watched him, Sveti squirmed away, her words shook out, "No, we are not doing this." She spotted a shirt on a chair and scooted to the end of the bed to get off and get it. "*Ohh!*"

He snaked out an arm, lassoed her and brought her back and pulled her onto his lap. Wrapping both arms around her, he cuddled her to his strong torso. His lips butterflied across her face, he brushed her hair aside and cupped her jaw lifting it to connect their eyes.

His voice severe, he said, "Svetiessa, only minutes ago you were more than willing to go have some stranger fuck you and you would have been tied to him for life. Or, wait for your perverted brother to sell you to a monster, or, commit incest with him. I can't be worse than any of those things."

He tilted her head and lightly sucked her top lip then the bottom. Softening the roughness in his deep voice, he contended, "Svetiessa, I am not worse than those. I will protect you with my life, you will never want for anything. I might be an aggressive tyrannical bastard, but," he kissed her, "I will never hurt you. I will take care of you, honey."

He looked into her quivering blue eyes and admitted, "I came to the fortress of the Amphicyonids, the grizzly-dogs that day with the sole purpose to rescue you. I told everyone, you, including myself, that I did it so I could punish you. That was so far from the truth.

"The truth was I couldn't get you out of my mind since that day of the party. I had searched for you. When I heard the damn grizzly-dogs had you my heart literally stopped with dread fear for your life. I had to save you. I dove into a fucking raging river for you, you think I would do all that for just anyone?"

"You claim you won't hurt me? You just ripped off my blouse, my pants!"

His lip twitched up. "I didn't hurt you, Svetiessa, just disrobed you. I told you, I won't rape you but you needed a little nudging."

Indignant she snorted, "Nudging? You-"

His mouth closed over hers taking her into a heady, heart-thumping kiss. As he plunged into her mouth, her body betraying her oozed in his arms.

Dev lifted her and laid her on the mattress and quickly settled beside her. Rolling towards her, he caught her thighs and pushed them apart. Sliding his hand between them, he stroked up the smooth skin of her thigh to place his palm on her silk-covered sex.

She shoved his hand away and sat up, "Wait," she begged.

He sat up preparing for another argument. Sveti put her hands on his strapping chest, then unbuttoned a button on his shirt.

Dev looked down in surprise. Her elegant little fingers undid one after the other until they were all undone. She pushed aside the sides of his shirt and gazed at his heavily muscled chest covered with dark hair.

The room was quiet, white ruffled curtains closed out most of the light. Faint illumination came from the door Dev had left partially open. He held his breath as Sveti drew her palms down over the hair, and let it out when she sifted her fingers back up through the thick matting.

"It's kind of rough and soft at the same time, Sire," she murmured, running her palms all over the thick hair.

"Devilos," he mumbled, watching her sitting half-naked, pet him, exploring the rocky slabs and sinewy hollows of his muscular chest. She struggled to shove his shirt off his brawny shoulders; his eyes on her he easily shrugged it off and carelessly tossed it.

Her hands strode up to stroke over the hulking shoulders then down his biceps where her fingertips prodded and skimmed each powerful taut muscle. She slid her fingers down his burly forearms then up to graze his pecs.

Leaning into him, she traced the strange tattoo on his neck with her tongue, followed it down to words tatted on his collarbone, then she bent and sucked a nipple into her mouth and teased it with her tongue like he'd done to her.

"Zues, woman," Dev shivered and gripped her arms, held her back. "Your first time has to be gentle, I need all my will power to hold back," *and to keep the beast at bay*. He pushed her on her back and enclosed her breasts with his hard hands.

Lowering his head he licked the swells of her full globes, lathed then suckled her nipples.

With a tiny mew, her body writhed under his tugging mouth and stroking hands. He moved to catch her panties with his calloused fingers and dragged them down her slim hips and slender legs, dropping them on the floor.

The contrast of her so dainty and him so rugged excited him like he'd never felt before with another woman.

Forcing himself to be gentle with her, spend time in real foreplay to get her ready, he was astonished to find he was truly savoring this, relishing every touch and taste of her sweet body, the adorable sexy sounds she made. Finally, his fantasies, his dreams of being with her were coming true.

It was imperative that her first time be perfect, so she would desire it again and again, not cringe with fear every time he reached for her. Because, there was no doubt, he would be reaching often for this extraordinary beauty, and a willing Sveti would be so much more enjoyable than a resisting one.

Because this was it, he was taking her, mating her whether it was what she wanted or not. She would learn in time to accept him, accept them.

Modestly, Sveti pulled her legs up, he gently pushed them down and apart. He laid a heavier muscular leg over one of her willowy limbs to hold her secure and drifted his fingers up her thigh, softly trickled them around her core without touching it, a seductive tease.

His touch like the softest feathers, swirled around and around until her hips were squirming and she was crying, "*Devilos, ah,*" her legs widened and her hips lifted seeking his intimate touch. He lightly stroked a finger up her sex. She jumped with a gasp, her head rolled. "Devilos, I…" a sigh slurred out of her pillow lips.

"What, sweetheart, tell me." Dev fingered her slit, brushed around her tightening woman's bud then applied pressure before running his fingers back down her slit. Her silk poured into his hand. It was out of this world amazing watching her become aroused, seeing her innocence flowering.

She gasped, "I don't…know."

He painted her silk around her core, circled her clitoris then gently pushed just the tip of his thick finger inside her. Her legs stiffened.

"Shh, baby," he crooned, "I will pleasure you, just go with it. Relax and just feel." When her legs loosened, he nudged them further apart, let her silk surround his finger before he slipped it inside her.

Her hips jerked, he stopped, she was too tight. Too small. He'd had many women in his time, but never one so tight and delicate as Sveti.

He was going to have to be so careful. And he wanted to be. He wanted to relish this time with her. He wanted her to love what they do, he wanted her to want him, want this, for eternity.

Dev shuffled down the bed, gripped her thighs to hold them apart, and covered her entire sex with his mouth.

Sveti bucked and cried out, "*Devilos!*" Hitching gasps quivered through her. "You can't," she heaved, her throat chafed with rapid, sharp inhales, she tried to pull her legs together.

He lifted his head, long black hair spread on her ivory thighs. Dipping his finger in her, he soothed, "Trust me, baby," and dropped his mouth to lick up her slit and take her bud in his mouth. Flickering his tongue over it, her hips jerked up with a sharp cry. He licked and sucked, carefully thrusting his strong finger in and gently drawing it out, her natural lube making it easier with each stroke.

"Devilos," Sveti sighed, closed her eyes, heat swirled like a whirlpool around her core, and sizzled up her body to coat her brain. Her hips moved with his finger, his mouth sucking her swollen bud dragged whimpers from her rasping throat. The heat burned and built in her core until she felt about to explode.

"Devilos, tell me, it- it's," she groaned and writhed under his mouth, her hips thrust at his finger that was suddenly plunging faster. He slowed, inserted a second hard digit, stretching her and curled them both in her silky channel, searching for those spots that would send her to the moon. And he when he found them, he thrust his fingers faster.

Her body grew rigid, toes curled, she gripped his shoulders, digging her little fingers into his tough flesh her hips bounced uncontrolled with her sudden agonized weeping, skin flushed bright.

"Go baby, let go, I've got you." His voice a faint whisper he told her, "It will hurt honey, just for a second, it's nature's way, then, I promise it will become bliss."

He thumbed her bud and shoved his fingers deep and she bolted up, knifing forward with a wheezing squeal, her spine arched sharply with a harsh inhale, his name a silent scream on her lips as he tore through her maidenhead right as she climaxed.

He paused his fingers letting the writhing orgasm mingle with the pain of her tearing hymen confusing her body's pain/pleasure receptors, Sveti fell back flat on the bed, chest hitching and heaving.

When her lungs filled with gulps of parched air, she lay twitching, he plunged his fingers and pinched her clit, and she thrashed asunder, her body lurching into a second orgasm and she knifed forward again with a jagged cry.

Dev moved to a knee as Sveti undulated and fell over his shoulder with gasping strangling sobs. He'd never heard a more beautiful sound.

Chapter Eighteen

While Sveti's body still trembled and her skin flushed a shimmering pink, Dev laid her back down, and moved off the bed.

Quickly shucking his pants he climbed back on and between her legs. Forcing her thighs wider he lowered down over her.

But he was drawn to watch her. Her long lashes fluttered over heated round cheeks, tiny tongue swept around parted lips that still panted, her bosom still rose and fell rapidly, the soft breasts swelling and shifting, nipples tight pink knots.

Flaming curls waved in disarray around her beautiful face, spreading like fiery streams over the mattress.

Her eyes rippled open, she saw him gazing at her, his pupils fixed, irises voltaic white. Her blues widened like plates at the horns growing out of his dark hair. The horns grew more, even as she stared at them in her ascending fright. She glanced down at the big hands on her thighs, his claws were just barely digging into her skin.

"Svetiessa..."

Then she saw the fangs, they descended further when he opened his mouth to reassure her. Her body stiffened. Bracing her palms on the mattress under her she pushed to sit and wriggle from him. Her pupils huge and brilliant onyx in her terrified orbs galloped around the room and to the door.

"Goddammit Svetiessa," he barked at her grabbing for her leg to hold her. "I can't help it," he growled, dragged her back and pushed her down. Leaning over her, he kneed her thighs wide, set his palms beside her head.

Scowling at her hands that moments ago had caressed him tenderly then gripped him with such abandoned heat, were now pressed in fright against his chest.

He said harshly, "I told you, you need to trust me, I won't hurt you." He saw her gaze fall to his penis, the blue orbs spiked wider at the thick heavy club and she hit at him.

"Dammit Svetiessa!" he yelled at her.

"I need to go, Dravidian, let me go!" The panic rose in her voice, tightening it. "We can't, I won't go find another man, I promise, let me up."

Her fingers crunched into fists, she punched at him. "Just let me go, somehow I'll come up with the money and pay off the warrant, the bounty, you'll get your money, please-"

Dev knew his shouting and scowling at her wasn't helping, she was only becoming more afraid of him. He caught her wrists and pinned them down by her side. Her chest popping with frantic short breaths, the blue eyes gaping at him actually shook with her fear.

Lowering his voice, he said softly, "I'm sorry, I didn't mean to yell at you. It's just part of what I am, I come from an infamously vicious stock." *Okay, not the thing to say to calm her.* He held her tight when she fought for release.

"Svetiessa, calm down. Take a breath." He waited, her chest still panted with agitation, lashes flapped with hysteria.

"Sire, please," she pleaded taking a deep breath, squirming under his steel hold. Her breasts jiggled with her jerking, she saw him glance at them, the eyes that had settled back to obsidian sparked white, he quickly raised them to her face. She was so vulnerable lying naked while he held her immobile.

"Svetiessa, I am Devilos. Stop calling me sire." He knew she did it to keep a distance between them. "Calm down, honey," his voice soothed. "I told you, I am not going to rape you, but we are going to make love. Right now."

He couldn't let her go, they would never get back to this point, she would find a way to escape. There was nowhere out there safe for her, but she was too naïve to realize it.

Sveti jerked her body, tried to wrench from his grasp. He held her secure but not enough to hurt her. "Devilos, please let me go, I'll pay you, I swear."

"Goddammit!" he exploded. Shoving his face down to glare at her, his hair sweeping over her, angry breath misted her lips, he said, "It is not about the money. I have more than I could ever want, or spend. This is about us."

He had to calm his own self down, his anger and frustration did not diminish his horns, or claws, fangs or, he could feel his shaft straining hard as an iron drill wanting inside her.

Moving her hands to up beside her head, Dev lowered his body onto hers, and just barely let the hair on his chest nuzzle her breasts. He didn't show his smile at the hitch in her breath, the hardening of her nipples. Her body was reacting to his, perfect.

Her wrists staked to the bed, Sveti's fingers flexed straight then curled. Dev felt her stop fighting him. He lightly rubbed his chest over hers observing the pink flush her cheeks.

He dipped his head to kiss her temple, her jaw, still holding her wrists; he licked her lips, top, then the bottom, the seam between them. The long black hair brushing her face like a fringy caress, he cosseted the seam until she opened her lips to him. His tongue snaked in and took command of her mouth.

When her tongue feathered against his, Dev released her wrist to drift his hand down and palm her breast. He controlled the urge to squeeze it hard, bite her nipple, instead, he massaged it gently, savoring the supple feel of her, his long fingers compressing the luscious flesh between them.

The hand he released stayed beside her head. Dev let go of her breast and strolled his hand down to her core. Her body flinched.

"Shh, Svetiessa, let me," he whispered and fondled her sex, caressing her slit, thumbing her bud, until he felt her silk fill his hand. He slid a finger inside her, she protested, shifted her hips away from his hand.

He ignored her stiffening and pushed a second finger in her, carefully stretching her and tickling the inside of her sheath, teasing over her woman's erogenous dells.

A breathless squeak sucked in sharply before oozing out in an *uhhh* moan, her hand went to his chest, her fingers splayed, then scrunched, clutching the fur over his rocky pecs. Enjoying the slight tugging pain of her dainty fingers, Dev palpated and stroked his hand over her feminine core until her neck arched, her hips rotated with her rending whimpers.

He brought her to the edge. Her shoulders hunched, neck arched so far her eyes slit in inferno throes rolling to the ceiling. "*Devilos*," she exhaled in need, thrusting her hips to his hand, but he paused, moving his hand to her thigh and trickled his fingers over the soft flesh.

Zues, he loved seeing her losing control. She was magnificently gorgeous, rosy cheeks, lips like dew on morning apples, her chest already in paroxysms, tiny hard nipples like cherry drops on mounds of fluffy vanilla ice cream. Aye, she was the richest of desserts. He will never tire of her, never.

His own orgasm twinged and bundled in his balls, ready to shoot out. He brought her again and again to the crest loving the way her body writhed under his adept hands.

Finally she cried, "Devilos, please, let me, let me," she gasped pleading, shoving her hips at him, but he backed off each time. Until her breathing was ragged and shallow, her face pained, head flopping back and forth on the mattress. A line of blue shimmered from beneath lids heavy with want up to him, "*Devilos, please*," she begged.

He licked the side of her face, behind her ear then whispered in it, "Tell me, Svetiessa, tell me you want it, you want me, inside you. Tell me and I will take you to heaven."

He built her up again until she was keening in her need. "Tell me, Svetiessa, say, 'Devilos, take me, please,'" his hand kept working her. Her chest billowed with her panting breaths.

Their faces so close their breaths mingled, he could see the myriad of color in each lush lash; flame, gold, sun. He whispered, "Say it, Svetiessa."

"Yes," she gasped, her eyes clamped shut hard, her pouted lips pulled in, beads of perspiration slid down the sides of her face.

"Yes what, baby?" He pumped his fingers harder.

She licked her lips, croaked, "Yes, take me, Devilos, please," she gasped, writhing at his ministrations.

He brought her to the edge again until her hips bucked wildly at his fingers seeking release, then he removed his hand and nudged her knees wide.

Bracing on an elbow, he fisted his shaft and pressed it to her opening. Rubbing the head over her soft nether lips getting him lubed and keeping her primed, he murmured, "Okay, baby, tell me if I hurt you and I'll stop. Okay?"

She didn't answer him, just nodded, raising her hips to his.

He pushed inside her ever so slowly. His cheek next to hers he felt her grit her teeth, her legs stiffened, but she said nothing. Pausing, he brushed tangled hair off her damp face, sweat gathered at his own temples. "You okay, sweetheart?"

Keeping her eyes closed, she nodded.

So tight, the grip of her channel clung so tightly around him, Dev pushed inch by agonizingly slow inch until he was finally buried deep inside her silken sleeve.

The strain of holding back tightened the skin around his eyes and mouth, temples damp, he braced on both elbows to look down at her. His biceps bulged holding the weight of his torso off her small body.

Her face creased in pain, long lashes splayed on hot cheeks, little spurts of air puffed from her tiny lips.

"Svetiessa?"

She sighed, "I'm okay, Devilos. It hurts, I'm so full...but it...feels...miraculous." Lids down, her breath frayed, suddenly concerned, they flew up at him, she croaked, "You- we- we aren't using...protection, you have to stop."

"Aye. We are not using protection. We are to be wed, Svetiessa, it doesn't matter, and my...kind, does not carry disease. You said you wanted a family." He stroked her face, murmured gently, "You will make a wonderful mother, my Prințesă."

Sveti's eyes cracked open. He filled her so much she thought she'd break, but as she relaxed, she could feel him throbbing against her inner walls. His hot gaze blazing at her screamed his desire, but it was tempered with clear concern for her.

She studied the huge warrior with the harsh face that killed with ease, yet had been so careful with her. She knew he could have easily forced her and taken her virginity and been done with it, the same as any male Krystian sold her to would do, or what he himself planned for her.

But, Dev had taken gentle time to coax her and make her enjoy their sexual union, and get ready to be able to take in his pounding manhood that stretched her to her limits, and now pulsed deep inside in her.

She smiled at him, combed her shaking fingers through a swath of his black hair. She didn't flinch at the bolt-bright white eyes that flared in even more intense desire at her.

The breath he let out at her sweet action released some of the tension in his broad shoulders. Dev drew out, slowly, then he rocked back into her, his penis throbbing like a hot breathing animal against her tender walls.

He continued thrusting carefully in and drawing out slowly, until he saw the flush cover her chest and creep up her neck. He plunged faster, deep, all the way to the end of her, pleased when her slender hips bucked up to meet his with equal intensity.

"Sweetheart?" Question in his voice, "I'm going to go, uh, harder. Okay?"

"Um," she nodded, licked her lips, her eyes stayed closed. "*Uh!*" she grunted with his sudden hard thrust. He barraged her with another, then another, each one harder and shoving deeper than the last.

Dev felt her silken channel squeeze him after he thrust, it almost undid him. His plunges steeping faster, then slowed, then fast again, short hard thrusts then long, his face strained, teeth clenched from holding back. He wanted this to last, enjoy the sensation of her for as long as he could.

He shoved grunts out of her with every hard drive. "Devilos, I feel, uh," she groaned at his drilling shaft shunting all the way deep inside her and dragging back out.

"What, what do you feel, baby?" he growled, his mouth near her ear, he pumped a hard strike, she groaned.

"Bumps...I can feel, bumps...on your....manhood," she sighed and grunted at his stabbing thrusts.

"Aye, only my kind have them. Called pebbled bins." He chuckled. "Like your cute nipples, only harder." He bent and licked a nipple, then pushed in her, paused for her to feel his pounding shaft, hard bumps raised all over it.

Sveti could feel each and every one of them as he dragged from her and slammed back inside, a low wail slid out as every hard bump lathed through her, rubbing against her soft sheath. His lips on her neck, he sucked, nipped down to her shoulder, licked her skin.

With his charging thrusts, penetrating her again and again, Dev's horns elongated. Sveti couldn't see them, but they had turned from facing his back to curve over his head and over her, then grew longer until they were over her shoulders.

As he sucked on the flesh of her neck, his fangs descended, the tips barely touching her skin. He suddenly shifted so his phallus dragged its bumps directly over her clitoris, then shoved back in with a twist raking them faster up her sweet sheath.

Sveti's breathing grew like a falabella bounding up a mountain about to catapult over the top, hurtle off the cliff and free-fall. Her nipples like hard points, little gasping cries evulsed when her hips lurched up to buck at his, she clung to his shoulders as if hanging on for dear life.

Dev's own breathing, husky heavy inhales, he growled at her, "Svetiessa, look at me, see the man who is bringing you to rapturous torment, open your eyes, see your husband," his rhythm slowed to an almost stop.

The claws protracted from his fingertips, he encircled them around her full breasts and dug them in holding the round soft pillows in a forked clutch.

Sveti's lashes blinked over blurs of dazed blues, "Devilos?" she whispered breathy, her gaze a befuddled cloud at the man with the hard face, glittering white eyes spearing her with his intensity.

"What...*uh*..." He slammed in hard, her eyes closed then split open, pupils flared at him, a soft groan purled from her heaving lungs. Her spine curved in at his claws digging into the flesh of her breasts, bringing on strange spasms of agony, pleasure, agony.

He covered her mouth, tugging her lips into his, then pulled away and drank her in. "Look at me, Svetiessa." He waited until her disoriented eyes swerved up to his and he suddenly pounded into her, so hard he had to release a breast and move a hand to hold her shoulders to keep from thrusting her away from him.

He watched the blue irises solder and then blur, her head rolled back.

As he drove into her, his horns raised over her back, his fangs hovered over the side of her neck. Piercing her breast with his claws, he felt her start to undulate in his arms as her climax began, he stabbed his horns into her back, under her shoulder blades as she arched, and sunk his fangs incising just above where the soft flesh met her neck and shoulder.

Sveti sucked in a constricted breath, her eyes flew wide, she screamed from the profound pain cleaving with excruciating pleasure, her spine bent into a spiked arch, her body jolting so sharp and hard almost bringing her clear off the mattress.

Her body filled with the sun glowing brighter and brighter, so heated she's going to explode, Sveti could feel every atom of her- golden and burning like the sun. Her brain static into insanity, a blinding light shrouded her- Dev's manhood literally vibrated inside Sveti- another of his differences.

His name on her lips she screamed again and again from the exquisite, unbearable, agonizing pleasure of it.

Detracting his horns and fangs, then his claws from her breasts, Dev grabbed her face to force her to look at him as she came, bursting into fragments of extraordinary joy in his hands.

As her body convulsed around him with her rushing cries, he let himself go. Wrapping his arms around Sveti, holding her fiercely tight, his teeth grit, a vein at his temple hammered as he pistoned into her with unbridled violence.

Feeling his body blistering from the inside out, on the tip of a bomb, with a guttural grunt, he roared her name and exploded, his seed blasted from his engorged phallus, surging into Sveti's delicate channel.

He mindlessly pumped and pumped until he shot his everything, then paused feeling his body contracting and emptying with jagged seizing spasms.

Yet, he couldn't stop impaling her, she was his obsession, she stole his body, his brain, his heart, he thrust so deep he pounded against her womb. Growls gouged up from his heavy chest, and he collapsed on her soft giving form with heaving growling grunts.

Under his panting weight, Sveti squirmed for air.

His heart pounded out of his chest and into hers. Dev shifted slightly so she could breathe. Still inside her, his hand found her breast and latched onto it, a leg stayed sprawled over hers. She wasn't moving until he let her. He had never experienced a climax such as this before, unimaginable, unmatching.

Dev had never cuddled in his entire life. The word, the action had never even been in his vocabulary. Not with a familial caretaker, and not with any woman he had sex with.

Months ago if someone had said anything so absurd to him that he would be in a very feminine lavender room with white ruffled curtains, embracing the most breathtaking creature he'd ever seen, a human no less.

And after having the most mind-blowing sex he'd ever had, and was now holding her, wanting to keep her tight to his chest so she couldn't leave him, so they could imprint upon one another. Add to that they had technically wed with their act, well, he would have sent the men in white coats to take that person away.

It was unheard of, that the Principé Devilos Dravidian, great great grandson of Lucifer, had a heart and *wanted* to hold this woman in his arms. Other than his close friends he'd known all their lives, he shook his head, he had never had feelings, cared for another soul, until her.

As he rolled to his side to look at Sveti, his manhood slipped from her incredible body.

He had wanted her since the second he'd laid eyes on her. He knew he'd have her, it had been an internal fight to wait and not take her by force. Every day his beast fought him to just grab her, fuck her, claim her. His breathing slowed, he hugged her tightly.

Dev acknowledged that she hadn't been fully willing, but he couldn't wait any longer. The longer he waited the closer to danger she crept.

She was partially turned towards him, her eyes drifting closed. He had known from the start that she would be his. After seeing her at that party, he would never admit, even to himself, the back of his mind was endlessly plotting and planning how to find her, get her. Steal her if he had to.

Even when they weren't speaking after the river incident, he never stopped scheming how to win her, keep her. And she, them together, it had been even a thousand times more amazing than he thought it would be. His body, brain, still rang with the intense tumult of his release.

Dev's face relaxed into a pleased smile, and her intensity, damn, she was made for love, for him. He'd never enjoyed the sexual act as much as tonight, when they'd shared pleasure, he didn't just take what he wanted and move on.

It was just so different, with her; he wanted to give so much more than receive. His heart clenched as if in the grip of a fist at the sight, the very thought of his Svetiessa.

Brushing the flaming hair back behind her shoulders, drawing each lock through his long fingers, he asked quietly, "Hey, Prințesă, you okay?"

"Mmm," the murmur was part awake, more asleep. He had depleted her young virgin's body.

Smiling, at least she seemed all right with what they had done, hell, she'd screamed her release until she was hoarse, her little nails had dug into his back. His gaze traveled down her body. He glanced at her feminine folds, and quickly away, or he would be in her again in a flash. She needed time to rest. She would be sore.

His hands itched to play with her tits. But he saw the pinpricks of his claws around the soft mounds, those, as well as the marks from his incisors and horns would disappear shortly. Thank Zues, she'd freak if she saw them.

He had penetrated more than just her woman's channel, and gave her more than just his semen, but she didn't need to know about that right now, not yet.

His horns. He was going to have to explain what he'd done, without asking her, telling her first before he did it. But not now. He reached his arms around her to pull her close, nestle her softness against his chest.

With a sated sigh, Sveti cuddled into his embrace.

He palmed the back of her head lifting it to gaze at her. Her eyes were closed, she was already asleep. Zues, she was pure bliss. His bliss.

Snuggling her back in his arms, his hand slid down her silken skin to cup a rounded butt cheek, he squeezed it, holding onto it firmly, possessively, as he drifted off with her.

Chapter Nineteen

$\mathcal{D}$ev broke consciousness feeling a soft warm bundle in his arms. He had never literally slept with a woman before. He wouldn't have liked it before, it would be creepy waking up next to someone, even one he had fucked. But surprising himself, he sure as shit loved it now.

Still asleep, Sveti rolled on her side burrowing her bottom into Dev's already hardened erection.

"Sweetheart," he whispered in her ear, lifting her shiny curls, caressing them between his coarse fingers he sifted them under his nose. He brushed the tendrils back and forth, inhaling her scent, feeling the satin of her tresses against his rugged skin.

Settling her hair behind her so his lips could find the silky flesh of her neck, he licked then sucked, loving the smell and taste of her, his animal instincts were already showing themselves.

She didn't wake. Sliding his hand over, he coiled his fingers around a sweet breast and clutched it, kneaded it softly, tranquilly. A murmur hushed from her lips but she still didn't awaken.

He gently tugged her nipple with his thumb and finger until it peaked, then moved to the other, over her shoulder he watched them pebble. He skimmed his palm over the plush curves, and down her thin ribs to splay over her concave belly. "Damn, woman," he muttered, "you need to eat before you get sick."

Lowering his hand he curled his fingers over the tender folds of her womanhood. Her hips wriggled, she sighed but didn't wake.

Dev whispered, "I need you again, baby, I tried to wait, but having you once, hell, now I crave you worse than ever. Like the red in my blood, you've woven your beautiful soul into mine," he took a breath and cuddled her. "I find ease and comfort, release and searing desire when I'm with you, Svetiessa."

Her sleek back rounded into his massive chest. Dev never thought he'd be so gentle with a female, never thought the word 'sweetheart' would come out of his mouth, unless of course in sarcasm.

He stroked his fingers over her sex like he was playing a harp. Light yet strong, slow and fast, the melody he plucked entranced her hips to furrow imperceptibly against his hand with his cadence, but she still slept in his arms.

Although asleep, her body responded to his manipulating fingers. When her silk oozed into his hand, he nudged her legs apart, fisted his thick shaft and carefully slid it in from behind, forcing himself to move slowly into her tight woman's channel.

Dev maneuvered her slightly to bend forward with her back arching so he could go deeper. He played her clit like feathers beating a drum, phallus sluicing deep until he was entrenched inside her, paused, then eased back out.

His rhythm increased, but he still moved carefully to not startle her or unduly hurt her if she was sore from earlier. He was big and she was so small, and so pure and fresh he just couldn't get over it.

Sveti stiffened slightly. "Devilos?" her slur drowsy.

"Aye sweetheart," he acknowledged, surging his thickness slowly into her, feeling his flesh glide along the satin walls of her tight sheath. His balls gently slapped her skin, his breath a slight breeze against her ear wafting wisps of flaming curls.

He moved his hand from her tender genitals to brush the hair off her face. His deep voice rumbled a slight tease, "Were you expecting someone else's hard cock inside your sweet pussy?"

In a sleep heavy voice she murmured, "Hmm, what are you…*uh*," his harder thrust pushed a soft grunt from her. With a quiet sigh, her tush nuzzled against his hips, forcing his shaft deeper.

"I'm sorry, baby, I couldn't wait until you wakened, are you okay?" His hand covered her lush breast, fondled it with his big fingers and hard palm before slipping back to stroke her clitoris, speeding up his rhythm.

But she was still more asleep than awake, "Mmmm," her languid shimmy against him made his dick throb. Even as he plunged harder and faster, she slipped back into sleep.

His lips smiled into her hair; if he didn't have a strong ego he would think he was boring her. But she was still healing, gaining her strength back, she refused to admit it, but she still tired quickly.

He held her hips taut and thrust faster, feeling the seething vortex of tight tension building in his testicles.

Dev forced himself to keep his fangs and claws sheathed; he didn't want her to wake suddenly to acute pain. She hummed and grunted slightly as he plunged faster into her delicate body until the heat boiled over and he started to come.

Hissing Sveti's name in a roar muted in her hair, he wrapped his arms around her holding her tight, his body went rigid and held, then he convulsed into her, his seed spilling into her female's cleft.

As his body spent in her, panting, his hands roamed all over her body, stroking, caressing every beautiful curve of her luscious skin. Dev prayed one of his seeds would take root in her womb.

He feared their linking was tenuous, he was well aware he had deliberately seduced her last night when she was in a fragile state of mind.

She was so terrified of going home she was frantic to figure a way out, and he had with intentional calculation taken advantage of her panic. And when she realized it, she may try to run again. But if she was with child, his child, it would tether her to him. He wouldn't have to fear her ever leaving him.

Petting her, Dev smiled, he had never in his life thought he'd have a woman of his own, much less a child. He pictured little children with her flaming curls skipping about, and drifted off to sleep while still inside her.

When Sveti woke she felt as if steel bands encircled her. She shifted and the bands tightened. A warm breath stirred the hair next to her temple.

Her body stiffened, *the Dravidian*. Last night came hurtling back to her. She had tried to leave, he wouldn't let her, offering himself, well, he didn't exactly offer, he *told* her they would mate.

Right now she felt his powerful chest pressed against her back with his rhythmic breaths. She was caught in his embrace, and one of his legs pinned her to the bed as if he thought she'd leave, and he wasn't going to let her go.

She felt his semi-erection pressing into her bottom. He was asleep and he was still hard. She shuddered remembering last night.

How could he still be hard? He had broken her virginity, they'd had sex, amazing, excruciating, out of this world sex. Her body shuddered again recalling the...second orgasm he'd wrung from her while inside her.

Like a rough violent amusement park ride, her body had riddled with sensation, she felt as if she'd reached the sun and flown straight into it then exploded into sharp radiant splinters from the inside out.

Her fingertips touched the side of her neck. He had...bitten her, sunk his fangs into her flesh. Odd, she drew her fingers over the area, the puncture marks were gone. He had scored his fangs into her and it hadn't hurt badly. On the contrary, sensation had rained into her with exquisite pain, so on the precipice of pain and pleasure, her body had been bombarded as if by electrifying shooting stars.

Even as she felt the heat rise now between her legs in remembrance, the wetness gathered, she frowned. He had tricked her. Her sex suddenly clenched with wet heat rippling through it.

And, it was hazy, but she faintly felt when he had taken her again while she flickered between blurred awareness and sleep. His huge manhood slick with her silk sliding in and out of her relaxed body from behind, he had played her body like a sonata on a piano.

Sveti had fallen back asleep, but her body felt the memory of his coming inside her, hard and full and fast, his roar of release muffled in her hair, spilling his seed, claiming her again.

She only vaguely felt him cleansing her with a warm damp cloth before tugging her back into his strong embrace.

He had stripped her clothes from her against her will, but hadn't forced her like he said he wouldn't. But, her fists clenched in anger, he had beguiled her like a fat worm dangling on a fishing line with his dark velvet voice, and his skilled mouth and hands of magic.

Her cheeks flamed as she remembered she had begged him, like he said she would, to take her. He'd made her do that, forced her to beg him to penetrate her virgin's body.

The anger built as she concluded that he had purposefully seduced her. *My Goddess Satrine*, they were wedded, by chemistry, a biological attachment. He was not only a vicious fiend, he proved he was also ruthlessly sneaky.

Why had he done it? What was in it for him except a ball and chain around his ankle? What about his other women? She shifted again, but his arms tightened more and his rumbled sigh pulsed over her ear.

Well, she wasn't standing for it; she would find a way out of the marriage. Even as she contemplated how, she knew she couldn't fight the chemical binds. But that didn't mean she would have to stay with him.

Yet she knew those were the rules, the principles of what they'd done. He said he expected her to stay with him, he owned her now. Damn him.

Regardless, she would find a way out of it. Gingerly, she slowly unwound from his arms and wriggled out from under his heavy leg. Squirming without jostling the bed, Sveti worked her way off until she was on her feet.

She paused and looked at him. He was sprawled on his side, his big arms flung out as if searching for her in his sleep. The long tousled hair, a spray of black showers on the lavender pillow and spread over his enormous bronzed shoulders. He would put a Greek god to shame.

Even in repose his face was darkly harsh made up of hard planes and severe angles. Dark whiskers covered his strong jaw. The only thing soft on him was his lips, yet they were ruggedly carved in masculine beauty.

Her fingers ruffled over her lips remembering the lurid assault of his mouth on hers. The sheet rumpled just below his hip, his muscled back bare, she could just make out the dark hair that covered his thick chest. He was fearsomely, dangerously, beautiful.

Her body stirred as she stared at him, remembering his strong body wrapped around her, over her, pounding into her. He was all strength and hot aggression, he had brought her to heaven as he'd promised. Her breasts felt swollen, aching from his rough caresses, his lips, teeth on them.

Thinking about his thick male member thrusting so fiercely hard inside her, her nipples tightened crying for his fingers to pinch them, his tongue to lap them, her sex was damp. She wanted to- no, she shook her head, no, he was a cheat, and she wanted no part of him.

All she had to do was remember how he'd easily held her captive with his great strength and effortlessly ripped her clothes off her body ignoring her protests.

She turned on her heel and hurried into the bathroom. A quick shower, get dressed, and she was out of there. Since he was with her, there would be no guard outside the door. This was her chance to escape.

Dev jerked awake. His limbs stretched out reaching for…her. Before he opened his eyes he knew she was gone. The bed was cold, empty. His lids slit open. He could hear the shower running. She should have waited for him.

He slid off the bed to his bare feet. Dragging his fingers through his hair, he scratched the mat of hair on his chest and headed for the bathroom. He grabbed the knob to turn it, it was locked.

"Son-of-a-bitch," he cursed, "she locked the goddamned door." Huh. Well, his little wifey will learn there will never be locked doors between them. She was not shutting him out. Ever.

He twisted the doorknob right off the door, tossed it and pushed his way inside. It was steamy, he could just make out her body through the mist on the glass doors.

He could see her nude silhouette, her luscious curves moving in scintillating languor as she bent and stroked soap over her legs and up over her arms.

He brushed his teeth with invisible speed, and grabbed up a bar of soap off the sink, he was as hard as a rock before he reached the glass doors. As quietly as possible, he opened the door.

She was humming while she ran her soapy hands all over that incredible body. Fuck, it sent goose bumps streaking up his cock.

The water sprayed the entire chamber, he rubbed the soap until his hands were filled with bubbly lush lather then set the bar on a dish, and crept up behind her.

Her hands were raised as she re-pinned loose hair, Dev slid his foaming hands around her and cupped her breasts. She let out a squeal.

Sveti screamed. Big hard hands covered her breasts with foamy soap. Before she could grasp them and pull them off, he was feeling her up, mauling her ripe globes, his head bent to her, wet black hair slid over her shoulder as he growled in her ear.

"Godsdamn, Wife," he nipped her earlobe, "a glimpse of your body detonates my cock to iron, these bounteous tits, ahh," strong fingers squeezed and caressed, "soft and fat and lush, how did I ever live before without my hands so full of them?"

His erection rammed against her butt, brawny chest pressing her slim back, hands hard and hungry, clenching and massaging, sliding up and down her body and back to reclaim her plush breasts with his strong, aggressive grip.

Trying to break from him, she cried, "No! Stop, Devilos, we are not doing this!"

His fingers gripped her succulent fruit holding her immobile, he pinched her pouty nipples with his tough fingertips while he rubbed and squeezed, the soap still foamy and luxuriant. His voice rough and as steamy as the bathroom, he murmured, "Aye, we are, sweetheart."

"No," she protested trying to twist from his groping hands. "You tricked me last night, but you won't again. Let go of me!"

His hand slid down to cup her sex while the other continued its soapy fondling. "Ah, Wife, I told you I would expect my husband's due when I wanted it. I want it, now." His fingers played with her slit, circled and pinched her tight bud.

"Devilos, I said no." She bit back the moan that slithered from her taut throat. She knew he heard it, his grip tightened; his mouth went to her neck and latched on. He sucked so hard it was almost painful, but not quite. His thick finger, slick with water, probed into her.

"No," her half-hearted protest ended in a quivering sigh, it was too late. He was only on her a few seconds and already he had her body on fire.

Feeling her surrendering, Dev clutched her breast, thumbed her clit and thrust his finger in and out before adding another. His fingers curled inside her, he gripped her mound tight with his palm, pulling his fingers harder against the inside wall of her sheath.

Her responding moan a low *grrr*, her neck arched as her legs buckled.

Turning her to face him, with hungered need he lifted her to straddle his waist and moved to the tiled wall. Licking her lips, his minted breath huffed against them, he said, "Put your palms against the wall to brace yourself. I have you."

Already delirious and heady with passion, her brain was shutting down and her body was taking over, Sveti did as he said.

Dev gripped her ass with both hands, lifted her and slammed her onto his cock as his mouth plundered hers, taking her shocked gasp into his throat. He waited, to see if she was okay, if he'd hurt her. He felt her sheath clenching all around his hard flesh that filled her tender channel.

Her head fell back, lips parted, eyes closed, nipples beaded to tiny pink marbles. Goose bumps covered her body as a mini-orgasm spiraled through her surprising both of them with the quick suddenness of it.

He watched her succulent breasts rise and fall rapidly, the female pillows wriggling, and her hips bucked to his. *Ah, she wants it.*

Dev wasn't going to last long. He crushed her bottom in his hands and lifted and slammed her again and again on his shaft until little wheezing squeaks chopped from her throat, a flush rose over her chest.

She pushed off the wall to throw her arms around his neck and wedge her breasts against his chest, to rub up and down on the thick hair and graze his nipples with hers as he moved her. The bumps sprouted on his shaft as he plunged, twisting and boring them against her walls.

He could feel her rising to peak, reaching the crest, he covered her mouth with his to feel, taste the vibration of her release. Her gutted cries raced down his throat as her body undulated under his hands and around his shaft.

Eyes rolling back in her head, her breasts bobbled against his furry chest with every thrust. Dev felt the flurry of spasms shake through her body with her climax, her sheath squeezed the length of him, he couldn't hold out. He let go to his own release.

He lifted her up and thrust her down on his erection again and again until the frenzy blew up from his balls to the tip and he thundered into her.

His mouth went to her neck, his fangs already descended, he plunged them into her flesh and heard her shuddering sob as another orgasm ripped through her. He pounded in and out until his cock jerked and convulsed, shooting his seed into her womanhood, his deep groan growled, roiling from his chest, reverberating against her body.

For several long moments they didn't move, couldn't think much less move, just chests heaving in heavy pants against each other as their brains cleared.

When they both quivered in winding after-shock tremors, his fangs retreating, Dev let her slide down his body to her feet.

Her trembling knees crumpled, he caught her up in his arms and moved back into the pelleting spray. He rinsed them both off again and carried her out of the shower. He set her on the rug and grabbed a towel, slung it around her, and rubbed her gently with it.

Her big eyes blinked at him as the throes of her orgasms receded and her brain once again started to take over. Immediately, her brows drew down, lips pursed and she pushed at him.

He gripped her towel in his fist, in front of her.

Holding her tight so she couldn't move, irritated bits of gravel in his deep voice, he commanded, "Nay, Svetiessa, stop. Not now. Let us catch our breath, get dressed first.

Chapter Twenty

Sveti was pissed. Not only had he seduced her again when she said no, now he held her immobile like a child while issuing commands. He might be captain of his ship, and prince of his planet, but he was not her boss.

She jerked from his hands, grabbed a second towel and padded out of the bathroom leaving him standing with a scowl, unsure if she was listening to him or not.

In her bedroom, Sveti quickly pulled on a short light skirt and blouse that had no buttons. He had already ripped apart two blouses and a pair of jeans. *Gah*, he was such a savage, and she'd bound herself to him. She needed to figure a way out of the stupid marriage.

She was rubbing the second towel over her hair when he came out. Naked as a jailbird. The man has no modesty. Sveti tore her eyes away from his masculine beauty. There was nothing that was going to entice her to have sex with him again.

There was some vestige of truth in Dev saying once she had sex with him she'd want it forever. Her body already burned for his, keeping her back to him, she combed her hair.

Dev gathered the clothes he'd worn the day before. Since she wouldn't look at him, he said to her back, "I have to go get changed. You can start packing up your things."

She swung around, mouth agape, against her will her gaze shot down his naked body. He already had another hard-on that could drill holes into granite, and his horns were swelling right along with it.

While dark red crept over her face, her eyes bounced up to see erotic fire burning in his dark orbs that were jagged with white.

A bit sheepish, he pulled his jeans on over his huge erection. "Sorry, it has a mind of its own when it's anywhere in your vicinity. And, apparently you are unwilling to couple until we both are truly satiated. Not that there is a chance in hell of that happening, pun intended, still, at least we could try."

He muttered under his breath, "Might take a hundred years, but likely not even close." Dragging his shirt over his head he stepped into his boots and moved to the door.

Pack? "What? Wait- what do you mean pack my things? I thought we were going to be here at the station for a while." Setting the comb on a dresser she couldn't stop her gaze from wandering over his insanely virile body. Powerful shoulders, lean sinewy hips, and that chest.

Remembering his male fur rubbing over her naked beasts as his big hard body hovered over her, his knees pushing her thighs apart, Sveti felt her panties dampen with a quiver, her nipples pebble.

One hand resting on a hip, Dev pronged his fingers over his scalp through his wet hair. He took a deep breath and shuddered, his lips bunched. "Just a little FYI Svetiessa, I can smell your arousal. You are fighting yourself as much as fighting me."

At her embarrassed scowl, he frowned. "We are going to be here for some time. You will want your things with you. In my suite. Our suite now."

The flaming brows boomeranged to her hairline. "What? No!" She vigorously shook her head. "There is no reason for me to leave this room. I am quite comfort-"

"Nay. You will stay with me. I made it clear last night, Svetiessa, you will be with me. In my chambers, in my bed, no matter where it is. This lavender haven was perfect for our initial coupling, but my suite is larger therefore more comfortable for the two of us together."

He turned his back as if ending the matter. A pillow flew past his head hitting the wall, he swallowed an irritated grin. Of course, he knew she was going to kick about it. Not that it was going to do her any good.

Sveti cried, "No! You are a dictatorial monster; I will not be married to a monster! You tricked me, that has to be illegal, so the marriage will be null and void. We will get an annulment. I will find another prince, a *gentleman*-"

He reached her in three long strides and gripped her arms. His face growing as black as his hair, his eyes flickering white, flames sparked at his heels.

"It is too late, sweetheart. You shouldn't have flaunted your plans to be with another man, prince, whatever, in my face. I had to take you before you went to another male. Besides, no sissy gentleman is going to give you what I did. You'll see, you will become addicted to sex with me, like I already am with you, you won't even think of another man. Especially that milk toast what's his name."

Her nose in the air, she said haughtily, "His name is Ryen. He is not a milk toast, he is sweet and gentle."

Holding her tight in hands like steel clamps, his thumbs stroked her bare skin under the short sleeves. He said with arrogant conceit, "Sweet and gentle won't make you scream like you did in my arms with my cock fucking you."

"Oh! You are such a pig." Struggling to make him release her, she cried, "You tricked me, you seduced me. It wasn't fair. Let go of me."

His fingers wound tighter around her arms as his anger grew. "Honey, just because a man is seducing you, doesn't take away your responsibility. You gave in." His smirk all cocky and smug. "Like I said you would. You're just uppity because you begged me for it, like I said you would."

"Uppity! Why you- you pompous jackass!" Shades of red way darker than her hair flushed over her entire face and neck and chest with her embarrassment and fury.

"It wasn't fair! You used your experience to break down my- my- uh, innocence. You knew I would not be able to deny you after you had your hands and mouth all over me, which you did force on me," her mouth snapped shut seeing the white flame strike in his eyes.

She jerked from his grip and rubbed her arms where he'd held her.

"Whatever," he said. "It's a done deal. Stop whining like a petulant child. I put my fluids into your body, from my fangs and my horns, my dick, there is no removing them, they bind us, sweetheart. All of which, by the way, you thoroughly enjoyed if your shrieks of rapture were anything to go by. I bet even right now you're visualizing our love making, and your wee little pussy is getting dripping wet thinking about my mouth on it."

He smiled at the tell-tale color that flushed her ivory skin. "Am I right? Maybe I should ask for my husband's rights, right now. As I told you I will insist on them, and I don't expect you to balk when I do. I'm obviously ready." He lowered his head indicating his raging hard-on, and smiled up at the appalled look on her face.

A black brow angled in a leer, he said, "Go ahead, take your clothes off. I'm sure you don't want that blouse ruined too." His gaze lowered and burned with lascivious intent. "You can leave the skirt on." He reached his hand to go under her skirt. "It's hot that I can just push the skirt up and yank those panties down and shove my cock right into-"

"No!" She jumped back from his grasp with a furious huff. "I told you, we will never have sex again. Your deceit will make it null and void and I will find another-"

He grabbed her so hard her breath was knocked out of her. Furious himself now, his eyes narrowed into fierce slits, his words grit out of clenched teeth, "Fucking stop saying that, Svetiessa. You are mine now. You will never, trust me, *ever* be with any man but me. Unless you want to see that man die. Do I make myself clear?"

The color drained from her face leaving it stark white. She knew he was capable of murder. Her lips moved but she couldn't push any words out.

He had told her she would be even more terrified of him, and he spoke the truth about that, too. She was scared to death of his capability to do lethal harm to anyone he chose to. She had pushed him too far.

Dev dug his fingers into her arm, and her face, holding it up to his. His tone deadly silk he said, "We are technically married. You cannot undo it. We will be formally wed tonight."

His fingers gripping her face, pulling her closer to him, he told her, "You will not ever leave me, Svetiessa, you do and you know I will come for you, and I will find you, and trust me, you will not like the consequences."

His grip loosened slightly when she spoke softly with a frightened catch, "I don't understand, Dravidian, why, why did you do this? What do you get out of it?"

He stared at her so long she thought he wasn't going to answer her. Then, he said, "I get you."

"But, Sire, I-"

His mouth closed over hers. One hand slid to cradle her head, the other splayed across her back to pull her body right against his. The kiss he forged on her was angrily brutal and volatile with lust, and she was a victim to its pull, like a sucking bog, she couldn't get out of it.

His mouth slanted, clamping a harsh seal over her mouth, holding her prisoner while his tongue drove in seeking hers to take it captive as well.

When she moved to be released, he pressed his thumb in her cheek, his fingers strung around her head, the hand on her back forced her curves to mesh into his steel chest. His rampage fueled like a struck match in oil.

Sveti could feel herself spiraling away under his fierce onslaught, unraveling like a cold knot into a long, melting ribbon of hot butter. Her knees weakened and she shoved her hands into his hair and clutched handfuls of it.

The hand on her back thrust around and savaged her breast with grinding desire while he bent his knees to press his engorged penis between her legs, and shoved hard up her woman's cleft.

Oh Goddess Satrine, her body was suddenly on fire, her sex screamed for him, she wanted, needed him inside her so badly, she felt as if she would die if they didn't- The chill thought came to her that he was again forcing himself on her and seducing her to shut her up, it stopped her dead like being hit with a bucket of ice water.

She suddenly shoved herself from him. Not expecting it, she was able to wrench out of his fiery clench. The back of her hand covered her heaving mouth, she warily watched him over it.

Befuddled with clouds of lust hazing his eyes, he stood with his hands still raised, confusion smothered his dazed expression then anger cleared it all away. "Svetiessa, what the hell-"

"No, what the hell, you, Dravidian. You are trying to use sex on me to shut me up and I will not have it."

Chest huffing, slicking back a fallen lock of hair, a sly sneer curled his lip as his gaze took in her pink cheeks and glassy eyes, her panting chest. His eyes tapered at the taut nipples that poked at her shirt.

He palmed his erection that was fair to bursting out of his pants. "I am using sex, Svetiessa, to show you what we have."

The black streaked with white eyes rose to her blues. "If you would give it a rest for a second you would see what I say is true. What is between us is blistering wildfire, trust me, you won't find anything else like it."

The flaming curls that matched her heated cheeks swished back and forth as she shook her head. "I don't believe anything you say. You continue to try to deceive me."

"Huh." His grunt sarcastic, "How's it feel?"

Brows drew low, her jaw rigid. She said with affronted ire, "I have not deceived you. You are well aware it was Krystian who sent you that transmission for the trade that day. He tricked me as well. He told me I would only be escorting Miles back to your ship. I didn't know what he'd done until I was back with him."

Forehead furrowing with a glint of suspicion, she asked him, "Is that what this is all about? You wanted revenge, this is your way of punishing me? By tricking me into a marriage I don't want? I still don't understand, you have only shackled yourself too."

"Oh my Zues," he groaned, his hand slapping his forehead Dev looked to the ceiling. "Of all the females of all the solar systems, you had to make me irrevocably desire this one?"

Shoulders hunched as she slammed her hands on her hips. "You want a different female? Go get one. I can't see why when you could have any female in the universes, princesses, queens, the most gorgeous of the gorgeous, why would you tie yourself to one woman? Why me?"

Dev stood, baffled, weary of this debate. He lowered his head, strung his hands over the back of his neck, then looked up at her.

So small and feminine, the epitome of grace and sweetness, huge, angry, bewildered, stunning crystal blue eyes regarding him as if she was trying to figure out a puzzle.

Sighing deeply, he said, "Enough of this, Svetiessa. I have explained, I don't want any other women, I want you. Only you, forever. Done. We will not talk of this again."

As she opened her mouth he waved a dismissive hand. "We are wedded. You are mine. You will do as I say, and I am telling you, number one," he stepped to her ignoring her cringe from him, "we are finalizing our union tonight at seven.

"Bowie purchased a dress for you that you had admired when you went shopping. And two," the ebony in his eyes glittered with threat and a scowl, "you will call me Devilos or Husband, or an endearment. I hear Sire or Dravidian again out of your mouth and there will be punishment. Mark my words."

"What? What is this, the dark ages? You would punish me for- for something so trivial?"

"Aye. Go ahead and test me."

Mouth a mutinous purse, she sneered, "What kind of punishment could there be for something so…stupid?"

His frown perturbed, he said harshly, "You are my wife. It's bullshit for you to call me Sire or by my last name. You do it deliberately to keep a distance between us, keep us less personal, preventing intimacy. It's not happening again."

Now he smiled, his lip curled in a smirk, he informed her, "Regarding the punishment, I'm partial to spanking. You that is, not me. I'm thinking of tying you to the bed, on your stomach, ankles and wrists, you know, spread eagle," his grin rose nasty at her eyes widening in disbelief, anger, shock, then fright.

"Oh, and completely naked of course, there would be nothing between my hand and that sweet, plump ass of yours, or anything else of yours." The dark eyes were now almost bone white. His brows lowered and the smile hardened. "If you don't believe me, just go ahead and try me."

Taking a step back from him, her voice hushed, "You wouldn't dare."

He moved a step to her. "Go ahead and say sire or Dravidian, call my bluff."

Her arms crossed protectively over the front of her, she looked up at him, saw the long black hair of a warlord drying past his shoulders, shoulders bunched as he set his big hands arrogantly on his hips, and she could see he was no longer angry. No, pure lust gleamed at her from his dark eyes like white torches, daring, *wanting* her to say it. Her mouth opened in an O, then it snapped shut.

"I didn't think so," he said smugly.

Scowling, Sveti tightened her crossed arms replied belligerently, "It's not fair, you are using your brute strength to control me."

"Ah, precious, no one said life was fair. Aye, I do have the strength over you, and therefore I do have the upper hand. I am stronger, so I rule."

"Oh! That's- so archaic!" She couldn't believe what he was saying.

"So? I am archaic, honey, you have no idea how much. You are mine to do with in any way I see fit." At her swift inhale of disbelief, he said, "Now, unless you want to have sex with me right now, and I'm okay with that in case you're not sure," stroking his erection, his mouth quirked facetiously.

"I'm going to go change, I have things to do before tonight." He waited but she remained mum. With a shrug, he turned and started down the hall to the living room.

Sveti stared after him, then, she ran after him. He was at the door. "Wait a minute, Sire- uh, Devilos."

He pivoted with a smile, his hot gaze raking her, his hands went to his belt buckle. "You want to fuck? I'm ready, babe."

She came to a rigid halt with a frown. "You are crass. No. I told you we are not having sex again." Her lids levered down over angry eyes. "You said Bowie bought a dress. That means you have been planning this- this, uh, seduction."

The realization continued to climb with her voice, "You didn't just happen to be here and stop me from going and getting a prince on my own, you- you planned all along to-

to trick me into wedding you." The blue orbs paled, turned bleak. "But why? Why would you do that?"

Grabbing up his holster, he opened the door with an exasperated sigh. "For mercy sake, Svetiessa, I have already told you. I wanted you, and you were going to run off and let some fucking alien animal screw you and likely hurt you or pass you around to others, or kill you afterwards. And if you didn't do it yourself, your brother was going to. I did you a fucking favor.

"So get the hell off the trip, woman. Bowie will be here to bring you at seven. I have a captain ready to complete our vows," solidifying her suspicions that he had planned the entire seduction.

His voice hard but his eyes were tender, before she could speak he said, "There will be no more arguing about this, Svetiessa, none. Mara will come to help you dress. Be ready at seven. You don't come willingly with Bowie then I will come and get you. Consider how embarrassed you will be slung over my shoulder as we march through the station."

She said with a sad grunt, "I'm supposed to be happy about that? Being forcefully dragged to my wedding, with no talk of- love, how am I supposed to accept that?"

Dev closed the door, his lips pulled in then he blew them out.

"Svetiessa, if I had the time to romance you, I would. I don't know how, because I've never romanced a woman before, but I could have gotten pointers from that rogue Bowie. But, you pushed the issue by going after danger.

"I knew it was only a matter of time before you fled. Between that and your *séantóir bráthair,* uh, your perverted brother, time was running out. I," he rubbed his hands over his face, scrubbed his fingers down over his whiskers.

Now he looked bleak. "Svetiessa, I am not capable of *drogaste,* ah, love. It isn't in my makeup. I told you, I come from a vicious, coldblooded stock. But, as I also told you, you know that I adore you, and I will take care of you, protect you, and, you already know the sex is out of this world with us. Isn't that enough?"

She said quietly, "No."

They stared at each other for several silent seconds, then he said coldly, "Well, it's going to have to be."

Uncaring it seemed, of her desolate expression and feelings of entrapment, he opened the door.

Keldon was standing to the side, he didn't move a muscle. Dev had told him previously, with his fists, that he was not to look at Sveti unless necessary and was never to be alone with her or touch her. His presence dashed Sveti's hope of fleeing after Devilos left.

Dev told her, "Get your shit packed. You will stay in my suite. There will be no further discussion that you will not be in my bed every night. And," his lip rose at the corner, he closed the door slightly in Keldon's red face, "we will have sex, daily, undoubtedly more than once or twice or more a day. You will spread your legs for me whenever I say. Hopefully, you will come to me wanting it."

"But," his smile harsh he went on, "I will never lose my desire for you, Svetiessa, never. You make me hard just thinking of you. So, get over your hurt feelings at being deceived and accept that from now on, you are mine and our lives will be spent together." *Forever.* She didn't even know the half of it yet.

His gaze swept her shocked, irate, and unhappy face before he stepped out and closed the door.

Chapter Twenty-One

*H*ours later, Sveti opened her door to Bowie. His cheerful grin did nothing to lighten her morose mood.

"Hey, Sveti, how're you doing?" The affable blond lieutenant entered her living room with a garment bag on a hanger slung over his shoulder. He hung it on a hook by the closet door. Glancing around, he saw a suitcase by the door. "Oh, good, I see you're packed. I'll get that to, uh," his voice softened seeing her misery, "uh, Dev's suite."

"He's given me no choice." She scowled at the suitcase.

Bowie was well aware of what transpired between her and Dev. Dev had told him everything when he saw him earlier.

His commiserating with her would do her no good and make him somewhat disloyal to his best friend, so he changed the subject. "I've, uh, brought your dress."

Her lashes lowered covering her eyes but not before he saw how crestfallen she looked. Bowie started to go to her when she put up a hand as if to protect herself.

He stopped and raised his palms. "Hey, honey, come on, you must know I would never hurt you. We're shopping buddies for Pete's sake." He tried a little levity with a half-grin. Then sobered. "Please don't be afraid of me, Sveti."

Her body was partially turned away from him, she wiped her eyes then turned to face him. Seeing his expression so earnest and worried, and hurt that she feared him, her stiff lips softened into a small smile.

"I know, Bowie. I'm sorry, it's just…him. He's so…cold, and lethal, and domineering, I'm afraid all of you are just like him. But I know you are not."

He nodded grimly thinking, *well, I kinda am.* Thankfully she wasn't his woman so he could treat her like a friend. Of course, Bowie realized, if she was his, he would be just as dictatorial, it was in their blood, and he already is nearly as lethal, and he hid his innate coldness behind the affable demeanor.

Pulling on a smile he said cheerfully, "So, don't you want to see your dress?" Her skin darkened so quickly and the blue in her eyes deepened. *Oo-kay, not happy about the wedding.* "Sveti, you need to-"

"He tricked me, Bowie, into giving myself to him. He is forcing me to marry him." A tiny tear slipped out, she dashed at it.

"He said he would never love me, Bowie. What girl wants to be chained to a loveless marriage with a domineering brute? I'd have been better off being sold to a horrible creature who would rape me and then kill me, at least it would be over." She wiped at more tears.

"Hey, come on," Bowie coaxed, moving to her, "you need to give Dev a chance. He thinks he's incapable of loving but he would do anything for one of us, his friends, he would die for us, and he would suffer immeasurably if one of us died. Sveti, he charged into that dungeon and dove into that river to save you. Hell, he carried you on his back up a damned mountain. He cares for you, it's just in a cold, violent way." He smiled at the description.

"Bowie, really," she snorted, "he wanted to get the warrant fee for me, I was dollars rolling away with the current or down the mountain." Sveti didn't mention the dungeon.

She still couldn't figure that out. She assumed he took her to punish her, but he had yet to set an injurious hand on her. Dev told her he'd been obsessed with her, he came to save her. It was all so confusing, he was deceitful, nothing he said could be believed.

Bowie folded his burly arms over his buffed chest shaking his head. "No, it wasn't that. He is wealthy beyond all means, trust me. He was only picking up your warrant case because he wanted to safely see you to your brother. A less savory type would have done you harm, trust me, before delivering you."

"But he did just that, Bowie, he did me harm. He took my…" pink deepened on her cheeks, "virginity. Knowing full well it would tie me to him. He wanted to…own me. He wanted to punish me."

His lips bunched. "But, Sveti, aye, he did what he did, but did he hurt you? No. Not physically. Another male would not have been gentle and, uh caring. You were with the Amphicyonids, those fucking, beg your pardon, grizzly-canines, you can imagine what a creature from another galaxy could have, would have, done to you. Seriously, he has your best interests at heart."

"That's just it, Bowie, he knew what my brother planned and was still taking me there. If he cared at all about me he would have figured out a way to-" She broke off thinking about what she was saying.

"Aye, you see? There was little way out of your predicament, Sveti, and he wedded you to save you."

"Ha! He said he wedded me because he wanted to bed me. He just coerced me into doing it so I couldn't cry rape or foul play later and try to get out of the union. Which I still don't understand why he would want to bind us together." One brow lowered over a squinted eye. "So, then who saves me from him?"

They were quiet for a few minutes. Then Bowie said, "Honey, you need to get dressed. Dev will be waiting." He glanced at his wristband to check the time.

She snorted again. "So? What will he do if I'm late? He's already threatened to spank me." Pink suffused her cheeks at his description of how he would spank her. Naked, tied spread-eagle on her stomach.

Matching red streaked across Bowie's sharp cheekbones. "Uh, TMI, honey. Just, let's just go. Get dressed. It's a pretty dress, I told Dev I bought the one you admired, but," his shoulders bumped with a grin.

"I thought it was too modest for your wedding, so I purchased a different one. Don't worry," he said at the look on her face, "Dev will love it. He may be cold-blooded, but he is a red-blooded male, and you will be a knockout in the dress. Of course," he grinned with a sly wink, "you would still be a living doll wearing a paper bag, and he would still want you."

Before she could respond, he went and took the dress off the hook and brought it to her and placed it in her arms. "Go on now, I'll take your stuff to Dev's," he hesitated at the mutinous curve of her mouth and lowered brows. Dev had told him Sveti did not want to stay with him,

"Uh, that will give you some time to get ready. Okay?"

A knock at the door gave him some reprieve. Letting out a heavy breath, Bowie opened it and Mara, Sveti's maid came in.

"Oh, good, you're here," Bowie said in a rush, "I'll be back in a few," and he raced out the door.

Mara beamed at Sveti. "Hello, miss, I mean, I guess that's missus now." She gave Sveti a big grin avoiding the bleakness in Sveti's sad eyes.

Mara was aware of the prințesă's reluctance to marry the Dravidian, he had warned her before he'd sent her to tend to Sveti. And, she didn't blame her one bit. He was big and tough and rough, hard as steel, lethal aggression radiated out of his very essence.

She'd heard the rumors about how he was in bed, she shivered half in fear, half in desire, they said he was violent, very violent. Not hitting the females, just his, acts were violent.

But, Mara shrugged, she heard the ones he'd been with begged him for a second shot but he always refused. The little prințesă was the only woman he had ever had stay in his chambers. And, Mara swooned just a tad, he was marrying her.

Everyone that knows him said they didn't believe it, not the powerful, cold, brutal spawn of Satan. Women had been trying to snag him for centuries.

She peered at the young woman with the flaming hair. She could see, if it was anyone, it would be her. The prințesă was the polar opposite of the Devil warrior. He was all tough iron, arrogance and icy masculinity. Whereas she was soft and sweet, kind and elegant.

Studying Sveti, Mara smiled. They had some things in common though. They were both courageous and stubborn.

"Come, Prinţesă, let's get you ready. Mr. Bowie got you shoes that will be perfect for your gown."

Wearing his dress uniform, a black tunic and slacks with almost imperceptible filaments of gold threading through, his hair in warlord braids as befitting his status, Dev stood waiting for Sveti.

He couldn't believe he wasn't fraught with nerves, not that he has ever been in his life, but still. He was binding himself to a woman, one woman, forgoing all others forever. The thought did not bother him a whit. Sveti was more than enough woman for him.

He had only lived with men before, Brahms and his lieutenants, his friends. He couldn't believe he was about to share his residence, his bed, his life, with a female.

Aye, he should be totally freaked, but he only felt utter calm, peace. It hadn't been easy, but he'd gotten what he wanted. Svetiessa was about to fully become his.

She already was, from the fluids that now surged through her beautiful body, but they were to be lawfully joined in front of the world. Zues, he wanted to wake up every morning with her in his arms.

It would all be perfect if not for that one pesky little thing, she did not want to be married to him. Ah, she will get over it, she will get used to him. It was a chauvinistic, self-centered thought, but he had never pretended to be otherwise. Although, he did feel a tiny twinge in the back of his heart that the woman he chose, did not want him.

The grins of his closest friends, Tomi, Lukas, Connar didn't help the matter.

To the background tune of quiet chattering and light music, Dev fought to not look at his timelink on his wrist. He already knew she was late. A frown pulled his dark brows down, she better not be refusing to come with Bowie, yet Bowie would have sent him a message on his link if she had.

His brows slashed down further, unless Bowie was struggling to argue with her to get her to come on her own. His hands fisted, well, if that little female, his fucking wife, thought she would refuse her husband- the chattering diminished as the crowd took in the groom's black countenance.

Alarm twittered throughout the chamber at the brutal anger in warlord's hard face. Sympathy sprouted from a few for the little bride he was marrying. No one wanted that fierce anger directed at them.

His features harsh and jagged with ire, Dev started down the steps then stopped abruptly.

She was here.

The room was decorated in lavender, pink and white, and filled with all of the personnel on his ship, his warriors, their wives, girlfriends, a grand hush fell over the room.

Bowie was grinning like a buffoon at Dev, but Dev only had eyes for Sveti. A shiver literally ran up his spine.

Her dress was a soft, sheer, shimmering pearl. Faint embroidered flowers and a curved design danced over the voile. Tiny pearls strung sewn along the low bodice, although fully transparent almost to her nipples, it was embroidered with a lace and curlicue design, as were the cap sleeves also trimmed with miniature pearls.

The middle section slightly opaque showcased Sveti's hot little figure, the design ended just past her thighs then flared out to elegant, sheer chiffon in a mermaid style.

Dev knew that wasn't the dress Sveti had admired. Bowie had described it, said it had been blush and nowhere near as damned risqué as this one. Freezing the frown that threatened to make his face even stonier, there was no way Sveti would be wearing this dress again.

It was so light and delicate, his big thick fingers would have it in shreds no matter how careful he was. And he would be taking it off her, his dick flared right along with the sheer skirt.

She was so sexy in it, it was all he could do to keep from striding to her, throwing her over his shoulder like a troglodyte and carrying her to the nearest closed room, tear the dress off her and fuck her up against the wall. His mouth quirked up at the corner, Bowie, the bastard, had gone to the store and made his own choice.

Dev glanced at his friend. His grin as big as ever, Bowie winked at him. Bowie knew exactly what Dev was thinking, the bastard. Dev shook his head at him, then returned his attention back to his stunning bride.

Sveti's flaming hair was swept up to a soft twirl to the side of her head with three fat, loose ringlets, one rolled down the front of her, the other two down the low cut back of the dress. The lowlights shimmied off the dress and her fiery hair, and over her lush breasts that molded above the bodice.

Feeling his erection swelling, Dev quickly raised his eyes from her glorious tits that Bowie had decided to put on display for every asshole present to enjoy, and looked up to her face.

Her head was high, spine regal, those that didn't know her would think she was royally composed, with the bearing of the true princess that she was.

But, Dev could see the apprehension that wavered through her eyes as she looked around the room with astonished surprise at the people gathered there. All of whom were smiling at her. Her gaze drew to him.

He tried to smile at her, help ease her, but he couldn't. His heart was in his throat clogging the air to his brain, and he was busy fighting the erection that the damned dress gave him.

But now relief was clearing the tension in his shoulders, fear had tightened them with worry that something would transpire to prevent the wedding from happening. Hmm, his mouth nicked in, he had never worried about anything in his life before.

The strain of desiring her without being able to consummate it at this very minute only made his harsh face more fierce. A shiver ran through men and women alike but for different reasons. His severe toughness made men nervous but titillated the female gender.

Dev had never craved a woman like he did Sveti. His knees were almost weak with the depth of feeling he had for her. The very thought of life without her made his stomach twist empty in pain.

His brows twitched. Was that love? Nay, he was not capable of possessing that emotion, he blinked the foreign thought away.

Soft music played and Bowie was bringing Sveti to him. Dev could see under Bowie's smile, he was whispering encouraging words to her while propelling her up the aisle. If not for the blush Mara had swept on her round cheeks, she would be pale as a swan's down.

It was fucked up that his bride had to be dragged to her own wedding, and looked at her husband with terror, and a shade of anger too for him forcing this on her.

But, it was what it was, she had to marry him or face the unknown which, since males were bidding for her online, didn't bode well that any of them weren't dangerous sickos.

It didn't take long for them to get to where Dev waited with Brahms on one side of him and a captain who would do the ceremony, the room wasn't that big. They were standing on a small raised alter.

Bowie walked Sveti up the three steps then tugged her cold hand that was clinging with a death-grip to his arm and placed it on Dev's. Before she could pull it away, Dev laid his hard hand over it.

Bowie stood beside Sveti as her witness. He gave her a quick wink. She stood towered over by the four immense warriors.

Dev gently turned Sveti so they faced the captain.

Captain Horatio read the necessary words, and Dev and Sveti said their vows.

Dev spoke his in a low gruff voice. After the captain having to prompt her, Sveti was barely audible, her hushed voice had a tremble in it, and she said her vows to his shoulder, not looking him in the eye, even when he squeezed her hand trying to get her to.

Except when he got to the part where Dev had the captain add in the old fashioned 'obey your husband' part in her vows. Her flaming brows spiked down and she flashed a scowl at him, then, with a smug smile, she finished her vows without saying the word 'obey.'

A sly grin tugged up his harsh face as he mouthed the word, 'punishment' to her.

A flicker of fear trickled over her face along with what looked to Dev like a shock of sudden lust that darkened her baby blues.

Ah, his bride was thinking about the spanking he'd promised, but less with fear and more with, could he hope- desire? Damn, his hands were sweating, the games he was going to teach her…

The captain droned on, Sveti's lips parted in surprise when Brahms held his palm out with two wedding bands on it. What little color she had drained from her soft complexion, her eyes darted up to Dev. He regarded her solemnly.

For the first time she spoke to him, "I don't think rings are necessary." She whispered, "You certainly can't fight with one on your finger, it would hinder you, and so I don't need to wear one either." It would be so much harder to flee from him with his brand on her.

His eyes directed hard and level right into hers, Dev took the smaller ring and pushed it on her finger quietly reciting his marriage promise. When it was her turn, she hesitated.

"Svetiessa," he murmured.

She picked it up and with nerveless fingers pushed it on his thick finger, with her head lowered she repeated the promise.

The cool mellifilia metal felt strange on his skin. He looked down at it, then at hers, he smiled, then looked up at her. He wanted his claim on her to be crystal clear to any male that would think to hit on her. She was his. Her eyes were fixed on him, her thoughts unreadable.

"You may kiss your bride," the captain announced with a broad smile.

Dev had chosen to have the ancient ceremony of the Earth, being the chauvinist that he was, he liked the old fashion tradition of it.

Sveti was staring at the round piece of exotic metal on her finger. Dev cupped her face with both hands and gently lifted her head to seal his lips on hers. The fire that was always ignited whenever he touched her, especially those cherry lips, burst into flames. He had to keep the kiss short or he'd be embarrassing himself walking out, and the small stage would truly be on fire.

"Please welcome, Principé and Prinţesă, Mr. and Mrs. Devilos Dravidian!" Captain Horatio announced loudly.

Dev disregarded the look she shot at him that he deigned to force her to take his name, it was so outdated, but again, he liked the old fashioned Earthly aspect of it.

Her acquiring his name made him feel they were more blended as one, and that she was now, in all ways, his. She could fight about carrying his name all she wanted to later, but it was on their legal documents and she would have to go by it.

Dev took her hand and raised it in the air to the cheers and clapping, and good wishes circulating in the room.

After the ceremony, there was food, drinking and dancing. Teeth grit, Dev had to watch other men, his best friends included, claiming dances with Sveti and keep his cool. Whatever. It was for the last time.

His bottom lip bunched. Bowie had grabbed her up and the bastard was holding his wife as close to him as he could. He was doing it on purpose to rile Dev, and it was working.

Dev paid no attention to the babbly women he held while circling the small floor, all he could think about was Sveti's tits mushed all over Bowie's chest, their pelvises and thighs touching, he wondered if her nipples were hard, poking into- shit, he couldn't wait for the night to get over and he could have her alone.

A few dances later, as soon as it was polite, Dev strode over and snatched Sveti out of Connar's big arms. "Sorry bro, it's time for us to leave."

Ignoring Connar's leer and Sveti's suddenly white face, Dev took her hand and led her through the crowded room, letting people give their well wishes, and lewd comments for the new couple.

The fierce powerful warlord, horns pushing up through the braids all over his head showering down his shoulders and back, and the dainty, angelic but sinfully built, prințesă. Men put their hands on her and gave her kisses until Dev thought he would fucking explode. Finally they were out.

Holding her hand, Dev led her along the main boardwalk of the sphere-enclosed station. A hundred thousand people resided there on a fluctuating basis.

They passed shops and bars, a green park, until they were back to their section. They continued in silence strolling the long corridors and elevators to his suite. The closer they got, the stiffer her hand became in his hand and the slower she walked.

She was trying his patience. She acted like he was a monster for fuck's sake and she was on the way to being slaughtered as a sacrifice or something. Okay, so technically he *was* a monster, but still, she didn't need to be so goddamned terrified of him, and she clearly did not want to be wedded to him, or be alone with him.

Pique scraped his mouth into a rigid line, his jaw working, he shoved his cardkey into the door, it slid open. When Sveti tried to hold back, he bent and lifted her in his arms.

"Sire! What are you doing!" she shrieked.

"Goddammit woman, what did I tell you about my name?" Growling his irritation, he carried her over the threshold, another ancient tradition. She was soft and curvy in his arms, he unconsciously held her closer to his chest drawing in her heady woman's warmth and fragrance.

Remembering his threat of punishment, Sveti exclaimed, "De- Devilos, please, I didn't mean anything by it," her arm swung around his neck or it would have gotten crushed against his chest. The one ringlet bounced over her chest, the other two trailed down her back and over his arm. They were both reminded of when, he, fully dressed, had carried her almost naked to her bedroom.

"I know. Your nerves are wrung tight." He strode through the small vestibule into the living room.

Still holding her, Dev looked down, his heart quivered at the raw fear crimping his new bride's face. "Please relax, Svetiessa. I promise, I won't do anything you don't want me to tonight. We can just go to bed, I mean just go to sleep. I would of course like to consummate our joining, but," he sighed gently, "I hate to see that damned palpable fear of me in your eyes."

He wanted her to fear him on one level, he needed her to obey him. He had lived centuries, she had only lived a short life even for a mortal, he knew the dangers of the world that she was so innocent of, and he had to protect her.

She had been about to trot down the avenue and throw herself at the first prince, stranger, she came to, for Zues' sake, thinking it would solve her problems.

Long lashes curled around the big blues gazing up at him. "Thank you, Devilos," she said quietly.

He waited for more, when she said nothing, he set her down. "Here," he said, moving to a bucket on a table and drew out a bottle of champagne with a towel wrapped around it. "We can at least toast to our union. Okay?" And maybe the alcohol would loosen her up a little.

He quickly unbuttoned his black tunic, shrugged it off and tossed it on a chair then rolled up the sleeves of the white shirt. Lifting the bottle, he twisted the wire off and the cork out and poured the bubbly liquid into flowing flutes. He set the bottle in the bucket and handed her a glass and then picked up the other.

Sveti lifted the glass to her nose then giggled.

"What?" he asked, stupefied by her giggle. He'd barely heard it before and it was musical, sweetly girlish, and bubbly like the champagne, his groin and heart ached as one.

"The bubbles, they tickle my nose." She grinned at him and he felt his heart flip over and bang against his ribs.

"Uh, aye." He cleared his throat and raised his glass and said, "To us, my beautiful bride." He waited for her to lift her glass to clink with his. She did, murmuring, "Um, to us."

Dev slugged down half his flute while she just watched him. "Drink, Svetiessa, there is no point to a toast if you don't drink after."

She looked down at the pale golden bubbles. "Um, okay. But, Devilos, I really haven't drunk liquor before."

"You had wine at the- you know when we danced that first time."

Shaking her head. "No, I never got to drink it, that man, Charlie, took me right away to dance-" She stopped at the darkness that crept into his skin and through his eyes. "Okay." She quickly tipped the glass to her lips and drank several mouthfuls, and then choked and sputtered as the bubbles tickled down her throat.

Laughing, Dev patted her gently on the back. "Slower, honey, you need to sip slower." He took a sip of his own glass then when she didn't drink anymore he said, "Slower, but drink, it will help take the tension out of your bones." *And make your legs more spreadable for your husband.*

She complied taking a more careful drink.

Grabbing up the bucket, he tucked it under his arm and grasped his flute in one hand, he said, "Come," and held his hand out, "let's go on the balcony."

She put her small hand in his and he took her across the room and through glass doors that swished to the side as they passed through.

The suite was up high; they could see much of the space station. It was night, but people were prowling the restaurants and bars. The complex teemed with all kinds of creatures making their way to somewhere.

Leaning against the railing, Sveti took a sip and smiled. "This is a great balcony, Devilos, you can see forever. Even through the clear dome I can see the evening sky and stars." She held her glass in both hands staring in awe at the scenery beyond them. Dev set his fingers on the bottom of her flute and lifted it to her lips.

"Okay," she laughed, "I get the hint." They leaned against the railing and for the first time, chatted comfortably.

She asked, "Your parents, do you, uh, have any?"

One big shoulder shrugged. "Not in the respect that you have, or could understand. I was in training as soon as I could walk. That was throughout my growing years."

Her lips pushed to a pout. "That sounds…lonely. Don't you have any siblings?"

He nodded, the braids flopped over his chest. "Aye. You will meet them at some point. My brothers trained as I did, but we never lived in what you would call a…house as a family."

"Hmm. A home. A building you live in is a house, the people you choose to live with are your home."

Dev wiped his fingers and thumb down the side of his mouth and pondered her, and her words. His deep voice quiet, he said, "You are my home now, Svetiessa."

Those long lashes flowed up, then down to cover her thoughts, then rose so he could see them. "I…" she didn't know what to say. It was the most profound, nicest thing he has said to her. Did she hear longing in his voice? Her lids narrowed at him, but he appeared fully without guile. Which was funny, because by his own nature, he was cunning.

Chapter Twenty-Two

After a sip, he set his flute on the wide railing, without looking at her, Dev commented coolly, "That's a real, ah, pretty dress, Svetiessa."

She looked down at the sheer lacy voile with wry chagrin. "You think so? You said Bowie had purchased a dress I had liked, but I sure did not admire this one. It is too-too-"

"Sexy?"

The color seeped into her cheeks with her slight nod, she set her glass beside his. "Yes. I feel a little, um, I don't know," she stared at the soft gown, raised the flouncy hem a bit, it fluttered like an early spring breeze.

"Sexy?" he repeated and turned to her, his heated gaze ruffled down her form, he kept his lids lowered so she couldn't see the white streaking in his dark eyes, and willed his horns to not grow.

As soon as she would see the telltale evidence of his arousal she'd find a reason to bolt. He casually lifted a long ringlet off the front of her, his fingers faintly swept the bare swell of her bosom, and dipped slightly into her cleavage.

Her cheeks flamed, she didn't know if he'd done that on purpose or not. She peered up at him suspiciously through the end curl of her lashes. He was calmly sifting the ringlet through his fingers, but his eyes were on her bodice, which made her cheeks burn hotter.

"So," Sveti said feeling awkward, "is Brahms going to be here tonight? Will he come and, um," her gaze drifted up to his head, "undo your braids? Or do you sleep in them?" Dev looked about to plunge into the neckline of her gown any second.

He settled the ringlet behind her back and this time, deliberately stroked his fingers over the top rounds of her breasts. "Nay. I don't sleep in them but it is our wedding night, he will stay in his own chambers. We will have total privacy."

The pads of his fingertips sifted softly over her mounds making her nipples pop through the sheer material. His pupils expanded, he didn't look up at the rebuke sure to be directed at him. She was flypaper, and he, aye, he was the fly. He could not resist touching her soft skin, her sweet breasts.

She stepped out of his tantalizing reach, her hands trembled. "Devilos, you said you wouldn't, force, uh, push me tonight to…"

His rich dark orbs ablaze with white rose to her unsteady blues.

"Devilos, you said-"

The huge shoulders hunched, his sigh heavy and deep, he tucked his hands in his pockets. "Aye, I did promise you I wouldn't push you. But," he said with a cheeky grin, "I won't say no if you want to follow tradition and tell me you want to consummate our marriage," his brows wriggled at her.

He dug his hands deeper into his pockets. "But, Zues, Sveti, that dress," pupils dilating, his eyes swooped down her body to her feet and back up, his chest swelled with a weighty inhale.

"You're already temptation beyond belief, but you look like heavenly sin, so fucking hot in that thing, I, I don't know." He knew he should say it would be best if he left, went and bunked with Bowie, but hell, it was their wedding night.

The air fell out of his chest with a beleaguered sigh, he couldn't make his mouth say the words or his force his feet to walk out the door.

Sveti picked up her flute and drank half her glass of champagne with nervous gulps. "How about I undo your braids for you?"

"Really?" He looked so boyishly surprised, an unnatural, but to Sveti, an endearing look for him.

She nodded. "Yes, I'd like to do that. Can we do it now?" She was bewildered at her own urge to touch him; his hair should be...safe.

He perused her for a moment, then picked up the bucket and said, "Let's go in where we can sit comfortably," gesturing towards the living room with his flute in his hand.

At her shaky nod, he led the way back inside. Setting the bucket on the coffee table, he went to the wall controls and dimmed the lights just a bit, set soft background music barely audible.

When he walked back to Sveti she was standing awkwardly, unsure of what to do.

He took her hand and settled her on the same sofa he had attacked her on that day he'd been mindless with jealousy. Then he stood, unsure, knowing if he was on the sofa beside her he was unlikely to keep his hands to himself.

She sat gracefully and set her glass on the table. When he just stood there, she said shyly patting the couch, "Here, sit down, you know I can't reach you if you're standing."

It appeared to Sveti that he was warring with himself, questioning whether he had the will power to be so close to her in that flimsy dress and not jump her. When he sat down, she let out her held breath.

He turned his back to her. Moving her skirt aside, she got on her knees on the firm cushion, and slowly, gently, untied the braids she could reach, drawing her fingers through each one combing the kinks out. When not braided, his hair was bone silky straight. "Mmmm, Devilos, your hair is so soft."

"You are surprised?" he asked with a chuckle.

One shoulder bumped in a half shrug. "Well, everything else on you is so hard. Your chest, your shoulders, your big rocky arms, even your face, everything is hard-" She broke off feeling the heat rise up her body, knowing what he was thinking. His horns swelled above the braids.

Watching them, she wondered what they felt like. She tentatively stroked a finger like a breath over the curve of one. It jumped, as did the rest of him.

"Shit, Svetiessa!"

"I'm sorry, I was...curious, did I hurt you?"

He grunted, giving his body a settling shake. "Nay, they are sensitive, like my, uh, they are somewhat parallel to my...manhood." He'd never been bashful to speak frankly about such things, except, now, Sveti was so sweet, shy, untouched except by him.

Hmm, he rather liked the thought that he was the only man to ever have been with her.

241

His horns pulsed from her caress. Normally he didn't care for women touching his horns. Those that did without asking were given a warning bite, and not a sensual one.

His mouth hitched up at the edge in a short smile. "Feel free to touch anything on me you want, honey, just know, the hotter I get, the less control I wield."

"Ahem," clearing her throat, she murmured, "uh, there, I've gotten all the ones in the back and to the side, you need to turn around and bend your head over."

He twisted around, saw her telltale pink cheeks and knew she was well aware her comment made them both think about how hard his shaft could be, and at the moment, was. He bent his head so she could reach the top of it.

His loose hair glided around his shoulders veiling the sides of his rugged face. Unfortunately, he was now eye-level with her cleavage. "This, uh," he took a stiff breath, "this is the first time anyone other than myself or Brahms has unbraided my hair."

"Oh really? None of your, um, other women did this?" She tucked the tip of her tongue out of the corner of her mouth as she plucked the twined hair apart.

He glanced up and saw her tongue. Damn but he wanted it in his mouth, to suck on. His snort was of inconsequence. "Hell no, I never stayed long enough with a woman to-" Of course no woman had ever offered before, not that he would have let anyone other than Brahms groom his hair. But, Zues this was sweet, fucking intimate.

"Svetiessa, I don't want to talk about other women. As far as I'm concerned, there were none before you and there won't be any after. I did not marry any of them, I married you. Let's not bring other people into our wedding night, okay?"

"Hmmm." It made her stomach pinch picturing her warlord with his Greek godlike body with another woman. His lips on a voluptuous, robust woman, Rianna perhaps, the kind he likes, and his strong, demanding hands groping her enormous breasts while sucking a nipple into his handsome mouth.

"Devilos, um, I am not like your other women, the type you like. Why have you saddled yourself to me?" Her hands paused on a braid.

An annoyed growl brewed, he curled a finger under her chin, meeting her perplexed gaze. "Svetiessa," he growled and took a breath.

"Wife, I have explained that to you. Those kinds of women were easy and fast, a source of release only. You," he slipped his fingertips through the side of her hair and brushed her lips lightly with his, his voice lowered sensually, "are different. Special, what I want. You make my blood boil like none ever has. You eclipse all thoughts of other females, forever.

"You are the most beautiful creature I have ever seen in my life. Now, stop going there. Stop bringing other people into our life that is only ours now. No one else's." He kissed her lightly again then lowered his head for her to finish.

She only had a few braids to undo. Unwinding the last, she lifted her arms to comb her fingers through the loose locks. With her hands over her head it caused her breasts to bunch together and wiggle with her movements. Dev groaned out loud.

She immediately dropped her arms. "What? I'm sorry, did I pull your hair?"

"Listen, Svetiessa, I know I promised I wouldn't push you, but, there is no way I can be this close to you, and you in that dress, and sleep next to you without," his head shook dolefully back and forth. He looked up from her cleavage, his skin darkened; the vein at his temple was going nuts.

"How about," his voice soft and moltenly rough, "if I tell you up front, that," he brushed back the ringlet that had drifted back over her chest, "I have been dying all day to kiss you, and touch you," his gaze dipped to her breasts.

"What if instead of pouncing on you, or methodically seducing you, I ask you. My wife," he said quietly, "can I kiss you?"

Sveti looked at him in astonishment. This powerful dangerous warlord who took what he wanted, when he wanted, was asking his wife, who he had every right to kiss, if he could. Her gaze roamed over his face.

His head was twice the size of hers, skin more tanned than weathered. Tough jaw, dark with manly shadow, cheekbones sharply defined, indomitable. He had a beautiful mouth, really, full lips but sculpted purely masculine. Firm but so, so, soft.

Brushing her fingertips over his pointed ears, she slipped them under his hair and cupped the sides of his head, and pulled him to her. Their lips met, his didn't move. Smiling, she realized he was letting her truly chose what she wanted.

Shyly, she licked his lips like he'd done to her, it always gave her shivers, and it had the same effect on him. Then she slanted her head slightly to the side and pushed his cooperative lips open.

Her tongue slipped just inside his mouth, she tasted his teeth, explored his mouth, then with tiny shy stabs, she stroked his tongue.

It was all he could take. Dev curled one hand around her head, the other on her back to pull her closer and taught her how to fire up the kiss. In moments they were both panting.

Pulling from him to catch her breath, Sveti could feel the dampness between her legs; she didn't have to look down to see if he was hard.

"Svetiessa," he huffed roughly, "I want to touch you, say yes." The dress was scooped low across the front leaving her shoulders almost bare, the lightly embroidered sheer sleeves started just at the curve of her shoulders.

Dev put both hands to the sides of her head, his thumbs brushing the hollows under her cheeks, to keep touching her but not seducing.

He looked so earnest, so dying to take her, the strain of holding himself back was apparent in the clench of his jaw, the narrowed eyes, the struggle to keep from digging his fingers into her face with his tenseness.

As downright scary as he was, Sveti sighed, he was equally gorgeous, in a tough, aggressive, fierce kind of a way.

She did something next that stunned him so much he froze.

Chapter Twenty-Three

She hiked the dress up a bit then climbed on his lap and straddled him. Sveti smiled inwardly at his sharp inhale.

The color in his skin deepened, his voice husky, Dev rasped, "Svetiessa, honey, I can't play like this. You sit like that and I have to tell you, warn you, I'll be all over you. No seduction, just pure action." His hands fell to her hips. "You need to get off-"

She grabbed his head and pulled his mouth to hers and burned his lips up with a scorching kiss. His groan went through her lips and down her throat, so rumbly deep she felt shivers to her core.

He mumbled against her mouth, "I'm taking that as a yes," and dove into a potent tongue-lashing kiss. He waited a few heartbeats to make sure she was acquiescing then he moved his hands slowly to cover her breasts over the filmy material.

When she didn't protest, or move her lips from his, he gripped them harder. She shivered in his hands. His big fingers clenching her supple globes, Dev leaned back from her and took in the beauty on his lap. She looked dreamy, her eyes closed, lips parted from their kiss.

Sveti slowly opened her eyes to see his blazing silvery back at her, his hard hands cupping, fondling her breasts.

When she shivered, his voice a silky rasp, Dev said, "This dress is as fine and delicate as you. I will try my best to not destroy it while I peel it off you." His long arms reaching around her, he pulled the invisible zipper in the back all the way down, slowly.

He had studied the dress the entire reception trying to figure out how to get it off her without destroying it. He trickled his fingertips up her bare arms as he moved his hands to her front.

Sveti felt his fingers shift to the neckline and pull it down. The dress had a built in bra. The cool air chilled her already puckered nipples stiffening them to hard little berries. But it felt oh so good, the air sliding over her bare breasts.

She watched Dev's snow white eyes lower to drink them in as his hands went back to cup the fullness of her woman's flesh. His fingers clenching her breasts, his thumbs rubbed over her nipples, they both looked down to watch his dark hard hands caressing, then crushing her full creamy flesh.

His hands full of her plump flesh, squeezing, his groan low and rough, hers quieter, more feminine yet equally erotic.

Dev let her plush pillows go to pull the sleeves of the dress down to bare her completely to the waist. His eyes glowed at her fair bounty.

"Ah, God's Zues, *má drogaste, má ádainn prinţesă,* my love, my beautiful prinţesă, you are more breathtaking than the night's sky with all its diamond stars glittering in it." His head lowered, he licked a nipple, bit it until she gasped, then sucked it into his mouth to lick it harder.

"*Ohh*," the moan scraped up her throat, her head fell back, tiny tremors rolled over her shoulders. Opening her eyes, Sveti reached for the buttons on his shirt. He had to move his hands for her to undo them.

His palms fell to her thighs while he watched his shy little bride unbutton each button. When she reached up to his shoulders to push the shirt back, he grasped her breasts again making her giggle.

"You are a wicked man, Devilos Dravidian," she accused, arching her back, her feminine purr mingled with his deep gruff growl at his hard hands kneading her soft flesh.

She moved her hands to stroke her palms up his bare chest, his hands dropped to her thighs thrilling at her tentative strokes growing bolder.

When she reached up again to shove his shirt off his shoulders, his hands slid under her gown and up her thighs to pet her core with his thumbs over her tiny silk panties.

Audaciously, he lifted the hem of the dress to peer at her panties, and smiled. "Ah, nice, Wife, white silk with lace trim, fucking virginal hot," he pushed the skirt all the way up past her thighs.

His shoulders so broad, she still struggled to get his shirt off, he shrugged out of it tossing it to the floor.

"I like this position, baby, you straddling me, your dress all bunched up around your waist, I can see, and touch your pussy and," he leaned over and swiped his tongue over a nipple, "lick your tits at the same time."

Suddenly shy at being so exposed in front of him and his bold, crude language, Sveti moved a hand to cover her breasts and the other to primly shove her skirt down.

He caught her hands and held them back. "Uh huh, you can't just give me a glimpse of your naked beauty and take it away."

Holding her hands, he said seriously, "Svetiessa, I'm really too, ah, far gone to stop. Please don't try to make me." His gaze swept her bare breasts down to her panties that were sheer enough he could almost see through them, then up to her heart-melting pretty eyes.

He let one of her wrists go to cradle her head, and see what she would do. She hesitated, then reached for his belt. A smile curved up his hard face, he let go of her other hand and she unbuckled his belt.

Sveti smiled shyly up at him through her fringe of lashes. Keeping their eyes connected, she unbuttoned then unzipped his pants. Bolts of white lightening shot through his dark orbs, his jaw worked, vein thumped at his temple.

When she reached her hand into his pants to wrap her small fingers around his raging erection, his shredded groan graveled out, sparks of flames danced along the back of the couch.

"God's Zues, Wife," he moaned.

Using both hands, Sveti pulled out his engorged member. She spread his pants open, pushed his briefs down to get a better grasp of him. She wrapped both hands around it.

He made a strangled sound that sounded like he was dying, she looked up at him, he was staring at her hands, then his head fell back, eyes closed, and he groaned.

Dev wrapped one of his big hands over her small one to show her how to grip him, and moved her palm up and down on his hard flesh.

Sveti had never seen a man's shaft like this, up close and personal. Except for when she and Dev had sex, but then she was too unnerved to take a good look at the huge thing. He released her hand to let her freely stroke him.

Wanting to see what he actually felt like, she stopped pumping to lightly draw her fingers down his shaft, around, and back up, his growl deepened when she circled the tender top. A tiny tear of cream spooled from the end, she dipped her fingertip to touch it, his body jerked.

"Svetiessa, I think that's…uh…enough…uh," he ground his phallus into her hands as she gripped him hard. Her fingers coiled back down his length, she slipped her hands under to cup his balls, see what the heaviness of them felt like in her hands.

"Shit, Sveti- ah," he groaned and leaned forward, he grasped her wrists to move them, smiled weakly at her. "I want more baby, I want to come inside you."

As Dev talked quietly he slid his hand in her panties to finger her clit. Her hips shifted on his lap, he wasn't sure if it was to move from his touch, or to it.

Zues, she looked so incredible, naked from the waist up, her breasts soft spherical gleams in the low light, her head arched back, her thighs spread open over his legs baring herself to him, as she now definitely pushed her hips at his fingers.

He titillated her slit with his fingers, pinching her bud, her hips shimmied with her silky whimpers, when she reached up to gently stroke his horns, her thighs spread further. That did him in.

With a hoarse grumbled growl, he wrapped his hands around her waist and lifted her as he stood. She was surprised as he set her on her feet and before she could react, he slipped his fingers in the dress that was now bunched around her waist.

Kneeling, he very carefully, never feeling more lugging and clumsy than he did at that moment trying not to rend the sheer fragile dress with his big rough paws, slowly pushed the dress down over her hips, down her legs to the floor.

If she were any other woman he would have just shoved the skirt up and fucked her. But this was Sveti, and their wedding night. She probably wanted to preserve the special dress, and he didn't want to be the wild animal he had been before.

Not until down the road when she could take it, would *want* to take it.

"Nice shoes, babe," he huskily complimented the very high white peep-toes. "I'd love to feel them stabbing into my back, maybe later, but for now," he lifted a leg and peeled off one shoe then the other, and sat back on his heels to gaze at her standing there in only her sheer white panties.

"You are a vision, *má ádainn prinţesă,* the daintiest thing I've ever seen in my long life." Lifting off his heels to kneel upright again, he gripped her breasts.

"Devilos, what are you-"

His manhood was iron hard and thick sticking partially out of his open pants, he apologized, "Sorry baby, I can't get enough of them, it's unlikely I ever will." He kneaded her plump flesh for a moment, gazed longingly at them then turned her around to face the couch and pressed her to her knees.

"Uh, Devilos," she whispered, unsure what he was up to, she was nervous again.

His hand on her back he gently bent her and moved her arms to rest on the couch cushion.

"Don't move, sweetheart," he murmured enjoying the sight of her panty clad butt up in the air. Zues, but she blew his mind. He palmed her ass, squeezing, enjoying the perfect roundness.

"Every part of you, Svetiessa," he sighed, "*ahh,*" squeezed harder, "is so fine, so damned perfect…"

He quickly shucked his pants, briefs, socks and boots and knelt down behind her. He slipped her panties down to her knees, but she didn't budge for him to take them off. "Baby, I don't want to tear these," he smiled when she moved her legs so he could remove them.

"I'm not sure, what are you doing, Devilos?" The uncertainty of her inexperience wavered in her hushed voice.

"Ahh, sweetheart, trust me. I do anything that hurts you or freaks you out, you tell me, I will stop."

Bending, he kissed her bare bottom, kneaded it, then gently slid his thumbs in the lower part of the crease, and sucked a deep red mark on her fair skin with his teeth and lips.

"No, Devilos," she objected faintly but wriggled her cheeks against his hands and mouth with a slight shuddering moan.

His soft chuckle wisped against her skin. "Okay, baby, no worries." Kissing her bottom, he stroked his palms up her back relishing the softness of her tiny waist and slender back.

He caressed and kneaded her small delicate shoulders, then drew his hands lingeringly back down to cup her ass and squeezed gently.

Sveti's arms on the couch, her bottom stuck up in the air in front of his face, her skin was flushing with mortified red. His rough hands came around the front of her to grope her breasts then he skimmed his palms down her ribs to her pelvis.

He nudged her legs further apart with his knees and stroked her core. Her soft body quivered under him. Dev leaned over her, his chest brushing her back, and stroked her clitoris, pinching and prodding her hardened bud.

When she moaned slightly with a grinding writhe of her hips, he slid a finger inside her. "Ah, good, baby, you are wet, ready for me."

He played with her sex, smoothing her silk over her slit and circling her bud with his thumb while moving his finger inside, stroking over her sensitive erogenous bits, added a finger, and in and out of her until louder cries of urgent excitement eked out of her beautiful lips.

Her hips reared at his hand, he dropped his lips to her neck, moved her ringlets aside and licked her skin, sucked her flesh, pinching with his sharp teeth.

He brought her to the very edge then pulled his fingers from her. Fisting his throbbing granite hard-on, he brought it to her core's opening.

Dazed, her voice woozy, "Devilos? Please, let me, uh, go, uh, come," her breath rasped up her constricted throat, her hips strafed at his phallus.

His groan so deep his chest reverberated like a hungry bear, Dev started pushing into her. "Baby, I want your orgasm around me," he growled in her ear, "if you want me to stop, *ah*," he groaned at her slick tight sheath clutching around him, he couldn't finish his sentence.

Her hips abraded his pelvis helping him push slowly into her until he was fully embedded. He grinned, she was liking it. He paused for her to adjust to his bulk, his thick hardness, then whispered, "You okay, baby?"

Her fists bunched on the cushion as she struggled to adapt to him, he felt different, was deeper than before. His shaft stretched her, her body strove to accept his substantial rigid length.

Braced on one hand, he moved carefully out then pushed back in slowly, his fingers found her sex and stroked her. He could feel his organ as it slid out and back in, his tight testicles slapping her thighs.

His thick chest brushed her back, expanding into her with every heavy breath. But she was not responding as she had been.

He gingerly pulled out of her, lay down on the floor on his back and brought her to straddle him.

"Wha- what are you doing," her breath gushed with the sudden movement, hair swept around to spiral on the dark hair of his chest. He wrapped his hands around her hips.

"I was giving you more pain than pleasure, sweetheart." He brushed a ringlet out of her face. "You are so small, tight, we'll wait until we have more…experience before we do that again."

Her tense smile softened, slender thighs hugged him. "What do we do now?"

He lifted her hips and said, "Put me in you, try it," he nodded at the unsure indenting of her brows.

He held her up, and she was on her knees, it was difficult, he was so big, but she maneuvered him so the tip was against her opening and he lowered her down on his phallus, he groaned. "Okay," he voice shook, "lean over, let me feel those tits on my chest," he waited while she did.

"Oh, Devilos, that's nice," she oozed, rubbing her bare breasts on his fur.

"Aye, okay, grab ahold of my horns."

"Really?"

Nodding, he murmured, "Aye."

She leaned forward to hold onto his horns. He winced at the wave of sheer pleasure that roared through him at her touch. Holding her hips, he brought her down on his shaft, then raised her up, sliding through her juices.

"That, um, is," she grunted as he pulled her down on his rod, and sighed as he lifted her up, his horns throbbing like crazy in her hands. "So weird, but, hot, erotic," she giggled.

"I feel like I'm riding a horse, Devilos, bareback, lying naked on my stomach and holding onto the saddle horn, my, um, privates rubbing on- *ohh*- actually the saddle horn is," his pull on her hips drew her down harder on his rod.

He did it a few more times, then suddenly flipped her as he rolled so she was on her back and he was on top of her, back inside that sweet sheath.

Hovering over her, he pulled the pins out of her hair, then combed his thick fingers through the long curls fluffing them and spreading them around her head on the carpet.

"This position is called 'vanilla' for its commonness, but it's my favorite, I like seeing you lying spread out under me. All vulnerable, achingly feminine, baby," he rocked into her, loving the way her breasts bobbled with his hard thrusts.

"You just like being dominant, Devi- oh!" her gasp sharp at his sudden deep thrust.

"Aye," agreeing, he came down to brace on his elbows and whispered, "I'm going to go fast and hard, baby, tell me if I need to stop," before his words were out he plunged deep into her and rapidly pulled out, thrust in faster, the bumps on his penis rose, they scraped along the inner walls of her tender channel.

"Uh," Sveti groaned loudly at the bumps rolling in and around and out of her. She matched his rhythm bucking her hips to meet his as his plunges grew wild and manic, hard and deep.

The flush started to blossom up her chest, her eyes rolled in the back of her head, groans mixed with whimpers roiled from her parted lips.

He grasped her knees, lifting them to wrap her legs around his hips, and churned into her like a corkscrew to rub his penile bumps over her hot spots, and run over her clitoris as he pulled out and jammed back in.

Clutching her bobbing breast, he pinched and tugged her nipple, twisting it in his fingers, and leaned to suck on her neck.

Her fingers strung in his hair gripping handfuls, Sveti's back arched in rising euphoria. Feeling his mouth stroke her neck, she tilted her head so he could bite her. The climax climbed up her like a fiery pearl necklace bumping up a jagged ladder.

The heat racing through every cell, her heart quickened in a rush, peels of cutting cries whittled up her throat. When Dev sank his fangs into her neck, her body like a spinning top went airborne, exhilarated cries crashed out of her.

His horns elongated and stabbed into her back, her brain spiked and shot like a jetship rocketing through the galaxies, the stars blinding spangles of light igniting all around her.

Dev's shaft vibrated inside her making her entire body vibrate with her climax, his concrete torso impacting against her soft curves as she undulated as hard as a flag flapping in a hurricane.

Pumping into her silk, withdrawing his fangs and horns, Dev held on long enough to watch Sveti scream into the abyss of unconsciousness with the intensity of her pleasure.

Zues, she was amazing, his body coiled with brilliant, almost unbearable desire for his dainty wife screaming her release in his arms.

Thrusting wildly into her, he let go, his own release, a free-fall feeling of skiing downhill, down the ramp accelerating faster and faster until he hit the curve at the bottom and shot off to soar into the sky exploding into a fireball, his roar of her name reverberating in her hair, his seed erupted, surging into Sveti with his plunges.

Still mindlessly thrusting in her with stinging sensations ratcheting throughout his body, Dev wrapped his arms around Sveti crushing her so tightly to his chest he feared he'd break her.

His brain fried, Dev had to force himself to stop thrusting and drop beside her. Still inside her tender channel, he kept his arms clenched around her sinuous body holding her against him while his penis continued releasing tremors, throbbing against her satin walls.

It took considerable effort for a dazed Sveti to lift her weak, quivering arms to encircle Dev, they lay together feeling as if they were floating on air.

His fingers netting her face, looking her in her drowsy eyes, Dev said quietly, "You all right, Svetiessa, with what we did?"

He prayed she would say it was, but even if she said no, she was his wife and he was so hot for her, they would be having sex daily, he'd make her like it.

"Mmm," smiling, her lids heavy over shining blues, she mumbled, "yes."

"Svetiessa…"

"Hmm?"

"We need to talk about this."

Her eyes flickered, heavy lids lifted. "About what?"

Not stifling his groan, he said, "Our marriage," and struggled to sit up. "You are staying with me, we will have a true marriage, we will have sex regularly." His stated words sounded like commands, but the question was there, was she willing?

She opened her eyes and sat up pulling her hair over to cover her nudity. Her gaze traveled his tousled hair and over unbelievably broad, thick shoulders, hairy chest she could sleep naked on, those kissable lips, iridescent eyes still half white half black.

She glanced down and blushed. He was already hard again. And that impressive manhood.

She sighed. "Yes, Devilos. I take responsibility for the choice I made. I could have refused you. Although you made it pretty impossible for me to do that. But," she hurried on at the annoyance that crept into his rich orbs, "I accept our...marriage."

Bending forward, he twined his fingers and rested his arms on his thighs, frowned. "You don't sound too overjoyed about this...us. You need to reconcile yourself to being my wife. I expect 100% from you."

Her brows arched. "What does that mean? A hundred percent of what?" She pulled her bare legs to the side, draping a slender arm over her naked sex.

Under hooded lids, Dev watched her trying to hide herself from his greedy perusal. A bit of red tinged his hard planed cheeks, he took a deep breath, expelled it.

"I expect you to work with me to make this marriage successful. We are a couple now, I want us to act like one. In private as well as in public. I never desired before to ever have a wife, now that I have one I want it all. That cuddly shit that couples do, you sitting on my lap while I feel you up, kisses in front of others," his head ducked uncharacteristically embarrassed, "uh, holding hands, all that romantic shit."

A pretty laugh gurgled out of her. "That's such a nice way of putting it, Devilos." Her mouth firmed but her eyes twinkled. "I will, I promise."

"Uh huh. That means you honor me-"

She barked, "Don't you say it-"

"Obey me," he smugly kept going, "and like I said before, I expect my husbandly rights, when I want them."

Her brow furrowed hard over her spitting blues. "That is so ancient; I'm not going to obey you just because you're the *man*-"

He cut her off again reaching for her, "That's *husband* to you, babe, and, I want my husbandly rights again, right now." He slid a big hand behind her head and crushed her lips with his while hard fingers glommed over a soft breast.

She struggled, pulled from him. Irritated with his highhanded attitude, yet she felt the heat incinerating between her legs, her nipples were stiff peaks already, passion quaked and thickened her tongue. "Wait, we need to discuss this further, Devilos-"

He grabbed her up in his arms and stood up. Striding naked to the bathroom, before he latched his lips on hers, he said, "We'll talk about it in the shower." His grin evil, "Actually, sweetheart, I have something better you can do with your mouth, I'll show you," his lips covered her objections.

She sighed in his big arms, twined her hands around his neck and surrendered to his plundering lips.

Chapter Twenty-Four

As it turned out, they spent almost week in their suite. They ordered in, or to Dev's delight, Sveti was a superb cook. He even enjoyed just watching her prepare food, she was at ease, her motions graceful, she hummed.

They watched movies, and had sex, a lot. Occasionally they took a walk on the main boardwalk at night under the starry dome.

As she promised, when he took her hand she didn't resist him holding it as they strolled and occasionally dined out. But mostly they stayed inside christening all the rooms, and furniture in the suite.

They were nestled in the bed when his wristband vibrated on the nightstand. Irritated at being disturbed, he snatched it up and snapped, "What?" He listened, then growled his pique, "Fine, I'll be there."

He clicked off the phone on the band and tossed it back on the nightstand. "Baby," he turned to Sveti a contented, sated, purring kitten lying half asleep next to him.

"Mmm?"

He sighed, his hand skimmed down the curve of her waist to cup her bottom. "I have to go meet the commander of the Deslite District. It'll probably take quite a while," his palm roamed up to wrap his long fingers around a breast, caressing the lush tissue. "You stay here, then when I get back-"

"Oh no," she sat up like a springboard. "I am not staying here. Without you," she smiled coyly stroking a finger down his furry chest, sighing when he grasped both breasts, "it would be too boring. I want to go out too."

His grip tightened painfully with his frown, when she squirmed, he released her. "Sorry. I forget my own strength. But where would you go? Nay," he shook his head, loose hair swished over his shoulders. "I don't want you outside without me."

Now she frowned and moved away from his reach to clamor off the other side of the bed. Standing, she insisted, "Don't be ridiculous, I am a grown woman, I can certainly wander around the station by myself. There's a rec room Bowie showed me where a lot of people hang out, I can go there."

His frown deepened into grooves between his eyes.

"Svetiessa," he started, seeing her put her hands on her hips in defiance he sighed. "Okay, one of my team can, no wait, they'll be at the meeting, the guard," mouth pursed, "shit, he's on leave, and I don't trust anyone else to-"

"Devilos, stop it," she said with a pout, stomping her foot.

Dev was too busy watching her breasts bounce with her actions, his gaze lowered to her feminine apex, his eyes started glazing, a small smile curved the side of his mouth.

Already forgetting the argument, he got to his feet. "Come on, baby, let's go shower-"

His band buzzed again on the nightstand. He glanced at the text and read it with a pissed scowl. "Goddammit, I have to go."

Heading to the shower he said, "You will stay here, Wife, with the door locked. I do not want you to leave this room. End of discussion, I mean it."

He glowered at the angry blues that glared back at him, gave her a short hard smile as warning then went into the bathroom.

She got dressed as fast as she could. They had taken several showers every day, she didn't need another one. He would head straight to his suite for Brahms to do his hair into his war braids. As soon as she dressed in a skirt and blouse, she hurried out of the suite and down the hall.

A tremble of apprehension coiled up her spine wondering how her new husband would react when he found out she'd left, disobeyed his 'order.' Humph, some nerve. He had threatened a spanking before, but he was kidding around then. Maybe.

Her browns tugged down, Devilos was known for his lethal temper, she'd seen his beast. "Oh Goddess Satrine, what have I done?"

Well, it was too late now. She kept heading to the rec room, she'd face the dragon when she had to. Her mouth twisted in a wry grimace, literally, a dragon.

It took her fifteen minutes to walk to the hall. It was a big area crammed with games, food, drink, and people. People were playing at all sorts of games, video as well as cards, billiards, ping pong, along with visiting, some were dancing on a tiled floor off to the side.

Sveti wandered for a while checking out everything until she found something that looked interesting. She joined a rousing game of pickle ball, they had to teach her but she got the hang of it after getting teased and laughed at. After that, she played a few hands of cards before checking out some of the video games.

She wanted a drink but didn't have a paycard or wristband to pay for it.

"Hey, Prinţesă," a male voice greeted her with friendly cheer.

Sveti turned to see the man she had danced with, Charlie, grinning at her. He was quite nice looking, sandy hair parted on the side and combed over, friendly green eyes that showed his evident admiration of her. He wore black slacks and a tan shirt.

"Hi, uh, Charlie, right?"

He grinned pleased. "Yeah, you remembered. So," he glanced around, "where are all those big lugs that are usually hanging around you like a wall of muscle?"

That made her laugh. "They are all at a meeting, I'm on my own."

"Ah," his grin deepened, he said, "my lucky day." He nodded at her empty hands, "Hey, you don't have a drink."

Chagrined, she shrugged and explained, "I left in a hurry without bringing money." Not that she has any anyway, something to discuss later with her husband. After he got over his inevitable snit of her disobeying him.

"Oh well, shit, we need to remedy that right now. Come on." He grabbed her wrist and started walking her to the bar.

"Oh, no, I can't, please," she protested, trying to stop him but he cheerfully dragged her along.

At the bar, he rested a forearm on the counter and asked, "What would you like? Wine? Something harder? Something sweet, like you," he winked.

"Uh, no, thank you, Charlie, really, I can't-"

He flagged down the bartender, told him, "I'll have a gin and lemon, and a rosé for the lady." He grinned big at her showing lots of white teeth. "See, I remember, that's what you were drinking at the dance."

"But Charlie, no, I can't accept anything." Gosh if Devilos saw her at a bar accepting a drink from a man, he'd likely kill one or both of them. She had already seen his jealousy rage out of control, remembering the vision of the beast, she shivered. "Please, Charlie-"

Charlie was already paying the bartender. He picked up the wine glass and handed it to her and turned back quickly to get his own drink. He did it so fast she had to take the glass or it would have fallen.

When he turned back to her, he clinked his glass against hers and said with a wink, "Here's to good friends," and slugged down half his gin.

"Listen, Charlie," Sveti spoke firmly, quickly. "I'm married now. I married Captain, uh, Principé Devilos Dravidian, he's at a meeting and I don't think he-"

He reached out to push her glass to her lips. "Yeah, I know. The big fucker, fierce looking warlord with the war braids. The word is that he forced you into marrying him." He shrugged, took a sip.

"Well, not exactly, he-"

"I believe it. The guy is a ferocious brute. Listen," he crept in close to her and whispered in her ear, "what he doesn't know won't hurt him, huh? We can still be...friends," his gaze slid down the top of her blouse as he set a hand around her waist.

Sveti tried to jerk from his hand with an exclamation of protest, "No, listen, please, I told you, I am married, I can't, here please take this wine, I need to go!" She was appalled that this man would ignore the fact that she was married, and disregard her objections.

"Aw sugar," he nuzzled his lips in her hair, near her ear, "come on, he won't know, you said he was at a meeting, let's have a little fun," he squeezed her waist pulling her against him.

Sveti was getting mad, how dare he ignore her wishes, but she didn't want to cause a scene. She said through clenched teeth, "Charlie, let go of me right this minute and take this wine-"

Moving his head seeking her lips, Charlie cajoled, "Oh come on, honey, he'll never know, let's-"

"You heard my wife, get your motherfucking hands off her or you will lose them."

His voice such a low chilling growl, Sveti felt ice flow over her. Beside her, Charlie stiffened, he dropped his arm, his body instantly shaking.

Dev snatched up her hand, held it in front of Charlie and fingered her wedding band. The voice of a dragon he snarled, "You see this you fucking asshole? She's taken. Claimed. Married. To me." He leaned into poor Charlie's stark white face, clutched his shirt in his tough fist and pulled him up on his toes.

The enraged warlord's eyes as blinding as a blizzard, his voice deep and harsh with his wrath, "You get the fuck out of here before I rip your head off and shove it up your ass. I ever see you near, talking to, *touching* my wife again, I will ignore her compassionate pleas and fucking kill you where you stand. You understand me?"

He released Charlie with a shove, the man staggered backwards, just barely stopped himself from falling down.

Charlie's body shook like a leaf in a storm. Gawking at the flames that sparked up around Devilos, he stammered, "Y- y- y-" at the incensed warrior.

"Fucking move it before I disregard my wife's desire that I don't remove your head from your body." Before he finished his sentence, Charlie was a blur. Dev turned his furious, piercing white gaze to Sveti. It fell to the drink in her hand.

"Um, Devilos, I-"

"A married woman does not accept drinks from men in bars." He snatched it out of her hands and slammed it on the bar uncaring half the contents spilled.

"But, I didn't, I- I tried to say no, he shoved it right in my hands, Devilos-"

A voice from behind them said, "Prinţesă Ritrova?"

The couple looked to the person joining them.

Dev's voice as a deadly rattler about to strike, he thundered, "She is Prinţesă *Dravidian*. What the fuck," he turned to Sveti snarling, "do I have to tattoo it on your forehead?"

The beast was wavering around his body, the horns thickened as his ears grew sharper, his height increased, the broad bulk of his chest and shoulders was growing bigger about to split the long-sleeved dark blue shirt. His lids drew down so low the penetrating white was a mere streak of lightning.

The anger rolled off him so hot Sveti felt singed by it, she cringed at the sparks of fire that burst in crackling snaps of flames around them.

The man interrupting them turned as white as Dev's eyes. "I- uh, I'm s- sorry, sir, I apologize, I saw her alone then with another man and now you, uh," he slid a knuckle under his collar and tugged to get the stammer out. "I, that is, I thought she was alone, and if she turned you two guys down I might have a chance-"

"Sir," Sveti warned, "you should leave, now, quickly," her eyes slew to her livid husband.

Dev was fighting to keep the beast down but it looked like vapor was steaming out of his head with the effort, his face setting hard and coarse like dark cement in his fury.

Near the door she caught sight of one of his lieutenant guards, Dev must have sent him to search for her earlier when he realized she'd left the suite. Undoubtedly he had been there most of the time she was inside playing.

"Uh, yes, I see that," the man shook his words out, blanching further at the warlord clearly struggling to keep from lashing out at him. "I- I work in transmissions, they were trying to get ahold of you, Prinţesă, there's a message for you-"

"You have one second to get the fuck out of here," Dev growled so base he sounded like a rabid animal.

"Wait," Sveti put her hand on Dev's arm. She said to the man, "What message? From who?"

The man's eyes darted from Sveti to Dev.

The outline of the beast hovered around him growing larger and more solid by the second.

The man sputtered quickly, "Uh, there's a- a Ryen, uh, Rembrandt, Ryen Rembrandt, a message, you have no wrist-cell for Transmissions to contact you. You have to call them to-"

Dev grabbed up Sveti's arm and ushered her away from the frightened man who was about to piss his pants, led her across the room, people moved out of his way like he was a typhoon roaring through, and out the door.

He was moving down the corridor so fast in his blistering rage Sveti had to hurry to keep up or he'd be dragging her.

"Devilos, please, slow down, I can't keep up with you." She tugged at her arm but he held her like a vice. "Please, I haven't done anything wrong and I resent you treating me like this!"

He stabbed the button on the elevator, swung furious eyes at her. "You did, you trotted around like a fucking whore, accepting drinks from strange men in bars, and now, now," he took a deep gritty breath, his fingers tightened around her arm.

"Your fucking boyfriend is calling you. That's a bunch of shit, Svetiessa, a fucking bunch of shit. I won't fucking stand for it. You are my wife."

The door pinged and opened, he practically shoved her inside. She stumbled into the car, he reflexively grabbed her arm to hold her steady.

Inside, a riled Sveti snatched her arm from his grasp. "No," she said with heat, her eyes narrowed irately at him, "*I* won't stand for it. I will not be treated this way. Your jealousy is out of control, I will not be cursed at like that or treated like-"

"A whore?" He pushed her up against the wall of the elevator, crowded her with his hard body.

Furious, Sveti swung and slapped him across the face. Then blinked rapidly when he didn't even twitch at the strike. It had hurt her a lot more than him. Holding her stinging hand, she demanded, "Do not call me that again. Ever."

He leaned into her without touching her, his face in hers, eyes spasmodic white-black-white, his mouth ticked up in sarcasm. "Or what, little girl? What will you do? Put me over your knee?" Towering over her in breadth and strength accentuated the ludicrous suggestion.

"Just," her brows in a scowl, she kept her head lowered, "get out of my face. Leave me alone."

Dev slammed his palm on the emergency stop button and grabbed her arms pinning her against the wall. The elevator came to a complete halt.

Sveti's eyes flew to the door that wasn't going to open, trapping her in a cage with her enraged husband that was half-man, half-beast.

She raised her apprehensive eyes up to him.

Hard angry fingers wound around her arms, his dangerous face flushed dark with daunting wrath, he ground out, "Leave you alone? Don't you tell me to back off, *Wife*. I give the orders here, and I do what I want." Flames sparked, licking and crackling around the encasement without touching anything to burn.

His voice still low grew louder with threat, "You have men hanging all over you, your fucking boyfriend is calling, have you forgotten who your husband is?"

"Devilos, stop acting like a jealous-"

"Fool?" His black brows arched as his eyes turned vilely white, his horns swelled, the flames billowed. "Now you're calling me a fool? I will remind you who your husband is, Prinţesă Svetiessa *Dravidian*."

He smoothed the ire from his face making it an implacable mask and yanked a cloth out of his pocket, reached high to tuck it over the video cam.

Turning back to Sveti who had nowhere to flee, her back against the wall doing her best not to cower from the raging demon she had married.

Dev curled one hard hand around the front of her neck, the other reached down to the bottom of her skirt and pushed it up.

"Devilos-"

The beast wavered, rising and spreading around him. "Me, Prinţesă, I am your husband. I am the only man you will ever be with," he moved his hands to shove her blouse up and harshly gripped her breasts.

"The only man who touches these," groping them roughly, he let go and jerked at his belt unbuckling it, tugged his pants open.

"Devilos, stop this! We're in a public place, stop!" Sveti hit at his chest.

He kept her immobile with his arm as he unleashed his pulse pounding hard-on, rigid with fury and lust. Then he lifted her to force her legs around his hips, braced her back flat against the wall, one arm under her butt to hold her up.

His face mere inches from hers he snarled, "Your husband, Prinţesă, only me," stuck his hand under the bunched skirt, fisted her panties and ferociously ripped them off.

Stuffing them in his pocket, his face was so close to hers he could smell her fear, her femininity. "See, Svetiessa, if I was a real bastard I'd strip you naked, but I'm not, that will wait until we are in our suite. Aye, and then I'll tie you down, naked, you won't be going anywhere." If he wasn't so frighteningly furious his mouth would have been raised in a grim smile.

Her palms flat against his chest, she pushed, he was such an iron tank it made no difference. "Please, Devilos, don't treat me like this," her plea a whisper, hoping to calm him.

"Like what? Like my wife? You need a lesson, honey, on who owns you. You're going to get it right now." He gripped his shaft and pushed it at her opening.

About to brutally ram his steel beam of man's flesh into her without care or making her ready, glaring infuriated into her pale face, seeing her baby blues wavering with burgeoning tears, he paused.

Sveti laid the side of her face on his shoulder, his shirt roughly soft on her cheek. Her hands clutching his huge rocky biceps, her voice tight with emotion, as fearful, and angry as she was, he still lit a fire in her. Between her legs she burned for him, but not like this.

She spoke in hushed stillness, "Husband, please don't take me like this, in anger, in violence."

His rigid manhood in his fist strained against her core, Dev didn't move a muscle. Then he gently let her slide down to her feet.

Without looking at her, he tucked his stiff penis in and did up his pants, then grasped Sveti's blouse and silently tugged it down then fixed her skirt. Hearing her sniff back tears, he raised his head, the corners around his eyes crimped deep with his remorse.

He cupped her chin, murmured, "Baby, Svetiessa," a deep breath filled his chest down to his throbbing erection. "I...ah, I'm sorry. I," he lifted her head so their eyes connected, his were drifting back to black, hers were blue blurs from the unshed tears.

"Shit, Svetiessa, I've never cared about a woman like I do you, I've never felt jealousy before, it just takes me over. I'm," he kissed the tip of her nose, another deep, slow calming breath exhaled.

He said slightly embarrassed, "I'm terrified, huh," a sad chuckle with a shake of his head, "terrified of losing you."

He brushed a thumb over her cheek still red with anger and fear. "I can't say I won't behave this way again. I most likely will any time some other asshole is sniffing around you. It's not in my genes to not protect and fight for what's mine."

Her smile a weak squiggly line she informed him, "Devilos, I am not a possession."

The corner of his mouth tweaked up, his hand slid to embrace her face. "You can say that all day long, my sweet, but you are mine. Your feminism aside, I can't change who I am and how I feel. But," he sighed ruefully, "I will try to keep a tighter lid on my temper. Okay?"

When she smiled, he bent and cupping her face with both hands gave her a soft, on the edge of steamy kiss. Lifting his head, he smiled at her, the darkness in his face and eyes lightened, the beast was gone. "Let's go before the gendarmes come to check out why the elevator car has stopped."

He took the cloth off the camera and stuck it in his pocket, then pushed the button and the elevator progressed to their floor.

When the door opened and he nudged her out, she hesitated, said embarrassed, "But, Devilos, I'm not, you know," she whispered, "not wearing any panties. You took them."

His horns swelled. "Aye, I've been struggling to not think about it." He gave her a devilish leer, and patted her butt, then caressed it. "We'll take care of that when we get back to the room."

As soon as they were in their suite, Dev turned to her and pushed both hands up under her skirt to grab her bare bottom, his mouth went right to hers to covet and forage while he squeezed and kneaded, crushing her hips to his, his fingers creeping into the crease between her round cheeks.

"Wait," she pushed from him. "I need to find out why Ryen called. He wouldn't I'm sure if it wasn't an emergency."

Dev's skin darkened into a scowl. "Fuck, Svetiessa," he reached for her, "I need you, *now*." His erection bulged in his pants, his eyes were flickering black and white.

She danced from his hands. "No, I have to find out if something's wrong."

Ignoring his growl and fisted hands, she hurried to the wall com and dialed the Transmissions.

Chapter Twenty-Five

"Hello, Ryen? Hey, it's Sveti. Why-" She moved away from Dev who was hovering over her. Her mouth dropped open. "What? He did what?"

"What? Who? What's he saying?" Devilos followed her.

She held a hand up to ward him off, her head shaking back and forth with disbelief, her eyes scrunched in worry. "I can't believe he would," she claimed, then blinked hard lifting her head, "yes, of course he would. Listen, Ryen, of course," she nodded as he spoke.

The cell was tight against her ear blocking any sound from seeping out so Dev couldn't hear Ryen.

"What? What Svetiessa? Answer me?" Dev bellowed as he followed her around the room.

She turned her back to him, said into the phone, "Of course, Ryen, I will do all I can, I will come-"

"Oh fuck no." Dev grabbed the phone out of her hand, barked into it, "Rembrandt? What the hell, my wife is not leaving this station! Hello?"

He listened, heard nothing, repeated, "Hello? Rembrandt, you there?" When the phone clicked silent, he slammed it onto the holder on the wall and swung around to her angry face.

"I don't give a fuck if you're mad, Svetiessa. What does he want you to do?" His dark brows lowered at the guilty look on her face.

When she didn't answer he gripped her arms, gave her a little shake demanding, "Answer me, what did he want?"

She said calmly, "Let go of me and I will tell you." She ignored his scowl and held her ground.

He let her go, then ordered gruffly, "Tell me."

A guilty rose colored her cheeks, she looked down. "Well, apparently Krystian has, um, taken him prisoner, and wants to trade his life, for," her eyes flitted up at Dev then quickly away.

His voice dark, growling, he asked silkily dangerous, "For what, Svetiessa?"

She hesitated, swallowed hard, then said quietly, "Me."

"What!" he exploded. Scrubbing his fingers down his face in lieu of bashing his fist through a wall he shouted, "Nay! No fucking way, don't even think about it!" Seeing the set of her face he barked, "What? You are not considering it, Svetiessa, no!"

"Devilos, he is my dear friend, he wouldn't be in danger if it weren't for me, I have to do what I can to help him."

The hammering vein in his temple looked about to rupture, he yelled, "I don't care if he's the King of the galaxy, I said nay, no, you are not going anywhere! How you could even think about doing such a stupid thing? You know what your *bráthair* will do to you, he wants you in his bed, Svetiessa."

His voice dropped, "And he will hurt you in revenge for your helping Miles, and for leaving him, for marrying me, you have to know that."

Sveti knew that. She corrected him with a mumbled, "Half-brother." Even though she was no longer a virgin, Ryen told her Krystian craved her, wanted her still. But Ryen was pretty sure he planned on punishing her for marrying Devilos.

A shiver rifled through her, Krystian was a vicious, sadistic man. With her own eyes she has seen him discipline, punish people for even looking at him funny, many did not survive.

But, her lips firmed, he had Ryen, he would certainly mutilate if not outright kill him, she had to do what she could to save her friend.

Seeing the wheels spinning in her head and the determined set to her small pointed jaw, Dev grabbed her arms again, held her taut.

With a quiver of fear in his voice, he demanded, "Stop it, Svetiessa, stop. You are not going there. I sent our mixed DNA per your virgin's agreement to your *séantóir bráthair,* sorry," he held a hand up, "your perverted *leasbratháir,* half-brother.

"He will see the langistine from my horns is there, it won't make him immortal like you, but with the spell he will be more powerful and dangerous than he was before. He got what he wanted, he wasn't cheated. Baby, please," he could hear the fear in his own voice, "you are not leaving this station."

He shook her, the flaming curls flurried down her back. "I will restrain you, Svetiessa, I swear to Zues, I will chain you here until my ship is fixed, and my team and I will go to save your Ryen. Without you."

Her lips pursed, she demurred, "No. He is powerful, he will hurt you. Kill you, I can't take that chance. He may hurt me but I don't think he'll kill me."

Dev exploded, "You don't think he'll kill you? For Zues' sake, girl. And me, do you forget already who, what I am? He can't harm me. My team will go, you will stay here, out of Krystian's reach." His head dropped trying to get into her face. "Svetiessa dammit..."

She opened her mouth to retort, then, she recalled the words he'd previously uttered. Her eyes bulged suddenly, brows lashed over them, she asked, "Langistine, what is that? What do you mean, immortal? What did you do to me?"

His mouth shut, clamped into a hard line. But a speck of color hit his chiseled cheeks, hell, he was going to tell her, just not for a while. Later, after their relationship was stronger.

"Devilos? You answer me right now!" She tugged her arms from his grip and crossed them.

"Ah." Wiping the back of his hand across his forehead, not looking at her he muttered, "Well, uh..."

She insisted, "If you don't tell me I will ask someone else."

"All right, the ah, all right." Exhaling heavily, he explained, "Langistine is a...gene, a chemical, enzyme, I don't know what you humans would call it but, uh, I have it. I am, um, immortal. I uh, when we made love that first time, I...well, you probably don't know, stabbed my horns into your back. When I did that, the langistine was released into your system, and then, well," he shrugged with his palms up.

"Well what? Damn it, Devilos, tell me what it means."

"You will be...it takes about a year to come fully to fruition, but, you will become immortal, Svetiessa."

Stunned, her face paled with shock. "You- you did that on purpose? Without asking me? You didn't even tell me that you did it! Why? Why did you do that to me?"

Getting angry, brows daggered down between his eyes he said, "Because I am immortal. You think I want to watch you shrivel and die of old age someday, or get shot or knifed, or some disease or accident takes you? Nay," he shook his head, the black braids swinging back and forth, face grown hard and defiant.

"I will not face eternity without you. You are my mate, there will never be another. It's a done deal, it cannot be undone." The brief guilt left, replaced by his anger.

Sveti just stood, shock rattling her body, her eyes wide with accusation. Then her expression sickened, turned shaky ashen. "The- your- claws, fangs, the monster that invades your body- will- will I-"

His jaw flexed at her repulsion of his attributes, he shook his head. "Nay, they are intrinsic to me, only to males."

She lurched back from him when he reached for her hand.

Dark eyes narrowed in anger, he had to concentrate to stay calm, speak gently with a slight cajole, "Baby, listen, when you digest it, you will be fine with it. It's just that right now it's, ah, freaky to you. But, trust me, you will be-"

"Trust you! I can never trust you! First you deliberately seduced me, now you altered my body, my- my destiny, ancestry, my damned DNA!" Her arms bowed, eyes tapered furiously at him, she ground out, "How dare you play God!" Spinning from him she stormed across the room.

Dev threw out a hand but she stalked past him. "Baby, Svetiessa, wait, listen-"

Her angry steps clicked down the hall in her heels, he heard the door to one of the extra bedrooms slam closed.

"*Gah*," he grabbed handfuls of his braids and jerked on them in consternation. "Women! Shit," his lips pursed, his growl pissed and frustrated. "It doesn't look like I'm getting any tonight. Fuck."

Of course he could with no effort take the bedroom door down and then take her, but, he sighed, that would push their relationship and trust issues back further. Hell, nay, he couldn't force her, she might not forgive him. She was so squeamish about forced sex.

He rubbed his eyes, but right now he almost didn't care. He was about to implode with sexual need of her, and she was his wife dammit, she is supposed to give it to him whenever he wants it. All day through his meetings and repairs he hadn't been able to push the thought out of his head of her lying under him crying out his name.

He rolled his shoulders to release some tension. If he whined to one of his friends they would tell him to either just fuck her without her consent or go take another woman.

Hell, he already decided not to force her and, his tongue stuck out, he had no desire for another woman, not that he would cheat anyway. He was mated, to Svetiessa, married for life, betrayal was not in his DNA. Adultery, *that* she sure as hell would never forgive.

Striding with heavy feet to the small bar, his gnarly sigh hewed to a shallow moan. He had to admit he preferred her willing.

A short smile curved half his lip, he loved it when her dainty little hands trailed all over his body, wrapped around his dick. The other night she'd licked and sucked it, so innocent and inexperienced, damn it was hot.

He had been lying on his back, she was naked, on her hands and knees between his thighs facing him, fine butt up in the air, those precious tits dangling down, swaying with her movements.

Plump cherry lips on his shaft, she had looked up through her long curly, flaming lashes, all sweet and shy and eager to please him, he'd almost shot his wad then, but he wanted to be inside her.

Later, when she rasped his name and exploded in his hands, he shook his head, that was the most stupendously extraordinary thing he ever experienced, and he wanted it again. And again. For fucking eternity.

"Crap," he spat, his erection swelled uncomfortably, painfully in his pants. He poured a big drink and gulped it down, then poured another.

Dev spent the next two nights alone in his big bed, he ate alone, and hung around the suite alone. Sveti had refused to emerge from the bedroom.

He had to go out occasionally to meet with his team and check repairs on the airjet, that's when she came out and ate then went right back in the room before he returned.

He could have gone and dragged her out, but she would just be sullen and give him the silent treatment. The third day he slammed into Bowie's room without knocking.

"Hey, bro, what the hell?" Bowie was watching a sports game on the vidcam with a beer in his hand. A grin split his handsome face at Dev's pissed expression. "Ah, the groom has finally left the marriage bed, and by the looks of you, the honeymoon is over."

Stomping to the kitchen to get a beer, Dev muttered, "Fuck off."

Going back into the living room, he flopped on an easy chair and put his feet up on the coffee table, yanked open the beer and guzzled most of it down.

"Whew, Dev, what's going on? You look like shit. The little woman withholding?" Bowie snickered.

Shooting him an irritated scowl, Dev polished off the beer then went and got another one. He brought Bowie one too then plopped back down.

Sprawled in the chair, his knees bent, long legs spread, he groused, "You won't believe it, Bow. First off, she was furious that I injected her with my langistine. I made her immortal, for fuck's sake, at least in a year she will be. But, can you believe that- she's mad at me because I gave her eternal life! I don't fucking get women, Bow, never will."

Slugging the beer, he growled with frustrated exasperation.

"Hmm, I bet you didn't mention it to her before you did it, you didn't ask her if she wanted it." His smirk irritated Dev.

Observing his friend's face darken with guilt, Bowie said, "And, you undoubtedly, cowardly, didn't even tell her after that you did it. How does she know now? I bet she's pissed as hell."

Dev's dark skin flushed. "Aye, yeah, well, no I didn't. I did it without telling her because I didn't want to argue about it, and, she might have said no. And," he raked his fingers down his face, "even if she'd said no, I still would have done it and she'd be even more furious."

He shrugged, "So, I did it anyway without telling her ahead of time. You know, ask for forgiveness after rather than permission before that could be shot down. I was going to tell her when we were on a more solid foundation in our relationship. But," he sighed, his shoulder bumped, "I slipped and accidentally spilled it. Aye," he shook his head, "pissed doesn't begin to explain it. She's slept in one of the extra rooms the past two nights."

He absently rubbed his palm over his cock thinking about how badly he wanted her.

"Uh huh. You said that was the first thing, what else did you do to her?" Bowie asked with a chuckle.

Dev snorted. "Huh, I am not responsible for the other thing. Get this," he leaned over with his forearms on his knees holding the beer bottle in both hands, his braids dangled over his hunched block of shoulders.

"That boyfriend, the wimp she left on her planet, his name is Ryen Rembrandt for fuck's sake, what kind of an absurd name is that?" his snort indicated he considered Ryen a sissy.

He went on, "So, her fucked-up pervert of a *bráthair* snatched Ryen and said if Svetiessa doesn't go trade herself for him, Ritrova will harm him, probably kill the poor sap. I told her the bigger ship is in for repairs, as soon as it's done we, as in you and our team not her, can go get the Rembrandt guy. But she won't wait for that."

He huffed in annoyance, And, she thinks she has to go because *I* will be in danger and that *she* must protect *me*. What a bunch of hogshit, huh?"

"What?" Stunned, Bowie's feet dropped to the floor, his dark blue eyes widened then narrowed at Dev. "You can't let her go, that's fucked up, her brother will bang her and then seriously hurt her."

"Duh, I know. Try to convince her of that. She feels the need to be everybody's savior. Hell, she traded her life for her little *bráthair* with the grizzly-canines knowing full well it was a death sentence at the time. This would be just as bad.

"I told her I'd chain her to keep her here, and I will, goddammit." The color drained from his face, leaving his dark eyes bleak.

He swung his worried gaze to his friend. "I can't lose her, Bow, I can't live without her, I-" the words were on the tip of his tongue.

His blond brows arched with some humor. "Say it, bro, it won't hurt, I promise."

Dev's celestial black eyes shone in wonderment at Bowie, they widened in astonishment. "I...love her, Bow, I fucking love her. How did that happen? I thought I was immune to that senseless emotion. But, shit, Bow, I get a horrible pang in my heart when I think of her in danger, being harmed, of losing her."

Bowie nodded with a shit-eating-grin at his stunned friend. "Where is she now?"

"Ah, she's hanging in one of the other bedrooms sulking." The sides of his mouth nicked in with a short laugh. "Probably planning her escape."

The color suddenly drained from his tan. "Shit, because I was there I didn't put Keldon on the door-" He jumped up and ran out of Bowie's suite.

Dev raced back to their suite, threw the door open and went straight to his bedroom, of course she wasn't there. He checked the other rooms, empty.

He ran back out and down to her old room. She wasn't there either. Digging the heels of his palms into his forehead, his fingers clutched his hair, the frustration and terror of what she might have done was gutting him.

He clicked his wristband shaking his head. All the women in the universe and he has to choose the one that needs to be a selfless rescuer that puts her own life on the line to save others.

Not even big and tough, he thought as he pushed for Transfers, no, he has to choose the most petite, delicate, damned dainty female he'd ever come across. And she has no damned clue or hesitation to her own fragility.

"Sire?" a voice came through his band. "Bren Simmans here."

Running down the hall Devilos commanded, "Simmans, stop all ships from leaving the station. All, every one, commercial, private, military, everything."

"Copy, Sire." About to relay the message to the entire station, Simmans commented with good nature, "It's a good thing the prințesă left when she did, huh?"

His feet stopped like they were suddenly deep in mud. His heart pounded in his throat, his voice stiff with sudden terror, Dev rasped, "Fuck. Simmans. The Prințesă Svetiessa, *my wife*, she left the station? How did she leave? With whom?"

Hearing the fierce growled danger in Dev's tenor, Simmans' voice raised a few octaves, "Uh, Sire, the interplanetary ship dropping off commissioned personnel on leave was just firing up when she, uh, intercepted them, that is, she banged her fist on the ramp door. It was opened and I guess she asked for transport because she boarded and that was it. Left not five minutes ago. Sire, what would you like for me to-"

Dev clicked off.

Pressing the pads of his palms into his eyes and roared, "*Goddammit!*" His curse so crushing fierce and loud and forged with fear, people passing by gingerly skirted around him.

Chapter Twenty-Six

Sveti knew Devilos would blow a gasket when he realized she left the station without even telling him, but she had to. If she had told him, he would have prevented her from leaving.

He said he and his team would go for Ryen, but, she would not allow him to risk his life for something that was her issue.

Krystian would for sure kill Devilos and his men, she shivered, wrapping her arms more tightly around herself. Besides, his ship was going to take a long time in repairs and Ryen may not have much time. No, she had to do it this way.

"We're almost there, Prinţesă," one of the crew announced cheerfully.

It had been two weeks since she boarded the airjet. Sveti sighed, glad it was almost done, but scared to death of what Krystian would do to her when he got his hands on her. Then she'd have to worry about Devilos coming for her.

She was his wife, he considered her his possession, his property. A warrior hunter, he would unquestionably come.

She would need to communicate with him when she got to her planet to tell him to not come for her. A tiny snort erupted, yeah, like he would listen to her.

She'd had to charge the trip on his account, she had no choice. She would pay him back, if there was ever a way for her to do so. That would be doubtful, Krystian will likely keep her in chains for the rest of her life.

Sveti had quickly packed a small bag before she'd run out of their suite. Their suite. Sveti felt her heart twist. She finally realized what Devilos meant to her. He was her world.

She didn't want to leave, the breath she sucked in literally stung with pain. She wished with her entire being she was back in his big bed, with him poised over her about to plunge inside her body, that smug, arrogant smile on his hard gorgeous face.

Her sigh deepened. It didn't matter now, she would be Krystian's and Krystian would never let her go once he had her.

"Thank you," Sveti told the crewmember politely. She was standing by one of the windows watching the stars flash by gulping back tears that threatened to fall. "Devilos," she cried in her heart, "I'll miss you, forever, I'll never forget you."

The ship was landing. Sveti had contacted Krystian as soon as she had boarded the ship to advise she was coming to trade herself for Ryen to stop him from doing anything rash.

Gosh, she could only pray that he hadn't harmed Ryen yet. She'd had to bite down on her impatience every time the ship stopped to let someone off on a different planet, or space station.

Twenty minutes later, with a group of other passengers she disembarked the ship to her home planet, Qoph. The station they landed at was the largest one on the planet.

All chromia steel and unbreakable glass. People bustled in and out of the station, as aircraft soared in and out and around from the back landing field.

Straightening her spine and her shoulders, Sveti pushed her long curly hair back and strode firmly to the exportation border post where she had to pass through to get out of the station. Getting in line, she hoped they would allow her to pass as she had no ID.

When it was her turn, she smiled at the officer behind the stand. "Hello, sir, I am Svetiessa Ritrova. Unfortunately, I left in a hurry and didn't bring my proof of residency."

He shook his head as his eyes lit over her body, up and down over the slacks and blouse outlining her astounding figure. "I cannot allow you to pass without your proper identification. I am aware of course," he reddened slightly, "that you are the Prințesă Svetiessa, but, I could be arrested if I do not vid your identification. I-"

"That is not necessary, officer, we will take charge of her." Two huge, stiff-faced bulk-muscled men in red and blue uniforms suddenly flanked her.

"Well, uh..." the officer blanched, unsure how to proceed.

The guards didn't wait for his response, one took Sveti's arm, the other her bag, and walked her though the boisterous throng and out the door.

Outside, five more guards waited. Sveti bit back a smile, Krystian had expected trouble, assumed that she wouldn't have come alone as he had commanded.

The guards ushered her into a small airjet, three guards climbed in with her, while the other four boarded another one to follow them. They were airborne in seconds. No one spoke.

Thirty minutes later the airjet slid into a garage station attached to the castle and parked. The two guards helped Sveti out and down the few steps to the ground.

They ushered her to the entrance of the ivory granitium castle.

Without pause or ceremony, they brought her inside, through the grand, polished marble antechamber, down a corridor to a huge salon. The back was all glass, floor to ceiling.

White and gold extravagant furniture sat atop snow-white luxurious carpeting, hedonistic opulence ran amok throughout the grand palace.

Krystian stood in the center of the room, like a statue. A tall, strong, auburn haired, sapphire-eyed psychopathic statue. His face was a handsome blank veneer.

But Sveti knew him well. His eyes were raging storms of vengeful fury, and she could see in them and the cruel curl of his lip the promise that he was going to hurt her. With triumphant joy.

Sveti walked to her half-brother with her shoulders straight and a firm trod. But she carefully stopped several arms' length from him. "Krystian," she said flatly, looking him in the eye. She watched his lip curl up higher in a vindictive sneer.

He wore a dark burgundy tunic that should have clashed with his hair but didn't, his pressed slacks were as deep blue as his cold merciless eyes. "What," he snarked, "dear baby sister, no hug for your brother?"

She didn't move. Sucking in a solid breath, Sveti let it out slowly. "Half-brother, Krystian. There is no need for us to pretend any affection. I am here as a trade for Ryen as you ordered. I presume he is unharmed, alive?"

The side of his mouth edged up, his snake's eyes glazed with malevolence. "Ah, you are not quite the timid little girl you were before you allowed that savage to fuck you."

Her lashes whisked over her cheeks at the slur before rising to meet his bestial gaze. "I married Principé Devilos Dravidian, Krystian, as you know. Per your deal, you know the one, selling my virginity to the highest prince bidder, Devilos paid you and sent you our DNA. It was what you wanted, we did not cheat-"

"It was *my* decision you bitch!" his fury bellowed.

Stepping to her, lids low hiding half his psychotic furor, he thundered, "It was *my* choice to sell you or keep you, not yours. I would not willingly have sold you to that demon creature from Nasitar, he was not...malleable."

His hands clenched into fists, spit flew out with his rage. "Whatever prince I chose to fuck you was supposed to come here," he swung his hand in an arc across the front of him. "Marry you here, so I could get my spell done then kill him and keep you."

Krystian swept his palms over his auburn hair, smoothing the thick waves back, collecting his composure.

Forcing her trembling body to not back away from him, she said quietly, "I'm sorry you are displeased with the arrangement but-"

"Oh, darling," his smirk pure evil, "you will find out how displeased I am. You are lucky I still desire you, or you would be dead already." In a flash Krystian slapped her so hard she flew back and slammed to the floor.

He bent and grabbed her hair jerking her to her feet.

Before she caught her balance he gripped her face, nails digging into her flesh, he pressed their mouths together so hard Sveti's teeth bit into her lips. His brutal kiss, with depraved cruelty punctured blood from her soft mouth.

He released her suddenly, wiped the back of his hand over his own mouth. Seeing the pain crease her face, the trickle of blood over her swollen lips, with a malice tainted smile, he sneered, "That is infantly tame, darling, compared to what I plan on doing to you, after I mete out your punishment. Yes," he nodded ghoulishly.

"You will be severely disciplined and then I will fuck you, in every possible way, every day, forever, dear sister, like I have always desired, always planned."

Sveti put her hand to her bleeding mouth and stumbled back from him but he grabbed her chin, jerked her forward and squeezed it with ruthless cruelty.

"You will bear my heirs, Sveti, you will never be free of me again. If you try to escape, I will slaughter your, *our*, entire family."

Hauling his hand back he slapped her again hard enough to knock her back down to the ground. She landed with a breathless sob.

Staring down at her curled on the floor leaning back on one palm, Krystian snarled to the guards, "Take her to the cell I prepared."

To Sveti he said without inflection, "You will stay in the cell for...let's see," his eyes rolled back and forth as if thinking, "a long time without food. I want you meek and eager to please me when I have you brought to me. After that, a maid will help you dress into what a princess of your standing, one who is worthy of me, should be wearing. You will quickly forget that satanic freak you married."

Her hand on her aching face, her contempt for him sprayed from belligerent eyes. "Do what you will, Krystian, you can batter my body, but you will never beat out of my thoughts of Devilos, my husband, from me."

He propped his fists on his hips, taunted, "What you don't know, my sweet, is that I will kill that bastard thereby ending that meaningless marriage of yours, make you a widow setting you free to wed me."

He leaned over her, dark blue eyes spitting grim hell, he snarled, "I will burn that demon from your brain. Mark my words." Standing straight, he nodded sharply to the guards.

Her face stinging, Sveti didn't fight the guards that pulled her to her feet and took her from the salon. They brought her to a cell, thrust her inside, and locked the door.

Stumbling, Sveti set her hand on a wall to catch her balance and looked around.

There was nothing to see, three steel walls and a door with a tiny window in it covered with bars. That was it. Not a chair or blanket, nothing. A tiny hole was dug into the stone floor for waste.

Sveti sunk to the cold stone floor, wrapped her arms around her knees, then let the sobs roll out.

True to his word, Krystian had no food, only water, brought to her for a time long enough to break her. She was lying on her back, half delirious when the guards came for her.

They took her to a chamber, led her inside, followed her in and locked the door.

A thin, nervous woman waited with a shaky smile. Twisting her fingers together, she bowed. "Hello Prinţesă," she cleared her voice, eyes skipping to the guards and back to Sveti. "My name is Vania. I am to help you bathe, dress, do your hair for your bro- uh, Principé Ritrova."

The woman dressed in a floor length white gown, was in her forties and wore her dark hair in a tight chignon.

Sveti had returned to Qoph expecting, knowing what was going to happen to her. She couldn't run, or fight, or balk, she couldn't think about Devilos ever again or she would completely die inside over the loss.

She had to believe that Devilos would remain safe and if there was a God, he would set off on a mission where he couldn't come search for her and hopefully he would eventually forget about her.

Krystian would annul their marriage under abandonment decrees and then they would wed. She needed to accept her fate with as much grace and endurance that she could.

Starving and weak, Sveti nonetheless smiled kindly, "Thank you, Vania."

The maid helped her to bathe, wash her hair and set it, then she dressed Sveti in an opalescent powder blue, gossamer-light shimmering gown. When she slipped the pastel blue ballet slippers on, Sveti was ready to face her future.

The guards brought her to Krystian's chambers. In a cobalt blue tunic and darker blue slacks, his auburn waves perfectly coiffed, he stood facing the door with his hands clasped behind his back.

Handsome face frosty with arrogance, his smile harrowing, he took in the shining curls flaming down her back, brilliant blue eyes now haunted with loss, the plush lips tight with fear, the feminine dress skimmed the still lush curves of her slender, now thinner than ever figure down to the slippers.

"Ah, so beautiful, my darling sister," he murmured moving towards her.

Seeing the quirk of her lip, Krystian smiled. He loved calling her his sister, got a perverse sick thrill out of it, especially since he knew it disturbed her, and everyone else. Sveti didn't move.

He looked at the severe curve of her slight waist with shake of his head. "Too bad about the starvation, sister, but you need to learn who your master is. The good news is," his lewd grin aimed at her chest, "skinny as shit but you still have the finest tits in the fucking galaxy." His hand suddenly whipped out and he slapped her.

When she staggered backwards, he shot his hand out and clutched her bodice, pulling her back. Holding onto her dress, his face a sick warped smile, he slapped her again and again and again until she could no longer stand.

When she crumpled to the floor, he let her go.

Bending over her he spoke calmly, "No, you don't get off that easy, darling. Don't move," he chuckled at that then went to a closet and came back with a cane.

On her butt, her elbows bent, Sveti leaned back on her palms, her eyes wide at the cane. "No, please, Krystian, we're- we're family, you can't-" She broke off with a shriek at the strike on her arm.

"Oh," he sneered, "*now* we're family. This past year you did everything you could to refuse me as your brother. You avoided me, stuck that little nose of yours up in the air whenever I came into a room." He lashed wickedly at her other arm with the cane, his lips twisted with sadistic satisfaction at her choked scream.

"You rebuffed all my advances, no one else ever had the fucking balls to refuse me, well, Svetiessa, my baby sister, that is done." The sick nasty grin deepened as he swung the cane, striking her everywhere as she tried to get away from him.

She covered her head with her arms, he saw her ring flash. "What the hell, you still wear the barbarian's brand?"

Krystian crouched with his hand out demanded, "Give it to me."

Sveti's eyes closed as she clasped her hand to her breast holding it with the other and shook her head. Tears streaming, her voice hoarse from screaming, she rasped, "Never."

Frowning, he slid a knife out of his pocket. "I will cut your finger off, give it to me."

She stayed huddled into herself, holding her hand tight to her chest. Her whipped body ached, screamed in pain, her skin burned in agony from his whipping.

"You bitch," he swore, grabbed her arm wrenching it so hard she cried out. He pried her finger up, snapped it and then ripped the ring off, his mouth pulled in gleefully at her hoarse shriek, it seems he broke her finger. Oh well.

He unclasped a gold necklace from around his neck, slipped the ring on it, and put it back around his neck, smirking at her sad horror, her bereft eyes on her wedding band.

He stood up. "All right, I wasn't done yet," and he viciously whipped her until the dress was in shreds and her blood flowed. The sapphire eyes glowed with lascivious insanity watching her writhing in agony on the floor at every lash. Her skin was covered in red weeping lacerations, blood streamed over her body from everywhere.

Curved in a tight fetal ball, her tortured skin rippled and quivered in pain, her sobs had weakened to wheezing gasps, Sveti's brain shrieked for relief from the burning torment. His last strike accidentally scraped across her cheek.

"Fuck," he grunted, "I did not want to mar that beauty of yours. Oh well," one shoulder shrugged, "it will heal. Now, come," bending over her he held out his hand.

Tears and pain blurring her vision, huddled trembling on the floor, Sveti stared at his proffered hand. She was too weak to reach up to it.

Sighing, he smiled, "Fine, I will help you." He bent over further and took her hand lifting her to her feet.

Grinning cheerfully, he said, swinging their hands, "Now the real fun begins."

Chapter Twenty-Seven

Krystian half walked half carried her down the corridor to a vast chamber of smoky grey walls and marble floor. The immense room contained only dozens of guards, and a divan placed in the middle, no other furniture, or ornamentation.

Sveti was so hungry and is such pain, she didn't notice the stares of the guards, ogling her in the shredded gown.

The smile no longer present, Krystian cursed then told her, "You humiliated me by leaving me and marrying another man, so now I will humiliate you. I will strip you and fuck you naked in front of my men. They will enjoy the show of my cock perforating your gorgeous ass."

He held his hand out to a guard, the guard set chains in it. Krystian's eyes gleamed with horrid glee at the terror wreathing her waxen face, her panicked eyes on the chains.

Holding the chains in one hand, he slapped her, knocking her down. He turned sharply and glared at the murmur that passed through some of the guards. Then he bent, snatched his fist in her hair and wrenched her up.

Sveti wobbled on unsteady feet while Krystian grasped one of her wrists yanking it behind her back.

Wrapping a chain around it, his lips in her hair, he murmured, "You have the most delicate wrists, darling, beautiful hands, such dainty fingers," he jerked her other wrist back ignoring her gasp of pain and chained her wrists together.

"I particularly like the swollen ring finger. Breaks hurt like a bitch, don't they, my darling sister?"

Spinning her around, he ripped the already torn dress across her chest and shoved the pieces back off her shoulders, exposing her breasts in the miniscule scrap of lacey bra he had sent for her to wear. The shredded skirt of the gown was now mere pearlescent, powder blue strips.

Holding her upper arms with a painful grip, Krystian's deviant eyes, like immoral blue spotlights, glimmered over Sveti's breasts.

He bowed his head, kissed the swell of one of her lush mounds, then licked between her cleavage, then bit her, not hard enough to break the skin, but enough to leave an angry red imprint and rent a scream through her raw throat.

He threw his head back with a degrading, guttural laugh ignoring the men murmuring around him. Most of them were hoping when the principé was done, he would turn her over to them, many chops were being licked. Others were appalled at his brutal treatment of the small female, and his own sister.

But today, sadism was his, and he viciously hit her again and again, having to hold her up by her neck as her body gave out and she hadn't the strength to stand.

Dragging Sveti to the divan, Krystian put his hands on her waist, lifted her and set her on her knees on the divan. She cried out in pain when her beaten knees hit the couch.

She wobbled on the cushion unable to level her balance with her hands retrained behind her back, waves of dizziness assaulted her bruised brain.

Watching her breasts bounce as she struggled to keep still, with a smile he chucked her chin to get her attention.

Her brutalized head lolled, he gripped her jaw to hold her head up. Limp tousled curls draped over her battered face and down to spiral over her almost completely bared breasts. Her blood pooled, soiling the divan beneath her.

"First, darling," Krystian told her, "you will suck my dick dry, you will choke on it, gag on it as I shove it down your throat and you will swallow every drop. My cock stuffed in your pretty mouth will show you who is master, who has won. When I recover from my orgasm, I will fuck you to bloody gore."

His chuckle so sick every person present felt disemboweled of their sanity, unexpectedly frightened from the pure portent evilness of his vow, his sadistic smile chilled everyone to the bone. "I mean you're already bloody on the outside, your insides will soon match that lovely crimson red, eh?"

He climbed on the divan and faced her. Sitting sat back on his heels, he opened his pants. Tugging his erection from his trousers, he fisted it then wrapped a hand around the front of her neck to hold her immobile for his rapacious brutal kisses while he pumped his cock to get it stiffer.

Laughing guttural grunts, he slid his hand around to grasp the back of her neck, and forced her head down to his penis.

Then he paused, allowing his victorious grin to shine. "I think you need to be naked for this, my beloved sister, the degradation must be complete."

Releasing his member, he moved to wrench the rest of her tattered gown and lingerie off before he shoved his shaft into her mouth.

At that second, the entire back wall of glass shattered, and suddenly, Devilos was there.

He had moved so fast he wasn't even discerned busting in from outside. Bowie materialized beside him.

Dev's cloaked airship was invisible and off radar, he'd flown in undetected and landed behind the castle then used an x-ray radar to locate where Sveti was inside.

Shocked, Krystian shoved his dick in his pants and scrambled to his feet dragging Sveti with him. "What the fuck is this?" he squawked with anger and confusion.

If he wasn't holding her, Sveti would have collapsed on the cool marble floor from her hunger and brutal beatings.

Krystian gripped her hair and held it tight to keep her head up, forcing her to look at the demon that was her husband.

But all caring and desire was gone from Dev's face. His expression implacable like a sheet of dark iron, he stared at her with blank black eyes. Then a flicker of hurt and rage pulsed in the rich orbs sending chills down Sveti's spine, before going back to a blank slate.

His long black lashes dropped over his eyes. When they lifted, his deadly gaze was a ruthless white current slicing across the room to Krystian.

The guards shifted, unsure what they were supposed to do until Krystian gave orders.

Seeing the threat from Devilos, Krystian released Sveti's hair and pushed her back onto the divan. A slow, sinister grin cut up his face. "Ah, you must be the savage, the demon husband. Good, good." The grin widened with his nodding head.

Palming his waves of auburn hair, slicking them back off his forehead, he said, "You couldn't have done any better. Except for the damage," he frowned at the broken glass, then shrugged.

"This is exactly what I wanted in the first place. I got your DNA blend, and my spell, my power and strength have increased twenty fold, and, I can kill you like I had planned, and keep Sveti for myself."

A guard was standing in a hidden alcove, he stepped out with his flashgun aimed at Dev.

Krystian grinned more broadly, nodded at another guard who turned and rushed out of the room.

Dev stood and calmly scanned the chamber.

Losing the grin at seeing the unperturbed demon warrior, Krystian snarled with an aggressive grimace, "What, you think you can break into my home and take what is mine?" His clenched fist and brief scowl cast from Dev to Sveti who was struggling to stay conscious.

"No," Sveti cried weakly, rasping in pain. "Please, Krystian, I did as you asked, I am here." She drew a ragged breath spoke with ragged hitches, "You promised that you would let Ryen go and not retaliate against Devilos. You can't hurt him-"

"Shut up!" Krystian thundered at her.

Dev's eyes narrowed at Krystian's neck. "You wear my wife's ring?"

Smirking, Krystian fingered Sveti's wedding band on the chain around his neck. "Yes, I didn't notice it until this morning. She refused to give it up. I was going to cut her finger off to teach her a lesson, but alas, I could not make myself mutilate her beauty." His glance at Sveti showed no remorse.

"However, I might have broken her finger getting it off. Next time she will be more cooperative, eh?" He smiled at her, said silkily, "Won't you my sweet?"

The guard who had rushed out of the room returned with an armful of chains.

"Chain the demon prince!" Krystian ordered with loud commanding triumph.

The other guards raised their flashguns at both Dev and Bowie.

Dev was shoved roughly to sit on the floor.

As the guards chained him, Krystian explained, "Yeah, I know you are as strong as…the very devil himself, but," the grin was back, "these are made of a new updated graphene. Atom-thin layers of carbon arranged in a honeycomb pattern making it 500 times stronger than steel by weight. The chains made of this particular metal and along with a spell are indestructible, even you cannot break them."

The guards finished binding Dev.

Moving away from Sveti and closer to Dev for his taunts, Krystian mocked him, his mean voice dense with enmity, he told the bound prince, "You will be forced to watch me take possession of your…*wife*," he snarled the word, "fucking her again and again while caning her in between rapes. You took her from me with a trick, well, now I reclaim what is mine!"

He cast a cruel glance at Sveti weeping and shuddering with pain, bleeding on the divan. "She will rue the day she threw her defiance in my face and let you, a filthy alien hunter fuck her. And you will regret the temerity in coming here thinking you can just waltz into my castle and take her back. Ha!"

His sneer gloating, he said, "Once I make Sveti a widow she will be free to wed me." Grinning with satisfied glee, he expounded, "And she will bear my children, as many as I can get on her."

"You are going to die, Ritrova," Dev said calmly matter-of-fact. His eyes shifted to Sveti and lowered to the bite mark on her breast. Flames sparked around his head as his ebony eyes flashed brilliant white.

Her wrists bound behind her, she struggled to stay upright on the cushions. Lids heavy with fatigue and pain, she was unable to maintain eye contact with her husband.

Moving tauntingly closer to Dev, Krystian tapped his own chin with a finger while speaking, "Big words, nothing to substantiate them, asshole. When Sveti is so…used, she can no longer stand, after I've made her observe me torture you, I will force my baby sister to watch you die. And it will be a long, horrible agonizing death, to teach you both your mistake in fucking with me!"

His malicious laughter echoed through the room. Then, his laughter shriveled in his throat, his eyes widened, as he watched Dev jump easily to his feet.

Dev's powerful chest pumped, his enormous biceps bulged, he slowly straightened his arms, the chains stretching with them. His ominous grin nicked up one corner. "You are correct, you sick fuck, I can't break these chains, well, I can, but it would take a while, but I can stretch them."

In front of the stunned audience, Dev's beast was emerging, he grew taller, broader, his horns, claws and fangs descended and grew.

His voice a roughened growl of the creature he was becoming, he told Krystian, "I allowed you to chain me only to lure you away from my wife so you can't use her as a shield or injure her further when I come for you."

Krystian appeared unconcerned. "I have dozens and dozens of guards you freak, you think you can fight them all? Ha!" he spurted, and waved to his men.

Shedding the chains, Dev let them drop to the ground in a clanking clatter around him. He said, "Bowie, get my wife to Protostar and to Geffry, when he declares her well, bring her to Nasitar. Tell Connar, Lukas and Tomi waiting outside to clear any innocents out of the building."

The soldiers started swarming Dev and Bowie.

Sveti struggled to sit up, get off the couch, but she was too weak, she screamed hoarsely, "Devilos, just run! Bowie, run!"

His brutal gaze lit with frigid emptiness on her, Dev said coldly, "Ah, Wife, you still doubt me. I will see to your penance for disobeying me when I return to Nasitar, for now, Bowie-"

Grinning, Bowie bashed his boot, breaking the knee of the guard beside him and slammed his fist into the jaw of the other one, then he streaked across the room to Sveti.

As Bowie moved, Dev spun into silver whirling dust, an almost invisible tornado spinning around the room slicing and dicing, stabbing his sword, cutting off heads, arms, shoving the blade into bellies.

Krystian stood dismayed at the slaughter of his men.

Dev was nothing but a glinting blur as he killed every guard.

When the last man fell, the blur slowed and Dev became still, morphing into his human form, he was standing a few yards in front of Krystian. He didn't take his eyes off him as Bowie pulled Sveti through the room, shielding her with his body.

"Devilos, he has," Sveti rasped painfully, "power. Run, leave me to my doom, he will kill you." Wrists still restrained behind her, her legs buckled.

Bowie swept her up in his arms and headed for the broken wall of windows. He hesitated, Sveti almost passed out, her head fell to Bowie's shoulder.

Once again, Dev's beast willowed and wavered, as a violent swelling vapor the creature spread around him. The vapor, like the shimmering sun in the hazy summer, he transformed into a gigantic demon, a raging fire-spewing dragon.

Most of his human looks were gone, taken over by the bloodcurdling monster.

His beastly mouth snapped open revealing voracious teeth and fangs, huge, razor sharp and gleaming, dripping with poisonous saliva. His arms raised, the claws descended as he roared at Krystian.

But, Krystian was also transforming. His body bulked and grew in height and power, his roar back at Dev indicated he was ready to war.

Fire burst in blazing flames all around them, crawling over the floor to lick at the dead bodies of the guards until they were ashes, and climbing up the walls to the cathedral ceiling to explode out the upper story windows.

"Time to go, sweetie," Bowie said cheerfully. Holding Sveti tight to his chest, he turned and strolled out of the chamber. Stepping through the open windows he hurried to the ship that waited behind the castle.

"Bowie, no," she gasped, "you have to help him, Krystian will destroy him, please, Bowie, help him." Her wrists still chained behind her, straining to not pass out, Sveti struggled in his arms trying to get loose.

"No, honey," Bowie grinned, walking up the short ramp to enter a ship, "Dev will be fine. You need to trust him. For once." A smaller ship sat at the ready next to the airship.

Inside the aircraft, Bowie set her on a cushioned chair then broke the chains with his sword and belted her in before she could get up.

She fought to get out of the safety bands, but she was too weak, too broken, too feeble to unhook them.

Bowie jumped in the captain's chair and buckled in while hitting switches and swiping digital pads.

The door to the ramp raised and clamped shut.

The engines ignited and they were gone like a spark from a star.

Chapter Twenty-Eight

*B*roken bones, lacerations, and internal damage, it took months for Sveti to heal and finally able to get on her feet.

Bowie had visited her that morning and Geffry deemed her well enough to travel. It was time for them to head to Nasitar.

Now, aboard an airjet, a burr of trepidation churned in her stomach as she stood by the window on the bridge watching the Milky Way streak by.

Every one of the crew was polite, yet remote to her. She had left Devilos, her husband, their principé, their captain, leader, sire, to some their master, to others a friend.

He had been the devil to be around after she had gone to trade herself for Ryen.

Unrestrained rage fueled him, temper gone wild he pounded his fists through walls, got drunk and into brawls while he had waited for his ship to be repaired to go retrieve his wife.

The people felt for his wrath, his hurt, his fear, but they stayed the hell out of his way.

Only Dev's close team was kind to her. They knew she had left him to sacrifice herself for her friend. She'd been told Ryen was safe and well, back home with his family. No one had given her any word about Dev.

She didn't know if he was dead, or injured, dying, when she asked, people averted their gazes and didn't answer her. Well, she thought, if he was alive, he would be burning with rage at her.

Rubbing the goose bumps on her arms, Sveti shivered. He had promised punitive action. Would he be any better, any worse than Krystian had been? Did she get tossed from the frying pan into the fire?

She had seen Dev's full beast in action, she had never experienced anything more bone-chilling terrifying in her life. Would he unleash the monster on her? Tear her to pieces with his teeth and claws?

"Buckle up, honey," Bowie said with an amiable order, "we are about to land."

Settling into her seat, nerves struck her, shaking every chilled bone in her body. She had never been to Nasitar, few outsiders have. They were a secretive, mysterious race.

She pictured the planet being starkly black, obsidian like Devilos' cold eyes. An apocalypse ruin overrun with vicious human-like creatures with horns and fangs tearing the throats out of each other.

A land of no safety, no peace, a dark place of constant battling amongst the dirty remnants of demolished buildings. No light, no flowers, no beauty, just a frigid lightless shell, with her infuriated demon husband at the helm.

She tried to take deep, calming breaths, but her body shook like a leaf.

Bowie landed the ship perfectly, smooth as silk, not a bump. He shut the ship down and then let Lukas and Connar take over the closing up and seeing to the crew leaving.

He unbuckled his belt and came to Sveti who was sitting still as a rock, her fingers twined, skin pinched white.

"Come on, sweetie, time to beard the lion."

"I take it he's alive? No one would tell me."

"Ah, aye he is. He had business to clear up here before sending for you. You were too ill to travel as you know, and he was out of the galaxy on a mission that needed to be completed before hundreds of innocent people were killed, that's why he didn't come to see you."

The relief that he was all right streamed over her in a warm wave, then the rigidity and shaking came back, she knew he undoubtedly hated her now. "Is he furious with me?"

"Uh, well," Bowie evaded the question, "let's just get going, come on." He unbuckled her belt for her and helped her up then led her trembling body out of the ship.

"Oh...my, Bowie," she gushed in awe as she stepped outside, "it's...breathtaking." Her eyes like huge blue saucers, Sveti looked around with her mouth open.

The land was a dark golden swath that rolled on softly forever. Gigantic, dazzling flowers of hues Sveti had never seen, flowed and fluttered over the gold. But she did recognize the spreading shrub of oval leaves with fragrant pink and purple flowers, the graceful honey myrtle, and the vivid red blooms of the rock rose.

The sky was the palest, pastel lilac. Homes like shining jewels scattered over the panoramic land in clustered knots, tucked in and around broad trees with umbrella branches that were covered in tiny sparkling leaves.

The ship had landed in front of a palace.

It was many stories high, but the levels weren't cut in geometric squares, but more of a saffron serpentine that rolled in waves up higher and higher. Numerous gilded towers jutted gently around the structure.

She could see several suns and numerous moons, blue spheres suspended in the amethyst sky.

In awe, Sveti soaked in the planet all shades of lush, of bright and soft pastels, vibrant colors, and calming dusty blues and searing greens. The polar opposite of what she had expected.

A feeling of peace and welcoming overwhelmed Sveti, until, she remembered her demon husband, beyond enraged with her was waiting inside to punish her for her deed.

Her sigh brief as she bucked up her inner strength, her life seemed to be a series of men that wanted to penalize her with physical abuse. Devilos likely didn't actually rescue her, more like cold-bloodedly reclaimed his property.

Bowie cupped her elbow to lead her, steady her, keep her from running away in a frightened panic.

Magnificent doors of ivory and gold slid open and they passed through into the majestic glimmering castle.

Servants and lieutenants lined the creamy atrium illuminated with vaulted ceilings, embellished with dramatic, red-rimmed windows way up high.

Reminiscent of running the gauntlet, every head was bowed, no one made eye contact with her.

Sveti felt part relief she didn't have to face their resentment, but panicked that they knew what hell she faced and didn't want her to see it in their eyes.

Bowie brought her into the throne room. Emerald and gold, the resplendent gallery was a sea of more people and officers.

Sveti swallowed her terror as the teeming crowd swelled then separated for them to cross the room. The long skirt of her gown brushed the emerald marble floor that was so polished everything reflected off it like a blurry colorful Renoir painting.

Sveti chose her outfit not for the pretty foil it made for her brilliant hair, but because the blouse that matched the ice-teal skirt with seashell stripes, had big round white buttons that went all the way to her throat, and she had every one of them closed.

Unfortunately, the clothes had been provided for her, the top was snug, hugging her plump breasts where she would have preferred to hide her figure as much as possible.

She knew Devilos would be incensed with her, but she didn't want him to also be sexually inflamed. He wouldn't be beyond taking her, forcefully, violently brutal to punish her.

At the thought, petrified shivers rolled up her arms and across her shoulders. What if he took her as the colossal beast? He would shred her apart from the inside out.

"Sveti," a voice whispered as they reached the end of the gallery.

Her head whipped around. "Daddy?"

Her parents and little brother Samson were there along with Ryen. Their smiles of love were laced with fear, for her.

Her father whispered in horrified awe, "He burned Krystian's entire compound and lands to the ground without so much as striking a match."

"Svetiessa."

The familiar deep, rough voice beckoned her with its glacial chill. Icy fingers trickled down her spine. Turning around slowly, she looked up.

There was no love, compassion, desire for her in Devilos' empty eyes of cold cinders. He sat upon a throne on a dais bordered by his consorts.

He looked every inch the imperial principé. Hair loose, not bound in the warrior braids, he was dressed in royal blue and violet, his enlarged horns were out and pointed and full of wrath, claws digging into the arms of the majestic throne did not bear good will for Sveti.

Fearing for the safety of her family, Sveti sank to her knees and bowed her head.

"Prințesă, stand up," his command devoid of warmth.

Raising her head but keeping her eyes lowered she plead, "Sire, please, do what you will with me, but I beg the lives of my family and Ryen." She didn't see Dev's glaring nod to Bowie beside her.

Bowie silently grasped her arm and gently pulled her to her feet.

"Bring her to me, Lieutenant," Dev's growl boded profound danger.

Bowie nudged her, but Sveti didn't move. He had to tug her forward, the blood rushing into her head deafened her to the cries of her family pleading for her life. Bowie brought her up the steps of the dais to stand before the Principé of Darkness.

When she lifted her long lashes to look up at the throne, she physically felt the fury radiating off her husband, but his rich prismatic eyes remained barren.

Still clasping her arm, Bowie watched his friend.

Although no one else could read him, Bowie could see Dev's arms twitch, itching to steal around his estranged wife, desiring to hold her so hard against him she would cry to breathe, beg for mercy, sob for forgiveness, plea for his embrace.

But resisting the impulse, Dev nodded imperceptibly at him. With a tight smile, Bowie released Sveti.

Without his support she swayed backwards in her stark fear. Bowie quickly pressed his hand to her back to steady her, then dropped his hand and stepped away from her.

The room was dead silent.

"Get on my lap." The harsh order surprised everyone. He still clutched the ends of the chair arms with his claws, knees spread, he glowered down at her.

Her eyes flew up to the principé. Still, his iron-angled face revealed nothing, eyes unreadable as black ice. Her feet glued to the floor, Sveti wondered, was her husband going to rape her in front of the filled room, in front of her family, his lieutenants?

Was he going to mock his prior words of how he wanted their marriage to be real? He had said he wanted her to sit on his lap in lovers' coziness while he felt her up, but the outrage in his eyes swore he planned more, so much more than that.

"Now." His voice so deep, dark, cold, not one civilian in the room did not shiver.

Dev's brow slashed down at Sveti's father's protest, forbidding any interference.

Sveti jerked her brain to obey, forced herself to move forward until she was upon him. She hesitated unsure of how she was to climb up onto his lap. He was a big man on a big throne, and she was as petite as ever.

Dev bent towards her, she put her hands on his knees to brace, he gripped her upper arms and helped her climb up.

She sat rigidly on his lap, her long gown covered half his legs, his arm was a steel band around her, his hard hand curled around her hip. The vast hall reeked of fear and deadly silence.

"Lieutenant," he commanded Bowie quietly, "clear the room."

Immediately, Bowie and the other lieutenants, Connar, Lukas and Tomi, herded the silent people, funneling them out the enormous arched doors until the immense glittering room contained only the throne, Sveti, and Dev.

Chapter Twenty-Nine

*K*nowing his eyes would be blazing venomous white by now, Sveti couldn't look at him, or keep the tremble out of her voice, "Sire, I-"

"Shut. Up. You do not speak." Dev could feel the granite in his graveled voice. So angry he could not control his horns, fangs, claws, but, he stared at her lowered head, *she is so beautiful, so self-sacrificing,* his stomach twisted.

The timber in his low tone dark and grim, he said coldly, "You left me. I ordered you to not leave the suite, the station."

Keeping her body sideways to him, tilting her head slightly, she lifted her flaming lashes, the anxious blues searched his white discs for any kind of compassion or warmth and found none. "I had to help Ryen-"

His hand gripped her hip, he roared, "Shut up!"

Dev worked to keep the beast from taking him over, inside his body it roamed and pushed, snarled and fought to come out. It wanted to lift her gown and impale her. Now. It had waited a long time and it wanted her now.

He growled, "I don't give a bleeding fuck about Rembrandt or anyone else but you. You put your fucking life on the line for a grown man who should have been protecting you from the start," the hand he put on her shoulder turning her to face him shook with rage.

"Sire, I'm sorry but Ryen-"

Keeping his temper from blasting out of control, Dev put his fingers over her lips. "How dare you put me through that agony, worrying that I wouldn't get to you before your fucking *bráthair* assaulted you, skinned you, burned you alive." The nightmares had tortured him day and night while she was gone, and he couldn't fucking get to her.

With a guttural sound he moved his hand to drag his fingers through his long loose hair. "You fucking have any idea what it did to me seeing you all…beaten, broken and bloody, barely conscious, in pain, goddamned bitten for fucking sake, with that bastard brutalizing you in front of his audience, about to violently rape you and whip you more?"

"Sire, I had to-"

He barked over her, "You do not talk! You deprived me of my wife, my husbandly rights, my comfort."

"Comfort?"

"Aye," he ground harshly. "Braydon Frasie, a friend of mine from the centaura Tamba-mer, was killed in an airjet explosion."

"Oh Devi- Sire, I am so sorry." She set her palm on his face, compassion and sympathy shone in her beautiful eyes.

He leaned into her hand for a second, then firmed himself.

Contrary to his words about missing her comfort, he said, "I do not want your sympathy. I want my rights you have denied me for ages. Get down, on your knees, and put your hands on the chair."

At her confused look he barked, "Do it! Shall I bring your family back in to bear the brunt of my rage?"

She went to move off his lap, but before she could, he grabbed her jaw and kissed her with all his raging fury, suppressed passion, aching heart, until they were both dizzy.

Letting go of her face he ran his lusting hands up the front of her and cupped her breasts with barbarous strength, squeezing, crushing, growling gutturally until she cried out from his roughness.

He set her on her feet and moved off the chair. "Kneel, bend over and put your hands on the seat cushion. We have time to make up for."

A fleeting glance at his leaden face, his slate eyes narrowed in acrimony, Sveti sank gracefully to her knees, bent over and placed her hands on the chair.

Chapter Thirty

Leaving his throne, Dev stood behind her staring down at her slender back, so delicate, elegant, the long flaming hair draping over the sides of her face. The most luscious ass in the world pushed up for his perusal and to take. And he was going to.

He grabbed the hem of her skirt and pushed it up to reveal pale pink silk panties. He was already hard from her sitting on his lap.

Her body shuddered at his touch. She was terrified of him. She should be. No one had ever defied his orders before, and lived.

The living hell she'd put him through, the agony of not knowing what was happening to her, the impotence to get to her, then the true hell of seeing her so...brutally injured. His big body shuddered with the dread he'd felt, the helplessness.

His legs on either side of Sveti, he bent over her, grasped her blouse and shoved it up as high as it would go to expose her pink bra. Unhooking the bra, he shoved the silk up too, exposing her breasts that hung like full ripe honeydews. Her nipples hardened with her fear.

Zues, how he had missed the sight of them, the feel of her supple globes in his hands. His dreams had been rife with images of them.

He growled, "I told you as your husband I would expect my due. You have denied me. That ends now. You will not disobey me again. You will never leave our residence without my permission. You understand?"

She didn't move.

He grabbed a fistful of her hair lifting her head. Her lips parted, eyes wide. He barked, "Do. You. Understand? I will not ask again." She nodded as much as she could. "Out loud, Wife, say it out loud."

"Yes, I understand you, my Sire."

Kneeling behind her, he let go of her hair and covered her breasts with his big hard hands. She wriggled, he moaned. Fondling them roughly, he pinched her nipples, clutching and squeezing her full flesh just short of causing her pain.

His cock rampagingly hard pressed into her ass, he pulled her body tight against his chest, relishing the feel of her safe in his arms.

But, she had disobeyed him and could have died for it. And, it wasn't the first time. His growl low near her ear, he could have lost her forever. Releasing her breasts, he slid his palms down her side and to her back, grasped the silk panties to push them down.

"Sire, please," she whispered.

He snarled bitterly, "You had your time to talk, woman, before you chose to leave me. Now you will be silent and give me my due." Dev heard her gulp back a sob. With a grinding sigh, he re-hooked the silk bra, shoved her blouse and skirt down to cover her, got to his feet and lifted her into his arms.

His voice a mere abrasive whisper, he said, "I warned you Svetiessa, what I would do if you called me fucking Sire again." He strode through the back passageway to his chambers.

Her voice small, Sveti replied, "I was giving you respect in front of- of your people-"

"Ha!" His scathing ire a coarse rumble. "If you respected me you would not have left me, not have thrown yourself at utter danger to go rescue your boyfriend. Nay, if you respected me, Wife, you would have respected me enough to trust me that I would have gotten Rembrandt safely away from your sociopathic freak of a *bráthair*. But, nay, you did not respect me. You have never trusted me to take care of things, of you."

The doors to his massive chambers whooshed open at his approach and closed behind him.

Dev carried her to his huge bed and set her on her feet beside it.

He brushed her hair back, and slid his hand around her jaw to hold her still for his plundering, riotous kiss, bingeing on the savory taste of her, the feel of the plush lips yielding under his tough mouth and scavenging tongue.

The relief to have her there, his mouth finally on hers again washed through him with a shudder.

He didn't bother with the buttons Sveti had so carefully done up like a protective vest, he grabbed the blouse at the collar and ripped it apart. At her gasp, he jerked the destroyed blouse off and tossed it.

He caught her wrists as she raised her hands to cover her breasts in the tiny bra. "Do not fight me, Svetiessa," spat sarcastically, "*Wife*." Releasing her, he spun her around and undid the back of the skirt and yanked it to her feet.

On his knees, he lifted each foot and removed her shoes. Sliding his calloused palms up her legs, up her thighs, her butt, he slipped his big fingers into her panties and with a hard jerk ripped them off. His eyes on her bottom, he clutched her round cheeks and groaned.

Bowing his head he rubbed his rough face on the smooth skin of her ass, pushed his thumbs into the crease to crush each cheek with his huge hands in a frenzy of anger and frustrated desire.

"Kneel," he commanded. When she hesitated, he moved his fingers deeper into the crease of her bottom. Without comment, Sveti moved down to her knees.

Dev unclasped her bra, she didn't fight him when he pulled it off, before it hit the floor his hands covered her breasts. He allowed himself a moment of enjoying their soft weight in his palms, clinching the chubby treasures.

Thinking of Krystian mauling her, his perverted hands on Sveti's tender body, biting her, his anger overtook him.

He put his hard hand on her back, pushed her to bend and face the bed with her arms on the mattress, and roughly nudged her legs apart.

Tearing at his belt buckle, he yanked it apart and ripped his pants open. When the zipper grated down, he felt her shiver.

One hand splayed on her back to hold her down, he grabbed her pelvis lifting it, then took out his cock, wrapped his fist around it and jammed it against her woman's opening.

"Devilos, don't-"

"I am your husband, I will do as I please," he stated coldly, so raging furious and blind with lust, he was about to just thrust his thick steel length into her, when she cried, "Devilos, please don't take me like this, with anger and hate. No different than Krystian. Your strength, you're too big, forcing me," a sob hitched out, "you will hurt me in your rage," in a whisper, "I will never forgive you."

His temper unconstrained, he paused, growled fiercely, "*You* will never forgive *me*? You forget, my wife, you left me. Will *I* ever forgive *you*?" His knees shoved at her legs pushing them farther apart, he reached down and palmed her woman's mound so hard she jumped.

A big hand spread on her slim back to hold her down and in place, he grabbed his cock to thrust into her when he felt her shaking under his palm with her silent weeping.

Drawing a hard ragged breath, he let go of his cock and wrapped his fingers around her hip. Lowering his other hand to slide down, he gently cupped her sex. She quivered at his touch. Whether in fear or desire, he couldn't tell.

Dev caressed her feminine folds, slicked his thick fingers up her slit and circled her clit with his thumb until he felt her silk ooze out into his hand. Feeling her relax somewhat, and the evidence of her body's reaction to his caresses, he reached for her breasts, cradled one, kneaded it, then the other.

His fingers stroking her sex, and gently groping her breasts, he felt her hips start to move with his fingers, a slight moan slipped from her as she wriggled against him, and more of her silk wet his hand.

Leaning over closer to her, he put his mouth in her hair, inhaled her fragrance, her familiar scent went right to his dick making it swell even harder and pound with the want to thrust into her.

His lips near her ear, he kept working his fingers on her core, and whispered, "This what you want, my sweet wife?"

He carefully slid a thick finger into her small passage. So tight since they'd only made love those few times then she left him.

Feeling the anger build again, his long finger penetrated her harder, deeper until she cried, "Please!"

"Please, what, Svetiessa?" He thrust his finger faster then added a second finger stretching her so she could take his engorged, broad length.

"Please Devilos," he snarled, mocking her, "I will never leave you again? Please don't stop, Husband?" Growling through rugged panting breaths, his dick shoved against her naked butt rubbing her harshly, "Or, please take me now," he shoved his fingers hard into her.

"*Uh-*" grunting from the dominant impact, moans burned her throat.

"Well? What is it, Svetiessa?" He whispered seductively in her ear, "Tell me you want me, tell me I can take you now." His thumb stroking her hard bud, his fingers rough inside her tender sheath. Squeezing her breasts he put his lips on her neck and sucked so hard a red mark rose instantly.

"Answer me, Wife," his heavy growl a harsh grunt from the strain of holding himself back from just savagely plunging into her.

Sveti writhed back against his throbbing manhood shoved between the crease of her bottom, then wriggled with mindless purling moans, thrusting forward into his roughly probing fingers, "Sire," her breath caught.

"*Devilos*, dammit," he smacked her bare butt with a sharp whack.

She bucked with a squeal, the smack punching her sex hard against his fingers.

He ground out, "Svetiessa, answer me. Can I take you now?"

Her gasping breath gushed the words out, "Yes, please, yes, Devilos, I- I want you." She lifted her head with a needy whimper as he bore his mouth back down on her neck, crushing her breast in his violent hand.

He suddenly removed his fingers, stood up with her in his arms and laid her on the bed. He positioned her hands palms up next to her head then gripped her ankles and spread her legs apart.

"Don't move," it came out gruff in his strained throat. His gaze licked every inch of her body like a flame.

He stared at her lying as if in surrender, her hands up, soft rounded breasts calling for his hands and his lips, her legs wide apart to expose that tender pink knot, the lady slit he had been dying long lonely months to plunge into.

Dev reached over his back to grasp his shirt and jerked it off his head and threw it. Crouching, he undid his boots, kicked them off, then his socks, standing, he shoved his pants down pushing them the rest of the way off with his feet.

She hadn't moved, just kept those baby blues on him, they slid from his blinding white eyes, down his massive chest to his sinewy hips. Her pupils dilated when they reached his rigid penis he gripped in his fist as he moved back to the bed.

Pumping his heavy cock, Dev climbed on the mattress, it sank and jostled slightly with his weight, he moved on his knees between her legs.

Reaching down, he trickled his fingers over her slit, and smiled as her silk dampened his hand. He took some of her natural lube and layered his seething iron rod with it.

Her small hips bucked up at his fingers massaging her sex, his fingers plunging inside her. "Devilos, *now*," her shy voice begged, emboldened with the desire he burned in her, her body writhing on the cool sheets.

"Aye, baby." His knees nudged her thighs as far apart as they could go, he dropped down on his elbows, his cock in his hand, voice a rough haze, he murmured, "You ready, baby?"

A bare whisper, "Yes."

He slammed into her. She cried out with a hoarse rasp that choked from the bottom of her chest and scraped out of her throat.

His cock only halfway in, he paused at her cry. "Svetiessa, are you all right?" Dark face tight with the strain of holding his throbbing cock back from blasting off, heavy groans rumbled in his chest.

Dev watched her face ripple in pain, he eased back, caressed her warm cheek. "Baby?"

Her gulp audible, she nodded with shallow gasps. "Yes, I'm fine, keep- keep going." Her serious gaze up at the tumultuous tornados that roared in his enigmatic eyes, told him of her own hunger.

"Ah, my wife." His tense grin relieved, still angry, hot as fuck for his bride, then he remembered something. "Wait," without leaving her body, he squirmed them as one body to the edge of the bed then reached over to grab his pants.

"Devilos?" He was squashing the breath out of her and she was on the pinnacle of coming, her body twisted and burned inside ready to surge into the sun.

He took something out of his pocket and dropped the slacks. He held it out for her to see.

"My ring?" her lips parted. "How did you-" her eyes darted up to his. "Did you...kill..."

The long black hair swung with the shake of his head. He lifted her hand and pushed the ring on her finger.

"Nay. His father, *your* father, rushed in and begged for his life. Svetiessa." White seethed in his enraged orbs.

"I was so fucking furious seeing your ring around his neck, I was about to rip his head right off to take it, but," he let out a breath, "your father interceded. Pleaded for his heinous life. So," a grin nicked up the corner of his beautiful masculine mouth, "instead of death, since he said he broke your finger getting it off," he shrugged.

"I felt it was only fair that I break his neck as I...removed the chain, which I then shoved down his throat. His next shit will be pretty, all gold and sparkly."

"Oh, Devilos, that's...sick, don't tell me anymore." She held up her hand to view her wedding band.

He gently stroked her face, said softly, "Krystian said you kept wearing it, refused to give it to him."

Swallowing the lump in his throat, his growl pained with his words, "It means everything to me that you wore it even after giving yourself to him. It means you didn't abandon me out of your heart."

"Never," she swore. Her gaze slanted up at him. "I just don't get it, Devilos."

"Hmm?" he murmured, resuming his slow push in her, still working his way through her tiny channel.

"Uh," a sigh pushed out of her with his careful thrusting. "You, I mean, that day at the river. You said you didn't want a commitment, then you turned around and deliberately seduced me into marrying you."

The corners of his eyes crinkled with his smile, he kissed the tip of her nose. "Foolish girl, you misunderstood me. I was saying that you were mine; that I will not share. You anyway, other women I could have cared less," he kissed her nose again and smiled when she wrinkled it.

"I was saying that day, Svetiessa, that you didn't need to worry about me not wanting commitment because once I took you, you would be mine, there would be no other people for either of us. That you didn't need to fear I wasn't committed to you, I was fully into us being together forever."

"But your other women-"

Sighing, he cupped a breast, thumbed her nipple and pushed his shaft almost to the end of her.

"I've told you, you are different. Always was, always will be. The first time I saw you at that party I was blown away, already knew I had to have you. The second I saw you on my ship, I was irresistibly, inexplicably, drawn to kiss you, like I would die if I didn't."

He took a deep breath and smiled when he was finally buried inside her to the hilt, then exhaled in relief that she was home, safely home, with him. "I've never felt that way before, and when you started disappearing I had to keep you there, I thought if I let go I would never see you again. I thought I could hold you with the kiss."

"It wasn't a strong enough physical hold to keep me from transporting."

"Aye, well, I will hold on stronger now," and he suddenly pounded into her hard and fierce like a powered trip-hammer.

He was driving so hard he was shoving her body away, he had to grip her shoulders to hold her, but only with one hand, he couldn't open his fingers to release her breast, so he held on, his balls slapping against her with every plunge, his hair splashing her face.

She wrapped her legs around his hips, groans peppered from her jolting body, breasts bouncing. He thrust so hard she gasped with a shocked grunt.

Fearing he was too rough, Dev slowed. "Am I hurting you?"

"No," she panted out, "more, Devilos, more," her hips strove up to crash at his, trying to make him go faster and harder again.

But he maintained a long, deep, rocking rhythm. "Devilos," her voice high and stretched, "please, please," then she shuddered feeling the bumps rise on his manhood along with the horns on his head.

She was on the brink, wincing with the strain of trying to make him move faster and push her over the top, her cry a dire rasp, "*Devilos, please!*"

"Tell me you will never leave me again, Svetiessa." His voice a chasm of hurt and fear, and tenderness, he whispered, "Tell me you love me as much as I love you."

She was startled at his words. He now moved ever so slowly, long lingering thrusts in way deep, long languorous slide out, the bumps rolling against every soft tissue inside her sheath.

Groans rushed with the burning in her sex, she moaned "*Devilos*," a shudder started at her core and ricocheted out.

"Tell me Svetiessa," he demanded, his penis scraped and roiled like a helix all the way in, and all the way out.

Sveti's body shook and shuddered, her teeth chattered with the intensity of the sensations he drew out of her.

"I, uh," grunting groan, "I love you, Devilos," her voice trailed off in the awe of the moment, she meant what she said, but she was unmistakably dumbfounded at it. Her fingers dug into his rock hard ass, her lids scrunched over her eyes as she fought to grind at his cock to make him move faster.

"Damn you, Devilos, you are so...uh," her throat clenched at a sudden hard thrust, but she wasn't coming until he let her, "controlling..."

With a chuckle, he socked his mouth over hers sucking out a voracious mind spiraling kiss, letting her little tongue slide over his descending fangs, then he drilled into her soft sheath.

He smiled at the small jump of surprise, she'd forgotten the fangs. The discovery of them on her tongue, with his hard thrust made her skin quiver, Sveti's body rippled against his with the sudden rush of heat that struck her.

Picking up his momentum, Dev plunged faster watching Sveti's eyes roll back, her neck arch.

"Ah, stay with me sweetheart." Thrusting harder, he panted, "Open your eyes, little wife, look at me."

It was a few more plunges before her heavy lids lifted and the blue streamed out already dazed. Their eyes linked, and wielding his man's club, he bore into her like a maelstrom.

Choppy *uh, uh, uh's* ruffled up her throat. "Devilos," she gasped, "you're tearing me asunder, no, don't stop!" her nails raked across his back, then staked into his biceps.

"Zues, baby, I love when you claw me, speaking of," he huffed, "my horns, fangs, you okay with all that? I need to know like, ah, right now," his voice deep with tension, his balls were on fire, they were binding up getting ready to shoot.

"Uh huh," she croaked, whimpering at his increasingly harder thrusts that forced deep shockwaves up her core. "Yeah," she groaned, "all of it, all of you, want it all."

"Open your eyes, Svetiessa," he urged, he had waited a long time to have her writhing under him again and he wanted to watch those beautiful blues when she blew up.

Her body jolting from the hard mass of him punching into her, her eyes levered up to his, glazed and glowing, burning so hot the blue melted.

"Ready baby?" his growl ended in a harsh purr.

At her glazed nod, he pounded into her as his horns rose and turned, curling over her back preparing to plunge, his fangs descended. Leaning on his elbows, he could reach her chest with both hands, his claws unsheathed and encircled her breasts.

A short scream flushed from her tight throat at their sudden sharp, painful stabbing grip, her back arched off the mattress, her pupils slowly flooded black over the blue irises until not a shade of color was left.

At that moment her body undulated against his with violent tremors, his horns speared into her back. As she went over the brink, her eyes shook and rolled back in her head as Dev's fangs pierced the firm flesh of her neck. He pushed her knees up and went deeper.

She screamed, "Devilos!" Her body bucking at his uncontrollably, screaming and screaming. With a sharp inhale she cried, "I can't withstand the feelings- I'm exploding from the inside out- Dev, the burn, the blinding brilliance!" and she shattered.

His fangs withdrew and he covered her mouth with his, her lids raised slightly to see his eyes ignite in black then pure white phosphorescence as he let go.

Their bodies gyrated together, he could feel her multiple orgasms shake and race through her body, one after another as her silken channel clamped open and closed with spasms on his shaft, grinding, wringing him, she couldn't scream anymore.

His roar of release reverberated in her mouth, down her throat, his balls erupted and his seed shot out of him. In the back of his mind he knew he needed to sheath his claws or he would pierce her breasts too much and injure her in his extreme intensity.

Growls of fulfillment strew from his rumbling chest as his horns, fangs and claws receded and he continued driving into Sveti until there was nothing left and he dropped on her, chest heaving, heart pounding.

Lying on his side, Dev pulled her in close, threw a leg over her and wrapped both arms around his wife to hold her secured to his chest, their rushing breaths slowing as they came back down to earth.

Zues, he was never letting her go, never.

Chapter Thirty-One

Dev woke with Sveti curled in his arms. Gently extricating her, he moved slightly to her side. Up on one elbow he drank her in. So beautiful, he loved her so much his heart about burst apart with it.

She lay tumbled, naked, with a sheet covering one thigh; her chest rose and settled softly with her sleeping breaths.

He couldn't not touch her, his palm covered a breast, the pink nipple no longer a tight knot. She squirmed slightly and sighed.

Staring hard at her, memorizing every pure inch of her lush body and gorgeous face, Dev knew what he had to do.

He had forced her to Nasitar, forced her to marry him Last night he had bullied her into his bed, and, his chest tightened, he had even forced her to tell him she loved him.

A groan burned in his gut. She had made it clear from the start she did not want to marry him and resented his tricking her.

She had only acquiesced to his commands because he made her. Probably hated mating with him too, all burly and rough, hard and violent. He dominated and pushed her around like a tyrant, as bad as her brother.

A small chuckle tripped from his chest tight with anguish, but she hadn't feigned her orgasms; there was no faking those screams and body breaking paroxysms.

Still, he sighed with the agony of knowing he had to do the right thing by her. He had to bury his selfish need of Sveti, it was time he put her wishes first.

Gently caressing her breast with his long fingers for the last time, he bent and softly kissed her sweet lips. Then he reluctantly pulled the sheet over her to keep the temptation away, and got out of bed.

Gone for half the day, when he returned with Bowie, Sveti was up and had prepared a casserole for dinner. Her face lit up when he came through the door.

"Devilos, where have you- oh, hi Bowie," she frowned at her husband's grim countenance.

"You need to go with Bowie," he said flatly without looking at her.

"What? Why? Go where?" Her head swung from one to the other in bewilderment. "What's wrong?"

Dev growled, "There is nothing wrong." He grasped her arm and brought her to the open door and pulled her out to the hall. Bowie, his face just as grim followed them out.

Confusion wrought over her pretty face, Sveti asked, "Devilos, what is going on?"

Now he looked her in the eye, his face drawn and pale. "I realized, Svetiessa, that it was wrong of me to make you marry me. But," he drew a hard breath, expelled it roughly then said, "I didn't want to lose you and you gave me no time to woo you." The fingers of one hand forked through his braids.

"I know, but-"

"It was wrong, and I don't deserve a woman like you. Damn, Svetiessa," his black brows scrawled low over pained eyes. "I even forced you to tell me you love me." The braids swung with the contemptuous shaking of his head.

"I've treated you so badly, acted the savage animal with you, I," he ran his hand through his scalp again, glanced at Bowie but Bowie was looking away.

"Anyway," he turned back to face her bewilderment. "I am setting you free. Bowie is going to take you to your family." His lip twisted wryly. "I was even so unfeeling, so drowned in selfishness with my own greedy needs to have you that I didn't even let you visit with them yesterday."

Sveti put out her hands to him. "Devilos, listen-"

"Nay, you don't have to kowtow to me anymore, ever again. While you're visiting with your family, I will have your things moved into your old suite so you don't have to worry about me assaulting you again. You can leave with your family when the ship arrives. I promise," he said quickly as she tried to speak.

"I will find a way to break our...bond. Our marriage bond, the chemistry. I will find a way to dissolve it and you will be free to, ah, find another...and be happy."

Dev's throat closed and he turned from her. "Take her to her family, Bowie," he commanded quietly then he took off with hard strides away down the hall, war braids flapping behind him.

Hours later, after a few meetings he couldn't keep his mind in, Dev hit a dingy bar a distance from their quarters so he wouldn't run into anyone he knew, and drowned his sorrows.

How the hell will he live without her now that he's known the pure angel that was Svetiessa?

The alcohol did nothing to dull the excruciating pain in his heart and crushing ache in his head from his loss. He had wanted her, he took her, fell in love with her, and lost her.

Only lowlife miscreants hunched in the foul tavern, even trashed and stupid, they were smart enough to stay away from the grievously brooding warrior.

A few more drinks and he shoved heavily to his feet and lumbered out of the bar. His steps slow and ponderous, he could barely lift his boots off the ground, he had no desire to go back to his empty suite but he had nowhere else to go hang around and pine for his wife.

He had made sure Bowie had taken Sveti's cardkey; he didn't want her coming back because she feared he would harm her or her family in retribution or some shit. She was free of him, and that was that.

At his door, he fumbled out his key and dejectedly shoved it in the lockspace and trudged inside. The suite was dark, cold, and profoundly empty, like his soul.

His nose lifted, he could still just barely smell her scent, it only tore more at his hurting, broken, heart. His mouth twitched with miserable bitterness.

Here he had never thought he would fall in love, want a woman to keep forever, and then get her and marry her, and now have to let her go.

He snorted miserably, now he could understand other people's pain that he had always sneered at.

Toddling into the bedroom, he didn't bother with the lights; the grey light from the station matched his grey heart. He dropped his cardkey and weapons on the nightstand then went to take a shower.

Not feeling the least refreshed after letting the stinging water beat at him, burn him with the hottest heat he could stand, he trod sadly back to his room.

He didn't bother to put anything on, he just climbed in the bed and pulled the sheet up to cover his hips and laid there trying not to think of his wife. Correction, soon to be ex-wife.

Ha, like he will ever be able to not think about her, not picture her smile, not dream about them together making love. Dragging his pillow over his head, he tried to bury his tormented thoughts.

Epilogue

*T*hat's where Sveti found him after letting herself in with the key she refused to give over to Bowie.

A shaft of low light sifted in through the window softly lighting parts of Dev's bronzed body, a buff shoulder, an angled cheek.

On his stomach facing the side, his arm was out like it had been when she had left him before, as if he was reaching for her.

The black hair loose now, Brahms must have been by, showered over the white pillow. She stood beside the bed watching the powerful warlord sleep.

When her fingers reached the first button on her blouse, his eyes shifted slightly open.

"Svetiessa?" his voice low and rusty with sleep, "what are you doing here?" He didn't move.

"I decided, Husband," a small calculating smile curved her lips as she unbuttoned a second button watching his gaze latch onto her dainty fingers. "That I was done with you telling me what to do. You even had the gall to tell me I didn't want you."

Still not moving his body, his baffled gaze rolled up to her shimmering blues.

The last button opened and his eyes dropped back down, a flick of white glinted in the blackness of his orbs.

"Oh aye? Yeah?" his croaky murmur crept out, his tongue snaked around, licking his dry lips as Sveti drew her blouse off and let it fall from her fingers.

"Yes." Smiling at the glow in his dark eyes now staring hard at her breasts, she said, "You are not the boss of me, I am."

She reached around and unclasped her bra, slid it down her arms and dropped it on the discarded blouse. Then she discarded her shoes.

Her breasts unfettered in front of him, those amazing pink-tipped globes he thought he'd never see again, Dev couldn't put a sentence together, he muttered, "So, you say."

He still didn't move but his body shifted as his cock swelled.

"Uh huh," she nodded and reached behind her for the button on her skirt.

Undoing it, she tucked her fingers in the waist and started slowly sliding the fabric over her shimmying hips then down her legs watching Dev's pupils spark, his Adam's apple bobbed with a hard swallow.

"From now on, Devilos, no one, not you or anyone, will tell me what I can and can't do, go where I want to."

Standing in a tiny triangle of pink silk, Sveti sifted her palms up to brush over her breasts then down to just barely touch her sex through the silk.

She kept on, her voice husky seeing Dev about to detonate, "Tell me whom to marry," sliding her fingers over her clit she almost grinned at the color that seeped across Dev's hard face as his horns swelled.

"Uh, yeah?" he mumbled, licking his lips, his breathing grew deep and rapid.

"Yup." She grasped the panties and drew them languidly down her legs, grinning at the strain on her husband's face. "And, no one, least of all you, will tell me who I can, will, *do* love. So," she said, stepping languorously out of the panties.

Wriggling slightly, Sveti skimmed her palms over her bare skin before holding her arms gracefully out at her sides. "Is that the striptease you said wanted that day you seduced me into marrying you?"

His gaze roamed up and down her nude body, eyes bright with desire, "Oh aye," he murmured and pulled the sheet back for her to join him.

Sveti put one knee on the bed, her thighs spread, his eyes devoured her glistening womanhood exposed in front of his face. He reached for her.

She climbed onto the bed on all fours. Dev couldn't have stopped himself if he wanted to, his hands closed over her hanging breasts, his moan quivered all over his body, shaft a thick, hard, pulsing club.

"Zues, Svetiessa, baby," he groaned with profound pleasure, and gratefulness. "I never thought I would have the blessing to hold these again."

The backs of his eyes stung with the threat of tears. Another new and unfamiliar sensation. Everything with her was new, and wonderful.

Sveti arched her spine thrusting her breasts into his hard grip, her own moans vibrating with his.

Climbing on him to straddle his hips, she waited while he moved to lie flat on his back, still kneading her globes, the full spheres throbbed in his hands.

Up on her knees, her sex was fully exposed, Dev released a breast to stroke her slit. When he rubbed her throbbing nub her body shook so hard her head fell forward, long strawberry curls tickling his chest.

He couldn't take his eyes off her beauty as she raised her arms to push the locks back to tumble in a curly flame down her back.

Sliding a finger into her, his groan unharnessed agony, "Baby, you are so wet."

"Yes. For you. Always, forever, for you, my husband. I love you, Devilos." She leaned forward to grasp his ramrod penis and put it at her soft opening, and sighed with a sensual mewl when she lowered herself on it.

Her hands settling on his powerful chest to hold herself up, Sveti set the rock and roll rhythm.

"I love you, Svetiessa, my beautiful wife, Zues I love you so much. We're finally home." Dev gripped her breasts, pulling her down so he could suck a nipple into his mouth where he lathed it, bit it, suckled it, making her sex clench and writhe all over him.

"It's time I put a devil-pup in you, baby."

Sveti nodded with a glorious smile.

Dev slid his hand behind her head to bring it down. He moved his mouth to take hers prisoner.

The rhythm was too slow for him; he grasped her hips then shoved his up hard, impaling her to the womb.

Her first scream peeled out.

His horns, fangs and claws emerged, and he drove more screams from her as he brought them both to heaven.

The End

Thank you for reading Devil's Prince. I hope you loved it!

Please review the following excerpt from my book, Devil's Seed, Book 2 in **Satan's Brood**.

DEVIL'S SEED

Chapter One

On the heels of the fleeing kidnapper, Kesindra Jasmari's stomach clenched in mortal fear that she'd lose him and the victim would die.

The suspect's shoes clacking furiously over stone and asphalt diminished as he moved further from her, out of sight into deeper darkness.

She could still hear him splashing in puddles, kicking and stomping on garbage as he raced down the alley. Alarm that she was losing him clogged in her throat, drawing a deep breath past her pounding heart was impossible.

A brand-spanking-new agent in the city of Ships Bay, near Boston, her confidence flagged. Kesi wasn't sure what to do.

The Glock 19 heavy and awkward in her small hand, it was not the subcompact she had trained with. Even then, she'd only had a few days of target practice.

"Just buck up, Kesi," she scolded herself, trying to peer through the dimness.

No longer able to hear his footsteps, her pace faltered.

Other than rusty pipes dripping plop-plops on the scummy broken-up blacktop and her panting, it was bone dead silent.

Slowing to a cautious walk, her head tilted listening for any sound to indicate where he went. *Where the heck was the rest of her team?*

Carswell was to stay back, and Richard, Jersey and Chris were to close off the exit to the alley. They had been instructed to only keep furtive eyes on the kidnapper, but Jersey had stared at him too long and the kidnapper made them as agents and fled.

Creeping to the end of the alley, she stood beside the dumpster, her held breath whooshed out. Darn, the alley didn't end as Richard had thought, he had read the map wrong, there were more corridors, more dark squalid corners for the kidnapper to-

She never heard him as he dropped from the dumpster on top of her slamming her to the blacktop-

The wind snapped out of Kesi as she crashed down flat on her stomach- the gun flew out of her hand and she was suddenly in a fight for her life. Skin scraping and gouging, she scrambled on her belly for her weapon, but his weight held her back.

"Oh no you don't, bitch," he snarled in her ear, "you're done." Heaving bear grunts and vile curses ground from him as he wrestled her to keep her down, but small and slender,

Kesi was able to squirm out from under him. Spotting the Glock she tried to make for it, he grabbed her around her knees, jerked hard, and she crashed again on the hard jagged asphalt.

"*Bitch, you ain't goin' nowhere!*" he yelled.

Before she could put her hands up in defense the man started pounding on her. He punched her in the side, in her head, ruthlessly pummeled his big fists like sledgehammers all over her body.

Literally hearing the crack of her bones breaking, Kesi screamed for help. Darkness rapidly enveloped her, pulling her under from the vicious beating. The agonizing pain blinding, then she caught sight of her gun again.

With her last bit of strength, she kneed him in the balls and when he cried out and folded double, she scrabbled on her belly. Her destroyed arms too fractured to hold her up, she still went for the gun.

But, gagging and groaning, he limped over, jumped on her again and grabbed her arm to hold her from reaching the gun.

Jerking her arm back, he broke her shoulder and snatched the gun himself. Her scream of agony withered to a pained hoarse gasp.

A voice nearby yelled, "Don't move, or I'll shoot!"

Kesi fought to stay conscious. Thank God, Carswell Cartwright was in the alley with his gun drawn.

Unfortunately, Carswell was as green and inexperienced as Kesi. His gun wavered all over the place, his boyish face sweaty and strained with fear.

"Okay, all right, I give up," the perp huffed. Straddling Kesi, he raised one hand in surrender.

Carswell commanded, "Uh, okay, don't try anything funny, get on your feet dirtbag with your hands in the-"

Bang!

The perp rolled shooting Kesi's gun. A red dot exploded between Carswell's stunned eyes, then he crumpled to the gritty ground.

"*Nooo*," Kesi cried, her shattered arms flailing uselessly at the killer.

He staggered to his feet with a sneering smirk. "You think to capture me you dumb bitch? Last mistake you will ever make," and he fired at her as she rolled trying to elude the bullet.

Feeling the hot steel slam into her, Kesi heard more gunfire. The kidnapper screamed.

Kesi thought, *good, got him*, then she felt the hot lick of fire as she went under, crashing into the black.

Chapter Two

$\mathcal{A}$ hand from the grave, the kidnap victim's fingers burrowed up through the cracked pavement. Skeleton of splintered bone, grey shreds of skin and tissue and ligaments clinging to it, blood dripped from the ghastly hand as it reached to grab her leg.

"No!" she screamed thrashing, trying to get away from it, but it clutched at her, scraping gnarled cadaver fingernails over her already skinned flesh.

"Wake up, Jasmari! Wake up, Agent!"

The voice kept shouting until Kesi managed to crack her sore lids open.

It wasn't the poor victim, mother of two tiny children; it was her FBI senior agent in charge, SAC Keith Dukes.

"Ah, ah, Jasmari, back from the dead." Sounding more annoyed than concerned, the agent sniffed with mild condescension.

She struggled to sit up but couldn't make her limbs move. The pain knifing everywhere through her body, unbearable agony, tears sprung.

The dry words barely a whisper in her parched throat, she asked, "Sir, what…happened?"

5

The fortyish agent plopped down in a chair beside the bed. "What happened? I'll tell you what happened. I sent the most green, useless, sorriest excuses for agents I've ever had the misfortune to be in charge of, to be a tiny part of a vital mission. Simple. So fucking simple."

He shifted in his seat and glared at her.

"You observe the kidnapper until senior agents come and follow him. He leads us to the victim, and," he snapped his fingers, "voila. We rescue said victim and lock up the sick perp for the rest of his miserable stinking life."

Trying to gather moisture in her scratchy throat, Kesi uttered, "But, I remember, uh," her mind blanked. Then, "Carswell, is he-"

The look on Dukes' grim face told her. She really had seen the agent die in front of her eyes.

"Yeah." The senior agent nodded regretfully. "Carswell didn't make it. You barely did." He dragged his fingers through short trimmed dark hair, then pulled at his rigid lips.

His long face all sharp angles and hollows under his cheekbones, his nose strong but not as jagged as the rest of his features, it evened out the elongated jaw.

With a sniff, eyes like brown pebbles regarded her with mild dispassion.

"But, I don't understand," Kesi mumbled, her brain beat against her skull. The pain struck with grinding jabs, her head vibrated from the ceaseless pounding.

"What happened was, when we located the kidnapper, you fucking inept agents were sent in to only watch him, not arrest, not chase, not kill him, just fucking watch him, keep him in sight." He glared at her as she lay immobile from her numerous, life-threatening injuries.

Hawking out an aggravated breath, he went on with his rebuke, "Let the seasoned team come in and take him down after we find where he stashed the victim. But no, you comedy gang of misfits decide to chase him down, against orders."

Blurry pictures straggled through her bruised brain. Sucking in a dry breath, she responded weakly, "But, we, he made Jersey and then ran. Chris, our team leader said we needed follow him. I," she took another gasping breath, licked her dry lips, her forehead winced in creases with the pain.

"I stayed after him, and Richard said they would block the exit, we would, catch him, and," her wheezing breath scraped at her lungs inflamed with thick fluid.

Sitting back, Dukes crossed an ankle over a knee and regarded her with unveiled contempt. Running fingers down his tie to straighten it, he said, "And, you idiots, Richard read the map wrong, there was no end of that wing of that alley corridor."

Her eyes clenched with physical pain, the mental pain was only just beginning. "I...remember, branches, there were other corridors."

"Yeah. To make matters worse, Chris led the rest of your bumbling team over to a passageway to wait in ambush, but stupid dolts, they weren't at the correct alley you were in. Carswell followed your screams. Apparently, when he tried to arrest the kidnapper, he waffled and the suspect shot and killed him."

Rubbing his angled jaw with a few knobby fingers, his voice softened slightly, he said, "Then, after he had already almost beat you to death, the suspect shot you. His first shot missed." He paused, shifted with some awkwardness.

Clearing his throat noisily he went on, "His second bullet caught you in the head. Ah," he cleared his throat again. "There was a can of spilled kerosene in the alley, the first bullet set off a fire, you were, ah, burned somewhat before the others could get to you."

His expression showed some sympathy. "Fortunately the docs were able to extricate the bullet from your noggin and they claim it hadn't hit anything dire, you should expect a full recovery. One shining thing at least. Eh?"

But Carswell was dead. He had family. Oh God. Her mind was swimming with stinging agony, dread and loss. Licking her dehydrated lips, she whispered, "The- the victim, did we save-"

He shook his head. "No. The rest of the bumbling team raced in with reckless abandon and shot the kidnapper dead. He'd had his hands up in surrender but they panicked. We found Mia Collins a week later in the trunk of the car he had stolen."

"Oh my heavens," Kesi cried, tears of sorrow falling. Voice a wounded rasp, she questioned, "A week? How long have I been here?"

He got up and paced to the window, combing the tips of his fingers in irritation through his hair.

Turning back to her with a frown, he replied, "You were critically injured. It was touch and go for a few weeks. We looked for family to call, but couldn't find any on record."

Tears eked out the corners of her scrunched eyes. "I have no one."

"Yeah, we found that out. Anyway, you've been here in mostly a coma for about six weeks."

Her lids flew up so fast it hurt. "Six weeks? Oh…" Her head spun, her apartment, what happened when she hadn't paid the rent?

Gaze flitting to him, her voice weak, strained, barely a raspy whisper, she asked, "Have I been on medical leave? Have I been drawing pay?"

"Really, Jasmari, after all this, that's all you have to ask, for fuck's sake?" Boomerang-shaped brows drew down. "No, you moron, you are too new. Hadn't even halfway completed the academy when we put you on this mission. You and the other misfits are only probationary agents."

His voice softened again at her look of despair. "We pulled you from the academy because we needed a person the perp wouldn't notice, a young-"

"Nondescript, plain female," she interjected with a sad sarcastic snort.

"Ah, well," sounding abashed, his long face colored somewhat. "I wouldn't go that far, but, yeah, pretty much. Hair always in a tight bun under a scarf, big bug-eyed glasses, baggy clothes, no one would look twice at you, you'd blend into the crowd."

It barely hurt her anymore. She'd always been told she was plain. "Plain as a wooden post," her mother used to say.

Her father would add, "Let's hope she has brains. She's too small and delicate boned to be any use physically, no sports scholarships for you, girlie."

Kesi had grown up home-schooled in an isolated farming commune. Both parents were killed in a flash flood. They had tried to cross a swollen river with cattle and all were swept away. She had no siblings and no other relatives.

Her parents hadn't owned the house they'd lived in, they only had the shirts off their backs. Mr. Thompson, the commune's appointed leader had told Kesi she was too small to do the hard work her parents did.

He had slyly advised her that she could work off her rent in another way, and he was very clear about her spreading her legs for him, or she could leave.

She had no job, no money for college, and was unable to rent an apartment with no funds or credit to her name. She had tried to leave a few times, to get regular employment when her folks were alive, but they had begged her to stay with them.

Kesi could relieve them of the burden of taking care of the household, cooking, cleaning, maintaining the home and doing menial tasks for them thereby leaving them free to do the farming heavy lifting.

With no options, after her parents died Kesi went straight into the FBI. She was a hardship case, they took her in without a college degree but with a contract that she would obtain her degree while working for them.

"Well," bending over her, Dukes said, "look on the bright side, you can't miss what you never had. You've never experienced the life of a beautiful woman, so," one shoulder rose in a 'so what' kind of a shrug, "it can't hurt as much now that you're disfig- uh-" he broke off awkwardly with a small cough.

"What? I have permanent damage?" The tears welled and ran over down her cheeks. She tried to raise a hand to touch her face but the pain was too intense just trying to raise her arm. All four limbs were in casts.

"Uh, well, the doctors have, uh, hope that, I mean they said the bones in your face would heal, but you would never look the same. At least all of your hair didn't burn off, since you have at least that one pretty, uh, element. Now that I've seen it loose. Uh..."

He stuck a finger under the knot of his tie and tugged at it, went on, "And of course, thank God, your eyes weren't damaged, the heat, they were afraid, I mean your glasses burnt over your eyes. They thought, you know, there was a chance of blindness..." he trailed off.

Then smiling, he said cheerfully, "They are a nice actually, um, an extraordinary color, kind of, uh, you know, amazingly sexy like, anyway," he rushed on, "now that they aren't hidden behind those ugly dark glasses you wear."

As her painful lids lowered, Kesi thought it was unusual everything wasn't a big blur like it normally was when she didn't wear her glasses. Must be the medication.

"So," she started, licking her lips, she was dying for a glass of water but she would never ask this stick-up-his-ass boss for anything. You would think he would see her distress and offer to help her.

Flopping back down on the chair, he crossed his legs and said coolly, "So, then, this is what happens next."

He waited until her lids rose slightly and her eyes slanted up at him. "The entire mission was one big clusterfuck. It gave the agency a big black eye. So, you, and the rest of the bungling team, are being sent to Původně."

"What?" Her mouth dropped with the question. "Where is that? I've never even heard of it?"

"Um, it's kind of a really tiny, third world country, it's pretty, uh, rural. Like jungle rural. The village is quite rustic, called," he pulled out his cell phone and leafed through his notes. "Brutální."

Blinking at him in bewilderment, she stuttered, "B- but, I don't understand. Why are we to be exiled to a foreign land, will we even understand the language?"

He looked slightly uncomfortable. "I think they speak English."

The senior agent leaned over her, frowning. "Like I said, you guys fucked the thing up so bad we need to get you out of the picture, way out of the picture. Maybe you can somehow redeem yourselves. If not, out of sight, out of mind, right?"

Confused and unnerved at his words, she made no response.

11

"Ah," he sighed. "Think of it as an extended vacation, well, a working vacation. You won't have to worry about the hustle and bustle of the busy dangerous streets here. Except, there have been alien sightings there. But," he shrugged, "that's to be expected out in the primordial jungle."

"Aliens? Are you serious?" Kesi drew a shallow wheezing breath. "I've only heard the occasional news report of them."

She closed her eyes trying to recall the information the authorities had given out regarding the intruders from outer space.

The reports indicated there was a truce of sorts between Earth and the extra-terrestrials. The aliens stating they were staying temporarily for observation.

To Kesi it sounded like they were visiting the zoo. When their curiosity was sated they would return to their own planet, or whatever they were from.

Hopefully they wouldn't desire to take any 'pets' home with them for entertainment or...further study. Like dissecting.

Darn, she was letting her crazy imagination get carried away. She has enough on her plate without worrying about aliens coming to abduct her and experiment on her.

The reports had also indicated the aliens were from the far future and considered earthlings to be quite rudimentary and backward.

They might even consider snatching a few humans to force them to do dangerous or dreadful, wearisome work for them.

Okay, Kesi thrust the frightening thoughts away. Her brain already hurt so much. She asked, "But- but, what would we do there?"

"Well, you would actually be acting sort of like police officers. You know, checking out petit thefts and shoplifting, stuff like that. However, there is some oddity going on out there, there've been vague reports of, well," his eyes flicked away from hers as he said, "entire towns disappearing."

"What? How can-"

"Anyway, you agents are really being sent out there to keep an eye out to look for anything suspicious. Might be some of those aliens fucking around. There have been two different species sighted. They may have some involvement in the disappearances. You and the rest of your misfit team, Christopher Carpenter, Richard Valsaint and Jersey Gerard, will go."

Kesi's anxious voice rose stridently. "But we aren't police officers, we are FBI agents-"

"Listen here, Jasmari, calm down." He leaned forward, glaring at her. "You fucked up, you guys need experience and need to get the hell out of the public eye, and the Bureau's. You just keep your eyes and ears open, take notes, do not, I repeat, do not engage and create another catastrophe."

Never knowing where to settle his hands, he smoothed his palms over his slacks, then forked the knobby fingers through his short dark hair. "It's for the best. All the way around. You'll see." He patted her arm not noticing her face crease in pain from his touch.

"At least you're alive, can't say as much for poor Carswell. You're lucky, you missed the funeral. Hell, it was long and boring and his young wife crying and carrying on, you-"

Speaking of pain, the intensity was creeping up, her entire body burned as if on fire. She cried through the excruciating suffering, "Agent Dukes, please, God I can't bear it," she shrieked hoarsely, "get the nurse!"

Quickly getting to his feet, thankful to get out of there, he said with awkwardly cheerful reassurance, "Yeah, sure, you'll see, it will all be for the-"

The torment roared out of her throat into racking hoarse screams.

He scurried out as fast as he could.